A Daughter is Given

Also by Faye Green

The Boy on the Wall	2012
Dicey	2013
Gertie	2014

July 2017

A Daughter is Given

For Maureen,
Enjoy!
Faye Green

Faye Green

© 2017 Faye Green

All Rights Reserved.

No part of this publication may be reproduced, stored in a retrieval system, or transmitted, in any form or by any means, electronic, mechanical, photocopying, recording, or otherwise, without the written permission of the author.

First published by Dog Ear Publishing
4011 Vincennes Rd
Indianapolis, IN 46268
www.dogearpublishing.net

dog ear
PUBLISHING

ISBN: 978-1-4575-5365-3

This book is printed on acid-free paper.

This book is a work of fiction. Places, events, and situations in this book are purely fictional and any resemblance to actual persons, living or dead, is coincidental.

Printed in the United States of America

Dedication

This book is dedicated to members
of the extended families that filled my
my life with happiness, respect,
perspective, constancy, support
and love—Beall, Poe, Watts and Green

༄༅

In Memoriam

Claudette Marie Latsko

1938 – 2016

Friend

Acknowledgements

Writing a book is an amazing amount of work. I could not do it without help and support from an unusual team. My team includes readers, family members, interviewers, reviewers, editors, proofers, designers and believers. Everyone who reads this acknowledgement will find that they are part of my team. The things you have done for me and this work are beyond measure. Thank you, everyone.

I am once again indebted to my editor, Connie Rinehold, and my manuscript readers, Claudette Latsko, Penny Reuss, Sunny Pritchard and Bill Byer. I appreciate their red ink, helpful comments, and most of all, encouragement. A special thanks goes to Ann Messina who did the final proof with unbelievable skill and diligence. She polished my efforts.

My cousins in the Beall family worked with me to produce my envisioned cover. Charlie and Violet Beall are a picture-perfect personification of the man and daughter in this story. Thanks to Gary Beall (who retired this year as a cameraman in the White House press corps) for walking out of his office and taking the picture of the White House.

Bill Byer saw this book as part of my life and shared every hour, day and week that I spent working on it. There were hours and hours, days and days, weeks and weeks…seemingly endless. But, with him on the journey, there was plenty of fun and endless optimism. I am thankful for Bill's support, his editorial work, but most of all, for his positive outlook and love.

While you are reading <u>A Daughter is Given</u>, I will be writing the next book. It's who I am and what I do.

PROLOGUE

1939

Snow started with Pamela Ross's labor—a typical February storm that began as feathers in the wind. By the time her contractions got to five minutes, a full blizzard blurred the world.

"Katherine Marie." Pamela Ross named her baby on the last push that brought the child into this world. Then exhausted, she exhaled one more gasp and turned her head away from the red, squirming little creature that was placed upon her belly.

James Ross watched from the corner of the bedroom and waited for the baby's cry—and cry she did—as tears ran from his eyes. Pamela should have been relieved, but after enduring labor pains without so much as a whimper, she wailed uncontrollably when she heard her baby cry.

"Katherine Marie," she repeated minutes later when the midwife placed Katherine in her arms. James stayed back. Mother and child had their moment. Pamela opened the receiving blanket and counted fingers— "Ten,"—and toes— "ten."

Her finger caressed Katherine's tiny cheek, outlined her perfect chin, touched the soft spot on her head, and lingered on open lips. The baby tried to suckle but, too quickly, the finger moved on. Pamela lowered her head to smell her baby. Her breath ruffled newly dried hair. Katherine's first kiss was quickly delivered to her forehead.

"Katherine Marie," Pamela spoke once again. Mother and child closed their eyes to the magnitude of the moment.

James stepped forward as the midwife motioned to him.

"Are you sleeping?" he asked.

"No." Her voice was sharp; her eyes flashed. Emergency and tension caused the baby's arms and legs to jerk, hyper-extended.

"James, take this baby. Take her now. I'm finished. Finished!" She emphatically lifted the baby into space and tendered her to him. "Tell the nurse to make a bottle. I'm not nursing." Her head turned away. Her body twisted. Trembling hands pushed Katherine to James.

"I'm giving her to you. Decide now—right now. Do you want this baby girl?"

"Yes! I've told you a million times. I want *her* and I want you, too. Please…Pamela."

James received Katherine.

Two strong hands took her to his chest. Baby Katherine relaxed in the warm manliness of his scent.

1947 Eight years later

Shaking off his reverie, James Ross moved his thoughts to the difficult task at hand. He had to have a plan for Katherine Marie, if anything happened to him. He had to ask the last person he wanted—his business partner, Senator KC Kingsley. There was no one else. No one—no family—absolutely no one else. It had to be KC and, more importantly, his wife, Julianne.

"Julianne." He spoke as he cleared snow off the windshield. She was the pivotal part of his deliberation and conclusion. Katherine would need a kind and a dedicated mother. "At least that." Julianne was the best choice. "If I die." His feelings about KC had to be set aside.

Annapolis was not its usual charming self on a snowy day. Clouds colored the water grey and the wind gave it texture. James arrived at the waterfront restaurant to meet with Senator Kingsley, who was delayed by diners fawning over the well-known and influential politician. Finally, politicking ran its course and the Senator took his seat. The meeting could not be delayed any longer.

"What's this about, James? You said personal?" No time for pleasantries—KC was an important and busy man.

"Katherine." James announced tersely.

"She's alright?"

"She is."

KC nodded and waited.

James ordered an oyster sandwich, and paused for the waiter to leave before he spoke again. "I'm concerned about Katherine's care if anything happens to me. We have no family to step up for her." He lifted his fingers and made quotation marks in the air as he said *family*. "Well actually there is an elderly great aunt, but she can't. We have no one—" James drew a deep breath. "—except you and Julianne. Isn't it ironic?"

"I told you a long time ago that I would support… do whatever…" KC looked directly at James. "You remember that night as well as I."

"Of course, I remember. I'm ready to put aside all that has been between us. I have to. It isn't easy. Not easy at all—coming to you, but the truth is, how I feel, what you think, is not important."

"I still mean what I said. And, I know Julianne will do whatever is needed…if it is ever necessary."

"I plan to be around, but one never knows…." His voice trailed off. It was so difficult—so painful—to offer KC this accessibility. "It is impossible for me to envision Katherine given to you; easier to think about Julianne caring for her."

"I understand."

"She loves the hours she spends at King's Trace. She loves the horses, the open space, and playing with your children." He paused and stared out at the grey, icy scene—composed himself and continued. "I can't allow myself to think of things in the past. This meeting is not about the past or how I feel. It's about Katherine. Nothing more. Only her."

"I'm sure you have thought this through. Tell me what you want to do and I'll make sure it happens." KC was running low. He could only deal with family matters so long and then his curtain came down. If only Julianne were here to handle this situation. But, she was not. "Just tell me." It was a demand from a position of power. KC fidgeted, needing some air and space.

"I'm drawing a will and directive. If I die before Katherine comes of age, I'd like her integrated into your family. She will be, by all standards, an orphan at my death. Her mother has no rights …or ability to choose for her…or care for her. She'll need a family, siblings, and a mother." He avoided saying, and a father. He just could not do it. "She's eight now. I'll stipulate adoption now and when she is older, remove that. I still have some details to work out in my mind."

"I see."

"Of course I'll arrange funds in trust for her. You will get a copy of the directive now and whenever it is changed."

"That's fine. We'll look after her and her inheritance. Don't allocate any funds for her if she is in our care, before she comes of age. Not necessary. Leave it all in trusts for her when she does. I hope by making these plans it will assure these arrangements will never be needed." With unusual compassion he added, "James, put your mind at rest. Nothing is going to happen to you." KC folded his napkin and took the bill. His exit was imminent.

They walked together toward the entrance and went into driving snow that was piling up on cars. Both were chilled to the bone when they got in their cars. KC called his secretary to arrange a fresh suit so he could resume his Senatorial duties.

Back at Greeley Development's office, James took off his suit coat and tie, rolled up his sleeves and went to work. He wished he felt better about the whole thing, but he didn't. He paused to pray…for Pamela, a victim who gave up everything and for Julianne, the most profound irony of all.

CHAPTER 1

1955

How could such a luxurious life be so hard? Sixteen-year-old Katherine Marie` roused in the large four-poster bed, stretched, and glanced over to her Siamese cat purring in luxury. The bright sun tore through the ruffled curtains; the smell of breakfast cooking seeped into the room. She kicked the comforter and pounded the pillow in rebellion. "Damn the sun. Damn the bacon," then fell back accepting and spent.

"Come on, Lady Fair." The cat humped its back in a long stretch. Katherine lifted the lovely blue-eyed creature on the bed so she could talk to her. "I live at King's Trace. You are my still my cat—this is my room, my bed, and my new life. I have a brother and two sisters now. And, I have a new name, too, so, don't call me Katherine anymore. At King's Trace, I'm Kathy." She nuzzled the lazy feline.

Six days ago, she had been Katherine Marie Ross, only child of James Ross. Today she was trying to be Kathy in the Kingsley family, permanently planted in this beautiful home with Senator KC Kingsley, Julianne Kingsley, and their three children, Brenda, Johnny, and Melissa.

"Kathy, you up?" Brenda, her new big sister, tapped at the door and poked her head in the room. "Forty-five minutes before we leave for school. Breakfast ASAP. Gonna make it?"

"Sure, Brenda, I'm up. I'll make it. Thanks." She pushed the cat aside, shedding her long embroidered gown as she headed for her private bath. She tiptoed across the always-cold marble floor and stepped into the modern glass shower square, recently installed next to the big claw-footed bathtub. As the water coursed from her head to her face, she allowed the only tears she would cry today. The big towel dried her body and tears. She had a lot to get used to fast.

Living in luxury was not new to her. She gave no thought to her bedroom and huge bed left behind in the apartment on Capitol Hill. That home, which she had shared with her father, was modern. This house was traditional—the only real difference. Katherine lived in Washington, DC. Kathy lived at King's Trace, Montgomery County, Maryland. The appointments of a room were of no importance as long as she had Lady Fair and felt safe.

Twenty minutes later she descended the wide antebellum staircase to the grand foyer. Inviting aromas led her to the breakfast room where Brenda and Melissa were wolfing down cereal, toast, and eggs aided by Suzanna, the ample black woman who did the cooking and whatever else she could to keep the household moving.

"Your mother'll be in the car waiting at 8:45. Mind you be out there."

Kathy looked around the table at the children and thought, *maybe your mother...not mine.*

"Good morning, Kathy." Johnny, who was her same age, greeted her and barely acknowledged his sisters as they looked up and smiled with various foods showing in their mouths. She was new enough. Johnny was still trying to be welcoming.

"Ready for a new school?" he directed his question to everyone.

"Yes," Kathy was the only one who answered.

All of them were enrolled in new schools. KC Kingsley decided it would be easier for Kathy if all the children entered new schools when Kathy came to live with them. She would not be singled out—all the children would be struggling in a new school environment. Tuition would have to be paid to attend out of their local district and Julianne would have to provide daily transportation—a small inconvenience to help the girl acclimate to her new family, new home, new life. It was KC's decision, and neither Julianne nor Brenda, Johnny or Melissa, had a say in the matter. Kathy could not help but wonder how Brenda felt about changing schools in her senior year.

"Eat up, Missy. Here, let me tie your shoe." Brenda took charge of breakfast, helping seven-year-old Melissa. All the children were nervous about new schools, but together they pretended to be unaffected by the changes in their lives. The big house echoed with sounds of a busy family trying to get everything together to meet their car-pooler-mother at the appointed time at the front portico.

King's Trace was a big house—a mansion, built in 1935 to look like a southern plantation house that should be next to a traversable river—not on a hill just west of Laurel, Maryland. The stately columns and broad expanse of porches enclosed on one side stretched across the lush lawn at the end of a long drive lined with a canopy of huge oak trees. Three stories of white clapboard made an impressive sight at the end of the drive.

Kathy moved in last week. It felt odd. She was now a resident in the home she and her father had been guests in many times. She had grown up with these children of her father's business partner. Brenda, Johnny, and Melissa were almost like siblings before the tragic events of last Tuesday made her a member of their family.

A temporary custody document was shown to her and presented to the school so Kathy could be enrolled by Senator Kingsley.

"I've taken care of everything, Kathy. Use the Kingsley name until things are settled."

"Yes, sir." She swallowed hard and held back a tear.

She disliked being called Kathy, and didn't want to be a Kingsley, but made no protest. The Senator was powerful and strong. She needed the home he was providing. No one doubted he would take care of her, least of all Katherine. She had the same feelings and attitude toward KC Kingsley that her father had had—aloof, reserved, and matter-of-fact. Katherine was comfortable in this setting with this family, but inside an undefined feeling kept her from embracing it. She knew KC and Julianne would make sure she had all she needed, yet some of her unsettled feelings were coming from being provided with too much. *Too many things tied up neatly—without Papa*, she thought.

Katherine did not understand her feelings and she could not explain the stirring in her stomach and swirling in her brain with all the hovering people. She needed time to grieve but did not know how to ask for it. *Stop! Stop giving me things I really do not want—a new father and a shining example of what a mother should be.* Even as those thoughts blasted her brain, she was happy to have the company of siblings after sixteen years as an only child. The masterfully arranged changes were accepted because she had to… and she had to be *somewhere*. She could only live in the moment, and right now, at this hour, she had to eat breakfast, get in the car, and go to school with her new brother and sisters…and mother.

A week ago last Tuesday, the night was rainy and raw when James Ross, CEO of GRK Properties, Ltd, and his daughter, Katherine, were coming home from the National Theatre. A van, unmindful of conditions, skidded through the red light at K Street. The accident seemed minor. James Ross shot his arm and body to the right to protect Katherine. They were thrown forward and then back, hitting the dash and ending with him across her in the passenger seat. She expected him to rise. Instead, he died there.

She was delivered to the housekeeper. "Katherine, child, are you alright?" Mrs. Martin's generous and caring arms circled the stunned and rigid child.

The officer answered for her. "She is fine. We had her checked out at Children's Hospital. Not a scratch or bruise."

Katherine went to bed in their apartment on Capitol Hill totally alone. This was not like the nights she was alone, with only Mrs. Martin, because Papa was away on a business trip. This was a black and deep aloneness. Her wonderful father—the center of her world—would not come home again…ever. She did not know what to do with her grief. Katherine undressed, picked up Lady Fair, got into bed, and gave way to crying.

Mrs. Martin lightly tapped on her door. "Katherine, Senator and Mrs. Kingsley'll be here in an hour to sleep in the guest room. Do you want to come out and see them or wait for morning?"

"Morning."

"Do you want me to come back when they arrive to see if you are still awake?"

"No."

"That's fine, child. I just wanted you to know you will not be alone tonight."

But Katherine knew she was alone even if her father's business partner, along with his wife, came and filled the bed in the next room. Julianne Kingsley always treated her as one of her own brood, but Katherine, unable to remember life with a mother, did not have a clue how to return her affection.

Katherine awoke and, for a short moment, was content…until the horror of the accident and the finality of it kicked her into awareness. *How could Papa be dead? He didn't look hurt—no blood.* She recalled telling the policeman he was wrong, "Papa's not dead," refusing to allow him to lift her father's heaviness from her lap.

Katherine opened her eyes to the first morning without her father. It was pure tragedy. She had to face the truth and go forward. The mirror showed nothing different; the same girl with brown hair naturally highlighted, blue eyes, peachy complexion. Katherine studied her reflection and thought of her father. *Daddy said I was lovely, and had classic beauty.* Then, aloud, she continued her reveries. "Even called me his Mona Lisa." She smiled at her own words. Katherine was never sure her father was right even when he hinted at her one day being a beauty queen. She thought all fathers said that.

She was not a girl given to easy smiles. She had wonderful strong straight white teeth and full lips. A smile would make these tragic days easier. For some reason, unknown to her, the reflection made her cry as she felt unbearable sympathy for the girl in the mirror. She began moving around the room, dressing quickly, wanting to get away from the reflection.

The Kingsleys were having coffee and looking out the window at the Capitol dome. Katherine took a chair, glad that they did not rush to surround her with arms that would have seemed monstrous this morning. She did not know what to expect, but she knew if her father could not give her a morning hug, she did not want it from anyone else.

KC, in his favorite flannel shirt, looked like a caring, nice man, not the hard-nosed politician and business tycoon he was known to be. Julianne was a tall woman, exuding a gift for organization. Softly permed hair was clipped to the exact round shape she desired. Her face was kindly, and taking care of people was the key to her life. "Come, Katherine. Eat and then we will talk, dear."

KC greeted her. "Have some breakfast, Kathy." He used the nickname he'd given her years ago and kept for times when she was at King's Trace. It was the first time she had heard it at the Capitol Hill apartment and it did not sit well with her today. "You need to eat something. Cereal? Toast?"

She was hungry so she would try to eat. "Toast, please." She asked for it and wondered how she would swallow with the awful pain in her chest that seemed to want to travel out of her mouth.

"Bring her milk and juice and let her decide which appeals." Julianne instructed Mrs. Martin.

"Kathy, we are here to do what your father said he wanted us to do if—" The difficult words were in the air beating Katherine's brain. "—you ever needed us. Would you come home with us to King's Trace today? If you aren't ready to leave, we'll stay here with you." *He's trying to make it easy.* But, her mind stormed. *I don't want to do anything!*

"Eat your toast and think about it." Julianne interceded.

Katherine tried to eat. It was hard sitting here with these two adults. She could not imagine the whole day stretched out ahead with the three of them looking at each other in these rooms, which spoke so loudly of the absent man. There were no chairs, no corners, no nooks that did not scream, *Papa,* to her. The best way to deal with her sorrow was to run from it.

"If I can take Lady Fair, I will go…with you…now." Relief spread across Julianne's face. She was thinking of the children at home who needed her, too.

"Of course you can. I'll help you to pack some things."

"I can do it." She stood to leave the room and hesitated. "I want to go see my mother. Can you please take me to the hospital?"

"I'll go and tell her," KC said with insistence.

"No, thank you. I have to tell her." Both KC and Julianne were amazed at her maturity and strength. Katherine was surprised at her own words, for she had not thought of her mother until this very moment when she agreed to leave the only family home she knew. She did not think of Pamela Ross when the police lifted her father out of her lap or last night during her darkest hours.

"Go get your bag, Kathy. We will go home and then I will take you to Catonsville to visit your mother. There are things we need to talk about." All three knew they had avoided the word *funeral.* "As soon as you are packed, let me know. No hurry."

The move to King's Trace was accomplished with two small suitcases, a cat carrier and two photo albums. In no time, Kathy was settled in her room. Dresser drawers were filled, her hair brush was parked on the shelf and her toothbrush dropped into the holder—all so simple and quick.

Lady Fair was unhappy and expressed her discontent, which Kathy knowingly echoed by mimicking the strange meow cry coming from the back of the carrier. The temperamental cat did not come to her and would not accept petting. "I'll leave you alone,

Lady, until I get back from seeing mother. Then we'll have a heart to heart."

     ⒺⓈⒼⒹ

The ride to Catonsville, location of the largest mental institution in Maryland, was beautiful, yet failed to brighten the way for Katherine and KC. He tried to think of things to talk about, but every topic was either too serious or too frivolous. "Kathy, would you like to listen to the radio?"

She nodded, and Perry Como and Patti Page hits of the day filled the void in the car until they arrived at the gates of Spring Haven.

The hospital looked like a small college campus, except for the fact that every person on the paths and benches had an attendant dressed in white. As far back as she could remember Papa brought her to visit her mother. Four times a year—her birthday, her mother's birthday, two days before Christmas, and Easter Sunday.

The Senator called ahead and the staff was ready for the visit. Pamela Ross and an attendant were seated in a private visiting room with two-way mirrors. KC took a seat beside the attendant, and watched Katherine go to her mother to give the usual unreturned hug. The beauty of the older woman and the resemblance to the younger was uncanny. They could be sisters. Her soft wavy hair fell around her classic face, which was without age or wrinkles, hinting that not a care in the world ever reached inside this place.

"It's not my birthday, yours either. Not Easter. Not Christmas," Pamela said in a flat voice.

"You're right, Mother, I wanted to see you today." Katherine made one attempt to put herself in front of Pamela's eyes and gave up. It was a gesture she made each time to no avail. Her mother would not look at her.

"Tell KC Kingsley to go elsewhere," Pamela demanded. They paused until he was gone, as if she might say something important after he left.

"I have come with some very bad news, Mother."

No response.

Tears slipped from Katherine's eyes. "Papa is dead," she said as she lifted her arms wanting to give and get a hug from her mother, but she had to let them fall back to her lap with such heaviness she felt she would never be able to raise them again. "Mother…he's dead," she repeated. "I'm sorry to tell you." Silence followed and seemed an endless few seconds of awkwardness. Katherine was accustomed to it. "A car accident, Tuesday."

"I'm going back to my room now." Pamela stood and shuffled her feet toward the door as if picking them up would indicate some kind of life in her body. The attendant was at the door by the time she touched the knob.

"I'll be staying with the Kingsley family now. They will take care of me," she said to her mother's back. Pamela was gone. "Good bye, Mama," the child inside whispered. No one heard.

Pamela Ross looked back to watch them leave. She wanted to call to Katherine but she couldn't. *Too late, baby girl.*

What little control Pamela had, slipped away. She could not tell anyone how the death of her husband tortured her. She screamed in pain—pain that went through her brain, down her torso and burned her loins. Pamela wanted to call to James, but she was not worthy. His name stayed deep in her gut branding her with immeasurable agony.

The attendants held her firmly and murmured soothing words to her.

Stupid people. You can't hold me together. She jerked, kicked and exploded with a laugh that was maniacal.

In response to the buzzer, another attendant came to help handle the seemingly frail patient and the outburst of emotion and rage, which often followed her daughter's visits. Her fit was unmanageable today, not only because of the news Katherine brought, but also because KC had come. Two more attendants were called to help contain their patient. Exhausted, Pamela stopped fighting and folded limply to the floor. As she was picked up, she whispered with a voice sore and scratchy from screaming. "No… no… not with KC."

CHAPTER 2

Flashback

Pamela Ross was in a box. The small window cut in the wall opened, and two little paper cups appeared like magic—one with water, the other with her rainbow pills. They made the box acceptable, air breathable, and time unimportant. She ignored the cup of water and swallowed the yellow, blue, green, red and purple pills. They scratched and hung as they descended her throat and she enjoyed the pain of it like a nightly punishment. Then Pamela reached for the Hershey chocolate bar waiting on the nightstand as a reward for doing as expected and went to her bed.

The rectangle bed fit the box—it was sparse, plain, and straightforward. The bed held her and kept boundaries during the night. Pamela crawled in, assumed the fetal position and waited for the joy of the medications. Tomorrow was another day, but in a few minutes, the rainbow of pills took away concern about tomorrow. She was over it. At bedtime tomorrow she will hate the box, but like Pavlov's dog, she will want the rainbow pills and the chocolate reward, too. Modern mental health treatments were a marvel in mid-twentieth century. The patient was managed.

Pamela Greeley Ross had not always been in a box. She was the beautiful and only child of a successful businessman who was developing land in suburban Maryland and amassing a fortune. She lived with her parents, William and Genevieve Greeley, in a palatial home in prestigious Montgomery County, Maryland, where the rich and powerful from Washington, DC were entertained. William Greeley, of humble beginnings and small stature, was becoming a big man. His wife, Genevieve, came from the same humble station as her husband, but except for a few middle-age pounds, failed to enlarge as her husband had.

Genevieve wanted the simple life. That dream was lost to her. There would never be a simple life for the Greeley family of fortune and influence.

William hated his wife for dreaming of less than he amassed. He stopped seeing her classic beauty and forgot the reasons he married her. William focused on her failure to promote him in the circles he desired. She would not join the Women's League or the Ladies' Social Club at their country club. He treated Genevieve with disdain, while their daughter, Pamela, was adored. His adoration had a dear price. William controlled his power with money; he controlled his daughter with love—smothering, frightening love. Pamela tried to ignore the confused and scared feelings that stayed with her day and night.

"Who loves you most of all?"

"You, Daddy."

Each time they had the familiar exchange; Pamela felt strings circling her arms and legs. She was like the puppets tied up in the huge puppet theater in the corner of her play room. William and Genevieve had separate relationships with their daughter. At a very early age, Pamela felt their tug in different directions. One of her earliest memories was a dinner when they argued over what was the proper meal. She was near her fifth birthday.

"Let Pamela choose for herself; I'm putting portions of everything on her plate."

"Good God, Genevieve, you'll make a pig of her. I don't want her to get fat like you!" Her father spewed the words as he threw the full plate across the room and put his choices on a new plate. "Meat and green beans, proteins and vitamins. Now, Sweetie, eat it all. Daddy knows best." He smiled an ugly fake smile, and pointed at the plate. "I love you most."

"Yes, Daddy, you know best. I love you, too." As she answered, urine spilled down her leg. The food was hard to swallow, choking and scratching down her throat, but she ate it. She dared not cry and so her bladder failed her. If tears could not give her release, maybe the warm liquid running down her leg would.

When dinner was over, Pamela stayed in her seat, waiting for her father to leave the room so her mother could help her out of her embarrassment. Pamela loved her mother and hated her, too. Even now years later, just before she took the rainbow pills and ate the chocolate, she remembered the meat and green beans. She had the same recurring thought, "Why didn't Mama stop him?"

By the time Pamela was twelve, she had the first symptom of mental illness—anorexia—but it did not have a name. She found ways to avoid or void food so her frame was, hopefully, lean enough for Daddy. Her plate had small portions of meat and vegetables and she rarely ate it all. Still, with her eating problem, she grew beautiful and her eyes seemed larger. She looked like a loveable waif when KC Kingsley first saw her. She was seventeen.

William Greeley had only two missions in life—to be wealthy and to control his daughter's future. Actually, in his mind they were one and the same. His success in business was for Pamela—the choices he made for her were irrefutable. They were a team. When she was a teenager, he took her to sit and listen during huge business deals to put department stores at busy intersections and more money in his pocket. Pamela did her homework in the car coming and going to the sites where their fortunes were being made. She learned to nod when he looked at her, to act interested when architects, builders and investors walked around the table where a new project was enticing them in three dimensions. And, most importantly, she gave him the answers he expected. William patted her fondly on the head and kept a supply of Hershey bars in his briefcase as treats.

Pamela often ate one as a substitute for a meal and if she had the opportunity, she went to the bathroom, put her finger down her throat, watched the dark liquid come up from her stomach and spill from her mouth to the commode.

Her requests for piano lessons or invitations to parties were pushed aside as unimportant. "We don't have time for that," was his emphatic and final answer. The only thing she did which displeased her father was to refuse to spend his money. She simply had no desire for clothes, records, and other teenage passions. It was easier to be William Greeley's puppy than a daughter with thoughts, ideas, and inclinations of her own.

William went to bed most nights self-satisfied.

Pamela went to bed to end the day, dreading the next morning. She prayed, "Now I lay me down to sleep, I hope I die before I wake…"

CHAPTER 3

1938

William Greeley watched his little girl slowly turn into a woman. He had to do more than expose her to his business; he needed a plan. Her future husband would be the man who would continue his dynasty. As much as he loved his daughter, she did not have the strength to take the reins in the man's world of business, finance, politics, and power. He needed a partner who could assure it for her. A light bulb went off in his brain when he came upon the solution. He sat upright in the bed he no longer shared with his wife, and said, "I need *two* partners." He had stumbled on the idea—one partner could take his place with his daughter. *A young partner. A husband for Pamela.* The thought was invigorating. *Another partner with political clout.* Greeley was smugly proud of his late-night revelations "Yes, two partners," he spoke out loud as he sat up in bed.

William climbed out of bed on that cold winter night, pulled on his robe and slippers, and went to his desk to outline his brainstorm. With several erasures and scribbles he drew a plan just as he had drawn for the latest development for the corner of University Boulevard and New Hampshire Avenue. His plan detailed Pamela's future. He was drawing on the back of some blueprints for a nine-story apartment building with shopping on the ground floor.

It was his most perfect business deal.

"Kingsley's my man," he proclaimed. Greeley had contributed heavily to the campaign for KC Kingsley's bid for the House of Delegates in Annapolis and in return, a fat contract was awarded for a major department store in growing Anne Arundel County. Kingsley would be the perfect business choice—a partner to reward and reap advantages. Then he remembered a young businessman who had helped a competitor win a contract over Greeley Development. What was his name? "Ahh, yes," he muttered out loud. "James Ross." *KC Kingsley. James Ross.* His thoughts were in order; he had to get them on paper.

Future needs - two junior partners

1. Kenneth Kingsley - Political future
   Young
   Strong future
   Family Man
   Understands Money and Influence
   Ambitious
   Real Estate savvy
2. James Ross
   Experienced developer
   Smart
   Young
   Strong work ethics
   Single (attractive?)
   Good reputation in industry
   Partnership structure
   23% to each junior partner
   54% retained by me to pass to Pamela
   After Pamela and James Ross marry, they will hold 75%

It was a simple and good plan in many respects. The business needed new blood and new ideas. It was time to bring in strong young partners. Suburban Maryland and Virginia were pregnant with opportunity and William Greeley was at the right place at the right time. He wanted government contracts and high-rise condominiums. He knew what he needed to keep it going for his daughter and he would set about securing it—just as he secured good building supplies. He was positive Kingsley would see advantages in the deal, and it never occurred to him that James Ross might not want to be part of Greeley's enterprise or that he would not want to marry Pamela—or vice versa. He took his chilled body back to the bed to sleep peacefully the rest of the night.

Kenneth (KC) Kingsley was the youngest County Councilman in Montgomery County, Maryland. His progressive politics, athletic prowess and family image made his first election to the Maryland House of Delegates a breeze. His good looks, with blue eyes set in a fair complexion, turned many heads. His ready smile, marked with parentheses on either side of the mouth, was permanently etched by the time he finished the first campaign trail. He knew the power of his good looks and envisioned women voting for him and wishing they could run their fingers through his dark, curly hair.

Young voters came out in droves to assure he would represent them in the growing county and replace the incumbent whose only drawback was his age. KC had a future in statewide elections and even national ones. William Greeley assessed him as he did building locations. The potential was obvious to the developer who had been dealing with local politicians, placing businesses in districts to get voters. He would build businesses, local economies, and give Kingsley all the credit…and future votes. Politics was all about money and Greeley knew it.

William set up a meeting with KC Kingsley and talked about all these things. The two men found they shared the same goals. No minor moralities or high values would stand in the way. They seemed to grow two sizes by the time they left their first meeting.

"KC, I'm offering you a partnership in my business."

"Mr. Greeley, I accept."

"Call me William and someday, I hope I can call you Senator." The deal was set and the men, of like nature, forged the future. "I'll be adding another partner soon—a young savvy partner who will run this company as efficiently as a General Motors. Do you know James Ross?"

"Don't think I do."

"He's presently employed by Parker Contractors building the new high school in Rockville. Len Parker speaks highly of him. Ross has already established a reputation for bringing contracts in on time and on budget. Just what I need as Greeley Developments grows. Since that school is in your district, I thought you could check and see if my instincts are right before I entice him to come join us."

"If he is the man you want, I'll look into it."

"I've read his resume and researched his construction acumen—excellent, but I haven't seen him. KC, this may seem strange to you.…but he has to be attractive. I'm not hiring a dog."

Strange. KC made a note beside James Ross's name—*handsome?*

As luck would have it, James Ross was good-looking. He seemed perfect, handsome in a studious way, serious and well grounded. William knew his daughter would not like a flamboyant man and in many ways, the clueless father found a very good match for his quiet, beautiful daughter.

The deal was far from settled when he met James and assessed immediately that he was one of those high-idealed intellectuals. This did not deter Greeley. Ross was equal in height to William Greeley. His soft complexion was lit by dark blond hair that seemed to have a mind of its own—always falling down on the forehead. His green eyes were penetrating and surrounded by full lashes and natural shading which made them look deep-set. His eyes laughed before his smile, but that would not show in this meeting.

"Mr. Greeley, pleased to meet you. Your offer surprises me. I'm not looking for a job."

"Mr. Ross...may I call you James?" He assumed so and continued, "An up and coming man like you would always be open to opportunities. Right?"

"Yes, sir."

"Let me be blunt. My company is growing beyond my expectations and I will soon be doing government contracts as well as major development projects. I need a young man with experience and you have what I need. My offer includes a junior partnership when the parameters I expect materialize." Greeley became animated talking of the future and began pacing the room. "I'm offering you a contract which includes the partnership. Your vision and reputation for detail are already known."

Greeley turned and pinned the young man with his gaze. "James, would you like to be a part of the development that is going to mushroom around Washington? All the height restrictions in the capital will not hold us back as we provide the office space, shopping, and apartments circling the seat of government. I don't need to tell you that government contracts are the only hedge against the depressed economy. We are in the right place." He became emphatic, "Exactly the right place—the only place. Give Greeley Developments one year. Prove yourself and your vested interest in my company will be assured. I want you to be in on the ground floor." William Greeley was red-faced with excitement.

James Ross lifted his glasses, wiped his brow, and pushed hair off his forehead. It was a tactic he often used to give his brain time to assess an important question. "It's an exciting offer, Mr. Greeley. I'd like to think about it and get back to you. Tomorrow?" The two men rose, shook hands and parted, each sure they would find their future together. William Greeley went to his palatial home in the suburbs to relish his, and Pamela's, bright futures.

James Ross went home to his small apartment and turned on the record player to listen to his favorite classical music. With a glass of wine, he contemplated his loyalty to the company he was working for, and the unusual offer to move ahead in his career. It was a no-brainer and he knew it. The only choice he had was to go with Greeley. Opportunities like this did not come along often. He had already spent years working and was still just one of many. James knew Greeley did not even know how hard he could work. "I'll prove my worth and make partner in six months!" he exclaimed to the glass he raised in a toast.

CHAPTER 4

1939

KC Kingsley and James Ross came into Greeley's business and he congratulated himself on the master plan for both *acquisitions*. James Ross was a quick learner and had organizing skills, which were perfect for developing properties. He was brilliant and understood property values and potential. KC Kingsley was a born salesman; he could sell sand to a sheik. Greeley had other criteria for hiring these men and taking them into his business almost as sons. Ross would be the perfect husband for Pamela and KC, not needed for day-to day work, would be groomed for high political office.

KC and James would be more than partners—they would be family. At last, there was something his wife could do for his business. She was receptive to socializing the Kingsley family and the young handsome man, James Ross. Pamela was barely aware of the new activities—barbecues and dinner with her father's employees. She had so much business pushed on her, it seemed these gatherings were just another major commercial development being staged…and in truth, she was right. But, she failed to see the implications for herself .She did take an interest in the Kingsley toddler, Brenda. As soon as possible, she drifted off in the direction of the nursery to play with the child. It was often KC who went to check on the baby. He noticed Pamela Greeley's quiet beauty and budding sexuality, laden with innocence—an irresistible combination.

William Greeley had to be more aggressive to get Pamela and James together. It obviously was not going to *just happen.* He arranged for James to pick her up after school and asked him to give her driving lessons. James was glad to do it. She was a shy, lovely, agreeable young girl. His chances to talk to her included exploring the arts and he was amazed at the lack of exposure for a girl with her advantages.

"Pamela, would you like to go to the theatre or symphony?"

"I would but Dad would never allow it. I'm sure." She was surprised when her father not only endorsed her outings with James; he encouraged them. Soon she was looking forward to times they were together and he shared those feelings. They skated at the ice rink, went to movies, and joined a choral group. Pamela was happy in her new life. It was magical for her and soon she had stars in her eyes for the gentle, handsome man who was giving her a world she never knew—with her father's approval. They stood together for ovations at the National Theatre and lost themselves in Beethoven and Schumann concerts at the DAR Constitution Hall. Often they walked back to the car without talking, still enraptured by the music.

"James, I never imagined such beautiful sounds. Thank you."

"Shall we stop for something to eat?" She even forgot her fear of food and accepted the milkshake brought to their table although conversation kept her from drinking all of it. James's feelings were growing strong for this girl eight years his junior, but he never forgot his responsibility to her innocence. They held hands while skating and when walking the cold sidewalk to the car. He was always ready to study with her for her senior exams. They bent their heads over the book until they touched, electricity passed between them. Her happiness brought more beauty to her countenance. The only thing making it possible for him to resist was her lack of experience, for if she had turned her lips up to him, he would have claimed her.

James worried about his feelings, but Pamela had no worries. She was in love. This was so different from the love she and her father had professed. It was a giving love, not a taking love. She could not give James enough of her time and attention. She would give him the world and she would give him herself...but she did not know how to do it...and he never asked. Every morning was exciting and glorious. Pamela had never looked at or noticed mornings before. A new day had dawned and James was in it. No matter what Daddy required, it would be fine because James would be there. Her breathing was easier. Her stomach stopped hurting. Her prayer finally changed to thanksgiving and hope. She was a new person, reborn to love James. Her joy was in small things—walking, talking, reading, and listening. She was beginning to live and revel in all she had missed in her short life. Pamela wanted so little and it was all hers—and now—she dreamed of passion.

James was taken aback when William called him into his office late one day. The current projects were ahead of schedule and coming in below budget. Business was doing very well and he was succeeding as partner. He could not have surmised the topic for this late meeting with Greeley.

"I know you and Pamela are spending a lot of time together." James pushed his hair off his forehead so he could think.

"I assure you, William, I have great respect for your daughter. I would not—"

"Easy, easy boy. I know you wouldn't take advantage. She will be eighteen in two weeks. I think it is time I make things clear to you."

"What things?"

"James, I'm most pleased things are working out as I planned. You are a fine partner and now we can go ahead and plan the marriage." In the Greeley business manner, William tied things up too tight.

"I beg your pardon?" James could hardly breathe or think. His hand went up again to clear his forehead and hopefully his brain.

"Marriage—you and Pamela. She turns eighteen in two weeks, graduates in June. We could move things ahead and have the wedding this Fall. You *do* want to marry her, don't you?" It was rhetorical, like asking if a landowner would like to turn an acre of land into a million dollar sale. "Pamela and you are part of the plan. As my son-in-law and partner, we can get on with the grand scheme. I picked and hired you to be the one who would marry Pamela and assure her future. As I said, I'm pleased this has worked so well."

James had to stop the world from spinning and get his mind around all that was being said. He could ask only one question. "Does Pamela know your, eh…grand plan?"

"Come, come James. You've been around her enough to know her limitations, especially where business is concerned. She's a girl that must be taken care of. No point in getting her involved in the strategy. She'll do what is necessary and if being with you makes her happy, what more can a father want? You *are* the man who can run this business and Pamela, too. Admit it. It's more than you expected when you came in to be a partner!" William leaned back in his chair and took a big drag on his cigar. His smugness and his cigar drained all the oxygen from the room.

James was without air to breathe. He wanted to run from the office or maybe give William Greeley a shot on the chin, but he held back, thinking of Pamela. He not only loved her, he was her only friend in the world. She could be damaged more than she was already. Her father's attitude made her insecurities very clear. James understood Pamela even better. This manipulative man had made his daughter his major development project. He poured his desires and expectations into her like cement footings. Steel beams had constructed a rigid frame for his purposes. She did not know her father or herself. Now, she was being given away. He wanted to take her from this vacuum, but no matter what he did—take her or leave her—it would be so terribly wrong. The trap made for Pamela was closing on James.

He could say nothing as he took the doorknob and left his senior partner gloating. "Like winning the Irish Sweepstakes, isn't it son? Take your time courting her, but we will announce your engagement soon. Yes, perfect."

His laughter followed James to his car. "You and Pamela." It was incomprehensible that the young partner would not take Pamela for a prize.

James could not eat dinner and doubted he would sleep. The clock called to him hour after hour until he finally gave up and went to the den. *What would hurt Pamela more, leaving, telling her, or going along with her father?* His mind pounded.

It was all impossible because James loved Pamela. *I want to marry her.* "Never!" he screamed. How could he even entertain the thought of doing as Greeley wanted? His desire to have her caused one weak moment. Now, it was gone as the word *never* died in the air. There was only one thing to do—he would stay with Greeley Developments long enough to give Pamela some guidance and maybe influence her future. "Thank God, I never..." James thought of all the times he wanted to hold and kiss her. He whispered "Thank God she doesn't know." The only course was to gently back away and let her go. He would try to talk her into going to college and possibly meeting someone else. His head, which held these contradictory thoughts, fell into his trembling hands. It hurt to think about leaving her, but as the sun broke the horizon he knew there was no other way. He would neither be a party to nor allow her to be blindsided into an arranged marriage. He wanted Pamela so badly his body ached.

Not many miles away in her bed, Pamela drifted to sleep thinking about the man she loved and feeling maybe he loved her, too.

She noticed the difference the next day when he failed to pick her up from school. "Daddy, where's James?"

"He felt there was something at the Fredericksburg job he had to oversee. Left this morning."

"When's he coming back?'

"Probably this evening."

James did not come back, that night, the next day or the following four days. She did not understand the panic growing in her stomach. After all, he had obligations and, although he had not gone away before, she rationalized his absence with knowledge that the business was growing fast. Three days later she saw his car at the office, but he did not seek her out. That brought on a bout of hyperventilating. When she called him to see if the concert plans were still on for Saturday's matinee, he declined. She went to bed crying.

James called on Sunday and suddenly all was well again. They went to a movie but nothing seemed the same. He had an agenda and seemed to be going over items as if they were part of a checklist. First he talked of his need to be gone more often for business. Then he explained that he could not plan ahead on the concert schedule. Even with Pamela's limited experience she knew he was letting her down, but she could not manage to be disappointed at the same time she was so elated just to be with him. These conflicted feelings took her back to her childhood and she ran to the bathroom to vomit food she had just eaten. James saw her red eyes and misread that she had been crying when in truth it was the horrible pressure of retching that bloodied them. He wanted to take her in his arms and comfort her, but instead went on with his agenda.

"I really want to talk seriously with you about your birthday next week and your future when you graduate." Pamela, who was skilled at pulling herself together after vomiting, smiled.

"Now, James…or tomorrow after church? We could take a long drive up to White's Ferry and walk the C&O Canal trail. Remember, we did that last fall."

"Yes, let's do that. I will pick you up at 12:30." She put her apprehensions aside and waited for tomorrow.

Meanwhile, James went in to see William. He thought very carefully what he would say to her father. He had so much at stake here and Pamela had even more. He understood that. He went right to the point.

"Pamela and I have never discussed marriage and I'm not going to make marriage a business deal. Monday I am going back to Fredericksburg and rent an apartment for three months. I will be there until the Shenandoah High Rise is complete. Nothing would make me happier than to believe that she and I have a future but not now—not this way. We have talked of her going to college. I think she is considering Towson or another small local one."

"Maybe *you* would risk her going to college and meeting someone else—I can't." Greeley was getting angry and red-faced. *Who's this upstart daring to suggest he knows what's best for my Pamela?*

Then James talked to the man in terms he could understand. "Mr. Greeley, I own 23% of this company and I am going to do what is best for it right now…and that is being in Fredericksburg. There are problems with our first high-rise with a shopping Galleria. If we don't bring this in under budget and on time we can kiss future projects like it good-bye. I can do it, but I've got to be there. Several Senators are investors in this building and future government contracts hinge on this success. Shenandoah had better be all it is projected to be or what security will you have for Pamela? You know I need to be there."

"Alright, go to Fredericksburg. You're right about the project, although I am not convinced you can't take care of things from here." James breathed a sigh of relief and then the old, cigar-smoking, big man said the worst thing James had ever heard. "Come home for her birthday. Sleep with her once. I know my girl; she'll be true to the man who takes her first. A quick romp in the bed and she will be over this college thing and ready for marriage. In fact, one screw and she'll forget college altogether." Greeley's ugly face folded up into a disgusting wink.

In that moment James hated his senior partner—the father of the girl he loved. It took all of his control not to smash his face with the fist he had clenched at his side.

Pamela did not know why, but her wonderful life was over. James said good-bye and left for Virginia. She prayed the old prayer again and thought of suicide.

William Greeley was so caught up in the importance of the Shenandoah high-rise that he failed to notice the change in his daughter. He often went to Fredericksburg himself and social engagements became low on his priority list. James Ross was doing an exceptional job, and even with his mental and emotional stress, seemed to be focused.

The graduation and birthday party for Pamela was handled by Genevieve. The light that lit her daughter's eyes recently was gone and she resumed the familiar aura of past years. She ate birthday cake and quickly went into the ladies room and pressed her finger against her tongue until it was expelled. People of no importance wished her happy birthday and congratulations. James was not here; nothing else mattered. The fragile Pamela was lost without him.

"Daddy, where's James. Isn't he coming to my party?"

"He's on his way. I talked to him an hour ago."

Her father insisted she celebrate with champagne. It was a dangerous mix with the antidepressant that her mother put in her mouth as she came from the bathroom with red eyes. One drink tasted good and made her melancholy for James, the second made life bearable. The third made life wonderful. The bubbles promised that James was coming.

KC Kingsley saw Pamela go out on the lawn. He took a bottle of champagne and two glasses and followed. She was sitting on the stone wall by the pool.

"A penny for your thoughts," he asked as he filled the glasses. She poured out her feelings for James, as more sparkling wine flowed—repeatedly—into her glass. KC's arms went around the floundering waif and consoled her drunken body as he moved her to the grass and told her, "I'm James."

She clung to him. His fascination with the boss's daughter was exciting the man and, without thinking of the consequences, he answered the passion that she had wondered about. When he asked if she wanted to do this, she closed her eyes and drunkenly replied, "Yeth, James."

Pamela melted into strong arms. KC lifted her dress and pulled her lace panties down. Her innocence demanded—*stop*. She wanted to be free, but his arms held tight and lifted her hips. She opened her eyes and screamed, "KC". His mouth engulfed hers and no sound went past the hedge.

Pamela shut down her body and let her mind go.

Behind the hedge, in a moment of drunken bliss, hot desire and sexual abandonment, she was doomed. The lives of countless people were changed. A virgin was soiled and the future Senator was tainted to the point that any claim he made of morality would be deceitful. Pamela slept on the warm lawn. KC zipped his pants and gently straightened her dress, being very careful not to touch the girl he had just ravaged. He looked down at the sleeping child and trembled. Lights from the house and music drifting out to the pool required him to pull himself together. Before going back to the party, KC stopped at the pool house to wash his face and hands, but he could not clean himself to be the man he was thirty minutes ago.

⁂

James sat in his car, unable to rush traffic, one hundred miles south, and wondered if he could get to Maryland and claim the woman who had finally come of age. While one junior partner was sitting lovelorn on the highway, the other one put his discretion aside, satisfied a hunger, and rode the crest of an orgasm as he would soon ride the crest of political power and success.

Eight weeks later, the work to elect a new junior senator from Maryland was underway. KC Kingsley beat his ultra-conservative opponent. William Greeley spent a fortune to secure it. Political funds were available, palms were greased and votes were promised. Nothing could keep the handsome, carefully selected candidate from being elected and seated in the most powerful government in the world—nothing short of scandal—and there was not a hint of that. With his pregnant wife, Julianne, and adorable daughter, Brenda, at his side, he claimed victory in the primary. He would have the votes to be Senator. He would have glory and power.

Pamela was at home vomiting; she had not eaten nor put her finger down her throat. Her small breasts were tender. The days of the month were counted and signs were tallied by the girl just as votes were tallied for KC Kingsley. The night of her birthday flashed through her mind as she covered her eyes and fell on the bed. It really happened; she did not imagine it. She and KC did roll in the grass; he did pull her dress up; she did scream while his penis did draw blood.

Pamela rose from her bed and went to the bathroom where she lifted her dress again, pulled her panties down to her ankles and knelt with a razor. She was a cutter and had scars on her arms from years of relieving unbearable emotional pain with physical pain. Tonight she drew the razor slowly and deliberately through her pubic hair to her skin. The pain of the cut gave her wonderful/terrible relief.

The superficial wound spilled blood on to the white panties and the royal blue tile floor to backdrop her despair. Everything was swirling red, white and blue like the bunting spread on the podium where KC and his family were standing at that very moment, claiming his primary victory. He would be his party's nominee for US Senator from the great state of Maryland. He would go to great heights.

If Pamela Greeley could look into a crystal ball she would see that within her womb, little Katherine Marie was perfect, lovely and untouched by the horror of her conception.

CHAPTER 5

1939

It was hard to say when it happened, but William Greeley's appearance seemed to change with his obsession with money. As a young man, he was not sure his expectations of wealth would materialize. He was a pleasant, average-looking man, brown hair, and a complexion dappled by long-gone bouts of acne. His eyes were hazel and seemed ready to laugh, and his sense of humor was his best asset. It helped him make friends with the mayor of Laurel, Maryland where he would attempt to bring a major department store for this bedroom community just twenty miles from Washington, DC. Together they picked a spot north of town and began acquiring land. It was a huge moneymaker as the first major department store came to the suburbs on his properties. Greeley laughed with his wife, Genevieve, and his daughter Pamela, about the rich future that would allow them to vacation in Ocean City next summer. Little did he realize, they would travel the world and vacation on islands in every ocean because the average American family took their money to shop in his ventures.

The fun of vacations and lovely homes, cars, and amenities soon lost its appeal. The man dreamed of bigger, better, more. His eyes seemed to move close together, or was it the face growing broader as pounds were added to his small frame? He looked sloppy when his suits pulled around his wide stomach and his thinned hair spilled over his collar. Bourbon puffed his face and deepened the acne pits. The smiles that once softened his demeanor were gone and in place were lines which held suspicion, cunning, and avarice. Because of his own nature, he suspected the same in everyone else. Greeley's bulbous nose seemed to cartoonize the man. He was so self-absorbed he never realized his wife and daughter brought beauty and refinement to his life. Greeley believed those attributes were in his money.

Family life was non-existent in the Greeley household. Instead, they had meetings run much as he ran his business, usually instigated by William. A unique set of meetings occurred on the day Pamela told her mother she was pregnant. Genevieve asked William to meet her in the library. He tried to put her off, but he could not this time.

"It's about Pamela." He reluctantly delayed leaving for the office and allowed himself to be beckoned.

The fat-faced, big-nosed, untidy man plopped into the chair. "Well?'

"Pamela's pregnant." Nothing prepared him for this announcement and Genevieve had decided not to soften the blow. "I don't know who the father is...she won't say. And William...she has refused to come in here this morning to meet with us. She *will not* talk to you and barely talks to me."

"Pregnant? Are you sure?"

Genevieve nodded.

"Can it be aborted? We can buy a doctor." His mind was looking for a way out, but his wife was shaking her head.

"I took her to the doctor yesterday. He wouldn't discuss abortion, she is too far along." Greeley rose from the chair and began pacing back and forth. It seemed as soon as a possible solution came to his mind, his wife answered it. "We cannot send her away. She's much too fragile. You know that."

He walked to the window to watch his favored colts run through the fallen leaves. His next idea was addressed in the same manner.

"She doesn't want the baby and even now wants to deny a child is growing inside her. I'm afraid for Pamela."

He took a moment to light a cigar and sit back down. "How far along? When could this have happened? "

"Late May or early June." Picking up the pad he kept at the side, he began to write notes:

Early June

Men????

James Ross

He looked up at his wife with a sly, knowing smile. "Genevieve, it has to be James. He's the only man I ever saw her with and they had this thing going before he went to Fredericksburg. It has to be James. This isn't a tragedy. They'll marry." He was suddenly elated. "Go get her! Make her come here."

"William, I don't think you should force this. We're not sure it's James and I don't think she wants the father any more than she wants the baby. We need to talk about care and adoption."

His back went up as it always did when anyone countered him. This stupid woman had no idea what was right for Pamela. "Get out of my way." He shoved his wife against the wall. "I'll get her. Go—do whatever you do all day. Leave this to me."

Genevieve fell into the chair, exhausted and lost. She had never stood up to him and she could not today.

Greeley called James and gave him two hours to come to Maple Hill. Then he marched up the stairs and threw open the door to the room where all the blinds were down against the morning sun.

Pamela, in her nightgown, sat on pillows in the corner staring into nothingness. Her head did not turn toward her father. She knew what would happen. She knew he would make her tell. She knew he would hate her. She knew James would hate her. She knew her baby would hate her. But that was nothing compared to the hate she had for herself.

"Pamela! Get up from the floor and come here." She did as he demanded. "Put on your robe—," she moved like a robot, "—and slippers." Pamela sat on the bed while he opened the blinds and took a seat in the rocker. "Are you pregnant?'

"Yes, Daddy."

"You know who the father is?"

"Yes."

"Tell me?"

She did not answer; she did not know how to say *no* to her father. She did not cry but sat with her arms across her stomach to hide the small bulge.

"I know who the father is," he announced.

"You do?" Confusion racked her brain. *Daddy knows. How could he know of the terrible thing that happened on my birthday?*

"Just relax, child. Daddy'll take care of everything. Who knows best? I love you."

"You know best, Daddy. I love you, too." She did not know how her father would solve this, but he rang Pavlov's bell for her response and she knew no other way than to believe him. He would make everything right. Now it was possible for her to crawl back in the black corner and wait. She did not have to think about the pink baby growing inside. She did not have to remember the red blood and KC. She need not cry the blues over James. She did not have to dread the yellow sunrise tomorrow, either. Like the magic in a rainbow, Daddy would take care of everything.

William Greeley was beginning to be delighted that the couple had taken things into their own hands since James had acted so high and mighty about an arranged marriage. *"James found it wasn't such a bad idea after all,"* he thought. Greeley was smug and optimistic, Pamela would be happy by dinnertime. While he waited for James, he decided to call KC and tell him of the plans for a wedding.

"KC, I have great news about Pamela and James. We're gonna have a wedding. You'll be elected senator and what's more, I am going to have a grandchild. Can't get much better than that." He was interrupted by movement in the foyer. "James is here. We'll talk later."

This meeting would be the most pivotal in James's young life. Nothing that came before or since affected him more. Nothing would be the same after William told James Pamela was pregnant.

"Pamela, pregnant?" It was hard to believe.

"It's alright, boy. I told you before, this marriage is what we want. It has to be as soon as possible. You don't have to apologize. We're not angry, as long as you do the right thing now. She is upstairs in her room, waiting for you."

Two things were sure for James he had not fathered Pamela's child—and he could not trust William Greeley. The truth would not be in anything he said.

"You're saying she named me? I'm not the father of Pamela's baby. If she is pregnant, isn't it important to find out who *is* the father?"

This took William Greeley back. "What are you trying to do? Are you trying to get out of responsibility for this? That's the last thing I expected from you, James Ross." The old man was getting angry. "My Pamela deserves a man! Be a man. Step up for her and the baby. Maybe you need a minute. Have you talked to Pamela?"

"I haven't talked to her and I have *not* had intercourse with her either. While you are trying to get her married to me, there is another man who is the father of this child. I care about Pamela, but there must be someone else who means more to her than me—enough for her to have a baby with him. Excuse me, but if that is what you called me here for I'm finished." He stood to leave this awful place and the man he hated.

This was not going as the old man thought. He laid his hand on James' arm. "Wait a minute." For the first time, he was trying to think. "She didn't name you. She hasn't named anyone." William Greeley softened as he saw his daughter's plight in its true light. As narrow and suspicious as the old man was, he knew James Ross was not lying. "You're her friend. Will you go see her and talk to her? We can't help her if she closes down."

He could not refuse. James was thinking about Pamela and had not begun to think about his own broken heart. All dreams he had of life with the woman he loved were dashed by this news. Not only was there someone else in her life, she was pregnant with his baby. A departing dream is like a death and requires time to grieve. His heart remembered her joy when they were together, her renewed health—both mental and physical—and the tempting vision of a future together. Now he was on his way up the stairs to her room to find out why it was all shattered. He was on his way to see if he could help the girl, not agonize over his own grief.

Pamela was reading a book when he tapped on the door. "It's James, Pamela."

"James." She ran to him overjoyed. Her father's solution was James! "You've come. Did father send you? I didn't know what I would do until father said he would take care of everything. You tapped on my door." Her voice full of relief. "He sent you. You!"

They sat together on the floor. "Pamela, I came to help you but I am not sure what I can do—except be your friend." He took her shoulders firm in hand and demanded her eyes. "You know I'm not the father of the child you're carrying, don't you?"

"Of course, I do," she said with great sadness. "I thought because of this—" She pointed at her abdomen, "—you would never want to see me again or be my friend." Her eyes welled with tears. "Please be my friend. Please…please…"

"No need to beg, Pamela." He took her hand. "It's always best in these situations to marry the father. Do you want to do that?"

"No. Can't and wouldn't if I could."

"Then you need to be honest with your parents."

"That's impossible, too." Her joy at being with him faded and she began to retreat to her black place. "Help me, James."

"I want to, but I don't know how. Your father wanted me to marry you because he thought I was the father."

She laughed a weird maniacal laugh. "I'll never marry you. Thank you for coming. I don't want to talk anymore." She was finished and he knew it. Pamela waved James away with the back of her hand.

After the door closed behind him, she threw herself against it and whispered. "I'm not worthy. I'll never marry. After this child is born—," she clasped her belly and bent her head to speak to her womb, "— my life's over." Then she spoke softly to the closed door. "Go James. I'm doomed."

A rare emotion boiled to the surface for James as he stepped back to re-enter the room. Pamela had barely drawn a breath when James pushed against the door, knocking her to the floor. He slammed the door behind him, picked Pamela up from the floor and placed her on the bed while gently brushing his hand over her face, to push wet hair out of her eyes.

Pamela was stunned when James kissed the tracks of her tears.

"As well as I know my own name, I *know* you did not take a lover. The father of this child must have taken advantage or even forced his way! It's all clear to me now. I should've known. I *should have* known when your father told me." He let his thoughts retreat to the terrible moments downstairs. His face darkened before he softened again.

"My sweet Pamela. You're suffering and have been suffering since this awful thing happened to you." His arms circled, held and comforted her. "Tell me." He drew her closer. "Tell me." Pamela melted against his chest. "*I will not leave* until you tell me."

"KC," softly burst from her quivering mouth. His name came on a hot, unnatural, propellant breath and lay in the tiny space that had just opened up between Pamela and James.

CHAPTER 6

1939

William Greeley was waiting at the foot of the stairs. James held back his impulse to rage at the man who, in some way that James could not define, was responsible for Pamela's tragedy. He wanted to run from this house and think. His love for Pamela had been a warm and gentle feeling until now. How could it hurt so much? How could it tear him to pieces and put fear in his stomach?

"I don't want to hear anything you have to say." He jerked his shoulder away from Greeley's touch and continued toward the door. James stepped on the portico just as KC approached the door with a smile on his face. It was more than the gentle man could take. The blow to the newly elected senator bloodied his lip and sent him to the ground. A photographer, who was following the first full day since the election, took the picture of Senator Kingsley on the ground, but fortunately missed the shot of James Ross's fist connecting with his chin. William Greeley grabbed the camera and demanded he leave the premises.

This gave James time to enter his car. A white flash on the side lawn caught his eye. It was Pamela running away from the house. A glimpse of her, nightgown flying in the wind, running across the lower lawn brought James to action. He tore out of the driveway to the dirt road that led to the pond and arrived as she reached the water's edge. Pamela looked at the water, then at James. A split second decision was made—not only by her but also by him.

"Pamela, come to me!"

He was her savior after all. She turned and ran to his arms. It was more than a decision not to go to the bottom of the pond—she decided to let James save her.

In that same instant, he decided to claim her, keep her, tend her, and love her. "It's alright, Pam. I'm here...and, I'll always take care of you."

As much as he hated to go back to the house where Greeley and KC were, he carried the broken girl in. She took the fetal position in his arms and did not open her eyes until she was settled back in her bed. "Sleep, dearest. I'm going downstairs, but I'll be back very soon. No one will come into this room, I promise...until I come back after your nap." His heart burst with love and concern as he looked down on the broken doll he placed in her crib. As he brushed her hair from her face a tear from his eye found a target on her flushed cheek. "Sleep."

"Yes, James."

He stood a moment outside her door to gather his thoughts. There was one thing on his mind and heart. He would take care of this precious girl. Greeley had to be told. He wanted to be strong and take her from all of this, but the reality was the baby in the womb. He could not grab her and run from the only source of income he had. He could not take her from Maple Hill without a job and the means of caring for her. James needed time to think and yet there was no time.

The den was full of men. James recognized the high political figures assembled. Besides KC and Greeley, he saw the senior senator from Maryland, Crenshaw, Senate Majority Leader Logan, and National Party leader, Bob McAllister. It was a full pow-wow. Greeley, seeing James, took a political stance and dismissed the earlier events as minor compared to the reason for this meeting.

"James Ross, our business partner, is joining us. Come in, James. You have an interest in this meeting, too. " He waved him in with a generous expansive arm. "I think you know these gentlemen." It was evident they were discussing the future of the newly elected Senator Kingsley.

KC was genuinely puzzled at James's attack and caught his eye with a questioning look. It was disarming to realize that neither Greeley nor KC knew the facts or the implications of the festering problem, napping in the upstairs bedroom. James stood in the doorway listening to references to KC's unprecedented landslide victory, his oratory skills, and impeccable family image.

They are making a plan to make him the next President of the United States. James could only shake his head.

"KC is in the national eye."

"Picked up by the networks."

They were planning his future, and discussing future presidential elections as if the White House was assured for their party and the wisdom in making KC Kingsley their party's candidate. James was the only person in the room who knew there was a reason to doubt that would happen. The baby in the womb had more power than these mighty men. Pamela would have to be sacrificed for such a big dream.

James waited and prayed for courage. As the last limousine pulled away, KC turned to James, ready to return the attack. "Now, what was this all about?" He questioned as he touched his swollen lip. James could not look or talk to him and instead turned to Pamela's father.

"Greeley, Pamela told me who fathered the child she is carrying."

"Who?"

"KC." James turned to face the Senator again. It was as if a swinging door hit both men. Greeley plopped his huge body into a chair and KC lowered himself slowly and deliberately onto the sofa. "Yes, KC—" he repeated. "—the new and perfect Senator from the great state of Maryland—the one who would be groomed to someday be President of the United State of America. He seduced Pamela and she is pregnant." He turned and looked at the Senator. "Not as pregnant as your wife, KC, but pregnant." If bullet words could kill, KC would be dead.

William Greeley's eyes narrowed even more. His face puffed and reddened. His pitted cheeks went to gravel. Greeley saw his power melt and his fortune dwindle. He lifted his gaze and looked at one man and then the other. Just as he would look for solutions for cement and steel problems, he would find a way to bring KC to the White House on time and under budget. KC was his baby. Pamela was his pawn and James Ross was key to it all.

KC was visibly shaken. The truth that James had thrown into the air was accepted by the business partners. There was no denial. KC held his head in his hands. *Julianne… I can't tell her this.* The unborn baby he was anguishing about was not Pamela's, but Julianne's—due soon.

William Greeley poured a drink and sipped it thoughtfully, his eyes calculating. A harsh quiet settled in the room, broken only by the movement of ice cubes.

Disgusted with both of them, James rose to leave the room.

"Wait, James. Where are you going? We need to talk." It was KC making a weak appeal to the man who had everyone's fate in his hands.

"I seem to be the only one who has any concern for Pamela. Her mother has closeted herself away. There's no one else to go to her. She's upstairs trying to hold on to her mind. I'm simply going to make sure she does."

KC was prepared for Greeley's wrath but it never came. His defensive moment was gone and since Pamela's father was not going to tear out his guts over this, there was no sense in him doing it to himself. His breathing changed, became more regular. The glass Greeley offered was taken with relief as he asked, "What do we do?"

Greeley was still thinking—centered on James Ross. Suddenly he blurted out, "That fool loves her." All was not lost. One good business deal and this would be just a bump in the road. His drink was drained in one happy gulp. "There is a way to handle this." He went up the stairs and entered Pamela's bedroom without knocking. James was sitting on the edge of the bed brushing her hair from her face.

Pamela stared up at James, all her love—all her trust—in her eyes.

Greeley's confidence grew as he walked to the bed and gave his daughter a kiss. "Pamela, you are going to be fine. I'll make sure. Didn't I tell you not to worry? James told me everything. I love you," he added as an after thought as he patted her head, slid a bar of Hershey chocolate on her bed stand and addressed James. "I'll be in the den. Come talk to me when you come down."

"I love you too, Daddy," she said as he left the room. She would take the candy, just as she always did. She would obey, just as she always did. He was sure; he was positive.

James was ready this time when the three men met in the den.

Greeley did not open with opportunities for suggestions. "There are several facts we all have to accept. The first fact is

Pamela cannot marry the father of her child. She is fragile and needs someone to care for her. This is no time for emotions and feelings. We need a good solid business deal." He pressed his forefingers into his temples to pull his thoughts into his hands. "James, I'm offering you senior partnership if you will marry Pamela and raise the child as your own. Your percentage combined with Pamela's will give you controlling ownership. The child's biological father will never be revealed." William rubbed his hands, satisfied with his perfect deal.

KC found his voice. Sitting beaten in the corner, he spoke to his shoes. "I'm so sorry." He repeated weakly. "If I could change what happened that one night, I would. I am sorry."

James had no pity for him. He was basically ignored as the other two men plowed through the situation.

Greeley continued as if speaking in a board room. "As far as I can see, this deal is mutually beneficial for everyone. I know you care for her, James. I saw it a minute ago in her room. She cares for you, too." He tried to sound concerned for Pamela but it was lame. "Are the financial benefits sufficient for you to accept that she is carrying someone else's baby? I asked you back in May if you wanted to marry Pamela and you were offended by my intrusion into your life. Everything's changed now. She has to marry."

"Shut up, Greeley." The more her father said, the clearer it came to James what he must do.

Greeley was silenced; KC raised his head.

"Pamela is not a business deal. The baby she is carrying is KC's—not just *someone's*. She's been wronged. Terribly, horribly wronged. Neither *you*—." He faced Greeley, and then turned to KC. "—nor *you* seem to realize that. This isn't just something that happened to her. It's something *you* did to her." He pointed to the Senator, who felt the pointed finger as if it had punctured his eye. "Somewhere there has to be accountability and... and," he searched for the word, "... apology." James paused. No one moved. "How the two of you can calculate her life as a business deal is abominable. I'm not a business deal, either. My care for her has nothing to do with benefits and rewards. You both are so arrogant. All you are thinking about is business. Business as usual. Shame!" James stepped to the center of the room. "I love Pamela and all that I do for her is because of that love. I'll take Pamela and the child because I love her and all that is her, including the child she carries." James paused again and took a sharp breath, taking to his core the decisions he wrought on the spot. "As for you, KC—" He looked over at the cowering man. "—meet me in the office at seven. We will talk in private."

James, KC and Greeley did not know that Pamela, pale and fragile, had slipped into the room. She did not hear James's profession of love and care for her. She only heard the next words he spoke with ice and hate.

"I'll marry Pamela and raise her child. I don't want to know what happened to her. With her shares and mine, I *will* run Greeley Developments. *You* will retire." He walked close enough to breathe on Pamela's father. "I will not... I cannot work with you another day." Face to face, he continued. "Consider this if you don't retire, I'll ruin you."

He glanced at KC for a bare moment as if he did not merit more. Greeley saw steel in James's unflinching eyes. "If you don't retire, Greeley—," KC saw the same untempered metal glaring at him. "—KC goes down, too. That's the only deal on the table today."

Pamela turned and ran back to her room, unseen. She had never heard James speak like that. His words and voice, so cold and hard, cut her like a knife. In that instant the tender connections she had to people around her were severed. Pamela left reality, sank into a hole and embraced nothingness. Lost. She thought of the bottom of the pond and knew, although she was breathing air, that was where she was.

CHAPTER 7

1939

At six forty-five, James entered the office and made a pot of coffee, letting the soothing aroma ease the tightness in his chest. He checked the clock and wondered if KC would come. Confrontation was not his style. This had been a day of confrontations and it exhausted him. "God, give me strength to…." He didn't know what to ask for and finally prayed, "…just give me strength." As he waited for KC, his mind wound around the path that brought him to this night.

―※―

He was eighteen when his parents and sister died in a hotel fire. The only asset left to the sole survivor was the family home. Up until that day, he had been a spoiled child, underachiever, and a rebel. The first few sleepless nights alone in the home gave him an epiphany. There was no one to tell him what he should do—it was all up to him. James was solely responsible for his choices.

He sold the family home to pay for the education that his postal employee father could never have given him in life. He finished the last semester of high school with remarkable grades and aced the SAT with a score that surprised his counselor. He was off to Yale, determined to pay for the first year and earn a scholarship for the next ones. All of his plans worked out. He liked the taste of taking on the unexpected and succeeding. James Ross became a man who was willing to take adversity, take charge, and take responsibility.

Through the years he rarely went back to those days but tonight, with only coffee to boost his confidence, he did—with a philosophical comment. "Come… on… life."

⁂

KC walked into the office at ten past seven. He looked tired, haggard, and hungry. The lines in his face were drawn and his demeanor had none of the elation of yesterday when the votes confirmed his senatorial seat. He could not face Julianne; he called her to say he had a meeting at the office and would miss dinner. KC sat for a long while in the car. Finally, there was nothing to do but go into the office where James Ross was waiting.

James lifted his cup and pointed to the pot as invitation. The recriminations, accusations, and heat that KC expected did not come.

He took his cup, took a seat, and said the only thing that could civilly open their conversation. "How is Pamela?"

James had to concede that the politician had said the right thing. "What do you want to know?"

"Is she going to be alright?"

"Well…she is going to carry the baby and birth it. Physically she may be able to do it. Mentally, I don't know."

Silence settled like a shroud. Neither knew where to go. James decided to leave it to KC to again come up with the right thing to say.

"I *am* sorry. …and it is so inadequate. You know it; I know it. This is way beyond a simple apology. Lives and futures are at stake." He paused to drink long and deep from the cup and reached inside himself. "I'm not thinking politically, although you know, I'll be thinking that way tomorrow." The Senator spoke without evaluating the political wisdom of his words. "Today, right now...I want to talk about Pamela, the baby, you, and me. It may be the only time I will be able to do it." It felt good to be honest. "I didn't know she was pregnant. This is... all my fault. Do you want me to tell you what happened?"

"No."

"What *do* you want?" KC was pleading with his hands. "Should I go see Pamela?"

"No."

"Must I tell Julianne?" His voice trailed down into hopelessness. "For God's sake, James, say something." He knew better than to beg or barter. And yet, he was pleading with his eyes. KC was a man who was, at this moment, ready to do anything to relieve his guilt as well as the uncertainty.

James knew KC's vulnerability and candor would not last. He felt a tinge of pity for the man who had built a façade of strength to cover his weaknesses. He could not ignore the fact that the child he was willing to raise was fathered in a weak moment by a man headed to Congress to govern the nation. It was a dichotomy found throughout history. Thomas Jefferson to Dwight Eisenhower and most in between had secrets that proved beyond greatness, they were just men.

Suddenly, James knew; it was all so clear. What KC did to Pamela last summer was done and could not be undone. Could not be paid for nor ignored. The only important thing in this meeting was the future. No matter how he rationalized, he, Pamela, the unborn baby, and KC would be connected forever. He wondered if KC knew that even if he wiggled out of the dilemma of this moment, it would never be over. Neither the Senator nor his planted sperm would disappear any more than Pamela and the resulting baby would. There was no way to break the biological connection.

For the first time, the baby grew in importance over the mother. James was not sure he could help Pamela, but he had every confidence he could save the child. He had to act now to get everything in order for the baby's future. As much as he hated telling KC exactly what he wanted to hear, it was the only course he had.

"Pamela is very fragile. I'm going to talk to some doctors about her condition. There were psychological problems before this happened and I'm not sure I can bring her back to the girl I knew. She has no emotional attachment to you, KC. She really believed she imagined your encounter until her pregnancy became undeniable. Don't ever talk to her about it. Promise that!"

KC nodded in agreement.

"No one is to know about this except me, you, and Greeley. Genevieve does not know and doesn't need to know. She already thinks it was me. I'm going to marry Pamela as soon as possible. She'll be my wife and the child will be mine. I'm sure this is agreeable."

The Senator nodded again.

"Nothing else is going to change. That will be best for Pamela. She does very well denying anything is wrong. She'll see you and your family. She cares for Julianne and Brenda, in fact, she asked for Julianne. The less change the better." James went for more coffee and took a long walk around the room to gather his thoughts.

"Now about Greeley Developments.... You know I run this business—have been for some time. The growth into high-rises and government contracts—is just too much for the ole man. I've been on-site and kept all the contracts solvent since I joined the firm. He could not run it without me now if he wanted to." James went for another coffee. "You need me and ironically, I need to keep our business partnership. While everything feels like it is going to hell—thanks to you—I won't let the business fail. Won't! Greeley is out; we will keep it going. If I can do that, you surely can, too. Agreed?"

For the third time, KC let his heavy head go up and down.

"Greeley's retirement is not a point for debate. That's the crux of the deal. If he doesn't give it up, you and he will have to buy Pamela and me out." James stopped talking long enough to contemplate the possibility that Greeley would refuse to leave the business. James repeated and put on a stern façade, "I *can and will* ruin him. I said it and I mean it. Greeley Developments will go down the tubes." It was in that moment that James realized he hated Pamela's father and blamed him for her plight—more than the man looking at him in amazement.

KC could hardly believe that he would leave this meeting essentially off the hook. It was the last thing he expected when he walked in an hour ago. He stood to leave, offered his hand, and drew it back as James stood firm. There was no point in trying to make friends. "James, I'm going to support you and Pamela. I'm not sure how…but, if you need me, I'm here. Pamela is fortunate to have you, and I'm indebted to you."

"I'm not doing this for you!" For the first time this evening, anger flared. He stepped into KC's face. "Don't flatter yourself. If I thought beating you to a pulp would help anything, you would be a bloody mess by now. You bastard!" James took his collar. "Go! Make something of yourself. I have heard all your rhetoric about making America strong in spite of Europe's mess. I listened to your promise of civil rights for everyone. Go. Do it. Don't forget—your aspirations are as thin as a baby's breath. They could be lost to you." James twisted his collar and blocked blood trying to leave his face and closed his wind pipe. KC's mouth flew open just as the death grip was released. He was shaken as he reached backward for the door.

James advanced again. "KC. Forget your part in the conception of this baby." He pushed KC out the door, symbolically pushing him out of the new life in Pamela's womb. "That child is mine. That's the deal."

KC walked slowly to the car, which was bathed in moonlight. He could see the eerie brightness of night through his tears. He sat and exhausted himself with soft, soundless crying. As he pulled himself together and started the car, fear gripped him. It went up his spine, raising the hair on his neck; it moved the skin on his scalp. Anxiety gripped his chest so he could not breathe. KC began to panic. *Am I dying?* Pant, pant. *No* . Then loud sobs came. He wept uncontrollably, each inward breath bringing gasps.

Breathe, he had to tell himself. *Can I drive?* Self-doubt overwhelmed his brain. He banged his head on the steering wheel and screamed, "Pamela." And, then he knew his fear was Pamela. That stupid, crazy girl would never understand the plan. "She's nuts. She'll never understand—never!" KC knew Pamela could never think clearly enough to understand the deal he had just made with James Ross.

For almost twenty minutes, he went over the last events and devised a strategy to protect himself from any damages Pamela could cause. He gulped air and swallowed his fear. Mental illness could cause the whole sordid mess to come to light. But, on the other hand, her insanity would put doubt on anything she said about the baby and its conception. He chastised himself for even admitting that he fathered her baby. In a guttural, almost inhuman voice, he said her name again and took hold of the strain of superiority that drove his life. No feeble-minded Lolita and her baby would keep him from his destiny. He forgot the man who cowered before James Ross. He sat up straight and said something else to the moonlight.

"Senator Kenneth Charles Kingsley of Maryland!" It was the first time he had uttered it, and it sounded good, strong, and invincible.

He put the car in gear and drove off the Greeley Developments parking lot feeling more like himself.

CHAPTER 8

1939

KC began his first term as Senator Kingsley. James prepared to marry Pamela. Katherine Marie grew in vitro. The smoothest transition was KC's silky slide into his congressional seat.

William Greeley died suddenly. A stroke seized him last nightabout the same time that KC entered the office to meet with James Ross. While James proclaimed that he could not continue the business association with Greeley, the man fell to the floor with his eyes wide in disbelief and death.

The old man's sweat and toil left a solvent business. Ironically, the precious money that he worked so hard to amass for his daughter's happy future would secure everyone's except hers. The highly successful development company kept the edges soft, and comfortable. William Greeley scratched, dug, worked, and schemed for the rich life he left his wife, daughter, partners, and unborn grandchild. The quest made him a hard, selfish man who was not mourned in death, except by Pamela.

Genevieve found new freedom as his rich widow. She had her own life now and set out to discover how to live it. She took great solace in James Ross's willingness to marry Pamela. His genuine care for the troubled girl gave her mother a chance to flex her wings. She hardly looked back as she bought a beach house north of Ocean City, moved there and let the newlyweds move into the home on the hill. She believed James was the father of Pamela's child, and with a Pollyanna attitude, thought this marriage would solve all her daughter's problems. She did not have a clue and therefore would never be able to help Pamela. She did know that without James, Pamela and a baby would have been her burden. She would have been as confined as she had been by William. She was not only confident that Pamela would do well in James's care, she was eternally grateful to the man.

KC went forward without looking back. Voters and fellow lawmakers were waiting for him to define his stance. At the Capitol he was assertive and confident. He was clear and profound when he had the opportunity to speak on the floor or to the press. Every opportunity was taken. Both the powerful and lowly applauded his positions on the issues of the day. The Washington Post even called him *courageous.*

At Maple Hill and in the business office with James Ross, he was quiet and unassuming. Over the years he had taken a lesser role in the partnership and now, just being in the office with James was awkward. Greeley's death might have affected KC before this election, but now that the party machine was behind him and he was feeling powerful, the only thing KC would miss was the man's donations to party fundraisers. There were always other *Greeleys* around waiting for political influence—others waiting to jump on a power train riding the fast rail from Maryland to Capitol Hill.

Greeley's death made James's demand that he leave the business a moot point. No one would ever know if the man would have given up his business to save his daughter. James took the reins without missing a beat. The junior partner was thrust into the CEO chair before he could marry Pamela. His first act was to change the name to GRK, Inc. It was a strong business that had been in his capable hands for a long time. There would not be any losses, any setbacks or construction problems. KC saw it. James knew it. He divided his life into two arenas - GRK, Inc. and Pamela. He gave very little thought to the deceased bulldog or KC. James was not a man to waste energy on negative influences.

Pending a wedding date and at Genevieve's insistence, he moved into the guest quarters on the third floor and spent every spare minute with Pamela waiting for the time to marry and move into Pamela's bed, claim her and hopefully save her. He was not positive but he was hopeful.

Pamela believed her father's stroke and death were caused by the demand that James made for the deal that included running the business and their marriage. She managed to pile more guilt on the swelling embryo and her weak psyche. Pamela suffered depression and went into the depths of despair over the loss of an anchor to her life. Now that her father was gone, who would ring the bell and give the rewards that assured her that she was doing the right thing?

Would it be James? He came to her to every day hold her fears at bay and asked her to marry. Her grieving prohibited them marrying immediately and James spent many hours and days holding her hand and waiting for her to accept his proposal. Pamela anguished over her love for him and the knowledge that the marriage was just another of her father's business deals. She never told James what she overheard on that fateful day. She never had a chance to tell her father how she felt about the arrangement and worst of all…she could not tell James to go away. She loved him. She needed him, too much.

"Pam, do you feel pressured by my living here? I'll leave if that will help you decide?"

"No. No, James. Stay." The thought of him leaving seemed to solidify her need for him. She could not imagine him being more than one flight of stairs away. "I want you here."

"Then marry me," he asked again, as he had so many times in the last month.

The swelling in her belly remained an obstacle that, although James seemed to be able to surmount, she could not. Again, she did not answer him. Maybe after the baby was out of her body, she could be Pamela again and they could walk the path at White's Ferry. She retreated to her room, but James refused to allow her to sit in blackness. He came each day, raising the blinds, professing his love and begging her to marry him. She was enticed out of the house to walk the grounds. Eventually she agreed to go to Baltimore Symphony concerts and visit the Walters Art Museum. James never gave up. He assured her that they had a lifetime ahead. There were times when he coaxed her to laugh and she seemed willing to be taken to a place of joy. She began to look healthy and rosy in his care. It took two months for her to accept his proposal.

"You will?" He was amazed. "Oh, Pamela, I'm so happy and I'll make you happy, too. I promise." James was ecstatic and optimistic that he could take her hand and together they could raise this child. Pamela managed a smile at his exuberance. But, even after she said *yes*, he did not know if she would stand beside him when the license was purchased and the clergy arrived.

On the appointed day, the pastor and flowers arrived at Maple Hill. The caterer came for the less than twenty friends assembled for the wedding. Pamela stood on the top step, looking down at the assembled people and could not begin the descent. At the bottom stair James waited.

Julianne pushed by. "I'll talk to her. Maybe I can help." Twenty minutes later Julianne led Pamela to the top stair and gave her a kiss on the cheek and a hug. "Smile, Pamela. James is waiting for you. Go to him. Shall I walk you down?"

"Julianne, tell James to come up here, please." Pamela sat down on the stair and watched him come to her with love and concern on his face. His bride greeted him through her tears with a slight smile. She looked beautiful and innocent in spite of her blossomed figure. James took her hand and sat beside her. For the first time, she spoke of the baby.

"James, we haven't talked about the baby."

"I know. Do you want to talk now?"

"Yes. It is a girl; I know it is."

"Good. I'd like a girl."

"Are you sure?"

"Yes."

"I've acted almost as if there was no baby. That's not fair, is it?"

"Fair to me...or fair to you?" He would do all he could to address her concerns.

"Fair to her." She pointed at her stomach surrounded by cream chiffon.

"We're going to be totally fair to our daughter. We're going to love her and we're going to care for her. Keep her safe and happy. Nothing else matters. Nothing." James wanted to touch her stomach but such intimacy had not been allowed before. Instead, he held his bride with his eyes. "You and I will be great parents."

"What about the truth?"

"Truth? There's no truth outside of us. We *will* get married and be her parents." He had to reach out and put his hands around her stomach—holding his breath until he realized she allowed his touch. "Our love will be true. She will love us—that is the truth." He brushed her tears away with the same wet finger that had dried his own.

It was a lovely speech but he failed to say, *I love you.* James thought he had expressed it, but Pamela waited for those three little words, and they did not come. It was truly an oversight in a tense moment—James loved Pamela with all his heart.

"Can we get married now?"

"Yes, James." She rose and took his arm. She married James Ross because she was nothing without him—even though he did not love her. As they descended the stairs, Pamela wondered. *Can you teach me to love this baby?* She hoped with all her heart that he could. It was obvious to Pamela Greeley that James Ross would love the baby girl.

⸙

The honeymoon trip down the Skyline Drive and up the Shenandoah Valley was two good friends traveling together. They did not share a bed and he gave her the privacy she needed by renting two-room suites each night. He was being thoughtful and she did not know how she felt about it. The first night she cried alone in her bed and he heard her through the thin walls. James knocked gently on the connecting door.

"Pamela, are you alright? Can I come in?"

She did not answer so he slowly opened to see the terrified girl, sitting against the head board, clinging to the blanket drawn up to her throat. Tracks of tears marked her face. He went to her and sat on the bed.

"Are you afraid?" She nodded. "You need never be afraid when you're with me. I'm here to take care of you. It would be better if you were not alone in here." She nodded again. "We are married and you'll never be frightened and alone." He went back to his room and pulled the covers from his bed and returned. James pulled her gently down to the pillow and tucked the blanket in before he lay beside her on top of her covers, and drew his own across both. Pamela Greeley Ross would have died happy right there. The peaceful night was interrupted by the constant kicking of the baby in her womb.

James and Pamela spent every night of their honeymoon wrapped in separate cocoons on double beds.

James worried about his wife and sought help. Pamela went back to ignoring her pregnancy and did not talk to him about it after the day they married. She went for her check-ups and followed healthy eating directed by James. The doctor patted her hand and promised a healthy baby.

Although his desire for his wife was strong; he agreed with her and her physician that intercourse should wait until after the February delivery date. The pregnancy was normal but James feared his wife would never be. He could not imagine consummation.

They played house. She made sure his laundry was done and the cook prepared his favorite meals. They ate breakfast together each morning, although he urged her to stay in bed. She groomed herself for her husband, but had all full-length mirrors removed from her chamber and the foyer. Occasionally they stayed at the Greeley apartment in Washington to see plays or concerts at the National Theatre or the DAR Constitution Hall, but it had to be cool enough for her to wear a full-length coat, which she held tight around her extended stomach. James tried to talk her into moving to the city and abandoning the huge mansion, but she was adamant to stay at Maple Hill. He did not make waves and acceded to her wishes, carefully stepping around her feelings. After Christmas with about six weeks to go, he had to address the coming baby.

"We need to set up a nursery."

"I know."

"Which room?"

"Either room on our hallway. You pick."

"We need to paint and get furniture—plus baby things. We could go shopping Saturday." She agreed but on the appointed day, she could not get out of bed.

"You do it, James. Whatever you pick will be fine." He hired a painter and had the room done in creamy white to save her from having to choose a color. The only thing she did to prepare for the baby was have the agency send over three applicants for a nurse. When the room was prepared and all the special things he bought were washed and placed, he went to Pamela. "Come see the nursery. Everything is ready."

"Later. I don't want to climb the steps right now."

It was the middle of the night when she crept from her bed to the room across the hall. She slowly opened the door and pushed the switch. Light washed the beautiful pastel arrangement of blanket, bumper pads and mobile. The pale yellow furniture had animal pulls that matched the pictures on the walls of baby giraffes, elephants, lions, and hippos. She went to the rocker and sank into the plush cushion. Tears streaked her cheeks as she talked to her baby for the first time. For eight months, she had tried not to love the child growing inside.

"Katherine Marie. I have something wonderful to give you when you arrive. You will have the most wonderful father in the world. He can make your life perfect no matter how I mess it up. I'll never understand why James loves you, but he does. You will love him, too. God must have sent you to give James the love he deserves. He'll take care of you, and I'll stay out of the way, I promise." She laid her hand on her belly and waited for the movement that was a response to the words she spoke. "Katherine Marie, remember this. Because I love you and do not deserve you, I'm giving you to James." She doubled over until her torso covered the extended abdomen, wrapped her arms around to the hips, laid her ear against her navel and waited to hear the heart beat and feel the kick that meant the wee little girl understood.

CHAPTER 9

1955

Three months at King's Trace passed quickly for Katherine. She came to love the pastoral setting, but still missed the illuminated Capitol dome. Her curtain was pulled back to see the stars at night and the sunlit or rain-washed fields each morning. Today they were glistening green. The beautiful pastoral scenes in her east-facing window brought her some comfort.

The mansion at King's Trace seemed to be perfect, just as the family inside appeared. Like the fields, each was separated by a fence, and Kathy felt the fences. No matter how the media painted a politician's family, reality was always different.

KC traded his family life for the political arena. He built fences and rationalized that everything he did was for the family. He was dedicated to the life he had twenty miles south in Washington, DC—confident that he was building a better world for his children—and he was, except here at home. Julianne dedicated her life to putting gates in KC's fences so a semblance of family could be created. To his credit, KC had one close relationship at King's Trace—his son, Johnny. They shared a love of horses and Johnny benefited from his father's need to escape the political scene occasionally and ride a horse over the hills. They rode together and both looked forward to caring for the animals and tack back at the stable where conversation flowed easily. KC only talked about Johnny's subjects—sports and school. An automatic switch turned the politician's attention inward as they climbed the back stairs to the kitchen. A gentle pat on his son's back made a promise for another ride—soon.

Katherine stood at her window and saw KC and Johnny walk toward the house. Her attention was drawn to a spirited colt galloping across the paddock and pulling to a sudden halt before he hit the fence, sensing the barrier and the problems that would be caused if he tried to jump or decided to collide. She related to the colt and felt a sudden chill up her spine. The colt raised a cloud of dust but did not hit the fence, his test aborted.

Katherine settled into her new life and held to the reality that living in the moment was the only way. When she was in school, she was totally engrossed in her studies. Time with the family was dedicated to the activity of the minute and trying very hard not to be a problem and, more than that, trying to be an asset by helping wherever she could—setting the table, gathering laundry, tying Melissa's shoe or carrying groceries. Julianne noticed her in the living room at the grand piano and complimented her on her dedication to piano practice, not knowing it was another of her mind-engrossing, time-filling exercises. Most of all, she tried to be invisible during the quiet times. She and Lady Fair sat in the beautiful bedroom and talked over the background music of the cat's loud purring.

Katherine said nothing to the new family about the things on her mind, but she was thinking. Living here was nice and very comfortable, but she did not want to be adopted or change her name. She did not want to be a Kingsley and she merely tolerated being called Kathy.

"My life here is a square, and I don't want to be in the Kingsley box," she told Lady Fair. "If I choose to be outside the box, I will be alone with only father's memory and a lifeless, sick mother who doesn't care if I exist." She was living a nightmare of nothingness. *Downstairs, the Kingsley family is ready to consume me.*

After three months, each morning was the same. She did not know, with her first waking thought, if she was inside or outside of the imagined box. She rose to shower and fix her hair before going to the plentiful closet to choose her clothes for the day—no more school uniforms of plaid and beige. Her books were neatly stacked to go and she went with confidence, knowing her homework would glean an A.

Brenda was assigned the task of bringing Katherine information. She was big sister to all the siblings, but felt she had not, in these weeks, found any common ground with the newest. Brenda could not walk into Kathy's room without announcing herself as she did with her siblings. She knocked softly on the closed door that kept Lady Fair inside. "Dad's in the library and wants to talk to you."

Katherine's walk down the circular three-storied staircase always gave her the feeling that she was making a stage entrance and had to assume a role.

"Hi," she greeted KC warmly, still avoiding addressing him with a name.

"How's school?"

"Good. It's very different from my old school." Whether it was luck or wisdom, putting the children in a new school was working. The students assumed they were a normal group of brothers and sisters, and Katherine seemed to find it easier to make a place among these strangers than with the family at King's Trace. "I'm making friends easier than I thought." She knew that a comment like this would please the Senator.

"Fine," he smiled, leaned back in his chair and continued. "I got a call from the lawyer and your father's will is to be read day after tomorrow. Do you have any exams? I can change the date if need be."

"I don't think so. I'll get my work for Wednesday and it'll be fine. Do you know what to expect?"

He liked this in Kathy. She was always working ahead and preparing herself for the unknown. In this, they were alike—he managed his life and affairs in the same way. He studied her for a moment and saw Pamela in her mouth and softly waving hair— for some reason, today more than usual. KC shook all thoughts of Pamela away and answered her.

"Mr. Ashford, your father's lawyer, will read it. I know he took care of things for you and your mother; we'll learn the details today. It'll be trusts until you come of age. The will lists many things to be held for you and many assets that'll go into the trusts for you and your mother. It may seem overwhelming and I fear, emotional. Bring something so you can take notes and jot down questions. Everything will be straightforward."

"Who'll be there?"

"You, me and a representative for your mother. Since she cannot speak for herself, she must have counsel. His name is Jonas Longfellow. I understand he'll go to Spring Haven to ascertain if she is well enough to attend. I don't think she will be." KC voiced what they both knew.

Actually, KC Kingsley had already called the hospital and talked to Dr. Sherman to make sure the patient would *not* be well enough to attend. Things were tightly knitted and Pamela Ross would not be allowed to unravel herself or anything else. He managed the situation at the hospital as he did everything –just another business deal that would have the outcome he expected.

Katherine noticed the plaque on the library wall behind KC's desk. She had not noticed it before. "Right Makes Might" blared across the top and in a small font under, it said: "Might makes Right." She took a moment to promise herself to discuss those words with Lady Fair.

Wednesday morning was a cloudy, gloomy day and the rain started as they left the driveway. It was exactly the same conditions that caused the accident that took James Ross's life and both were aware of it. KC drove cautiously, knowing what was on her mind. By the time they reached the county line, the sun broke through and conversation picked up in the car. KC enjoyed her animation when talking about her studies—the only topic she could comfortably discuss with him. Katherine was a natural scholar, well-organized and inquisitive. She had a natural aptitude for math and a keen interest in history, and KC remembered the same subjects were his favorites ages ago.

"Can we talk about the condominium?" Katherine changed the subject at the first lull in conversation. She brought up the one thing that had been on her mind and she could not imagine another time or place when she would be able to talk to him without others around. "I need some time there."

"We could stop on our way home. Would you like to do that?"

"No, I need to spend a day there before the movers come to put things in storage. I need to select some things to keep and maybe sort things to be discarded. There are many bits and pieces of our life there and I worry about them." The truth was she wanted to be in the space and former time before it was packed and gone.

"Kathy, you need not worry. Everything can be boxed; the storage company is very professional. Let me take you there today and you can get anything you want." His matter-of-fact manner tied her concerns in a neat bundle and dismissed them.

"KC...." she called him by name for the first time since the rainy night her father died. She could not imagine being adopted and needing to call KC by a more familiar name. She was never going to do that.

"...I should not have said I *need* to go there. I should've said I *want* to go there. I want some time in the condominium—" She gathered all her courage, "—alone." It was a demand.

KC knew about demands and he understood the thin demeanor of gentleness that he had assumed for his relationship with her. "That may be possible," he said in a very congressional manner. It was like sending something back to committee to get it tabled. KC was not sure if his resolve not to let her go to the apartment alone was because it could complicate things or if it was because she had made a demand. Either way, the conversation was closed. Katherine sat quietly listening to the radio while he parked the car.

The elegant office building with huge brass doors was impressive.

"Who pays for these lawyers? That may be a stupid question." It was another attempt to claim dominion over her life. Something told her she had to understand everything if she was to have any control.

"Not stupid at all. The estate can afford the lawyers. You know your father was wealthy. Nothing to be concerned about." He knew instantly that he had brushed her aside again, and he knew it was a mistake. *She wants to know even this detail. I've got to do better.* Katherine, soon to be seventeen, was determined to comprehend the intricacies of her position, so he resolved to give more attention to her questions and definitely to be more careful in his responses. *Too savvy to be passed over or patronized.* He would tread carefully—an unusual position for the Senator.

Katherine had her own thoughts about their exchange. *He doesn't really want questions. Why?*

KC took a controlled, generous, and very political position, almost as if he could read her mind. "Kathy, all of your questions are valid. Don't hesitate if you have one or don't understand anything that is said." The puzzlement on her face went unnoticed by Senator Kingsley.

The lawyer's office looked as if designed by Hollywood with chairs of leather, fittings of brass, and triple-matted prints of horses, hounds and riders in red coats crossing rolling hills. The carpet was oriental over dark-stained hardwood floors. Everything was shiny and polished and not a speck of dust would dare land.

Mr. Ashford made introductions around the table. Katherine wrote down the names and noted the young handsome stranger as he reached across the table to KC.

"Senator Kingsley. Nice to meet you." Then he turned to Katherine.

"Katherine Ross. Jonas Longfellow."

When they shook hands, he cupped his left over hers and said, "Nice to meet you, Katherine Ross." She liked him immediately.

Jonas Longfellow did not look old enough to be a lawyer; he looked as if he should have a basketball in his hand, dribbling down a court, instead of a legal briefcase ready for court. His chestnut hair seemed to go in all directions and his attempts to control renegade locks with his fingers were to no avail. He was unaware how often he tried to straighten his hair. Katherine noticed his handsome face and generous smile, the only one in the room.

Jonas managed to get his long legs under the table and began making notes before anyone said a word. Katherine sat across from him with her own notepad.

Mr. Ashford took charge of the meeting and addressed his secretary, "Those in attendance for the reading of the last will and testament of James Henry Ross are: Katherine Ross, KC Kingsley and Jonas Longfellow, representative for Pamela Ross, widow of the deceased." With those words, Katherine stopped writing and looked at him again. The proceeding began.

Here, in this pretentious office, she was Katherine Ross again. She wanted to be Katherine, but she knew she had to go back to the hill in Montgomery County and be Kathy. She shook those thoughts from her head and concentrated on the proceedings while refusing to address the fact that this was because she no longer had her father.

"Mr. Longfellow, for the record, why is Pamela Ross absent from this reading?"

"Pamela Ross is hospitalized at Spring Haven Mental Hospital, Catonsville, Maryland. She is not well enough to attend the reading of her husband's will. I have a statement from Dr. Sherman to that fact. I'm her representative."

"Before I read the will I would like to make a few remarks. James Ross revised this will three months before he died. Everything is in order. I advised him against giving his daughter so much responsibility at age eighteen but he was adamant. His confidence in her was unshakeable. That being said, I will read."

The estate was formidable. James Ross's stocks, bonds, real estate, and liquid assets were all passed to his daughter, Katherine Marie Ross—in trust, administered by Kenneth Charles Kingsley until Katherine turned eighteen. It seemed simple enough.

Both KC and Katherine sat up straight at Mr. Ashford's words. It was clear and exacting; everything went to his daughter when she turned eighteen. The money set aside by William Greeley for Pamela would continue in the trust department of Hamilton Bank and Trust Company. There were no surprises except the age when Katherine would inherit the estate and control of her mother and all trusts. Not twenty-one—eighteen. Everything, including care of her mother.

When he began to talk about the business that supported her wealthy father and the even wealthier Senator, she put her pencil down and listened, not wanting to miss anything. She would rely on her remarkable memory. James and Pamela Ross held the majority in GRK, Ltd. stock after it went public. It now belonged to a deranged woman and underage girl.

She paid close attention to directions for her care by KC and Julianne Kingsley. Her ears perked up when the will addressed her guardianship. KC stopped the reading to ask. "I was under the impression that Mr. Ross wanted Katherine adopted by me."

"There was a complication in getting Pamela Ross to agree to adoption. This will was revised recently and with Katherine already sixteen, he saw it differently. Mr. Ross appreciates that you can offer his daughter a safe and good home. One that she is familiar with, but he did not want to go the legal route to override his wife's objection. You are assigned guardianship until she is eighteen."

Katherine understood that it was important for her to accept and believe that her father needed her to live with the Kingsleys for now. It was the logical place since her only family were her mother and great aunt Maude.

Her notes were:

No Adoption. No legal name change.

At eighteen control of my trust, care of mother.

Contents of our home

Coin collection

Art and antiques

Stocks and investments – handled by Branbridge Brokerage Inc. until I'm 21

Value $12,428,773.00

Tax and accountant - W.B. Hughes and Associates

Her relief was great and she understood why. It made things simple to be Kathy Kingsley at school and at King's Trace. *I'm Katherine Ross; always have been and before long, I will be Katherine Ross in college.* Her mind wandered. Today and forever, she would be Katherine Ross. This made it easier to live with and be a part of the new family. They wanted her, she knew that, and she made a new resolution to be happy there. Surely, she was the cause of her own discontent and her father would be disappointed in her. For the first time she relinquished anger at him for dying and thanked him for the gift of independence, and wondered what her mother would think.

She counted the days and another note:

Try to be happy. 18th birthday.

Of all the facts flying around the room she held tight to the one that would get her back to being Katherine Ross in the not too distant future. She could do this.

Katherine doodled flowers and scrolls around an elaborate *M* and wrote *mother* on her note pad. She remembered how tender

Papa was in every reference to her, and she resolved to hold the thought.

At times Mr. Ashford and Senator Kingsley talked as if she was not in the room as points were examined and clarified. Katherine missed nothing. Her self-discipline to stay focused worked well for her. Some of her notes were reminders of points she was digesting.

Greeley company stock
Bank accounts - HB&T
Coin collection - safe deposit box
Art
Hospital endowment
Allowance
Probate

Other notes were questions jotted in the margin of the page.

Dr. Sherman?
How do I look out for Mother?
What does the administrator do?
Is Mr. Ashford my lawyer?
How did Jonas Longfellow get picked for this? She looked across the table at him. He returned a soft smile.

When the proceedings ended, Jonas Longfellow reached across the table and gave Katherine his card with a note on the back. "Call, if I can be of service to you."

As a final gesture, Mr. Ashford gave Katherine a personal letter from her father. She held tight to it until reaching the privacy of her bedroom and the comfort of Lady Fair.

This letter is to be given to Katherine Ross if I am deceased before her 18th birthday.

Dearest Katherine,

Taking care of you and being your father has been a joy. I loved you even before the first time you were placed in my arms. I have tried to arrange things in case you were not of age at the time of my death. I thought a long time about passing so much to you at 18 instead of 21—recommended by Mr. Ashford. I thought back to the time when I had to take care of myself when I was eighteen. It can be done and you can do it. You are a very mature young woman and I have been passing decisions and responsibilities to prepare you. I think you will be ready at eighteen, if the need arises. Your mother needs a champion and you are the only person on earth who can be that champion if I am gone. She will not be able to wait until you are older; she will need you immediately. Caring for your mother should not postpone the things you must do in your young adulthood. Do them! If your mother is still ill at that time, you will have great responsibility as well as great resources. You must work hard, be strong, be confident and assume responsibility for your rich heritage and your future. We have always talked of you going to Brown…but when the time comes, if you want to make another choice that is fine. Just go and do your best—as you always have. When you graduate, you will have the option of entering our business or going your own way. I have made you prosperous, but have left you responsibilities too. The Kingsleys will make your life pleasant but you must make it worthwhile. Take good care of your mother. Make sure that her care is befitting your mother. Always remember that she gave you life and made sacrifices for you and she deserves the same in return.

I love you with all my heart and soul. God bless you, my child

Papa

Katherine was in her bed with Lady Fair curled at her feet when she realized there was nothing in her father's will about the condominium. She sat up in bed, disturbed the sleeping cat to ask her, "Lady Fair, why didn't Papa's will mention the condominium?"

The next morning, before everyone gathered for breakfast, Kathy was up and dressed. She knew KC would be in the stable early. She needed to talk to him and she would not be put off. She dressed for school, stacked her books in the foyer and went quietly out the side porch to find him. He was filling the oat buckets and talking to the horses.

"Good morning," she warned him of her presence. He turned in surprise and a look of delight crossed his face. He was glad to see her interest in his stable.

"Do you want to help feed this morning? Johnny left for school early. I don't have my helper."

"Sure." She approached the inquisitive horse that turned his head toward her. "I went to riding camp many summers, but haven't been on a horse for almost three years. Are they all saddle broken?"

"Yes, you should ride again. Johnny and I ride. Brenda won't come near them. She had a bad experience when she was small and you know what they say about getting back on…well she wouldn't. Ask Johnny. He will saddle up and ride with you anytime, I'm sure." He was more pleased than he would admit that she loved horses. KC filled a pail and led her to the last stall. As she took a step up to pour the earthy smelling oats, she broached the subject on her mind.

"I came looking for you to ask a question that occurred to me after we got home yesterday. Why didn't my father's will mention the condominium? Was that an oversight?"

"No. It wasn't an oversight. Your father did not, never did, own the condominium. It would not be in his will."

She was surprised and in response asked the logical question. "Who owns it?"

"It belonged to your grandfather, William Greeley. He left it to your mother. Her trust, set up by him, pays all taxes and fees on it. That same trust pays for her care."

"Who administers that trust?" Her questions were becoming more incisive. He would have to be careful.

"The trust was administered by Hamilton Bank and Trust and your father. Now it is totally controlled by HB&T. It is sufficient to continue her care well into the future, with the careful investments the bank is making. Are you worried about her care?"

"Not really. There is plenty in my father's estate if that trust can't cover it. I wanted to know about the condominium and what will be done with it."

"Well, Kathy, without your mother's consent, it cannot be sold and you will inherit it someday. Your mother made a will a long time ago and left everything to you at her death. I didn't want to discuss it with you so soon but I think it should be rented to help meet expenses. Unoccupied it is a drain on your mother's estate...and it must be maintained. There are rental companies that handle the leasing and the maintenance. We could get some references and set about moving on that."

She backed down from the stall railing. He was going too fast and she could feel his control. This is what she hated most about discussing issues with him. Opening a topic seemed to give him leave to take over. She turned to face him. "Good. It won't be sold." She took a breath and continued. "I don't want to lease it." She poured the last of the oats in the feed trough. "I don't want to hire a management company." She dropped the bucket. "I don't even want our things packed into storage." She turned away from the horse and looked back again at KC. "But… I have learned lately that sometimes things you don't want—have to be done." Kathy started for the door. "Lease it for one year. No more. Time to eat breakfast." She was gone.

CHAPTER 10

1956

*L*ike the new day forcing its way through the curtains, making a multitude of promises, Katherine made one herself. *I've got to fit in. Try harder.* Her resolve was strong but she lacked motivation. She was too young to know that grief saps motivation and invites inertia. KC, Julianne, and her new siblings were doing all they could to make her happy, yet happiness was not theirs to give. The problem was not unusual. Most people who have a life-changing event cling to their former lives. Katherine Ross was doing exactly that.

"Come Lady Fair, let's talk this over." The cat reluctantly allowed her girl to lift her from the sunny spot on the window seat to the bed. "Now that I know my name will stay Ross, I'm willing to act like a Kingsley kid." Lady Fair seemed to agree.

"Julianne can mother me just as she mothers Brenda, Johnny, and Melissa." Katherine remembered the gentle touch that had brushed her hair from her eyes yesterday. She remembered, but did not know why, she objected with a slight pull-back. "I'll work on that." Lady Fair apparently did not think that was important so she closed her eyes.

The cat did not respond at all when Katherine began to talk about Johnny. "He's my friend. He makes it easier to live here. Don't know why."

Katherine nudged the lazy feline and insisted on her attention. "It's KC—." She stretched out beside the cat and put her nose in the warm fur, and continued, "Why does he make me feel so unsettled, wise kitty, eh?"

Going on with this discussion was difficult even with a cat. Katherine had to look for words to continue. Lady Fair tried to leave, but loving fingers scratched her ears and begged her indulgence.

"Here goes. KC looks at me... Oh, I don't know...he looks at me as if... he expects me to say something... or do something." She rolled over and held Lady Fair so she could not jump from the bed. "I'll bet he looks at Brenda, Johnny, and Melissa the same way." She rationalized her attitude. "He expects a lot from everybody, not just me." Katherine and Lady Fair settled almost into a companion nap. Almost. "If it weren't for Johnny—I don't think I could stay here—as if I had a choice."

Lady Fair stopped purring and waited for the chance to leap away from her tiresome girl. "Go vixen!" Katherine released her captive cat. "You weren't any help anyway."

Even when we were little, I liked Johnny best, she admitted to herself. *Probably because we are the same age.*

Katherine went to the stairs to join her new family, repeating her determination. "I'll try harder." With each step down the stairs, she repeated under her breath, "Try harder, try harder..."

Daytime determinations did not always translate into nighttime certainties. When the comforter was pulled up to her chin, Katherine became an insecure girl again. Resolve dissolved into the night. Two repeating dreams haunted her.

In one, her mother was walking in the condominium calling "James, James." The rooms were empty except for Katherine sitting in the corner, calling out, "Over here, find me." Pamela Ross walked by without seeing her or hearing her. Just before awakening, Katherine became the mother and woke crying, sweating and confused. In the second one Katherine was a baby in her mother's arms. She looked up at her crying mother and felt tears splashing into her own eyes, burning and stinging.

Tonight the same dream awakened Katherine screaming, brought Johnny running to her room and sent Lady Fair scurrying.

"Katherine! You alright?" He opened her bedroom door, calling to her. By the time she was fully awake, he was handing her a drink of water. "Musta been a bad one. Shall I leave the light on? Do you want me to stay for a while?"

"I'm okay. Sorry I woke you. Help me find Lady Fair. I scared her to death." They spent ten minutes searching for the cat that was determined not to be found. "Did she get out the door when you came in?"

"I don't think so. Look, the door is closed tight. I closed it because of her. She'd have to be very quick to get between my feet. Let's stop looking and see if she will come out."

Katherine and Johnny settled on the window seat and quietly talked, hoping the cat would either get curious or want the soft warm bed again. The two teenagers found much in common as they talked of academics, the emerging rock and roll music, and horses. They were both seeking a friend within the busy household. Their special friendship came to life in hours like this.

"Sometimes I have bad dreams, too. But as far as I know, I don't scream. If you ever hear me, come and throw a glass of water on me." Johnny lightened the mood.

"Well, I prefer the water in a glass.... and I hope I don't disturb you very often."

"Does this happen a lot?"

"More than I wish, that's for sure. One is too many."

"Want to talk about them? Are they the same?"

"You know, I think I just want to get back to sleep now—not think about what was in the dream."

"I get it. Look, here comes Lady Fair. Guess she is ready for that, too." The friends parted.

Katherine gave the midnight incident some serious thought and concluded Johnny was an important step in joining the family, one member at a time. And, then she thought, *Johnny's enough.* She came to King's Trace from a two-person family. She did not want or need more.

Her focus on Johnny and acceptance of her place in this family began to bring changes. It generated reciprocal feelings. Melissa learned to come to her for quiet attention; Brenda sought her for her typing ability when it came time to fill out college applications. The children found more and more things that they had in common now that Katherine was willing to be Kathy, let down her reserve, and make the best of the arrangement until she graduated and came of age.

Julianne immediately saw the difference. Katherine's new attitude made it easier for her to express her natural mothering instincts with her. She began to seek quiet time when they could talk away from the busy family. One evening after dinner she found her new *daughter* alone on the west porch, reading.

"Hi. Mind if I join you?'

Katherine closed her book as an invitation.

"We're very proud of the way you have settled in here at King's Trace and in your new school." Julianne took a deep breath and continued with words and thoughts she had planned for a long time. "I want to treat you just like Brenda, Johnny, and Melissa."

She reached out and touched Katherine's hand. "It's hard to hold back. But, I'll honor your boundaries. We want you to be happy, but I think maybe that's too much to expect. Contented? Can you be content here with us?"

"Yes. I think I can—*am*." She smiled. "I work hard in school and help in the family so you can see I appreciate—everything. I am grateful."

"I'm not looking for gratitude. I'm looking for…" she searched for the right word. "Joy. Joy, for who you are with us. Put down your guard, child. Stop trying to be perfect—everything to everyone. Let there be egg on your face…and please, let me be the one who wipes it off with my napkin."

Silence followed these words. Katherine knew she was at a pivotal place. Julianne waited a long minute for Katherine to respond. With a heavy heart, she rose to leave.

"Please, don't go. I want to say the right things." Katherine lifted her forefinger. "One minute," she asked, needing time to think.

"How about a coke?" Julianne provided the space Katherine needed.

"Sure," she answered with a broad grin—one Julianne had never seen before.

When she returned with the cold drink, Katherine was ready. She had put her book away and moved to the settee where Julianne would sit.

"Julianne, I'm feeling more content every day. And, I'm sure I'll be happy again. It's what Papa would want…and with your question, I realized—it's what I want, too. I'm so blessed to have this family, this place…" She drew her arm in a large circle to show she knew the scope of her good fortune. "I would be one sad lonely person without my family at King's Trace."

"Love is the key." Julianne took the coke from Katherine and clasped both of her hands, demanding her complete attention. "You can broaden your circle of loved ones without giving up love for those whom you loved before. Love your father. Love your mother. But, look to others you can love, too."

"Yes." Katherine repeated, "yes," with tears in her eyes. She leaned into Julianne and invited a hug—long sought—long missed. Julianne returned her affection warmly. Katherine softly cried. She cried for herself, for her father, and for her mother. And then, she cried with a wonderful smile for Julianne and her future.

"This is truly an important time for you and me." Katherine only nodded.

King's Trace became a good place with a caring mother, but what she missed most was a father and KC could not fill that void. No one could. *Something or some feelings* held her back. Katherine could not put her finger on it. Was KC really okay with her living here? For some reason she resented him...maybe because he was trying to fill Papa's place or maybe because he could never take Papa's place. Once, when they were walking out the foyer, she caught a backward glimpse in the huge mirror. He lifted his arm to circle her shoulder and withdrew it before touching her. All the day, she thought about that simple action and decided that he had a problem with her intrusion into his family, no matter how she assimilated with the other members.

Johnny was special. The ease that started their friendship continued in all areas of their lives—school, home, stable. The best times were with the horses. Johnny did not ride to escape anything, but he was well aware of the freedom Katherine sought. He encouraged her to gallop with him over the countryside.

Their birthdays were three months apart to the day. Once, while studying together in the school library, they were asked if they were twins. Katherine took a close look at Johnny and could see with the hair and eye color, plus the chin line, there was a resemblance—but not enough to be twins. Johnny could not see it at all, but took to calling her *Kat,* not short for Katherine but for Copy Cat. She loved it. For some reason it was special between them.

"What about college, Kat? Brenda is so busy getting ready to go and before we know it will be time for us to do the same. I can't decide if I want to go far away or to the University of Maryland."

"I'm going to either Georgetown or American U."

'"Are you sure—one of those?"

"Yes. I'm going to school in DC. I can't go far…my mother, you know."

This is the closest she had come to opening up about things that were on her mind. Even as she brought up the subject, she worried that she had made a mistake beginning a conversation about her mother. It was something she never did. It was tempting to talk to Johnny but her well-developed reserve pulled her back.

"I know." He knew Pamela Ross was in an institution, but he did not know why. He did not ask questions or tell her what he thought. Johnny only acknowledged that she had other things to consider when talking about the future.

"Dad wants me to go to Purdue." He dissolved the awkward moment by telling her all the pros and cons of Maryland and Purdue. She listened and he appreciated her attention. It was obvious he wanted to stay closer to home.

"Dad's very insistent. I will not be the one picking my college." He changed the subject. "Smells like dinner's ready and my stomach tells me I am, too. If you ever want to talk about your mother; let me know." He had not missed the importance of her omission.

KC was away much of the time. Little Melissa complained and Julianne was overheard commenting that he seemed to be away more this session of Congress than any other. He reminded her that next year was an election year and she must know what that meant for fund-raising and planning. She did, but Melissa did not. He was constantly in caucus, ad hoc, and party meetings. The pressures were mounting for decisions, but the biggest pressures were coming at the man from an innocent girl, upstairs playing with her cat. On a rare evening when KC enjoyed dinner with the family he asked Julianne to join him in the study after. The children were sent to their rooms for homework or studying. Melissa went to Kathy's room and played with Lady Fair. They were put away so Senator Kingsley could discuss something important with his wife, usually the last to know what he was planning.

Julianne asked Suzanna to bring coffee to the study. Brenda was put in charge so they would not be disturbed. "Here," was his simple invitation to join him on the sofa. These arrangements made her nervous. "Is everything alright?" she asked as she took the seat next to him. "Ken? Are you alright?" She used a rarely used tender name. He hadn't heard it much in the ensuing years.

"Yes. I'm fine. This is all political."

Julianne sighed with relief and prepared her coffee. These *political-things-talks* were always his little concessions for her to get her mind around what he had already decided to do. She could do that; she had done it for 20 years. Julianne Kingsley always made it possible for KC to do whatever he wanted. She made that a daily mission along with keeping her family sacred. It was her job.

"Before you tell me what is on your mind, I'd like to talk about the children, including Katherine."

"Sure." He took his coffee and tensed. KC hated discussing family matters. He much preferred matters greater in scope—preferably global.

"The children are doing well in the new school. Johnny and Katherine seem to have a special bond." She paused for emphasis. "They're teenagers…and I wouldn't want them to move beyond a family attachment." She was very diplomatic and she had KC's undivided attention. In fact, his heart skipped a beat as he waited for the next words.

"As soon as basketball is over, why not get Johnny on the Hill as an intern, or an aide to an aide—something."

"Excellent idea." Julianne had come through again. Concern about Johnny's attachment to Katherine was robbing his concentration. He would move on that immediately. "I'd love to have him with me more. Consider it done." Relief laced the next draft of coffee. A worry that dogged him was assuaged.

"Now, what's on your mind?" Julianne turned her attention to her very important husband.

"It's the White House again. They—the party— I'm up for reelection this year, which I will do. They want me to run for President in two years—before the new term is up. I'll have to resign as Senator and run. The decision to go for it has to be made now. I have to say yea or nay next week…although it will not be made public. I'll deny I have aspirations for the presidency, especially while running for my senate seat this year. It's a lot of time and energy on elections, Julianne—especially if I go for the presidency. A year or more of campaigning all over the country. It'll be hard on you and the children. That's how it is. It is not just my decision." As he said it, she smiled a knowing smile which he took for love, but was really her yield to his career.

How convenient for KC! He wants to run away from this family situation and he has places to run. She continued to smile in spite of her thoughts.

Julianne stirred her coffee, contemplating what this could mean to her and the children. She knew they could do this. She also knew they would all step into the history books when they went to the White House. All her little misgivings seemed insignificant. He wanted this and she was surprised that he used the words—*if I go for it*. She was a good mother; a good wife. They would make a beautiful first family. KC was an excellent public servant and she was proud of his accomplishments. She knew he was better suited to lead the country than this family.

Her years of support made her say, "Of course, you'll go for it."

CHAPTER 11

1958

Katherine's second winter at King's Trace was a record-breaker—coldest, with unusual snows for Maryland. Another storm in mid-February choked roads and threatened power loss in Montgomery County. A blizzard—a total whiteout.

Johnny brought wood and stacked it on the side porch. If the furnace went out the eight fireplaces in King's Trace would keep them warm. Katherine helped him distribute wood to each hearth before the lights flickered and went out. The snow and wind howled across the hill, wrapping the house in a white igloo.

"I'm going to the stable before it gets too bad." Johnny would take care of the horses.

"I'm going with you." Katherine found her boots.

They trudged down to the stable holding hands, supporting each other against the storm. The stable was warm against the outside. Extra hay and oats were poured into the feed trough and stall. Then blankets were stretched and secured over the animals.

"We've done all we can."

"Are they going to be alright?"

"Sure, they'll be fine. Let's check the doors again. The worst thing would be one of them blowing open." They worked hard arranging the stable to withstand the storm. Finally, tired and finished, Johnny pulled Katherine to a hay bale. "Sit. Rest before going back. It's all uphill and against the wind." She moved to the edge of the bale where he was already sitting. Misjudging, she slid off to the floor and melted into laughter. He went down on the floor beside her. They laughed together.

Johnny could have stayed with her—isolated by the storm in their snow-globe world—forever.

"It's getting deeper by the minute. Let's make the trek. I'm hungry. You?"

Johnny had to get up. They had to go. "Yep." He took a harness and secured it around her waist while holding the ring tight. "Stay close and don't let go." He grabbed a kerosene can before he secured the stable door and led her out into the storm. "Stay against my back. We'll head for the lights in the house. It's deep and the wind is wicked."

Katherine put her head down and pressed it into Johnny's back. They trudged though the snow. Within fifteen feet of the porch the lanterns, which Julianne had put in the windows, flickered. The house went dark.

Thank God we made it, he silently prayed.

When Julianne heard them on the porch she uttered her own prayer of thanksgiving for her two children out in the storm.

KC would not be able to come home. He could not call—the phone lines were down, but he knew Julianne's resourcefulness. King's Trace would withstand the storm. They would be fine.

The *storm of the century* raged with snowfalls measuring 36 to 50 inches in suburban Maryland. Fires were lit in the three big hearths on the first floor. Extra blankets and quilts were put on every bed, the lanterns were refilled. Suzanna opened the gateleg table in front of the library fire and prepared to serve makeshift meals where the heat and glow would enhance the oil lamps and give comfort while eating. Julianne, in her usual well-organized and coping manner, assumed the pioneer spirit. Children dressed in layers and came to dinner. Talk of snow sledding and skiing was quickly squelched until the blizzard subsided. "I don't want anyone outside in these conditions. Wait until morning and hopefully the snow stops falling. We will decide then; it's too dangerous tonight."

Katherine, in the excitement of preparing the house and family for the storm, forgot it was her birthday. Suzanna brought a cake in with eighteen candles blazing to remind her and the family of the milestone. "We planned a special surprise party for you at the country club tomorrow. But no one, will be able to get there. I hope you aren't too disappointed with this small celebration."

The small celebration suited Katherine—a party was not important. This birthday had been long awaited and anticipated. She had been counting the days since her life changed so dramatically. She was finally of age to begin managing her own life, although she would have to bide her time until she graduated from high school in June.

"On graduation day I will move to the Capitol Hill condominium," she reminded Lady Fair of her often repeated plan. The Kingsleys expected her to leave for college in the fall. Her decision to go in June would upset them. Katherine felt sorry for that, but did not waver. She came from the window seat and smiled at the blazing birthday cake. Tonight she would relax, stop thinking months ahead, enjoy the cake, the fire, the food, and the warmth of this family that had become so dear to her.

"Julianne, I'm not disappointed at all. The cake is beautiful and I don't need anyone *else* to celebrate my birthday with me. Everyone's here that matters except Brenda..." She thought quickly, "… and KC." Even as she said it, she thought of her mother, who expected a visit on her birthday. After the dishes were cleared, she asked Johnny if the phone lines were open.

"No phones. Who ya calling on a day like this? Missing a heavy date?"

"No. It's alright." He had no idea that she wanted to let her mother know she was sorry to miss her birthday visit. It was the first time. Many icy, snowy February days she and her father made it to the hospital, and she wondered, if he were still alive—would they have gotten to the hospital—in spite of this storm? *Probably not*, she admitted to herself.

The snow piling up and swirling outside made it easy to focus and believe the world was confined to this hill in Maryland. Julianne was braiding Melissa's hair and took these quiet moments to explain some important things to her.

"Melissa, Daddy will be traveling across the country campaigning for President. We will all be going with him a lot of the time."

"Where?"

"Well…he'll be going to almost every state. We'll go to some of them."

"Why?"

"Because when a man runs for President, the people want to meet his family, too."

Melissa listened to her mother's words and thought about them. Julianne gave her time. She knew there would be more questions.

"The President lives in the White House. Right?"

"Yes. When Daddy is President, he will live there."

"What about us? What about our house?"

Katherine smiled as she watched mother and child talking about important things. Julianne was an amazing mother, explaining and clarifying things for her little one. Katherine enjoyed being a sojourner in the room but was saddened. *Mother never braided my hair…or explained anything.* She quickly shook off the melancholy mood and pulled the quilt close to her chin.

The presidential election was in the fall and this summer would be filled with campaigning across the country. Johnny and Melissa would be on the podium with KC after school was out. Brenda would join them when she got home from college, and assumptions were made that Katherine would be in the circle. Each time she heard talk of the plan she shrank from blurting out—*not me, I'm not going.* Johnny and Melissa were excited about the places they would see—beaches, mountains, the Grand Canyon. It would be a family summer to remember and Katherine was opting out—they just didn't know it yet.

Katherine needed Johnny to help her tell Julianne and KC she would be gone before summer. *Maybe tonight was perfect to talk to Johnny.* She looked around the cozy room at everyone snuggled down.

"Johnny, a game of Scrabble?" They both enjoyed the game and knew it was the only way they could get a couple of hours alone. They rarely declined an invitation from each other.

"Ten minutes. I'll get a lantern and pull the card table up to the fireplace in the library."

Johnny's crush was becoming more serious, and he wanted every opportunity to be with Katherine. But she kept him at a distance, just as she pushed all the boys at school away. Johnny was special and she felt his attraction, actually enjoying his attention more than any of the boys at school. She knew if she ever let him kiss her; it could mess up her plan. The last thing she needed was a romantic attachment that would weaken her resolve to leave this home. It was not the time for her to discover happiness in the arms of a handsome boy. This was not a time of abandonment; it was a time of resolve.

"I need to talk to you," Katherine drew tiles.

"I figured. What's up?" He could tell from the frown that etched her forehead that this was serious.

"I need help. I have to tell your father something he doesn't want to hear… and I'm scared."

"I know that feeling…but, it's never as awful as you think. The ole man ain't so bad. Tell him what?"

She chastised herself for not thinking through what she wanted to say. She was poorly prepared. It was not only going to upset KC and Julianne, it was going to hurt Johnny. She reached over and took his hand. "I'm leaving King's Trace."

"In this storm?" He interjected some humor to lighten the mood and hide his inner turmoil. "Not a good idea."

She punched his arm. "Johnny, I'm serious."

"I know. Spill it."

"I'm moving to my condominium in DC as soon as we graduate in June."

"Classes start in September. You're going in June?"

"Yes. I need time to set up before school starts. I'm going to live there while I go to Georgetown, not on campus. I had to wait for my birthday to tell your father. He would take charge, you know that. I have my inheritance to live on and to pay for school. My mind's made up. I just don't know how to tell your parents. This has been my plan since I came here." She avoided saying *since my father died*. "I'm going to take responsibility for myself and my mother."

"That is a lot…for a teenager."

"I'm eighteen now…but, really, Johnny, I've never felt like a teenager." She took her turn. "I never planned to go on the campaign trail with you all. It's not for me. Face it, Johnny. It's time for me to go." They concentrated on the game. Johnny made a great play; she came back with a higher score. Each was thinking, not only about the tiles on their rack, but on the words they had to say to each other. They started to talk at the same time, smiled, and yielded to the other. She needed his words more than he needed hers so she waited for him. Her breaths were shallow and tentative. The tiles blurred on the rack until she blinked and brought her eyes to meet his.

"I can't say anything to change your mind?" He spoke in a soft pleading tone.

Katherine shook her head from side to side.

"I'm eighteen, too, and I know I could not strike out on my own." Johnny changed his demeanor and put a lighter voice to his words. "I'm not even sure I'll make it at Purdue. You're different, Kat. You're strong and determined and I know you can do it…if you must. I can't imagine life without you here and I don't want you to go—not one day sooner than you have to. Things'll never be the same." Johnny shook his head. "I always knew you would fly this coop as soon as possible." He played on a double score space and uttered almost as if to the thin cold air, "I'll ride alone."

"Things never stay the same, Johnny. I just learned it sooner than you." She wowed him with a triple score. "I'll come to ride with you when you're home. Call me. Oh dear, I just drew a Q. This'll be easier to play than telling your father."

"Honestly, I don't know what my Dad will say about you going in June. It's *odd* and he's always thinking how it looks to others. It's more *normal* for you to leave for college in the fall. Politically, he'll worry that it'll look like something is wrong in the family…but, we know that is not true, and he'll just have to deal with it. I think the best thing to do is tell him right out—the next time you see him. Maybe it would be good to get Mom in your corner. There's no better ally."

"She's amazing. I think she'll support my choices—always has."

"And you'll always have me." He took a long breath. "I love you, Kat."

"I love you, too, Johnny. You're the best brother in the world and it means the world to have you."

Her words broke his heart. Her profession of love was just a filial emotion and it sounded like it was etched in stone and sat on the bottom of his being.

Katherine thought about Johnny's advice to tell KC and Julianne and get it done. She resolved to find the first opportune moment. "I'll tell your parents as soon as KC can get through the snow,"

Two days later the lights flickered on and the furnace powered up. The family was awakened to the noise of snow plows. When KC was finally able to travel, he came with good news from the campaign and plans for a winter party. He wanted to celebrate the resilience of his family in the storm. It was decided to do a feature story for the Maryland Life program on the local channels. Reporters and camera crews from the networks filled the newly plowed driveway. His return was a media event with emphasis on the Kingsleys' ability to survive hardship as taught by the father of the clan. Good press; good presidential material.

A dinner and sledding party was planned to celebrate their return to normalcy. Sleds were assembled and waxed. Gloves and hats were piled in the foyer as firewood was piled for a bonfire. Lights were stretched down the hill behind the house. The tractor packed the snow for a perfect sled run. Water was pumped on the frozen pond to give a smooth skating surface. A bountiful feast was assembled on the sideboard as friends and neighbors arrived. Johnny found Katherine and Lady Fair stretched out in her bedroom.

"I found your skates before someone else claimed them. We'll have to fight for a sled. Come on; the fun is beginning. Get your snow gear. Time's a-wasting." Katherine could not resist the winter wonderland. She jumped into action and smiled a smile that Johnny would remember forever. The only thing that changed for her was the opportunity to tell the future President of the United States that she would not come into the fold in the White House. He would be told; she would go. As with all things political, it was a matter of timing.

The following morning Katherine wakened to the drip, drip, drip of melting icicles hanging by her window. The sun sparkled through the stalactites suspended from the dormer roof. Lady Fair batted at every splash outside the window pane. Katherine rose to her elbow and looked at the scene, now lit by sunlight. It was time to get to the things she had assigned to this day. The drifts on the side lawn and hills were unmarred by footprints. Her task would be like making the first steps in pristine snow. Katherine would leave her trail across the landscape and away from here.

Ironically, KC was waiting for Katherine. He had some difficult issues he had to discuss with her. The hour was late and breakfast was already cleared when she stepped off the staircase. "Kathy, please, come into the study. It's warm and your breakfast will be brought in here. I need to talk to you." His unexpected invitation unglued her.

"Yes, Sir. Thank you." She sat before the food tray but had no appetite. KC seemed tense and she wondered if he already knew what was on her mind

"Kathy, I hope you had fun yesterday. It was quite a snow-party."

"It was great."

"The reporters asked so many questions about you and your place in this family…I had to answer them. When in my position, unanswered questions cause more questions. Do you understand?

"Yes, I do."

"I only wanted to let you know in advance…the media will most likely cover your father's death, our business relationship, and your residence here. I wish I could have avoided putting you through this."

He paused, waited for her, but she had nothing to say. She only had the deep gnawing wish that she had never come here. It was a mysterious wish because this man and family did all they could to make her a home. It just never worked for her.

"The best I can do is let you know when the news or newspapers are covering this, and you can avoid them…if you like. I will ask my staff to give us that information. I'm sure this will be a quick flash of interest and hopefully pass…in a week or two." She listened to his words and tried to imagine how she would feel as her hardest memories were put across the TV and in papers. This defused her worry about telling KC she was leaving. Her announcement seemed mundane compared to his.

"I'll deal with this as best I can and I will appreciate the information your staff gives me. I'll avoid as much as I can." She took a deep breath and continued. "KC, this is the perfect time to tell you something on my mind."

He put down his coffee and raised an eyebrow.

"I'm moving back to my home as soon as I graduate in June. I hope you recall my determination to move out on my own as soon as my inheritance was available. I haven't changed my mind. In fact, I was coming to tell you today. Now, with your news, I think my going is good for everyone. I will not be on the campaign trail and I will not be moving into the White House, either."

"If I get into the White House…Kathy, you are part of the family. Your decision to go will leave a void. I thought you would stay until college starts in the fall. And—" he searched for words. "—wherever we go, you are expected, too."

"No, sir. I'm moving in June—to my condominium."

The Senator was uncomfortable. His political mind flew to all the possible implications of this announcement. Was it better to have her out of his family circle and media scrutiny…or would it be better to have her and the truth of her birth under his roof and control? It was the latter; it was definitely the latter—he had to have control.

"You should stay with us until college and if we move to the White House—think of the experience. Brenda, Johnny, Melissa and you. It's historic."

"I understand, but…"

He stood to interrupt. "Julianne will be crushed, even hurt… after all she has done for you." He waited for guilt to load into his demands. KC brought his imposing stature and senatorial rhetoric into the conversation. "The condominium is rented; a dorm room has been secured for you." He spoke to her as if she were one of his own children making a decision about college. "We're your family. Let this continue to be your home until you finish college. I insist. We will not tell Julianne, Brenda, Johnny, and Melissa about this conversation. Come, my dear." he took her hands, brought her to her feet and led her toward the door to end the discussion. "It is settled."

Katherine turned in the doorway, drew her hands away from his, looked into eyes that were exactly her color, and said, "No. It is not settled. I *am* moving the day after I graduate. I appreciate all you and your family have done for me. This has been home for me and I'm truly grateful. I love Julianne and expect she will understand and support me, Brenda, Johnny, and Melissa—." She paused,"—I hope they understand, too. But, I am going." She walked to the stairs, looked back at the amazed man. "I must. I will."

Katherine climbed the stairs trembling. Upstairs, Lady Fair allowed tears of doubt to wet her fur. *Can I do this?*

In the study, KC Kingsley wiped a tear or two from his eyes. He had to admit—he wanted his daughter close. He had doubts, too. *Can she do this?*

Katherine avoided the TV news mention of the fatherless girl residing in the presidential candidate's home. She did not see the newspapers. The details, as reported, were not brought to her attention. Friends at school soon learned that it was a topic she would not discuss. Her tunnel vision and concentration were well developed, as she managed to pass through the hoopla with exceptionally high grades and a pleasantness that belied the turmoil. More than ever, she needed to get out of the Kingsley spotlight.

A drive to see her mother would assuage the guilt she felt in missing her birthday visit. Repeated winter storms made travel difficult until the first signs of spring dotted the landscape with brave early buds. All offers from the Kingsley clan to accompany her were declined, but before she went, KC again summoned her to the study. Katherine anticipated the worst, but he was relaxed and smiling as she entered.

"Kathy, come sit for a minute," This was significant for the busy man who did not have time for others in his household. "I want to make sure our last conversation did not create a rift between us. I've thought about your decision to leave. Believe me, I was only thinking of the hardship this choice makes on you. You haven't told Julianne, have you?"

"No, sir. Only Johnny."

"It's your news to tell and I would suggest the sooner the better…for everyone to accept it…just as it took me a while. That being said, Julianne and I will support you in any way we can. Will you share your plans with me?"

"The lease for the condominium expires in March. It won't be renewed. I plan to commute to Georgetown for classes. I intend to pay more attention to my mother; she must be missing Papa, too."

He smiled, but could not speak. Fear constricted his throat and sweat wetted his palms.

"Please understand. I'm not going away from my ties to this family. I love each and every one. I don't want to lose my only family. I just have to do it my way."

KC gave her a weak smile.

⁂

The Senator called Spring Haven and asked for Dr. Sherman. He was rather nonchalantly notified, that "Dr. Sherman had had a heart attack. We are praying for his survival, but it is doubtful he will return to his office."

For the second time in ten minutes, he could not speak. He had managed to deal with losing control of Katherine, and now he had lost control of Pamela.

CHAPTER 12

1958

Mid-June came. Katherine no longer lived at King's Trace. She stood in the center of her living room and looked out the window at the Capitol Dome, illuminated against the black sky. White sheets covered all the furnishings, and nothing brightened the dark corners. There was only one thing to do—sit on the floor and cry. She was frightened and her grief for her father, which surfaced again, surprised her and flooded over all. Reality coated like dust and resounded in the still clock. Responsibility crept in. Resolve, like brown ooze, flowed out of her. She allowed the mood, drew one of the sheets from the ottoman to dry her tears and turned slowly until it wrapped her in a cocoon. Thus the first night back in her own home, she slept in her clothes—swaddled in a sheet, on the floor.

Knocking on the door startled her awake and brought her back to today and its issues.

"Hello, Miss Ross. I hope I'm not too early."

"No, no, Mr. Longfellow. I'm glad to see you." Jonas Longfellow had the same easy good looks that she remembered from their first meeting at the reading of her father's will. "Come in, pull a sheet and find a chair. I'm afraid I have not made any headway in making this place presentable. The painters covered everything and I haven't had time to uncover. It's a mess—me, too. Make yourself at home while I at least comb my hair." She excused herself as Jonas began uncovering and folding. Katherine could hear him snatching sheets and talking to the furniture, she smiled for the first time, comforted by his lighthearted approach.

"Aha, a chair. Another chair." He spoke loudly so she could hear him from her room. "A coffee table … glad to find you because I brought coffee." He set two steaming cups by the newly revealed sofa. The rich aroma brought her back to the room. "Coffee, Miss Ross?" Jonas invited, pointing his long fingers at the cups.

"Coffee, yes." She turned to look at him "Please, call me Katherine."

"Katherine," he smiled. "I hope you find everything in order. The furnishings in the storage and moving company are fully insured so go over the manifest carefully." He assumed a professional stance.

"I appreciate all you have done—settling with the tenants and getting our things home again. I'm glad I kept your card and remembered your offer to help, and I know this," she waved her hand around, "is not in your job description. Thanks for coming over this morning." She paused to enjoy the coffee before getting to the point. "I need a lawyer because uh … I want to take responsibility for my mother. You represented her and know more than I do about her situation. I'm anxious to at least understand my position, and hers, before I start college this fall.

"If you want me to be your attorney, I must clear some things up with Senator Kingsley. I'm a bit confused on his position in this. He's not your mother's guardian—what's he in all this?"

"I'm not sure. I thought she was a ward of the state after my father died. KC is not her guardian. One sure thing, Mr. Longfellow, I need your help. I need to be her guardian."

"Call me Jonas."

"Jonas."

Katherine and Jonas began their business arrangement and their friendship on this day. They uncovered furniture and rearranged rooms. She told of her life in the Kingsley household. He told of his limited success as low man in a power legal partnership. They settled mattresses and found boxes of linens. She would not sleep on the floor again. By noon when their Chinese food was delivered, the dining room table was cleared and clean dishes and glasses were placed for their meal. As they ate, she looked at him and studied his features…his square face, dark eyes, and ever-bothersome shock of hair. He seemed more suited to playing sports because his long legs had to be folded to fit under the table. She liked the way his eyes laughed.

Jonas wanted to talk about Pamela Ross, but felt it was up to Katherine to open the conversation.

"Did you actually meet my mother?"

"No. When I got to Spring Haven her doctor…uh, Sherman…had all her records for me. They said it would not be good for the patient to see me. Sherman had the final say in that. Well orchestrated. Senator Kingsley was not there, but his name came up repeatedly and his presence was surely felt. It was a formality, I understand, but it was very well set out—as was the reading of the will. I was alert to see if Pamela, or you, would have any issues but really, Katherine, your father did a good job of taking care of everything. Is there anything you are questioning?"

"Not really, as far as the will is concerned. I have a lot to learn about Mother's care and I want to know more about her condition. She has been the same for so many years, not better; not worse. Maybe she should be in another facility and be reviewed by new doctors. I want the best for her."

"I know you do…and what you say makes good sense." She walked him to the door as the setting sun filtered the light in the room. "Thank you, Jonas…for everything"

"Stop thanking me. I enjoyed the workout, so I don't have to go to the gym today. It was fun. Call me soon for a business appointment and we will get started on the work at hand." As she reached for the door latch, the doorbell startled her. She opened the door to let Jonas leave as Johnny walked in. All three seemed to sense the crossing of paths was significant, far beyond the casual greeting and meeting of boy, a stranger, and a young woman. Lives were defined on the threshold. The man with the briefcase was beaming with delight in the unaware girl.

Johnny did not know the girl standing in the doorway. She was different, no longer the outsider at King's Trace, unsure of her surroundings. He could see the difference. He had happy memories of riding across the Maryland hills with her, the wind in their faces, panting horses, and a hint of *something* that maybe could be. But, now Johnny could not hold them here—in this place—in this time.

Katherine was tired but she tried to stay animated as she invited Johnny in and showed him around. It was a weak effort. She could not see him in this new life and he felt a new distance between them, as he told her good-bye and prepared to leave for summer football at Purdue.

"Kat, everything suddenly seems so different."

"I know, Johnny. It is." She looked sadly at him as she took his hand. "You are special to me. You know that…and we both have a new life before us. College and all. Aren't you excited?"

"I will be—I guess—once I get there."

"Of course you will. Me, too. I hope." A special understanding flowed between them but, more than that, each felt a great, undefined gulf growing. Katherine reached for his hand as he took her into a parting hug that she kept short, too short for Johnny.

"I'll see you at Thanksgiving." She smiled broadly. Johnny would leave with no promise except that. It was emotional but it covered no new ground for the couple.   Knowledge of it would have made Senator Kingsley breathe easier.

Johnny paused on the threshold. "Kat…"

"I know." She answered.

The closing clunk of the massive door with the name *Ross* carved into the solid brass plate was profound.

Katherine felt better—a lot better than 24 hours ago. She took Lady Fair and her thoughts to her bed. "Lady, we are going to be fine here. Johnny will be fine at college. I'll miss him the most." Then with a sudden change in countenance, continued. "It's good to be home again, isn't it?" She took the quiet purr as assent and went to bed early.

The next morning the phone broke into her sleep. The clock said 8:46 as she reached for the receiver. "Hello?"

"Kathy, its KC. How are you?"

She hid her surprise. "Fine, KC. How are you?"

"I called to offer help. Do you need some…for moving and setting up things? I can send a staffer over for you."

"KC, that is nice but I want to do it myself, little by little. The furniture is placed and I'm the only one who will know what to do with the boxes. My bed is set up and dishes ready to eat on. Don't send anyone."

"Don't forget. Julianne and I are both in Washington this week. She expects me to help you and I want to. Please call for anything anytime. Okay? Oh, and I'm sending over my schedule so you will know where we are at all times. It will have phone numbers, too. We want to hear from you .Everyone misses you and Melissa is out of sorts each morning."

"It's nice to be missed."

"Are you happy with your decision to move back to DC?" It was one of the longest conversations she ever had with him. He even let her respond with positive comments on the condominium and her excitement about school.

She was even more surprised the next afternoon when KC rang her doorbell.

"I decided to drop the schedule off myself." He said as he stepped inside. "I need to give Julianne a personal report. She's really worried about you."

"No need to worry. I'm home again. Maybe I should invite her to bring Melissa and visit. She'll see that I'm fine." He came in and sat. She knew he had more to say and the awkward moment was already becoming painful. Without asking, she went to get him a glass of tea. "Lemon?" was the only thing she could think to say.

"I want you to know…I *will* be running for President." She was greatly tempted to say *soooo…* ? but she waited and sipped her tea. "The opposition will be ruthless. They are looking for anything to discredit me. They will delve into your grandfather's business. You know James and I were partners in the original company with your grandfather. They will grasp at straws, even your mother's illness, to find anything they can distort. Politics is often a messy business."

"Why are you telling me this?" She finally had to voice her concern. "I have nothing to do with politics. Was there something in the business?"

"No, no child. There was nothing to hide in the business, but they are not looking for the truth. I don't want to upset you. I only wanted to tell you so you will come to me if anyone questions you

...or bothers you ...or upsets you during my campaign. That's all. I told the same things to Brenda and Johnny away at school. That's all. Come to me, Kathy."

They sat quiet and let the cool drink fill the void between them. He stood to go, hoping she would offer a hand or touch, but she didn't. At the door he thanked her for the drink. "Good bye, Kathy. I'll tell Julianne you are doing fine."

"KC, don't worry. I understand about politics and media twists. It won't matter to me what may be said about the Greeley Company and business." She drew a deep breath. "But, I won't allow anything about my mother. I won't allow that," she repeated with strength and conviction. "She is my responsibility and priority now and I will protect her from any and everyone who would harm or distress her."

He went to his car and recalled the night when James had beaten him without blows and he could not drive from the parking lot at Greeley Construction. He felt like he had bee hit again, this time with blows to his heart and psyche. He knew, just like before, he could not fight back. Finally, KC had no choice; he started the car and became again the man his image makers created. The power that would come his way would not be used against Katherine.

"My daughter." He had come to love her; the torture was complete. He could have every dream but one. Katherine Marie would never walk hand in hand with him, neither respect nor love him as his other children did. Most likely one day, when he could no longer keep his balance on the tightrope, she would hate him.

CHAPTER 13

1958

The phone startled Lady Fair, who jumped to the nightstand to attack the intruder. Katherine noticed the steady rain before the second ring told her where she was and what she had to do.

"Hello?'

"Katherine Ross? Dr. McMaster, Spring Haven Hospital."

"Yes, this is Katherine Ross." It was rare to sleep so late, but the stress of the past days and the dreary morning invited slumber. *Mother's doctor*? she thought. She ignored the flip of her stomach and made an appointment to meet with him later that day. "I'll be there."

The cold, wet day matched Katherine's mood. For several weeks she had promised herself it was time to face the problems waiting at Spring Haven. She wanted to go to her mother. She wanted to know all about her condition and meet the challenges of her care but, it was hard to make the first step. Dr. McMaster did it for her this morning.

Katherine fell back on the bed to listen to the rain pelting the big window. The drumming was not the rain; it was her heart. Fear gripped her. It gave her a chill so she pulled the comforter up to her mouth to stifle a cry, and then up to her eyes to wipe tears she could not hold back. She gave herself fifteen minutes by the clock.

At 9:42, she reached for the phone and told Jonas Longfellow about the meeting.

"Call me if you need me. I'm in court this morning but, free this afternoon. You okay?"

"Sure, I'm fine—just scared. It's time to get started on this."

"If I finish in time, I'll meet you at the hospital."

Lady Fair yielded to a gentle nudge and moved to curl into the warm spot vacated by her girl. Katherine lifted her so she could make the bed. "Why do you ignore me?" She asked. "Do you deserve a warm spot in my bed, my room, my life?" As she chastised the independent cat, she nuzzled her nose into soft fur and made her own purring noise. "Ignore me all you want, I'll never give up on you." Lady Fair was deposited back on the made-up bed. "Neither you, nor Mother." Katherine proclaimed as she started for the shower.

※

Dr. McMaster sat behind his desk, looking the part perfectly. He wore a white lab coat over his business suit, shirt and tie. His eyes were gentle and intelligent; his chin square. The small goatee beard was well trimmed and speckled with gray. Katherine noted he was a handsome man. Robert J. McMaster was also a wise, caring man. He knew the young woman entering his office was scared. His first business was to set her at ease.

"Katherine Ross, please, come in." He pointed to a chair facing his desk. "I'm Robert McMaster, senior resident here at Spring Haven." He rose and extended his hand. "We're going to be partners in your mother's care. Since we'll meet often, I'd like to call you Katherine. Is that good for you?" His smile was pleasant; his eyes friendly. "I'll refer to your mother as Pamela. Is that's okay with you, too?" Katherine nodded assent to both questions as he continued. "I would invite you to call me Robert, but I know from experience that would be too difficult for you at this time, so we will leave that alone." He laughed gently and she responded with a smile and another nod.

"Thank you, Doctor."

He lifted a large file onto his desk and began the business at hand. "I do not recommend you see your mother today." His first words relaxed her. Her breathing became easier immediately. "We're in the process of reassessing her and changing her medications. I would describe her condition today as changing and unsettled. I assure you, she is fine and what we are doing will not constitute a setback. You may or may not know she has been exclusively under the care of Dr. Sherman and he died last week. I'm now her primary doctor, but she will be cared for by a team, assembled especially to meet her needs." He paused. "Maybe this is a good time for you to tell me what you know about your mother's care. Are you ready to talk to me or would you rather I continue?"

"I'm ready to talk about Mother." She decided not to tell him how scared she was so she went to her rehearsed words. "Everyone protected me from worry over her. My father died about two years ago and now she is my responsibility. I'm eighteen now. I'm all she has and I have to know everything about her illness and treatment. I'm ready." She began to tremble.

"That's an important first step. Excuse me a moment." Dr. McMaster saw she needed to compose herself, so he went for some water on his sideboard. "Water?"

"Yes, thank you."

"I want you to be comfortable when you come to Spring Haven, Katherine. We're here for your mother, just as you are. You're an important part of her team."

Katherine took a cool, calming swallow. "Quite frankly, Dr. McMaster, I've wondered. Will she always be the same as she has been in the years I've been coming to see her?" She voiced the fear that was strong on her mind.

McMaster was impressed at the way the young woman pulled herself together and said what was on her mind.

"Together, I hope we can find the answer to your question. The first change affecting Pamela is the team I mentioned. She'll no longer be under the care of one doctor. That's against hospital policy instituted five years ago and we, as an institution, should have noted and corrected the situation. Pamela will have doctors from many disciplines—including therapists that concentrate on both the mind and body. We need to confer and evaluate with all the best minds and experience available. Having you on the team is vital. It means you will be included in these conferences and evaluations. I also believe it's important for the family be part of the treatment, and surely, vital to the cure."

God, can there be a cure? she prayed silently.

He rose from his desk and went over and took her hands. Katherine immediately thought of her father and his strong hands. Tears spilled unchecked.

"You alright?"

"Yes, sir. Excuse my tears. I've never heard the word 'cure' before. You are encouraging. I'm excited to work with mother's team." *A cure*, her mind reeled.

"We're always working toward returning our patients to their families and a more normal life. We don't make promises, but I'd like to believe she will be better. Are there any other family members to consider?"

"No, none." He was surprised. She was alone.

"Friends or close associates?"

"My attorney, Jonas Longfellow. I trust him and need him as I sort through this." No other name came to mind as she reviewed her support.

"If he is trusted, and you are confident he has your and Pamela's interests, at heart, we will list him as a team member. Is that what you want?"

"Yes, sir."

"I'll have a consent paper drawn for you to sign," He made a note. "We'll set a weekly team meeting. Tuesday mornings—good for you? In the beginning it's important to be here each week. Hopefully soon you can stretch out your attendance and I'll send you reports. Rest assured; you are always included. There will be no secrecy."

"It's good we're starting now while my schedule is clear. In September I start classes at Georgetown University. When can I see Mother?"

"I'm sure by next Tuesday when you come again. Here," he handed her a file, "read this diagnosis. I have written it in layman terms. You may not understand everything but it will help you if you know what we are dealing with. I'm sure there will be questions—call me any time. I'm not always available, but I will return your call."

"Thank you so much. I feel much better. What a change from every other time I entered this place." Her fear of this morning yielded to hope.

It was time to end this meeting. He could see she was exhausted from the stress of the topic. Information had to be digested by both parties. "Take your time, read the file and we'll answer your questions when you come next week—unless you want to call in the meantime."

"Thanks again." She gathered her purse and the medical file.

"One more thing, Katherine, what is Senator Kingsley's relationship to Pamela? Did you know Dr. Sherman had been reporting to him?"

"He's not related to Mother. My father was his business partner. He's been getting reports on her since my father died. I suppose because he was executor of my father's estate." This was troubling information, for the doctor knew Senator Kingsley had been getting reports from Dr. Sherman since Pamela Ross was admitted. *Why?*

"Is Mother a ward of the state? My father made generous gifts to the hospital each year. I could not find any payment invoices for her care. Has she been a ward of the state since she came here… or just since my father died?"

"I do not have information that she is, or ever was, a ward of the state. My files are medical but I will check for you." Even as he said it, he knew, every court-controlled patient was duly noted on medical charts, but Sherman's records were sloppy. This meeting with his patient's daughter was bringing more questions than answers.

She sat back in the chair and sighed. He could see the past forty-five minutes had been hard on her. She looked younger—almost childlike as she gazed up at the doctor. Yet, her resilience and strength came forward.

"I *am* overwhelmed, but I want to know everything."

"Give me time to get some answers; I'll call you." He had no intention of hiding anything from Pamela Ross's daughter, but he had to be sure of the facts. She was not the only one who wanted to know more about the background of his new charge. McMaster was a good doctor and he knew, especially with mental illness, all the factors were important to unlocking the problem and looking for a cure.

Dr. McMaster called the hospital director as soon as Katherine closed the door.

"Jeff, I need to talk to you. I've learned some disturbing facts about Pamela Ross. I'm appalled. She was not seen or evaluated according to hospital policy. I have some serious questions about how Sherman treated her. He kept two sets of records on her. It's bad—worse than bad. Our best team of doctors is reviewing and evaluating her but, we'll be doing a lot of back-pedaling. Do you know the patient and her situation?"

"Not really. Her case hasn't come to my attention since I took this job last year. What red flags are you seeing?"

"Earlier today I learned Dr. Sherman sent Senator Kingsley reports on her, although he is not related nor does he have any rights to such reports. I met with her daughter and she couldn't explain either. Now we need to know why Sherman did what he did, and we need to know Senator Kingsley's part in this."

"I'll be right down." The director and the doctor found more questions than answers as they rehashed the information before them.

"Frankly, Jeff, I thought we could get the best medical treatment for this patient and go forward, but I see a lot more in this than we realized. Obviously, Sherman treated Ross for control. I do not see a program in place to improve her condition." He paused to shake his head and scratch his chin. "He was incompetent, no doubt, but was there another reason? I don't like this and I don't like Kingsley's part in it, whatever that may be. And…we are most likely talking about the future President. We could be sued."

"Tell me about Ross's family."

"A young daughter, Katherine—just turned eighteen. She inherited her fortune, and responsibility for her mother. Katherine Ross thought her mother was a ward of the state when her father died. That's not true. They are quite wealthy. Her care is provided by a trust and her husband gave generously to the hospital each year. I didn't know about Kingsley's interest until Sherman died. Get me information. We need to know everything. Do you think Pamela's husband wanted her institutionalized, lied to his daughter, and used his partner, the Senator, to influence Sherman? I'm going to go back and sort over Sherman's records. I obviously should have sooner. No more surprises." He shook his head. "Now, we need to be transparent and proactive. And, Pamela Ross deserves the best care we can give her."

"Let's move on this… but let's be thorough. A lot hinges on what we find and what we do about it—for Pamela Ross and the hospital."

"I agree."

"This is serious. Maybe there are some logical answers. Believe me, I want the answers, too." The director went to the phone. "Mary, seal Dr. Sherman's office. Do not let anything be moved from there; not even his personal belongings … and especially not his personal files."

He listened to his secretary. "I know she was. Call and tell her not to come for her husband's things yet. And, call Finance. Tell them I want every transaction on Pamela Ross. Yes, back to her admittance. ASAP! Oh, and Mary, call Frankel and tell him I need legal advice as soon as he can see me. Set the appointment. Thanks." He turned to the director, "Norma Sherman was coming today to clean her husband's desk. Sealed just in time."

"I promised to call Katherine Ross. Whatever the truth is, she deserves it…as does her mother. When she comes again, I'm sure she will bring her lawyer."

"Can you put off telling her anything until we figure this out? Is she bringing the lawyer because she feels we are culpable?"

"I don't think so. He's a trusted advisor. I want to be honest. She is upset and in a difficult position. Our position is precarious, to say the least. I'm not going to mislead her and there is no advantage in stalling."

"But, we don't know the answers yet."

"We will by next week," McMaster vowed.

Dr. McMaster was not looking forward to his next meeting with Katherine Ross. He had his own apprehensions. Even with the few facts he had, he was sure the Ross family would have every legal right to sue the hospital. Pamela's care was beyond reprehensible; it was criminal. The death of Dr. Sherman released him from responsibility, but in no way excused the hospital. A quick scan of the material assembled on Pamela Ross presented two important facts: She was not and never had been a ward of the state. Her bills were paid annually, on time, through an escrow account set up by the Greeley Corporation, and managed by the bank holding the trust fund. Senator Kingsley had no legal right to receive reports on the patient. They were rightly concerned about the feelings of the daughter and the advice she would get from her lawyer. The involvement of the senator complicated the issue beyond reason.

Walking from the hospital, Katherine was suddenly hungry. At a small nearby diner she ordered a grilled cheese sandwich and opened the file. It had words she knew; schizophrenia, bipolar, personality disorder, disassociation, paranoid, violent outbursts.

The fear that claimed her earlier came back with a vengeance. The sandwich sat cold and uneaten as her confidence evaporated. She felt more detached from her mother than ever before as she read the file. The name she had used for years—Mother—seemed lost in the clinical descriptions layered in the pages of the file. She closed the file, and for the first time, thought of her mother, as *Pamela*.

She paid her check and walked zombie-like back to the hospital grounds and sat on a bench facing the pastoral lawn. She was not ready to leave and she had to at least have a physical closeness to her mother—for a while. The file was pressed to her chest as if her body, blood and being could change what was documented there. All around patients with hesitant steps walked with attendants. She looked into each face searching for Pamela or someone who reminded her of her mother. Katherine did not know if she wanted to see the familiar face so like her own or not. And then, the most frightening thoughts came. *Do I want Pamela to get well… or not? Where would she fit? Was it easier to come here several times a year and know she was not changing, challenging, or requiring? Should she stay here—be a patient—have an attendant? I don't know her; she doesn't know me. What am I doing? What do I think I'm doing?*

An old memory came back. She was about four years old. She could even remember the blue dress with pink and purple flowers that she wore for her visit with her mother. It must have been Easter. It was so clear. They were walking this pavement at this very bench when she planted her feet and refused to go home. "I'm staying with Mama."

"Katherine, you can't stay. We'll come back soon." She heard her father's voice.

"If she isn't coming home, me neither!" Katherine said her line again and recalled the tantrum. Papa picked her up, and carried her, screaming to the car.

"I want my mother! I want my mother!" She also remembered the tears on Papa's face as he drove home.

The file slipped from her hand and spilled on the ground. "I want my mother!" she cried aloud. A female patient and nurse saw the commotion and approached. They gathered her papers and gave them back to the distraught girl. The patient patted her hand while the nurse asked if she was alright.

"Yes," she lied.

Her head was in her hands when Jonas arrived and sat beside her without saying a word. She threw her arms around the startled man and held him as if he were a buoy in a raging sea.

CHAPTER 14

1958

Jonas removed the medical files from Katherine's arms, took her hand and silently walked her to her car. She got in behind the steering wheel without making any effort to find her key. After a short pause, he went to the passenger side and slid in beside her.

"Jonas, where's your car?"

"Parked at the diner."

"Why are you in mine? Something wrong?"

"You can't drive. I'm waiting for you to come back from wherever you are." He gently touched her hair as she leaned into his touch.

"I'm not going to cry."

"Okay. We'll wait until you know what you want to do." He patted her head lovingly. "Take your time." As Jonas spoke he began winding down the windows, reaching across her with long arms, taking care not to touch her. "When you're ready."

The afternoon breeze cooled the car that had been sitting in the sun for hours. Katherine took the Kleenex he offered and wiped the beads of sweat from her lip. She did not raise her eyes to look at him and his eyes never moved from her. He saw her perfect countenance, the wisp of curl under her chin and the bright clean of her collar and hair. Jonas was more than willing to sit and wait.

She turned and looked out the passenger's window without seeing him. The confused and lost look on her face stunned and scared him. If she looked in mirror she would see her mother's haunted eyes looking back at her, and the same vacant look that she had seen four times a year—every year for her whole life.

Come back. Please come back! Jonas was afraid. Could he be losing something he never really had? That was not going to happen—not if he could help it.

"Let me take you home."

"Home?"

"Yes, home." Jonas walked to the driver's side as she slid across the seat. The drive to Washington was accomplished without words. When hervdoor opened with the key she dutifully provided, she went straight for Lady Fair and her room. Jonas went to the kitchen and made coffee. The warm aromatic brew failed to draw Katherine from her room. The door was slightly ajar and he took permission to look in on her. She and Lady Fair were curled together on the comforter. After covering her, he returned to drink coffee and continue his wait.

In the dark of night Katherine dressed in her gown, crawled into the bed and slept. She was surprised to find Jonas rumpled and sleeping on her sofa as the morning light teased the day. Kitchen sounds and bacon frying roused him.

She heard him stir. "Jonas, why you are asleep in my living room?" she called. "Scrambled or over easy?"

"Scrambled."

"There's almost a full pot of coffee." She poked her head around the door jamb. "Shall I heat you a cup? Why are you here?" she asked again.

He did not hear the last question. Jonas was in the bathroom trying to straighten his hair, wash his face and push his shirt neatly in his pants. None of it was working. All he could say as he ambled to the kitchen was, "Hi." He had never been in a situation like this before. He had seen it in the movies—awkward mornings after one night stands, but this was not that.

Katherine was singing a silly popular tune while she cooked. Her invitation to eat was done with gestures. He could sense she did not want to talk so they ate their bacon and eggs, passed the toast and butter with a strange kind of ease without conversation. The sun, and the silence, comforted the couple and lured them into remaining at the table—unwilling to go forward to anything. But this was not their life, each had daily requirements.

Jonas wanted to talk about yesterday, but he left it up to her to open a dialog. She did not. He got his jacket as she cleared the table. At the door she smiled warmly and touched his hand, causing him to turn squarely and look her in the eye. He knew in the instant that it was the first time she had connected to his gaze since they left the bench on the hospital grounds yesterday.

"Dr. McMaster is mother's new doctor. He has formed a team to treat her and I'm on the team."

"That sounds good."

"I put you on the team, too. Alright?"

"Of course."

Without invitation, Jonas stepped back into the living room. "Katherine." He spoke softly like a prayer. "I want you to tell me about yesterday. Can you do that?"

Something broke inside her, as if a veil fell away and his warm gaze pulled her to this side of hidden emotions. Katherine crumpled to a heap and began to cry uncontrollably. He picked her up and took her to the sofa and let her cry. After what seemed an eternity and a river of tears, she looked at him again.

"For the first time in many years, I allowed myself to admit—I want my mother. I want what other girls have—a mother." Her arms clamped empty across her chest. "Breakfast across the table from her. Sleep in the next room." Tears flood with each new thought. "I want to be fussed at. Laugh and make faces with her. Watch Milton Berle together." These quirky ideas brought a teary smile. Katherine took his hand so she could digest her own words with his support. "I thought I had moved on in my life without her." With a tissue still working to dry her eyes and nose, she said, "I haven't, Jonas. I haven't." He touched her blotchy face and she bent into it. "I read her file. Oh, God, that scared me." She crushed his hand with unusual strength. "He used the word *cure*."

"The doctor said she could be cured?"

"No." She thought back searching for the doctor's words. "He said cure was always the goal. Can I bring her home? It's so much," she whispered. "Too much." For the first time she was questioning herself. "I don't know if I can do it."

"You'll be fine, Katherine. I know you will do all that you can, but not alone."

"I feel alone."

"That's because you miss your father. Think of the people who want to help you. Dr. McMaster, the team at the hospital, the Kingsley family—and me. I'm here for you, and will be, every step of the way." Jonas took on her problem. "Stop looking at this in the whole. Let's look at it in tiny increments."

"Jonas, you've done so much and I do appreciate everything, but I've even failed to pay you a retainer. That just shows… I don't know what I'm doing."

"Can't I be your friend *and* your lawyer?" He wanted to touch her, but held back. "Right now, I'm your friend."

"Please." For the second time in twenty-four hours, she threw her arms around him and he responded likewise.

She pushed away, suddenly realizing that his body next to hers was stirring too many emotions. "I need a good friend. More than anything." Her walls went up.

"You're shedding so many tears. I had better get you a glass of water." He went to the kitchen and gave them time to regroup. He came back with a notebook in hand. "Let's make a list."

They began writing all the issues Katherine had about her mother. The items were called and entered randomly. "Now we'll prioritize them."

The work was good, it settled the distraught girl and the newly enamored man. She saw a semblance of order in the problem of her mother. The first three items were duly numbered.

1. *Search father's files for information and payment schedules to Spring Haven*
2. *Wait for the information Dr. McMaster is assembling*
3. *Go to Spring Haven next Tuesday for weekly meeting*

Jonas took her hands firmly, letting his support travel up her arms to her heart. "Remember, your mother is being taken care of while you are sorting this out. You're very fortunate. Your father has given you the resources to provide the very best for her. Some in your position are not so blessed. Your job is to make sure she gets the best. There will be some hard decisions but really, that is all." He reached over and took her pencil. "The best care for Pamela Ross." He numbered the list. "Make that number four."

"I'll make that number one." Katherine took the pencil back with a more playful air. "You're right, Jonas. Thank you. I think you were sent to be my guardian angel." She drew wings beside her list.

"Katherine, I'm not an angel, but I'm glad I represented your mother at the reading of the will. I feel connected to her, and to you. Let me be your guardian friend."

"Perfect," she smiled before changing the subject.

"Your car is still in Catonsville. I have some things to do, and I need to freshen up. What time would you be ready to go get it?"

"This afternoon."

"Call me when you finish what you have to do. I'll be ready." Katherine met his gaze. "Jonas, thanks again."

"Not a problem."

"And, I will spend the afternoon fixing a heat-up dinner for us, back here."

Katherine was her old self when he returned that afternoon. The weather had changed. Wind tossed the trees and driving summer rain came crosswise. Each was anxious to resume the day together but for different reasons. Katherine wanted to re-establish the friendly working basis with Jonas. He hoped for more. He followed her car back to her home and accepted her invitation to eat cream of broccoli soup and crusty bread.

"That is all I had on hand. But, I did have ingredients to make my famous chocolate peanut butter brownies."

They sat with the rain beating on the big window and rainbow prisms dancing around the lights of the city, eating one of the best meals served in the Nation's Capital that day.

With a cup of coffee, she took the conversation away from the general to the thing on both their minds. "I want to talk to you about yesterday," she began.

He said nothing as he focused solely on her.

"I don't remember coming home from Spring Haven. Oh, there are parts I recall. It was so hot in the car and so quiet. Lady

Fair was happy to see me and I dressed for bed in the dark." She rose to get the plate of brownies and came back to sit with him. "I was shocked to see you sleeping on my sofa. Watching over me?" She smiled and gave a small laugh.

"Yes," he said, relieved by her lighter spirit.

Katherine was pleased that he was going to let her go on with her thoughts. *He's so special*, she thought. "When I left Dr. McMaster, I was overwhelmed. The enormity of the whole situation and responsibility seemed to draw the breath out of me. I felt as if I was in an avalanche with white nothingness engulfing me. Where were the answers? What are the questions? Why is this happening to me? When I got in the car, the cold white avalanche was melted by the heat and nothing was left but me. For the first time in my life I understood where my mother goes." Katherine stopped. Her thoughts and words hurt. She took his hand, so she could go on. "I don't understand why she wants to stay there in that cold, silent *nothing*."

He looked into her eyes, further relieved to see that although she was in pain, she had not retreated. He did not see the terror of yesterday. "Do you want to talk about it? If you do, I want to listen."

It was a critical decision for her. If she continued to open her heart to him, she had to let the walls down and allow him into her life. Katherine wanted to run to the kitchen, do dishes, forget this conversation, and crawl in bed with Lady Fair. She looked into the eyes of the boyish man, with the unruly shock of hair over his brow and tenderness in his face. She made her decision.

"I want to tell you, Jonas." She invited him to join her on the rug as she moved and tossed him a pillow. "Let's get comfortable, I don't know how long this will take."

"I have forever," he countered, looking at his watch as if he could find *forever* on the dial and laughing to keep the lighter spirit. "Yep, forever."

"I have thought a lot about yesterday. While stirring the soup and melting chocolate, I was thinking about your cutting to the core of the problem—mother's care. That is really my only responsibility. And that is my focus. I'm going to see that she has the very best and I want her to know that Papa loved her and I do too. But, the terrible feeling I had yesterday made me ask the question. *What overwhelmed my mother so much that she sought a white cold avalanche and stayed in it?* That awful place I found myself in was *Mother's*. I felt her pain and understood how a person can find relief from problems by withdrawing. It was terrifying. I went there for a couple of hours; she has been there for two decades. I never want to go there again." She took a deep breath. "My mother wants to go there every day."

She put her head down on the pillow and let a tear slip from her eye. "What's so *terrible* for Mother outside of her tiny box-like world? Do you think I'll find the thing that has driven my mother all these years? Will it be too horrible for her? Or me?"

He waited, not knowing if her questions were rhetorical of if she wanted his opinion.

She took his doubt away. "Jonas?"

"Dear Katherine," he touched her face. "I don't know the answers to your questions but I am of the opinion you can handle it. Dr. McMaster is the best judge about the wisdom in going back to why Pamela has withdrawn. I would let him be the guide on that. In your quest to get the best care and answers for your mother, you must take care of yourself. Remember, you are not the cause of all this. You were a baby and have no guilt. Don't let yourself go there. I wonder if your answers lie with your father. Even though he is gone, he is part of this. Why not go to his desk and find what he wants you to know. Have you done that?"

"No. The storage company packed everything, even the daily newspaper on the table. I have not opened the boxes from Papa's office. It's going to be hard."

"I was so impressed with his detailed will and the way he had things set up for you and your mother. The answers you seek may be in his journal or personal papers."

"I never thought of that. You're so smart!" She was feeling renewed by thoughts of her father and the possibilities waiting in the boxes stacked in the next room. *Papa is here* trying to help; she could feel it. Jonas seemed to stumble on the idea that would invigorate Katherine. He hoped his offhanded suggestion would be correct. He even prayed silently, *God, please let those boxes help and not hurt.*

"You can handle the past because you have a future that your father and mother, both, want you to claim. Is there any more coffee?"

Lady Fair grew weary of Katherine's attention and haughtily climbed across Jonas' shoulder to pounce to the back of the sofa. Katherine noted that the cat had never ventured that close to another human being.

More coffee, another brownie, and talk of her class schedule ended as evening shadows crossed the Capitol.

She walked him to the door and allowed an embrace which impacted both more than they would admit to the other.

"I'd like to take you down to my family home in North Carolina before you start school. Meet my parents. It'll be a relaxing fun time. They love to spoil me with good food and porch sitting. Wouldn't time by the ocean be wonderful? Game?"

"I would like that. Can we go down and back in the same day?"

"No, that would be difficult, but Mom will have a room for you. My parents are always excited when I have time to visit. You decide. Saturday? Back early Monday.

"I can go Saturday ... but, let's make sure it is a nice day, not a day like today." She pointed at the rain on the window.

"Pack for two nights. Okay?"

"Okay," she said as the phone rang. Waving good bye to Jonas, she went to pick up on the third ring.

"Kathy?"

It was KC. "I would like to put a date on your calendar. Julianne is coming in for a luncheon in two weeks—Saturday the 22nd."

"That works."

"Good, my driver will pick you up. Noon. We are looking forward to seeing you."

She went to bed unsettled as to why KC's call could steal away the good feeling she had about her evening with Jonas.

CHAPTER 15

1958

Katherine awoke and recalled today she would have lunch with KC and Julianne and, more importantly, tomorrow she would have a day with Jonas. Both events settled easily into her mind as she called to Lady Fair. "Come sweet one, we need to talk."

The cat acknowledged her girl but did not move. Lady Fair waited until she could come of her own volition. Katherine smiled knowingly. "Please," she said as the cat decided to move. "Nice to see you are so contented. I'd be contented too, if I didn't have so much on my mind."

⎯⎯∞⎯⎯

The black limo, so identifiable in Washington, arrived for Katherine at the appointed time. She stepped from the elevator as Julianne walked through the door held by the doorman.

"Katherine! I'm so happy to see you." Julianne's greeting hardly expressed her feelings. She regretted Katherine's departure from the family circle. Her instincts were to mother her and keep her, but she understood. It was beyond her control. So, she took small moments with Katherine to heart.

"I'm happy and surprised to see you. I expected one of KC's staff to fetch me. This is better." Her steps hastened, showing her delight. "How's everyone? Fill me in."

Julianne laced her arm with Katherine's and led her out. The driver opened the door and stepped back so two smiling faces could pop out from the back seat to greet her. The cheers and laughter were infectious as Melissa and Brenda spilled onto the sidewalk to give and receive hugs from their *sister*. Julianne began organizing the scene, ushering them all into the car again.

"This must be a special occasion. Brenda, home from college? You haven't been gone a month ... not that I'm complaining." She looked at Melissa, gently pulling her ponytail. " No school for you today, either?" Katherine climbed into the limo and commented. "Everyone's here but Johnny"

"We're all skipping today for Dad's award, except Johnny. Mom's idea. Dad's only expecting Mom and you. We are surprises," Brenda pointed to Melissa as she spoke. "Speeches, applause, and a great meal. I'm here for the meal. Food at the dining hall isn't that good ... but, don't tell Dad I said that."

"Why couldn't Johnny skip, too? Football?" Katherine addressed Brenda quietly.

"Didn't return Mom's call." Brenda shrugged

Katherine relaxed and enjoyed the family banter, which she'd missed more than she realized until this moment. Brenda hugged her tightly as Melissa clung to her hand.

KC was being inducted into the Maryland Hall of Fame for distinguished service to the people of Maryland. The limo headed south to Route 50 toward Annapolis, turned on West Street and headed to mid-town. They would soon be seated in the gallery of the oldest continuously used State House in the United States. The honor was being bestowed today because he had to resign his seat to run for President.

Katherine paid close attention as dignitaries came to the podium to recount KC's leadership in Congress for urban renewal, arts, and education programs that benefited not only Maryland, but citizens across the land. The Governor introduced several attending congressmen, one cabinet member and local leaders. The Baltimore Chamber of Commerce presented the Frances Scott Key award for his work spearheading urban renewal at the Inner Harbor. KC received accolade after accolade.

The Kingsley children were quieted by the magnitude of the commendations to the man who was simply *father* to them. They had traveled the campaign trail with him and had taken the red-white-and-blue acclaim in stride. That was hullabaloo. This afternoon's occasion was different and they saw it, even little Melissa. Katherine was duly impressed and looked at her father's business partner with new eyes. *He's a different man here. So important!* She would have to discuss these thoughts with Jonas. She surprised herself with thoughts of Jonas.

Lunch at the Treaty of Paris Restaurant in the Maryland Inn was festive. Except for all the important people seated at tables around them, they could have been in the breakfast room at King's Trace. Melissa's school news dominated the conversation. After she extolled the teacher she loved, Brenda recited the heavy schedule that filled her year at Duke.

"Have you talked to Johnny? How's he doing at Purdue?" Katherine asked Brenda.

"Oh, he's doing fine I guess, but he isn't good about writing. Mom is put out with him. I'm going to rattle his cage when I get back to school. No excuse for him ignoring her call—should have been here today." Her brow wrinkled and eyes darkened. "His loss."

Soon attention turned to Katherine. Everyone was waiting for her report on living back in the city and school. "Kathy, how are you doing? Like school?" KC posed the question.

"My first class is next week. Georgetown starts later than most. I'm settled back in my home and after some crazy days, things are livable. The truth is—it's exciting. At first, I thought maybe you were right—maybe a mistake. I'm glad I have had some time before you asked. The answer now is *fine*. I wasn't sure I would be ready to start class, but I am. Dad would want me to." She took a breath. "I miss you all, very much."

"Will you come to King's Trace for Thanksgiving?" Julianne asked with her heart. She wanted Katherine in her family circle, even if only one day.

"I'd love to." It would be so good to resume the friendly association that she had enjoyed with this family since childhood, now that the attempt to assimilate as one of the Kingsley children was over. She understood her new relaxation with them, they did not evaluate it, they welcomed her on any terms—even the Senator—especially the Senator.

The lunch of crab imperial and Cobb salad worked the wonder that food often does with mixed groups. Visiting between tables gave the family a chance to be introduced to all the important people. It was a wonderful day for the Kingsley family.

Julianne and Brenda tried twice to start private conversations with Katherine but gave up as Melissa clung to her like a magnet.

Back in the limo, KC leaned back and released a deep breath. The full lunch quieted all the occupants until they got to the Senate Office Building and Julianne began directing.

"KC, get a taxi for Brenda. She has a flight in forty-five minutes. My car is over there." She pointed and bent to hug her husband. "A wonderful, memorable day, Dear."

She turned to Katherine. "The driver will take you home. So happy to have you with us. See you Thanksgiving—if not sooner." She kissed Katherine gently on the cheek. "We love you."

KC got out of the limo to bid everyone good-bye as he signaled the driver to wait. Then the distinguished Senator climbed back into the limo with Katherine and instructed the driver to proceed.

"Kathy, I wanted to talk to you. I'll ride with you. It will give us a few minutes."

She smiled. For the first time since her father died, KC's one-on-one exchange did not cause a pit in her stomach.

"I'm so pleased that you are ready to start classes next week. It would have been very distressing if you postponed your education. Julianne and I would have felt responsible. Making sure you went on to college was important to James and us." Katherine said nothing, so he continued. "I hope you enjoyed today."

"I did. It was great. You were very highly honored. Congratulations, KC."

He was surprised by how important and wonderful it was to get that compliment from her.

"Thank you." He touched her hand. "It was so good for all of us to be together. Well, all but Johnny." Disappointment crossed his countenance.

"I missed Johnny, too. I enjoyed lunch. Thanks for including me."

"You're welcome. I must say you look very relaxed and happy."

"Yes, it is much easier for me now that I'm back in my own home. I like to remember the old days when Papa and I visited King's Trace. I had a great time with Brenda, Johnny, and Melissa and went home to my own family. Like today. That seems more natural to me. I don't want to hurt anyone's feelings. I'm happy and I look forward to Thanksgiving; I really do."

KC listened to her almost as if he never had before. For a brief moment he let Katherine be the center of his world. She had, in her few words, outlined the relationship she could accept with him and his family. There was no room for him to adjust her attitude. The powerful man had to let her draw this diagram. He knew it would be her way or no way. And, he admitted to himself that he loved his third daughter and would do whatever it took to keep her as close as she allowed.

"We do, too. It doesn't seem right that you are alone."

The car stopped at the loading space in front of her building. The conversation continued.

"I'm not alone. Mrs. Martin is back with me and I have made contacts with old school friends who also go to Georgetown. I'll make friends at school. Brenda and I write to each other. I write to Johnny, too. We'll always be more like brother and sister than just friends."

KC lost his breath at her words but recovered quickly. "And, Melissa... she speaks of you often."

"I know. She's a doll." The smile that always came when speaking of Melissa lit her face. "I have another friend, Jonas." She added as almost an afterthought. "Jonas Longfellow."

"I have a favor. Would you call Julianne once a week?" He was asking for himself. He wanted to hear from her but would not presume to ask her to call him. "She fusses at me to call you but, really Kathy; I hate to admit, I run out of time." Julianne would add Katherine to her endless lists to keep him informed on family matters. He knew she would.

"I don't expect you to call me, KC. I'll call Julianne every Sunday. I promise."

She left the limo with a warm smile for Senator Kingsley. He leaned back more contented than he had been for a long time. His conversations with Katherine had no hidden agenda, no political impact, and no fear of media scrutiny.

Two minutes later the name *Jonas Longfellow* came to mind. *Jonas Longfellow? Sounds familiar.* He could not place it.

CHAPTER 16

1958

The bright sunny, cool, September day was perfect for a hard workout on the Purdue practice field. Johnny pulled off his football helmet and looked down at the mud caked on his knees. He did not see the young business-suited man approaching with a clipboard and pen. If he had, he still would not have suspected he was a news reporter looking for John Kingsley. The tired halfback was still thinking about the play Coach changed and a complicated receiver's pattern as he walked into the man who should not have been on the field. The clipboard and the man in the sharp well-pressed suit lost his footing and splashed on to the muddy turf.

The mud on the grey suit was beyond funny. It was Johnny's most successful block in this practice. Nothing delights like putting someone into the mud on the playing field. A quizzical smile came unbidden to Johnny. *Why in hell are you on this muddy field?* he thought, but courtesy kept him from asking as his hand went out. "Hey, Pal. My fault. Let me help."

"John Kingsley?" The reporter asked as he futilely tried to brush off mud.

"Yes, sir." Johnny hid his dismay. *Oh no, another reporter.*

Alex Fremont was a professional. It took only a moment to forget his clothes and get back to business. "Tell me your relationship to Katherine Ross," he asked to John's back. "I have an interesting fact to share with her."

Johnny couldn't think but the question made him stop walking and look at the man.

"Where is Miss Ross now?"

What's he asking? Kat? I'm not telling him how to get to Kat? "Sir. I don't have time to talk to you. Excuse me." Johnny became the well-trained-reporter-shy candidate's son, regained his composure, and sprinted for the locker room. His mind stayed on the muddy sideline. When the locker room door closed, the reporter was right beside him.

His instincts heightened his alert. "You can't come in here. Players only." His eyes flashed as he pointed at the restrictive sign. "Please!" he demanded as he pushed the door open and invited the invader to leave.

"Alex Fremont, Washington Post. Here's my card, John." He thrust the card into Johnny's muddy hand. "I want to talk to either you or Katherine Ross. If not me, some other reporter will find you and her. There are questions. She's copy because she lived with your family."

Alex Fremont, reporter
The Washington Post
1245 K Street
Washington, DC
201 555-6784 private line 201 555 6785

The private phone number had been circled. John turned the card over and saw a scribbled note:

I'm at Holiday Inn, 476-555-6758
give me fifteen minutes.

Other players filled the entry as Alex Fremont retreated.

The card was crumpled and dropped into his helmet but not forgotten. While Johnny showered and dressed he felt unsettled. *What is this all about?* At first he thought to ignore the whole incident, but he couldn't, so he went back to his helmet and got the card, pitching the helmet into his locker with an expletive. "Son of a bitch! You'll bother Kat if I don't call."

Johnny decided it would be better to talk to this joker than have him bugging Kat at Georgetown University. His mind swerved in many directions and under it all was a question that had been bothering him for a long time. *What was so unsettling while Kat lived with us? She felt it; so did I.* His eyes didn't miss anything about Katherine and he picked up *something* everyone else missed. *What was it? Did she hate Dad? She practically bolted when he entered the primaries.* Johnny sighed deeply and continued to shake his head as he dressed.

He'd never figured it out. Now, he could not ignore this Alex Fremont .By the time he was dressed and leaving the locker room, Johnny knew what he would do. He would call Fremont. He would answer his questions about the Kingsley and Ross families and brush him off. Easy enough. *I'll call Dad after.*

Johnny walked to the brick wall outside the dorm and sat for a while. When he started thinking about Kat, his mind traveled in leaps and bounds over the last couple of years. He fell in love with her the day she came to live at King's Trace. The little Ross girl was all grown up and beautiful and his teen-age hormones raged in a crush which dominated his life while she lived in his world. By the time they graduated he was totally and completely in love with her. Even now, while he was in Indiana and she in DC, Kat stayed in his mind and dominated his dreams. It did not matter that she kept him at arm's length. He believed someday they were destined to be together. He clung to her parting words when she moved back to her father's condominium and enrolled at Georgetown University. "We have four important college years ahead. I love you, Johnny." It was the same hug she gave the girls, but he put his own spin on it. He never admitted her actions and words were brotherly.

Johnny picked up his books and headed for his room. He spoke to the reporter's card staring at him from atop his books. "I'll answer two questions, maybe three. Simple. Anything to keep you away from Kat and off campus." The door closed behind him as he uttered more expletives.

Alex Fremont thought carefully about what he would say to John Kingsley. He knew his questions would eventually get to KC Kingsley, who was running a strong campaign for the presidency. It was not a human interest story; it was political—very political. He waited patiently for Johnny to come into Hamburger Hut, two blocks off campus. He got out of his car when he saw Johnny approach.

"Hi, Johnny. Thank you for seeing me. I'd rather walk out here, if it's alright with you." The reporter and the candidate's son began a walk that would change lives.

"Let's get this straight, Fremont, I don't want to talk to you, but better you bother me than annoy Katherine Ross." His attitude was as hard as the pavement. "Her father isn't running for President but mine is… so I'm here."

"I have a couple of questions about her relationship to your family. How—"

Johnny interrupted. "I'll tell you about her relationship to us without your questions. She's the daughter of my father's business partner. He was killed in an automobile accident two years ago in February. At his death, because there was no other Ross family member to care for her, my father became her guardian and she lived with us until she came of age in June of this year. The whole Kingsley family loves and supports her. She's at college now. We're the same age. You don't need to bother her because my father is running for president. I don't like being interviewed but I expect it because I'm his son." He paused and took a breath. "There's no excuse for you questioning Katherine Ross." He took Fremont's arm in a tight grip, pulling him to a stop. "Leave her alone. I'm telling you the same things she would say. There *is* nothing else."

"Thank you, Johnny but I knew all that. My question is a bit more complicated. James Ross wasn't Katherine Ross' biological father." He watched the boy's face. The shock led him to add, "I see this is a surprise to you."

"Wait man. God, where did you get that lie?" Johnny was getting mad.

"I can't reveal my source but it is reliable." As Alex Fremont said it he winced, recalling Dr. Sherman, the creepy rat who crawled out from his white coat to try to turn information into profit one dark night on K Street. Alex did his job, took notes and followed up on it. And the next week, Sherman died. There was no way to confirm it except through a tough reporter approach.

"I was going to ask the question—do you know who her father is? But I can tell from your face you are ignorant of the facts. Let me just say this," Alex Fremont took a deep breath, faced John Kingsley squarely, and demanded his gaze. "Katherine Ross is your sister. This fact came indirectly from her mother." He allowed Johnny time to comprehend and melt. "Your father is her father, too."

Johnny's first inclination was to hit Alex Fremont. He drew back his fist and advanced. Before Fremont could think of defending himself, Johnny folded to his knees and put his face on them, folding his arms around his head. He assumed the shape of a football inviting a swift kick. Somewhere deep in his gut where denial lived, lightning flashed and he knew what the reporter said was true. His mind raced back to the words he had overheard coming from the library a year ago. *"We can control this information. No one needs to know about you and Pamela Ross. Nothing to fear, KC. I'll take care; it's my job."* Johnny knew the voice of the party campaign manager. He hadn't remembered those words for almost a year, but now they were as clear as a bell tolling in his brain.

This time it was Alex pulling Johnny to his feet. His clothes were not muddy but his heart and soul were caked in mucky earthy debris. He could not rid himself of it any better than Alex could brush wet mud from his suit earlier today. The smeary mess grew and bubbled in his gut and spirit like the hot earth spat and spurted in Yellowstone Park.

Johnny was broken. Alex could see it. His face was contorted in pain. His face turned ashen and his lips brown. Johnny needed to breathe but his pain disallowed involuntary acts. His arms flayed out, forcing his lungs to let go of trapped air. With the slight strength he could muster, Johnny backed away as if distance, even a small amount, would make this less devastating. He was beyond pain.

With unusual compassion for a journalist, Alex Fremont wanted to help the boy. He felt guilty for not realizing his information could take a good young man to his knees. *Why so devastated? Beyond affect?* He wondered. As he pulled Johnny to his feet and saw tears streaming down his face, he whispered to the night.

"Lousy job." Did he mean his occupation or the way he handled it with this fragile young freshman? It was a moot point.

"Come on, Johnny. My car is on the curb. I'll drive you back to school."

Johnny allowed Alex to lead him. In the car all attempts to get him to talk failed. Finally, Alex took another tack. "Do you want to ask me any questions?'

Johnny jerked his head around, came alive and demanded, "I have to know. I have to be sure. Please," he pleaded.

"Let me say it came from Spring Haven Hospital. You know Miss Ross's mother is there?"

"Yes. I know." Johnny's head hung lower as he began to put puzzle pieces together. Pamela Ross—Kat's mother—an insane patient. Dad's strange behavior when Kat came to King's Trace. The way he tried to make her one of his kids and only failed because Kat resisted. Constant comments on his resemblance to her. Then he had a terrifying moment. *I tried to kiss her; to date her.* He started to realize what it meant. He screamed and startled Fremont. "Oh God." His body went limp with the next thought. *I'm in love with my sister.*

Attempts to bring him back from some distant plane failed and Alex Fremont was becoming alarmed. "John, are you alright? Who can I call for you?"

Alex watched as Johnny pulled himself together. He tossed his head back and wiped his face with his sleeve. With a cold steely gaze he came from the abyss and took a hard detached attitude. "Thanks for the ride," was the kindest thing he could say.

"Are you alright?"

"Sure. The ole man screwed up and got one more child than he figured. Big deal. If you want to make something out of it—it's his problem." The nonchalant attitude did not fool the reporter. "Gotta go now. Exams tomorrow." John reached for the car door.

Alex did not want to let the damaged boy go into the night. He wasn't sure what had happened but he was sure his careful recovery in the last seconds was worthy of an acting award. He thought fast.

"Tell you what, Johnny. I will not try to locate Katherine Ross. I'm going to sit on this for a while. If it breaks before the 30th; it didn't come from me. But, I promise you, some other source will find it—especially with the loyal opposition working day and night to hurt your father politically. When it does break, I will jump in the fray, it's my job. You do what you want with our meeting. Tell your father, whatever."

"Thanks."

"And, I'm sorry. We're out there looking for dirty laundry to hurt a candidate and its easy to forget innocents get torn up too. Nasty business. When I leave here, I will go back to being the lousy son of a bitch that I am…but you have my promise." Alex started the car. *That poor boy. I must be goin' soft.*

Johnny turned back and leaned in the window. "Tell me, Alex. How long do you figure before…."

"Several weeks. No more."

Dr. Sherman's fatal heart attack closed the door on the facts that took Johnny Kingsley apart. The doctor never made money from the revelation Pamela Ross made while in a drug-induced therapy session. Dr. Sherman went to his maker to be judged as the villain he was. The doctor could not substantiate the reporter's story now.

The only credence to the story was in the horrible reaction Fremont witnessed when he slammed Johnny Kingsley with the fact. Johnny did not know that this reporter's source and the story were dead. He continued to agonize over Kat and died inside because of what he knew and what he felt.

The story did not break. But two more people knew who fathered Katherine—Johnny and a reporter from the Washington Post.

CHAPTER 17

1959

Mrs. Martin gently tapped on the bedroom door. "Katherine. Katherine, wake up." She tried to keep alarm out of her voice but, in the middle of the night, alarm sneaks in. "Johnny Kingsley's at the door." Katherine brought herself from deep slumber. "Shall I let him in?"

"Of course, Mrs. Martin." She shook sleep from her brain. "….if you're sure it's Johnny."

"It is."

"I'll be right there." She grabbed her robe and started to the bathroom to throw some water on her face and straighten her hair. *Johnny, here? In the middle of the night?* It took only a few minutes, but when she got to the living room, Johnny, sitting in Papa's big chair with his head slumped down, asleep.

"Mrs. Martin, please put on a pot of coffee." Katherine looked at her distraught housekeeper. "And…go back to bed. It's alright."

"Are you sure?"

"Yes, sure."

"I'll leave my door open in case you need me, Katherine." She headed to the kitchen and quietly made coffee and set out the cake they had had for dessert earlier before adjourning to her bedroom.

For the first time, Katherine took a good look at Johnny and was aghast at what she saw. *He's dirty. His clothes are a mess.* She stepped closer and whispered, "Alcohol." That smell caused her to step back from the gentle touch she planned to give Johnny's forehead. Stepping to the center of the room, to give distance to the scene, she searched for a suitcase or bag. None. She pulled an ottoman to her place at the coffee table and waited for the coffee aroma to tell her it was ready. She looked closely—he didn't move, not even a hair, and his breath was noisy. Her movement to unplug the percolator did not disturb Johnny at all. *I guess we won't be drinking coffee tonight.*

Katherine had no experience to bring to the situation except scenes in movies. Drunken men awakened were unruly and incoherent. She would let Johnny sleep it off in the chair. The sofa, a pillow and blanket made her bed for the rest of the night. The clock struck twice and startled her from sleep again. She looked to see—Johnny did not stir at the sound; his heavy breathing continued. Katherine shrugged and settled back to get some sleep.

The clock struck three, four, five, six, and seven. At eight, Johnny jumped at the sound, rolled to the floor and stretched out along the sofa.

"I'm dead," he whispered. "I'm dead." Katherine opened her eyes to look directly into his. "Am I dead, looking at an angel?"

There were times when Katherine would have thought him joking but the dire sound of his voice and soulful look on his face told her he wanted to be dead. He was not being funny. Her stomach turned.

Johnny's face turned to panic. "Oh, God, no—not here." Tremors shook his body and tears sprang from his eyes. "Oh, God. Oh, God. Not Kat." Johnny turned slightly and took the fetal position to continue shaking and crying.

Katherine reached out to touch his back and he jerked as if her touch were a hot poker. He tried to roll away but the coffee table blocked him. She was on her feet before he could struggle to his. Stooping down, she tried to soothe him with soft words. "Johnny… Johnny… it's alright." She did not try to touch him again.

Soft words did not get his attention so she spoke up. "Listen to me!" She took charge. "The bathroom is down there." She pointed to the hallway. "Go, wash up, while I get coffee."

Johnny stood but he did not take her direction; he headed for the foyer. Katherine moved quickly and stood firmly against the huge mahogany door as he spoke the first calm words of the morning.

"Move, Kat. I'm leaving." He took an unsteady step and exhaled a deep breath that reeked of stale whiskey. He turned his eyes away. "I'm so sorry. I apologize for coming. Move," he repeated.

"Johnny, you can leave after you clean up and have some coffee…maybe some breakfast." She stood firm and pointed once again toward the bathroom.

He had a painful need to go to the bathroom and would not know if he took her direction because of that or because she ordered him to. Johnny went down the hall as Mrs. Martin came from her bedroom.

Before she could ask, Katherine filled her in. "It's fine, Mrs. Martin. I'm going to give him some breakfast before he leaves. Obviously he was partying too much last night. If necessary I'll call Mrs. Kingsley. But, all is well this morning. I would rather he not see you—too embarrassing."

"I'll slip out the back door…if you are sure."

"I am."

Katherine started for her room, calling to Johnny. "Johnny, I'm going to get dressed. Promise me you won't leave."

"I promise."

When Katherine returned Johnny was sitting in the kitchen drinking coffee and holding his head. "Johnny...," She hesitated and decided against asking questions that were bouncing in her mind like ricocheting bullets.

"The coffee must be cold. Mrs. Martin made it last night."

"I'm a complete idiot but I can warm coffee. There's some for you in the sauce pan."

Just for the advantage of time, she poured a cup, prepared it with cream and sugar before making a fresh pot.

"Kat, I don't know how I got here last night. Sad, but true. If I had been in my right mind I would not have come here. Forgive me."

"Nothing to forgive. You're always welcome here and especially if something is wrong. And, obviously, *something* is wrong."

"I don't know what to say..." His voice trailed off and she let silence compete with the gurgle of the coffee pot. "I quit Purdue. Only went to classes for two weeks." He waited for her to voice her dismay but she said nothing. "I don't want to be in Indiana. And now—" his voice trailed into darkness "—I don't have any place." Again he put silence in the room like a heavy wet blanket.

Where have you been if you only went to school two weeks? She thought but did not ask.

"Of course you do, Johnny. You have King's Trace. It's your home." Katherine emptied his cup and poured two fresh cups of coffee and sliced cake as she spoke. He was happy to eat cake and begin recovering from the alcohol. "You have your family and you have me."

"No. I can't go to King's Trace. I don't have a family and I certainly don't have you." His voice was emphatic. "I can't go back and I don't know how to go forward." He dropped his voice and head to talk into his cup softly, so she could not hear his words. "And, I can never tell you I love you." With his head still low, he spoke in hardly audible, dead tones. "I gotta go."

What did he say about love? Katherine really could not hear his words and her brain was not working well.

"Go where? Johnny, I can't let you go until you tell me what's going on." She took him by the shoulders and forced him to look in her eyes. "I love you, Johnny. You are the dearest and only brother that I have. Your parents, Brenda and Melissa, love you, too. We're all family."

"Stop fooling yourself, Kat. I don't love you as a brother…and, you were never a part of that family at King's Trace. Never will be." His face and eyes hardened into steel. "Dad tried to mold and control you… and you escaped. Lucky you…you had a place to go and you weren't dependent. I'm dependent and that dependency is killing me. The mighty Senator is a controlling monster—an animal." For his next words, he needed to look into her eyes so she could see his passion. "I hate my father and—" he took a deep breath, "—and, I can't go home."

"You don't hate your father. I'm not sure what we are talking about…." Confusion reigned in her brain as she grasped his shoulder, pressing her fingers into his muscles. *Love, control, hate?* She had to give him something to take from this morning but she wasn't sure what. "What are you ta—"

He tried to pull away from her hold but she held tight as he interrupted. "I'm talking about love, Kat. I'm forbidden to love you. How does that happen?" He jerked his shoulders quickly and broke her grip, maybe because his words weakened her arms and legs. "I love you, Katherine Ross. You know it; you have to know it.

I always have, always will." Johnny was heading for the door. She could not stop him with words returning his love, but she could not let him go into the world—not now, not like this.

"Stop! Johnny, stop! The last word on this is not today. There's the future." She stepped in front of the door.

"No future. You can't love me. Forbidden."

His words came out as if they were twisted in his gut. He puked them— acrid like vomit—hardly above a whisper.

Katherine was not sure she heard him correctly. *Forbidden? Did he say forbidden?* The room seemed to swirl around her. She was torn between taking care of him—clean him up—take him home— and figuring out what he was saying.

Johnny pushed her firmly out of his path to the door.

And then Katherine, thoroughly scared and upset, did the only thing that could keep him from bolting out the door. She began to quietly weep. Without a tissue or attempt to stop the flow, she let the tears run without sobs down her face and drip off her chin. Her arms were straight to her sides in total submission to the frustration in the air. Her head dropped forward and tears trapped locks of hair on her cheeks. She was a mess as she folded down to the carpet. He sat down with her and they were again fifteen years old, sitting on the floor playing gin rummy.

"You deal," he injected the first light moment of the morning. She smiled through the tears.

"Can't it stay this way, Johnny? I don't want to hurt you. Please let us stay as children for a while?" Her voice and eyes pleaded. "Johnny, I can't be your girlfriend now. That's not tragic or forbidden. I want to love you as a brother and keep all possibilities in the future. Who knows about the future?"

He was settled and his emotions were spent. Down at this lower altitude he seemed to be able to talk to her without generalities and innuendoes that had resounded in his conversation all morning. "Kat, I'd love to stay as we were—playing games and riding the hills on horseback, but we can't. I'd be willing to wait for you to love me differently, but that is not going to happen."

"Johnny I'm not anybody's girlfriend. That's not tragic or forbidden. I want to love you as a brother and keep all possibilities in the future."

"It is tragic and it is forbidden. There is no future." He looked at her with dead eyes and dead spirit as he repeated, "No future."

"You don't know that."

"Yes, I do. I know."

"It is not fair of you, Johnny. Just because I can't tell you today that I love you more than as a brother, you are throwing your future away. Not fair to put that on me. Not fair."

"Oh, God. You can't love me and I can't love you. Accept that, Katherine. I'm going out that door very soon. When you accept that, and I think you will, your life will be good."

"My life is not going to be very good if you throw yours away. I don't understand all that you are saying. Just tell me what it would take to get you to go back to Purdue and King's Trace."

"I've thought about that question and the answer is nothing."

"Your mother, Brenda, Melissa?"

Johnny was visibly shaken. "I love them."

"I know. Go home to them, your father is away. I saw him campaigning in Iowa on TV last night. Go home to your mother, Brenda, Melissa. And Johnny, don't hate your father."

At the mention of his father, Johnny rose from the floor. Katherine continued to talk but he was concentrating on leaving.

"Please go to King's Trace. I'm coming for Thanksgiving dinner."

"I won't be there." Johnny was talking over his shoulder as he moved toward the door.

"Are you making the rules?"

"I guess I am. We will not see each other."

"Come on, Johnny. That isn't necessary, is it?"

"Yes." He pulled her to her feet. The game was finished. "Have a good life, Kat."

"What are you saying? Stop acting like we won't ever see each other again. You are scarring me." Her tears started again. "You don't know the future or what we can mean to each other in another time and place. Today we are friends. Don't hurt me by saying we can't be friends."

"I don't want to hurt you, Katherine." Johnny let go of his favored nickname for her with a look of pain on his face. "But, it's impossible for me to be just your friend. I already love you. And I'm your brother."

She did not get the meaning of his words. She always thought living at King's Trace was a mistake and now, for some undefined reason—she was positive—it was. Katherine could not offer Johnny false hope. Not tonight. Not tomorrow. She took some of Johnny's agony and did not know why but, she believed him.

"Are you going home? Please tell me you are going home," she pleaded.

"Yes." He turned, his hand on the latch, "Stay away from King's Trace. You don't need it." He gave her a long, poignant hug. Even as he released her, she knew he did not want to let go.

The mahogany door closed between them. The thud of wood hitting jamb resonated as Johnny and Katherine leaned against the door on opposite sides of the universe.

CHAPTER 18

1959

Katherine went to her bedroom to find Lady Fair. She was curled in the window seat enjoying the sun and not in the least interested in what her girl wanted to talk about, but she allowed herself to be picked up. Together they waited for some sense of order to come to their disturbed lives. The cat found the crook of a willing arm while Katherine focused on the fall beauty on Capitol Hill.

"Lady Fair, what's going on with Johnny? He said some strange things."

Katherine buried her face in the warm grey fur of her best friend, "His face… his eyes…" she whispered as tears spilled on the cat.

"I can't ignore what he said like I have ignored his feelings for so long." Katherine picked up Lady Fair and looked into her eyes. The cat hung in air like a limp rag.

"What am I to do?" She begged of the unresponsive feline.

The cat suggested nothing. She just waited to be put down in a congenial spot so she could resume her nap and purring. Katherine curled beside her and closed her eyes but could not shut down her mind. *I can't solve your problem, Johnny. I'm not sure what it is. Too much—way too much for me.* She turned away from the morning sun and thought, *Mother*. Katherine pounded the pillow and proclaimed, "I refuse to think about Mother now," and gave into sobs. She cried loud and hard. This was not the time for soft tears because fear crept into her heart and stepped silently into the dark corners of her mind. She found her mother there, unbidden. "No. No. No." The sobs dried her throat and pain shot down her esophagus like lightning. The blessing of hard crying is that it cannot be sustained for a long time. Exhaustion put an end to it.

The morning bogged down to inertia when the phone interrupted.

"Kathy..." It was KC. "I hope I'm not calling too early. Have you heard from Johnny? He's not at Purdue and," he hesitated, "well, it's been over two weeks since anyone heard from him."

"Actually, KC. he just left here a short while ago." Sheer power brought her voice to a normal range.

"Oh, Kathy!" relief was in his voice. "Do you know where he went?"

"He said he was going to King's Trace, but to tell the truth, KC, as I think back... he might have said that so I would let him leave. Johnny wasn't himself. He talked as if he and I could not be friends. You know that isn't true."

"Of course."

"I was waiting to call Julianne later this morning. Have you talked to her? Did he go home?"

"She hasn't seen him and I'm concerned." Katherine noted his anxiety and recalled how he related to Johnny better than to the girls.

KC loves Johnny—yet, Johnny said he hated his father.

In her concern for Johnny and the terror she heard in KC's voice, all reservations were forgotten. Without going into Johnny's words, she told the events of the last twelve hours and finished by voicing her concern.

"Johnny was very upset and quite drunk when Mrs. Martin let him in last night. He went right to sleep and I kept watch on him so he didn't rouse and leave. I fed him coffee and breakfast this morning. He was not going back to Purdue or home either. I prevailed on him to go to King's Trace. He said he would, and I didn't doubt at the time that he was headed there from here. Please believe me, I was about to call Julianne. I didn't know where you were."

"I'm in the airport in Des Moines. I'll be home this evening. No need to call Julianne now. It will alarm her if he's not home and it will be okay if he is. I just hope and pray that he's at King's Trace when I arrive."

"Me, too. Please, let me know."

Johnny was not at King's Trace that day, nor in the following days. A quiet search was made for him as KC tried to keep his absence from the press. The family pulled together while worry prevailed in the home, on the campaign trail, and at Katherine's apartment.

Julianne came to Capitol Hill to glean news of her son. Katherine was generous and open, trying to help the distraught mother. Still, she kept the most disturbing words from the dialog.

"Katherine, did Johnny tell you he loved you when he was here?" She could see shock on the young girl's face. "I have known he was in love with you for a long time. It was a crush, but I could tell it became much more before he left for Purdue."

"I have too many responsibilities to think of love and it wasn't good, living in the same household."

"I know that, Sweetie. You were so good with him and I thought he understood."

"I thought so, too. He's wonderful and the dearest brother Brenda, Melissa and I could have. I never said we did not have possibilities for the future. But..."

"What?"

"That is what upset me so when he was here. He kept saying there was no future. He said that more than once and it scared me."

"He said that?"

"Yes—no future, more than once." Then she turned to face Julianne squarely. "He acted as if he knew something I didn't. I can't figure it."

"I'm afraid for him." Katherine's lips and chin trembled as last night's terror came again. Julianne moved to sit beside Katherine and fold her arms around her. "Me, too." She took a deep breath and voiced a small hope. "I hope that he will contact me or you—soon—very soon. This is too hard."

Supplications to heaven were their only hope. Julianne hid her feelings from Katherine as a cold icy fear gripped her.

"I must get to KC. Nothing is more important—we have to find Johnny now." She lingered in a long embrace with Katherine and tried to find words to reassure but could not. Julianne walked to the street as she silently prayed, *Please God, bring Johnny to me.*

The media accepted the idea put out by the campaign committee that Johnny was backpacking across Europe. They soon lost interest in the candidate's son as political issues filled the head lines. Old photos were released occasionally showing him riding horses or hiking in unnamed European countries.

Julianne's strength was tested. She hated every day that was filled with political requirements when she wanted to pull KC from the podium and scream, "We need to find Johnny. To hell with all this." Frustration and obligation exhausted her. Each day she spent several hours in prayer and meditation. Suzanna was assigned to stay close to the phone—every hour. When the campaign became too much Julianne came home to King's Trace to regroup, give all her attention to Melissa and wait.

KC's campaign trail moved to the southeast. It was hot and crowds pushed to shake hands with the candidate and his wife. Despite efforts by the campaign manager, Julianne refused to give speeches.

"KC, tell them I won't speak. I'm here. That is enough." She pulled his shoulders around so he could look in her sad eyes. "I have the necessary smile." He was forced to look into her grinning face and admit that it was planted there as carefully as media hype.

Suddenly he knew he was winning the White House at a great cost.

"Julianne. Julianne." He called her name and buried his face into her cold hard neck. She pulled back from his embrace.

"If it weren't for this damned campaign you and I could search every acre of this country."

Her words were cold hard steel, each formed like a bullet. "You've made a terrible choice." She quietly accused. "Listen to me," she demanded. "I have given and given to you and your career. I have put aside how I feel for the good of this family and for the good of your damned campaign. I cannot…. I will not continue to make allowances and sacrifice for you." Her voice rose to fever pitch. "Not Johnny. Never Johnny." Her voice lowered to an emphatic whisper. "There is nothing as important as finding him." Julianne took one step toward him and pushed her finger into his chest right at his heart. "Nothing."

"I cry for Johnny every day." Suddenly his knees folded and he could not stand. KC and Julianne went to the carpeted floor in the hotel in Columbia, South Carolina. They cried together for their son and the reasons that they were in this no-where hotel room.

KC raised his arms to embrace Julianne. She smacked them down. He could not touch her or her pain.

October 17th was Julianne's birthday. The celebration was quiet. KC flew in for overnight. Brenda could not come home. Katherine sent flowers. Julianne refused to go out to dinner in case Johnny called. She never told KC why she did not want to go out, but he knew she would not leave the phone today. The small family of three enjoyed barbecued chicken, cake and candles. The day ended and spirits plummeted lower and lower. The day that Julianne had pinned so much hope on was nearly over. Johnny did not call on her birthday.

The next day a soiled, wrinkled card came—postmarked Boise, Idaho. It was unsigned and a day late, but she knew it was from Johnny.

Happy Birthday to the best Mom in the world.
Unsigned

She was home alone when it came. In the bedroom she vented all her anguish and cried endless tears. She opened every fold, turned the card inside out and, deep in the center where no one would see it, Johnny had written *I love you.*

He was sure his sentiment would never be found, just like him.

When KC called about midnight, her first words were, "He's alive." It was the first time she admitted that she thought he was dead. Julianne grasped hope and gave it to her grieving husband, who had given up hope.

Together they cried on the phone.

The next day, KC hired four private investigators and sent them west with enough payment to keep quiet and be diligent in their quest. A reward was offered to the successful searcher.

Julianne pulled herself together and got very angry, even enraged, that the effort to keep Johnny's disappearance quiet meant that every possible means of finding him was not used. No all-points bulletins. No pictures over the TV or in the papers. No ocean-to-ocean search for her son. She was furious at KC. She abandoned *the good little wife* image. KC might be a wonderful Senator and he might become the best President, but he was not perfect. Through the years Julianne had not held on to his mistakes, had not kept an accounting and tried not to judge him. However, anger brought them now like salt to her wound—fresh and painful. There have been times when he was wrong—like today.

The previous tender moments they shared on the phone were the last ones they would ever have. Johnny's disappearance drove a wedge in their marriage. Julianne's strength always supported KC. Now it was mustered against him. All of his mistakes blasted to the forefront of her brain and stayed there. All of the disappointments she had in him festered to the surface. She knew his love for her and their children depended upon her willingness to make everything right for him. Julianne was finished.

KC could sacrifice a lot for the presidency—but not Johnny. Not without a price, and the price was the love from his wife. This was the last straw. She could not do *this* any more. She would not overlook, make excuses, polish his image or bolster his ego for the sake of the family. Certainly not for the sake of the nation. Without her support there was no love—there was only his high position. Unless she told the children he loved them, there was no love.

Unless I convince myself that he loves me, there is no love.

A long and loving relationship requires some blinders. It is a sad day when one lover removes all blinders and wants to see the truth. Truth is rarely beautiful. It is even rarer that the blinders can be donned again.

CHAPTER 19

1960

Election Day had to come. It crept in on a strangely warm breeze left over from October as if sighing from the campaign hype. The morning dawned warm across the country and the turnout at the polling places set records. Even Mother Nature favored KC Kingsley. The final weeks of campaigning were intense and the wife of the front runner was excused from public appearances. Julianne was spent, physically and emotionally. She could not continue with KC for the last six weeks of whistle-stop events. The ball was rolling and even KC had less to do by Halloween. Election Day came and KC Kingsley was elected by a strong mandate. The country united behind him and his party. Every corner of the nation celebrated except for the few hills in Maryland where the lovely mansion was missing its son.

KC came home to King's Trace the night before polling so he and Julianne could go to their assigned voting place for the traditional picture of the candidate and his wife casting their secret ballot. An entourage of party bigwigs came to King's Trace with KC. Four black town cars lined the driveway—ready to speed the President-elect to Annapolis for his acceptance speech as soon as his election was assured.

Julianne found KC asleep in the library that evening with the newspaper across his lap. She sat across the room in the leather wing chair and studied her husband.

President. The White House. Her mind settled on the big thoughts. *I know you, KC Kingsley.* She studied his brow and handsomeness. He exuded confidence. *You can do this. Of course you can.* Julianne shifted around in the chair, pulling her knees up to a tight bundle. She held on tightly; she would not tremble. *Can I? Without Johnny… and without loving you any more?* She checked to see if he was deep asleep before she allowed tears. "Brenda, Melissa, Johnny…and Katherine." she whispered as she cried. "I can because I must. It's bigger than me—even bigger than you, KC. We're part of history, now." She went to him and watched his eyes quiver and his lips move in silent speech. His profile—identical to Johnny's, his mannerisms in sleep, were nostalgic. Julianne stored the memory and walked out of the room with her back as straight as a ramrod. The President-elect would not be troubled by her fears and doubts. He needed his rest.

The next day, **Kingsley Captures the Nation** blazed across the headlines subtitled: **Record Mandate**. In January he would be President. The secret service descended on King's Trace and paradise no longer belonged to the family.

Election Day was not as dramatic twenty miles south. Katherine waited for Jonas, with surprising anticipation. The knock on the door made her run to let him in and then she settled into nonchalance when she greeted him.

"Hi." Nothing in her voice gave away her growing feelings for him.

"Let's turn the TV on. East coast results are already coming in. Aren't you excited for KC?"

She could not tell him she was more excited to be with him than she was about the national election. "Sure, I am. He has assured us he'll win. Guess I believe him. Turn it on. I'm making dinner."

Jonas turned on the television while she stir-fried vegetables. They would play Scrabble and let the results be background. The meal was set up in the living room on trays in front of the TV.

"The race isn't even close. What do you think about that?" Jonas was trying to understand her complicated relationship with the Kingsleys.

"I kinda accepted it as fact months ago. It'll be exciting for the family. I'm not thinking as much about the election as I am about Johnny. I wonder if he's watching this tonight."

"I hope he is."

"Me too…and I hope this doesn't keep him away. I'll never give up. He's got to come back."

Jonas could see her becoming melancholy. "Keep the faith… and take your turn."

The phone interrupted the game and her thoughts. It was Julianne.

"KC wants to send a car to bring you to Annapolis tonight. He'll proclaim his victory. Will you come?"

"Thanks for thinking of me but I think not. I'll see you all on TV."

"Katherine, we have to make adjustments now for the new life but I don't want you to isolate yourself from us. Promise."

"I promise. I'll be at King's Trace for Thanksgiving. Tell Melissa. In three weeks I'll be on break from school."

"How's school going?"

"Really well."

"And your mother?"

"Not much change there, I'm afraid. Thanks for asking."

The screen of normalcy was maintained. The surfaces remained smooth. No new thoughts or feelings were explored or expressed. Changes were coming to the Kingsley family and to King's Trace but Katherine planned to avoid the ripple effect. She would not be caught up in it. Emotionally, she was attached, but by keeping a twenty- mile separation, she could save herself. There was a strange feeling that if she went into the powerful presidential residence, KC would regain the control he wanted over her. Katherine valued her independence too much. She had decided months ago—she would not be visiting the Kingsleys in the White House. In her mind, they were in Montgomery County and that was where she would see them. No mention was made of Johnny. As the phone disconnected, both Julianne and Katherine were aware of the void he left in their lives and even in their conversation.

She plopped down on the sofa beside Jonas. "I'm not a Kingsley. No need for me to go to Annapolis tonight. I don't belong there."

"Easy, Sweetie. You're preaching to the choir. It's okay."

"I know," she laughed lightly. "I have to convince myself that I have a good reason to tell Julianne no."

"You aren't telling her 'no', you're telling KC. I'm trying to understand."

"Ever since my father died, I have been pulling against him. Now that I'm out of King's Trace..." She drifted into thought. "I want to stay independent. Now he's President. Living in the White House. I must stay strong; stay clear."

"Wow. I had no idea how strong your feelings go."

"I'm really happy he was elected...but, I can't be drawn into—," she searched for the words, "—the excitement, even the glamour, of the world the Kingsleys have now."

Jonas gave her a hug of support and understanding as she leaned into him with rare response to his attention.

"When I go to King's Trace for Thanksgiving I'll make it clear to the family that I won't attend any inaugural events. I've decided…I don't want to be in that spotlight. Really, why should I? It's for the family. I've had enough time as a Kingsley. If invited; Katherine Ross will decline." She looked up to him, smiling and happy, "Maybe you will come and watch on TV with me that day."

"Sure. I'm available January 20th."

※

Thanksgiving was a somber occasion. Each person around the laden table hoped against hope that Johnny would enter the big front door. Katherine's joy at being with the family was lost as the minutes ticked by. Turkey and trimmings filled stomachs but the seat beside Melissa remained empty. After dessert was served, she knew in her heart, *Johnny's probably not coming home for Christmas, either.*

Katherine declined the invitation to be with the family at King's Trace for Christmas Eve but went for Christmas dinner. Maybe Johnny would come and if he did, she wanted to be there.

Christmas at King's Trace was like Thanksgiving, only worse. There was more missing at this holiday than Johnny. A lack of warmth was evident between KC and Julianne. There was no Christmas spirit. It was a somber occasion with a gallant attempt to make it fun for Melissa. But she was not convinced as she voiced the communal feeling and fear.

"Is Johnny dead?" Melissa asked as she touched his filled stocking hanging from the mantle. "No matter where I was, I'd come home for Christmas." She ran to her mother to cry for her brother. Brenda came from the sofa to circle her mother and sister in a tender hug.

KC did not move. He had forfeited his right to comfort and be comforted. So he rose and went to the window to look out at the stable and remember the many days his son was there tending the horses, often waiting for him.

Katherine took her gifts home and dropped them by her small tree. She did not turn on a light but rather let the city lights come through the window to give her enough illumination to get to the bedroom where she threw herself prostrate on her bed. Copious tears were interrupted by her repeated cries, "Johnny. Johnny. Johnny."

CHAPTER 20

1961

The White House, set behind a perfect lawn with imposing pillars and perfectly manicured topiaries, never appears as a family home per se, but the Kingsley family made it their home after inauguration, just as the Lincolns, Eisenhowers, and a long list of others did. Living in the lovely house was an amazingly beautiful symbol of an attained goal—an ideal.

As with most ideals, things were less than perfect. According to the Washington Post and other major newspapers, the new first family in the White House was as perfect as the house. KC was a bundle of enthusiasm and smiles. Julianne and Melissa came to their new home with forced smiles. It was a snowy day and they were not at all sure they wanted to leave King's Trace, surrounded by white hills and glistening trails, and go to a city—not even Washington, DC and the White House.

Everything necessary for the family went from King's Trace to 1600 Pennsylvania Avenue. Julianne, ever the organizer, supervised the activity when the moving van came up the wide driveway to pack the Kingsley family's personality and take it to Washington.

Three days ago the moving vans arrived. "I want my desk and the two chairs marked here." She pointed to the red notes stuck to the furniture. "Three beds from the children's rooms go, also." A soft shudder rippled up her spine as she remembered the discussion she had had with KC over Johnny's bed. *Of course, his bed goes to the White House.* She was so anguished she did not notice the pain in her husband's eyes. The schism grew wider and deeper. It became more painful because KC knew he could not give her comfort and he would not receive any, either. Johnny's name hurt when it was spoken and even more when it was left hanging in the air—unspoken. The very act of moving from Montgomery County made Johnny's return seem even more remote to Julianne. She would, at least, take his bed.

After discussion about Johnny's bed, KC walked away from Julianne. She was alone in the hallway outside their son's room. He went to the library, closed the door, and cried. The family was leaving the place where Johnny was a part. In the White House, it would seem the family was complete, but it did not include a son. It was a place where Johnny would never be a part.

KC cried again for his son. The not knowing was gnawing at him and tearing his wife and their marriage apart. Today he watched the movers dismantle the bed and began to believe his son would never sleep in it again. The thought took the very breath from the President-elect of the United States. His tears wrenched him into accepting the possible loss of his beloved son. If his expensive private investigators could not find him, no one could.

"Johnny. Johnny. Why? Why?" His mind traveled back to happy days at King's Trace where his ever-present, upbeat son believed everything was possible—the son who brought sunshine into his life—the son who held his dreams. "Where are you, my boy?" his sobs and questions brought a headache. He pressed his thumbs into his temples. The sobs relented as the male psyche, unable to maintain tears, finally closed the dam. His throat constricted and dried. His breath seemed to scratch in and out.

KC only allowed himself a few minutes, knowing demands would soon require his attention and strength, not to mention his leadership. They would be needed not only in the White House but here as his family prepared to leave King's Trace. He had hardly pulled himself together and dried his eyes when Melissa's quiet tap on the door startled him. It was not the strong rap of a Secret Service agent, but rather a gentle begging tap.

"Daddy?"

He pulled himself together and opened a book. "Missy. Come in."

Melissa crossed the room and took the book, which he held in reading position. "Mom is upstairs crying. I don't know what to do." Melissa was obviously distraught. "Come, see what's wrong."

KC rose from his chair and took his daughter's hand, leading her through the library door to the foyer. "Honey, it is hard to leave our home. I'm sure that's why she is crying." He delivered the lie to comfort his youngest daughter. "Go ask Suzanna to make hot chocolate and I'll join you as soon as I check on your mother." He dropped her hand. "Okay?"

Melissa took direction and assurance from her father and headed to the kitchen. Then she stopped and turned around. "I think she's thinking about Johnny." She delivered wisdom. "Just give her a hug, Daddy. That's what she needs. Maybe she doesn't want to move but, we'll like the White House when we get there." With a skip in her step she sent a final bit of advice. "A hug, and a kiss, too."

KC quietly stepped on the first step and deliberately advanced up the stairs knowing Julianne did not want consolation, understanding, or the warm touch of his arms and lips.

Becoming President and moving to the White House was more than KC and his family expected. It was also less than they expected. The first few days were a whirlwind of activity and constant directions. Julianne and Melissa had to find their place in it all. KC started and ended each day exalted and invigorated with *everything*. The election had been a landslide and public opinion was running exceptionally high in his favor. He grasped the reins of government and expected his tenure to be productive and historic.

KC was prepared for the job. He was at ease in international circles, enjoyed unusual support from governors and constituents. His party held the majority in Congress and he had a wonderful rapport with the minority. The journey started on an auspicious note. No president since FDR enjoyed such a nurturing environment in Washington. He was going to do it and do it right.

The first months of his term were challenging and rewarding. KC Kingsley was heralded in newspapers for spearheading peace negotiations between fighting African nations and taking an unyielding and non-compromising stance for human rights across the globe and civil rights at home. The newly inaugurated President stepped into his bubble of security confident of his ability to lead the country. There was no reason to believe otherwise.

CHAPTER 21

1961

John Kingsley had finally found a place where his father had no importance. Political campaigns, elections and inaugurations influenced life across America—but in Idaho's rugged country—not so.

Johnny rode across the valley following the fence line of the Proud Fool Ranch, He was a brown dot on the colorless landscape, occasionally contrasted to a red rock formation. His skin was brown, his clothes were dirty and his horse was a dusty chestnut. The beautiful mountain vistas to the east and west went unnoticed as he paused to take off his hat and beat the dust from it. His face was etched into a frown as he squinted to check the river for a safe crossing. *God, I'm filthy. Probably never be clean again*, he thought as he drew a red bandana across his face to mine dirt from the lines around his mouth that used to outline a handsome smile. John Kenneth Kingsley patted his tired horse's neck and leaned forward in the saddle to stretch the tense muscles in his back.

Clouds gathered in the south as a storm followed the river. The autumn sun was warm, but Johnny would need blankets and booze during the cold night.

"Guess we can stop here," he conceded to Pacer, as he stroked him again and turned him toward the stream so the horse could drink. Johnny pulled the reins and lightly tied them over a tree stump in a grassy meadow before removing the saddle. Then he threw a blanket on the ground and reached into his saddlebags for his bottled comfort. Ignoring the meager dried meat and beans, he pulled out two bottles of whiskey.

"Hi, ole friend." Johnny had drunk his way through the bowels of Idaho to nowhere. If only he could go somewhere. If only he could dream himself into the stable at King's Trace, or to the dining room table sitting next to Kat, or even to the football field at Purdue. "God damn," he cursed himself for even going *there* in thought. He picked up a stone and skipped it across the river. *Like me, a couple of skips and...kerplunk.* One sharp twist and the bottle opened. The amber, stinging, bitter liquor was the river—he was the stone. He thought of Kat and drank himself to oblivion.

John Kenneth Kingsley, son of the soon-to-be-elected President of the United States, was prostrate on the valley floor—ragged, drunk, and dirty. His only comfort was knowing the rancher would meet him tomorrow and pay him with more booze so he would continue to mend these fences.

When he first signed on as a ranch hand, he rode about ten hours, ate, boozed, and slept. Now he was riding less than five hours before feeling the call of alcohol and he often skipped eating, except for a few bites in the morning.

His beard was long and scraggly. His socks had worn through and his boots bent to the stirrups. Blisters on his feet had long ago turned hard and his hands were rough—his nails long and broken. He could not walk very far—if he wanted to or had to. His strength was gone and his prior conditioning for football was lost.

Johnny had passed out by the time the storm finally reached him. Lightning scared the horse. Loose reins released him and he ran. Johnny squirmed in the rain but did not awaken. The rising creek wet his feet, causing him to curl into the fetal position. The flash flood pushed a wall of water up and over the drunken man/boy.

"What the hell—" He awoke, coughing and sputtering, as he was carried down the gushing stream. His life flashed before him as he called out, "Daddy" and waited for his father to pull him from the water as he had on a summer day when he toddled into the deep end of the pool. Once more he called, "Daddy." Water filled his open mouth. It washed dirt from the crevices of his face and soaked under his finger nails. It cooled his hot tired feet and sweaty brow.

Johnny's father was not in Idaho to pull his son from the raging stream. The rocks along the river bed battered him. The current twisted him and filled his eyes, throat and ears. He saw Kat float by and tried to grab her but could not. "Kat," he called and swallowed more water. At times the flood weighed him down; at times it buoyed him up for air. An uprooted tree grabbed his jacket, threaded up and out the neck and kept him from drowning. Johnny hung there sputtering and cursing his luck. *It could have been over but it's not.* That thought bounced in his brain while he freed himself from the snag.

The next day unrelenting sun on the mountains and valleys of Idaho cooked Johnny's body and soul. He did not have enough strength to find his way out of this hell if he wanted to. *I'll walk... then I'll die*, he resolved. It did not matter that he'd been washed out of Idaho and into Utah. His horse returned to the ranch stable and a search along the fence did not lead to the ranch hand. After a couple of days, the rancher stopped looking.

Johnny continued to walk although his bare feet were bruised and bleeding. He began to wish he had drowned in the swimming pool at King's Trace when he was a toddler. Thoughts scattered through his brain. *That would have been good. Nice warm pool—King's Trace. I shoulda drowned in the pool—never loved Kat.* It was the first group of related thoughts he had had in his drunken world for months. Then he allowed one more fatal thought. *Dad and her mother—you bastard. How could you?* Johnny was tortured. He screamed and the sound was almost inhuman as it went to the cliff of the mesa and began to echo off opposite mountains. "Aghhhhagh." It came back to him from every direction. "Aghhhagh." "Aghhhagh." "Aghhhagh."

Johnny slumped over, curled up and waited to die. He embraced a vision of soft brown hair highlighted by the sun, blowing in the wind. He saw the hills of Montgomery County, Kat's smile, her challenge as she broke canter and raced before him. Kat shook the horse brush at him, throwing water. Kat waited for him after school. Kat took his hand when ice coated the portico. Kat shed tears on the last night he saw her. Johnny thought of her words. *"Nobody knows the future."* He answered her again. "I know, I know."

A dark cloud of emotion engulfed him. "One thing for sure…I'll never go to the White House looking for that son-of-a-bitch." Johnny believed his trap was set and set tight because his father would be the President. There was absolutely no way he could go to his father or confront him. There was no one in the library at King's Trace, no one in the stable, no one to talk to. Mom doesn't know. Kat doesn't know. "What's the point? Hurt those I love?" He knew why he was on the floor of the universe, wanting and waiting to die.

Johnny could not live with what his father had done. He could not live without Kat.

"Kat."

CHAPTER 22

1961

Katherine watched closely but could not see much difference in her mother since changes were made in her treatment. At times, there seemed to be a breakthrough, but Pamela remained resistant. Katherine, always hopeful, anticipated each Tuesday's visit.

"Hello, Mother," she said with a kiss on Pamela's cheek. Pamela stared out the window, unmoved by her daughter's tender greeting.

"Hello," Pamela said, in a soft, flat voice.

At the very least, Katherine would like to hear her mother say her name.

"Mother," she demanded. "Please…" Her voice trembled in the plea. But Pamela continued to study the window and pick atced the flowers on her dress.

Katherine wanted a smile. She wanted to be looked at—to be seen.

"Is it going to rain?" Pamela asked.

"No rain." Katherine responded dejected "No rain today. None yesterday—none tomorrow." Her volume trailed down to a whisper. "No rain, Mother." Katherine had enjoyed this exchange about the weather early on but this small glimmer of response faded quickly. It was repeated over and over and became another failure to connect.

Katherine had just come from the weekly team meeting. "Be patient," was admonished again today. The team saw and reported improvements. She did not see any. This visit would not be different. She saw it immediately.

Pamela's passive attitude changed as she became belligerent. She felt Katherine's demands, her disappointment and her requirements—none of which she would satisfy. "Why did you come? Don't you need to be some place else?" she asked.

There were no answers. So, Katherine put a record on the turntable and let music fill their space until time to go.

It was depressing. Month after month, Tuesday after Tuesday, Katherine left Spring Haven defeated. Today was especially frustrating as Katherine stepped out of the visitor's lounge and leaned against the wall. *She doesn't want me. I might as well be a stranger from the street.*

Dr. McMaster walked down the corridor toward her, frowning at Katherine's defeated posture. "Not a good visit?" he asked.

"Same as always, Doctor."

"Come let's walk together. Are you headed to your car?"

They went out into the bright day and the wise doctor led her to a bench where the sunshine could work some magic. "How are things at school? Schedule working well?"

"Yes, sir. I do plan to take four fewer credits next semester. I will take them in summer session. I don't want to be too busy—you know."

"Good plan. You're not getting much from your mother. Is that your frustration?"

Katherine nodded. "Each week the team boasts about her improvements, but she isn't showing me any. She doesn't want to have any feelings between us. I wish she would at least acknowledge me. I must have disappointed her terribly when I was little. I don't think she ever wanted a daughter." Katherine could not voice her next thought. *She gave me to Papa.*

"You aren't disappointing her. She knows she has let you down and if anything, *she* is afraid of disappointing *you*."

"Oh, Doctor, I just want my mother. She doesn't want me." Her lament was heart-wrenching. "What should I do?"

"I understand how difficult this is for you but I am confident—absolutely sure—your mother wants you. Just continue to be yourself…and continue to visit her. She's afraid to love, but fortunately…you are not."

That night, Lady Fair had to listen to her again. "I'm not sure I will ever get through to Mother." She stroked to the aloof cat. "She won't look at me…and yet, when I leave she gets a sad look on her face." Katherine picked up the cat and looked into her blue eyes. "This may be as good as it gets." Lady Fair was indifferent to the tear running down Katherine's cheek. "Mother's a lot like you. You won't look at me either. Heartless cat!" She lightly tossed her pet onto the soft pillow and smiled.

Suddenly, revelation dawned as she recalled her endless attempts to make sure the Siamese cat knew she was important. Her final proclamation put her on a new track. "I won't give up! I'll assume she wants me there—just as you want me here." She softly poked her finger in the furry belly, scratched and picked Lady Fair up again, forcing the lazy cat to look at her. With her greatest imagination she attributed love and a smile to the feline face. "I'll assume Mother loves me, just as I do with you, Lady Fair. And—" She paused. "—I will imagine a smile and love—" she breathed deeply. "—if I have to." The epiphany breathed new life into her.

The next week she went to the hospital with a lift in her step. Her determination boosted her spirit. Even after she and Pamela were alone in the lounge and attempts to engage in conversation were ignored, Katherine grew stronger. She saw side glances from her mother even though Pamela would not allow their eyes to connect. It was enough to give new hope. Katherine became more determined. *Okay, Mother. I'm here and I'm staying.*

Two weeks later, Pamela came to the lounge at the appointed time for their visit. Katherine was not there. The team meeting was longer than usual, so it was twenty after when she arrived at the lounge where Pam waited—her face stricken.

"Sorry, I'm late, Mother." Before she could make an excuse or explain she noticed a tear on her mother's cheek. At closer look she saw fear. She saw worry. She saw concern. It was the first time since she could remember that she saw anything but indifference on her mother's face. "I'm so sorry," she repeated.

Katherine rushed to her mother and folded down to her knees to be at eye level to look for the gaze she longed for so desperately.

Like an unyielding habit, Pamela turned her head.

"Mother..."

"I thought you were not coming." Pamela whispered as her head slowly, deliberately turned forward. Her pale face laced with fear and relief met the almost twin-like face waiting hungrily for her gaze. "You would not come again."

Pamela's gaze and words overwhelmed Katherine, lumped words in her throat, burned tears in her eyes. She trembled as she spoke. "Look at me. I'm here." Katherine wanted to touch her, wanted to be touched, but this was so much more than they'd had for eighteen years. "I will always be here."

Pam stood and squeezed by Katherine, who was still kneeling. "I have to go now."

"Now?" *Don't go Mother. Not now.* Katherine touched her arm. "Mother."

Pamela pulled away. "Yes, now." She pressed the bell and summoned the attendant.

Katherine made no effort to rise. Rather she prayed a prayer of thanksgiving silently as her mother turned at the door. "Next Tuesday?" Pamela's eyes were firmly fixed on her daughter for the first time in her memory.

"Of course, Mother. Every Tuesday. I love you."

Almost like Lady Fair, Pamela returned to her nest and curled into position to wait for love to force itself on her again next week.

Katherine knocked on Dr. McMaster's office door. "Doctor, Mother looked at me today and let me know she was frightened that I might not come. Our team meeting made me late."

"Significant."

"I thought so…and truly wonderful. But, she left almost immediately."

"She could not maintain the connection. It frightens her…makes her vulnerable."

He scratched his bearded chin. "Your mother has a deep-seated problem she cannot face. We—," he leaned forward. "—and you, cannot expect much improvement until she is willing to go back to what caused her to shut down. It may be much too painful for her. It means she has to go through it again. Some patients never do."

Katherine wrote the doctor's words down as he spoke them and wondered, *Do I have the right to expect her to go back and go through her pain again?*

"Doctor, does my mother blame me for something? Can I do or say anything to help her?"

"You are doing all the right things. Come as often as you can and show your love. I suspect she doesn't think she has a right to love you. A heavy burden for a mother. Your loyalty is important." He walked over and took her hand. "You have no blame. Don't complicate her treatment by taking blame. That won't help, I assure you."

Katherine left the hospital with a glimmer of hope, yet afraid to feel too much.

She took her dilemma to Jonas when they met for their standing Tuesday night date to discuss the weekly team meeting. Jonas did not care about the reason, he was always happy for times he had with Katherine.

"Sorry I missed the meeting today—court."

"Jonas, she looked at me and spoke directly to me!" Katherine's joy was spilling from her eyes. "I'll never forget this day. Mark it on the calendar—the 18th. I'm so happy to have her connect with me. When she did, I thought my heart would burst. Maybe that's enough." She paused to revisit her own words. "No, no…it's not enough. I want more." Her eyes dimmed. Her mouth drooped. "I don't think I'll ever be able to settle for so little from her." She looked up at Jonas. "Today was just a beginning—it has to be—just a beginning."

Jonas took her hand and led her to the sofa. "Just a beginning." He gave her resolve validation and endorsed her hope.

"I love mother so much." She wiped one more tear. "She doesn't allow it."

"Keep on keeping on. She'll see."

"I thought showing her my love would bring her around, but Dr. McMaster said she has to go back to whatever caused her to shut down—in order for her to improve significantly."

"Let Pamela be the guide. If she wants to talk about the past, let her. If not, live in the present with her."

"Well, Jonas, if she doesn't get well, she will never leave Spring Haven. She tells me it's her home. She doesn't want to leave."

"Your mother has few choices. It's one you might have to allow."

"As usual, you are right." Katherine leaned over to give him a glancing kiss on the cheek. "Your gentle persuasion—I appreciate that."

"Think about this... are you prepared to know the reasons for your mother's mental state? Just as lies affect everyone, so does the truth. You keep putting off going through your father's desk and papers? I know it is hard, but I've always felt the answers are there. Don't you think he wanted you to understand your mother?"

Katherine sat pensive for a moment. "He always gave me hints that mother was a victim of bad treatment. He *did* want me to understand. He demanded compassion for her and soothed my hurt when I felt rejected. I have always felt I was the cause of some of her pain. Maybe that is why I want to help her to be better."

"I think he would have written down what happened when you were a baby. James Ross did not leave loose ends."

"Right again. Am I afraid of what I might find? And yet, I can't imagine I hurt my mother...but when she rejects me, old doubts plague me."

"You have nothing to fear because of your father."

"You're right. I'll give his papers some priority. Maybe I'll even find the key to bringing her from Spring Haven."

"Oh, my dear, don't hold that hope so strongly. The doctors have said it is unlikely she will ever lead a normal life. You put me on her team and I have to be pragmatic about it. The doctors want her as strong as possible, but I haven't heard any probability she would ever be independent. Please don't set yourself up for disappointment."

"What am I to do?" Katherine was exhausted and her shoulders drooped from the weight of the discussion.

"Make her happiness and contentment your goal. Don't apply our *normal* to her. Everyone wants to be accepted for what they are. Your mother is no exception. Accept her."

"Jonas, I'm so fortunate to have you helping me. What would I do without you?"

He took her hand, pulled her to his chest. "You never have to."

As always, she let his tender words go unanswered except for the smile lighting her face. She did not pull away and Jonas took heart.

"It's a nice day, get your coat. Let's go for a walk." It was a perfect suggestion for them to continue the day neither wanted to end.

They walked to the plaza at the south entrance of the Capitol without talking. Finally Katherine broached the subject she had on her mind. It was time to put all her trust in Jonas.

"Jonas, there's something else I want to talk to you about."

"Come, sit on this wall." He led her by the hand. "Okay. What?"

"I need advice. I offered before to give you a retainer and make this business."

"And, again...let me say, I'm your friend who happens to be a lawyer. Tell me what's on your mind If something is bothering you, I want to know. We're a team."

She felt so cared for—so embraced by friendship and maybe love. *Yes, love,* she thought.

"Mother refuses to leave Spring Haven. There is no doubt she did not get good care while Dr. Sherman was in charge. The hospital doesn't deny it. There's no way to assess if she would be much better today if Dr. Sherman had followed hospital procedure with her. Common sense tells me she would be better but observation leads me to believe she has always been, and will always be, as she is today. Dr. McMaster and the team are giving her the best possible attention now. She's obstinate and I believe she doesn't want to get better. Mother's very intelligent and she manipulates the system to stay where she is."

Jonas' legal mind was going into gear. "Tell me. How does KC Kingsley figure in all this? What was found in Sherman's records?"

"Dr. McMaster has been very open. The only thing we have from KC was a request for her progress reports. KC did not request treatment plans or diagnosis or prognosis. Sherman's deposits from KC were regular. There's nothing to implicate him except his interest in my mother. It's a mystery. I've no idea how supportive KC was to my grandparents. Of course, he had a business interest in the company and my parents held the controlling shares. But, I know my father was never more than a business partner with him. Sherman seems to have held back on advancing treatments to assure he would have a patient that KC was interested in—and regular deposits. I would hate to think he asked Dr. Sherman to hold back her treatments."

"Nothing to show that KC did?"

"Nothing."

"What is your opinion, do you think KC asked Dr. Sherman to do what he did?"

"No, I don't think so. That would be very risky. KC is too smart to put something like that in writing. There was no advantage in that for KC or anyone as far as I can see. Why would he do something that extreme?"

"So, we have one doctor's greed."

"Looks that way."

"Tell me," he took her chin and turned her face to his, looking into her eyes, "how is your relationship with Kingsley? Could you ask him... point blank?"

"I guess I could but—" She didn't quite know how to say it. "KC and I are ultra polite to each other without a relationship. I think I am, umm... standoffish with him because that is how my father always acted—as if each had to tolerate the other. He's such a strong man. How could I ask without it sounding... sounding like I was accusing?" She slid down from the wall, folded her arms and walked a small circle. "I want to know why he paid Sherman for reports on Mother. It is hard to imagine questioning him. See?"

"Yes, I see."

Jonas allowed some time to put his thoughts together as Katherine beckoned to him to resume their walk. "Think about this, Kate. Money buys control and power. A politician knows this and one sure thing—KC is a skilled politician. I'm not suggesting anything except that his interest in your mother's care was more than *casual* and *passing*. He's certainly smart enough to know Sherman was and would continue to be *his* man in Spring Haven. He may not have asked but he knew what he was getting for his money. Someday someone is going to have to ask him—why?"

"And I need to understand why my mother chooses Spring Haven over life?"

Katherine was getting weary of the subject. Jonas could see it in her sad eyes that had been glowing minutes ago. He hated to go on but had to.

"Katherine, you know you have a good lawsuit against the hospital, don't you?"

"Yes."

"The hospital is responsible for its staff. Sherman's death does not relieve the hospital of responsibility."

"I don't want to sue." She paused for emphasis. "I won't sue. It is out of the question. What good would that do? I don't need the money for Mother's care. I'm sure Spring Haven knows there is a case against them. Her care has not been billed since our first meeting."

"Was there any mention of you signing a waiver and accepting this as compensation?"

"Yes, I recall something like that but I haven't signed anything."

"Good. You need to decide absolutely that you will not sue and call a meeting to make it clear. Then we need to see exactly what Spring Haven offers." Jonas was on solid ground now. His emotions were set aside. "I'll come with you. A lawyer in the room is always an asset," he quipped to lighten the mood.

Then he paused before putting the next difficult thought to her. "You don't have to get answers from KC. May I suggest you concentrate on your mother's current needs now—until, or unless, you find a reason to go into the past. Do you want me with you when you ask the questions that need to be asked?"

"Jonas, wait. There'll be no legal case. Why must I….." She stopped because she knew the answer. "You're right. I have to know—sooner or later. I'll meet with McMaster and KC, too—some day." She looked at him with relief as she admitted to herself she did not want to confront KC. "Yes, I want you with me when I meet with Dr. McMaster but when I see KC, I'll go alone."

He looked into her eyes, pouring support into her already strengthening demeanor.

"Have you considered that it could be important for your mother's care if you moved her? You are her guardian and have power to make that decision."

Katherine moved back from Jonas, back from their conversation and back from the moment. She struggled to say the words that came up her throat along with bitter bile. Jonas saw her transform from the lovely young woman he loved to a haggard overburdened girl he had not seen before.

"Mother will *never* leave Spring Haven." It was her hardest truth. Jonas tried to stop her from going on but she set her chin and continued. "I hate to think that she will live her whole life in that hospital but I don't see how I can get her out. When I suggested she come home until we find another hospital for her she went absolutely wild. It took three attendants to control her. As they dragged her from me she turned back and shouted. 'Never, never. Let me be, devil child.'" Katherine was embarrassed to cry in front of Jonas on the tidal basin promenade.

"It's alright." His arms circled her. "Cry." He held her tightly.

"Father did not put Mother in Spring Haven because she was a danger to anyone or to herself. She went there because she couldn't live in our world. In all these years she never asked to come home. Not once. Never wanted to be with us. I think I knew that from a very young age. Felt it was my fault." Katherine's tears flowed profusely. "Papa would set me on his lap and tell me she wants to live at Spring Haven. He would not allow me to think otherwise."

Without looking up, Katherine admitted with soft tones, "I'm sorry you are getting all this. It was three weeks ago and I... Oh, I'm sorry, Jonas" She took the handkerchief he offered.

"Don't be sorry. I want it all.' He continued to hold onto her, taking no small pleasure in the trust she gave him. He had never had such a welcomed burden.

Jonas thought his heart would break for her.

Suddenly he felt her stiffen and the sobbing stopped. Darker thoughts crossed her mind and she began to quake. To stop the terror gripping her, he took her hand again. "Leave it, Kate." He didn't know what was building up in her but he wanted to stop it. "Let's walk some more." He took her hands and drew her up to him as he again ventured to put his arms around her. She stepped into the safe, warm, and assuring place he made for her next to his heart.

"She called me devil child—" The crying pain in her throat tore at her soul as her sobs became gasps for breath After a few seconds, she fell silent. The stabbing words and wicked look she saw on her mother's face still affected Katherine when she thought of it. Right now, she wanted the comfort of Jonas' strong arms and she wanted nothing to distract except his strong warm arms holding her, keeping her from going into little pieces.

"I'm here."

CHAPTER 23

1961

"I can't put it off. Papa's desk today." Every excuse for not diving into her father's boxes was gone. Katherine spoke to the driving rain and sleet pelting the window. She watched an early spring nor'easter that had arrived from the Chesapeake, threatening Maryland and Washington, DC. The wind challenged her bay window. Although the storm lost most of its strength crossing the Delmarva Peninsula, the unrelenting wind surge pushed the tidal basins into the streets around the Jefferson Memorial. Ice coated the world. Government offices, schools, and college campuses were closed.

Today was the day. There was only one thing to do—inside projects—and for Katherine—her father's desk and papers. *No excuses. Today.* She would attack the six boxes pulled from the closet yesterday. The huge mass of papers was overpowering and she almost hoped for a power outage. Her venture into the daunting job was delayed by the phone.

"Hello."

"I have a long distance phone call from San Francisco. Will you accept the charges?" Before Katherine could answer, the operator continued. "I'm sorry, the party has disconnected." The line went dead.

She sat there knowing—feeling for sure— she *almost* had Johnny on the line. Her thoughts were deep when she was startled by another ring. She grabbed the phone, determined not to let him get away again.

"Hello, operator, I'll accept the call," she answered frantically.

"What?? Katherine, it's me..."

"Jonas. Oh, I just missed a collect call and I think it was Johnny."

"Johnny? How do you know?"

"I don't know anyone in San Francisco. I just have a feeling." She let her breath go. "I feel it."

"If it was, I hope he calls back. Are you tackling your father's papers today? Do you want help?"

"It's nasty out. But, if you can get here, I'd love help."

Katherine admitted she wanted Jonas here more than anything. He was filling a lonely place in her life, though she was not ready to admit to herself just how much she wanted him here.

Jonas arrived a long hour later. When she opened the door for him, her heart leapt and she was surprised at her feelings. "Let's do it." He was the burst of energy she needed for the job.

The possibility—the cautious hope— some discovery would be made, drove them until past seven with only two working meals—sandwiches amid files and files of papers. Both were beginning to doubt their quest.

"Are you beginning to think maybe Papa didn't know the answer either?"

"I keep thinking any minute the right paper will surface. Tired?"

"A little. Let's work until eight and call it quits, at least for tonight."

Jonas pulled another box over and cut it open. He had something else on his mind and only an hour to bring it to Katherine. Talk while they worked had been idle chatter; now he wanted to get serious. He put his hand across the opened box and stopped her from diving into it.

"We're great friends, Katherine...and I'm worried what I'm about to say will ruin our friendship."

She stopped fingering through the papers she had in her hand. "What could you possibly say that would do that?"

"Well, I could tell you my feelings go beyond friendship." He took the papers from her and slid the box aside. "I could say I care for you very much and I'm scared you don't share my feelings."

Katherine looked at him in wide-eyed wonder. She was truly shocked out of her perch, high above feelings. When Jonas reached over and took her hand she looked at it as if she could actually see electricity shooting up to her throat. Feeling in this special moment forced her to face a dream she had denied. *Jonas! Jonas!*

Her inability to say or do anything sent the wrong message. He pulled back, dropping her hand and leaving her lost. *Oh, no—big mistake!* Doubts flooded him.

"I'm sorry...I shouldn't..."

Katherine moved quickly to her feet, tripped over a box and fell into his arms saying, "Jonas! I think I just fell in love myself." They laughed together as he wrapped his long arms around her and shared the universe in a kiss. The kiss changed her. His lips pressed hers with longing and desire. Katherine had truly never felt anything like it. As he pulled back and looked at her, she felt emptiness where his lips had been. That feeling was as overwhelming as the kiss. She needed another kiss—desperately. Frozen to the moment, she remained with slightly parted lips until

Jonas brought the thrill back to her mouth. He held her firmly but not tightly. The territory had to be given, not taken.

"Jonas," she whispered like a prayer. "Jonas," she tried to repeat but he kissed her again on his name.

Awash with emotion, Katherine felt her face flush, her breath stumble, her heart trip and twirl in her chest.

Jonas was stunned by the new beauty he saw in her. In these few moments—a wonderful eternity—they became explorers on a new journey of discovery. They sat wrapped together until it was time to talk, claim their feelings, and face what had just happened to them.

"These last months have been the hardest in my life." Jonas found his voice first. "I've always been sure of myself, but I didn't have a clue what I was to you—lawyer, confidant, friend—none of which I wanted to be as much as your steady date and more."

"Oh, Jonas, just now, as you took your hand away, I realized I want my hand in yours. Guess I have wanted a kiss or two." She smiled and kissed him, this time long and tender. They lingered, savoring happiness—happiness in each other. The world had come down to the two people sitting amid a jumble of boxes and files. All seemed in disarray but actually a clear uncluttered view opened for the lovers.

"You're so protective of your feelings. I was terrified of scaring you away." He lifted her chin to look into her eyes. "Your walls are high, Katherine."

"I admit—true, but not for you, Jonas. Since Papa died I have not known who to trust. At the reading of his will, you were my only friend. You have become an important part of my life—truly the only part clearly focused for me." She allowed him to look into the windows of her soul without blinking.

"Dear, dear Katherine." His joy was without words as he embraced her again and pulled away. "Let's finish this last box and have a rainy night date. TV and your hand in mine, a kiss or more…"

"Popcorn and Pepsi." She laughed and finished his sentence.

"Sounds perfect. Next Saturday I'll come at eleven. Lets spend the day together and and have a real date. Okay?"

They should have skipped the pile of envelopes from the opened box. An envelope with Katherine's name surfaced and Jonas handed it to her. When she took the overstuffed parcel she seemed to sense it was important. In Papa's fine strong hand he had written:

Katherine Marie
To be opened after my death

Her hand trembled and suddenly she did not want to pull the envelope apart and see what it contained. "I have to open it, don't I?"

"Yes." The seriousness of the moment took romance from the air. "You must."

"Here's my birth certificate. I've seen it before. Here's Mother and Papa's marriage certificate. I knew she was pregnant before. Why is it important in this packet? This isn't a revelation."

"Go on. He's put everything of importance together. What else?"

"A letter to me." She carefully unfolded the paper and looked to the bottom to be sure her father had written it. "From Papa." She looked up at Jonas with sad, confused eyes. His heart broke for her.

"You can do this, Katherine. It's what you have searched and waited for. Do you want me to leave you alone while you read it?"

"Stay, please." She pushed back into the sofa, clutched a pillow to her stomach for security and began to read to herself.

Dear Katherine, my darling daughter,

You are the dearest person in the world to me. Every day you are entrusted to my care is wonderful. I believe God meant for us to be father and daughter. That being said, I believe it is important for you to understand your parentage. I am not your biological father.

Katherine stopped reading and took a deep breath. "Ohhh my." She ran her finger over his words before she continued.

Your mother was pregnant when we married. We could have handled this better for you if your mother had not been ill. She could not face the fact that she hurt you and me. We were in love and I married her because I loved her and wanted to protect her. Unfortunately she felt she hurt me too much. I was never able to convince her that I was her husband, and your father, because I loved her. My fervent prayer is – because of our life together, you know—I am your father in every sense of the word and more importantly, because I love you. Your question now is—who is your biological father? I promised Pamela I would not divulge the name. I think that would sever the thin thread that holds your mother together. I hoped that she would get well enough to relieve me of my promise, or that she would tell you herself. That seems doubtful. The possibility remains, he may some day come to you and reveal himself and it would be devastating to learn such an important thing that way. This pitiful letter is difficult enough. Needless to say, who he is is not important. I hope this is not too heavy a burden for you. You are Katherine Marie Ross. I hope you will always be the happy child I raised. You must have this biological information but it will not change the wonderful strong woman you are—my daughter.

My everlasting love,
Papa

She sat quietly with the letter loosely dropped on the sofa beside her. "Read it, Jonas."

Katherine went into the bedroom while Jonas read. She needed time to digest what had just been revealed to her. *Papa. Papa. I don't want anyone to come to me and claim to be my father. You're my father. I'm your daughter.* She pressed her hand to her breast. *You are my Papa.* She stretched on the bed and refused to cry. *Nothing to cry about. Nothing is changed. I'm Katherine Ross.*

She could not reconcile her feelings. She did not know why she was so conflicted. *Who was my mother's lover? Did he give me away?*

Her thoughts and quandaries were becoming deeper. *Is this why Mother is sick?* At last she pondered the question which really mattered and asked herself out loud. "Is this why mother is in Spring Haven?" She faced the reality of it—*sperm was placed—I was conceived. And it wasn't Papa.* "I was given to Papa because Mother couldn't look at me."

Jonas finished Katherine's letter and tapped on her door. "Are you okay? Can I come in?"

"Yes." She quickly sat up.

The room was dark and he could hardly make out her form on the bed as he approached and sat on the edge. Katherine immediately dove into his arms. She needed Jonas and his unwavering, steady support. She was safe and the thoughts whirling around seemed to find a place to rest—on his broad shoulders.

"I'm going to be fine."

"Of course, you are." He gently pushed his hand into her hair. She leaned into him.

"It just takes a while to take this in. Why didn't they tell me?" She took a deep breath. "Oh, I can see why…and, what difference would it have made?"

"You're the same person you have always been. And, your father loved you until his last breath. It's what a father does. A single act two decades ago does not a father make. You know that."

"Yes, I do. I'm going to look at this for what it may do for my mother. I owe it to Papa. It doesn't matter to me. I'm my own person now and I'll always be his daughter."

"You are… and never forget, I care for you—very much. One of the things I love about you is your strength…one of the things!" He pulled her to her feet before he took her in his arms. She responded with a hug. "Ready to come back to work?" he asked.

"Give me a minute to restore my face."

"Your face is perfect to me. A minute—yes."

As she stood before the mirror, strength, resolve, and confidence grew as she accepted the words her father wrote.

Another envelope, addressed to Pamela Ross, waited in the last box. Without hesitation, Katherine opened and read the letter her father wrote to her mother.

CHAPTER 24

1961

It was hard to wait for Tuesday and her regular time with her mother, but Katherine used the days to decide what she would say. The letter from her father stayed on her mind day and night. The only tears she shed over the contents of his parcel happened when she read her mother's letter. Katherine had wondered for years about his devotion and at times when she felt rejection and struggled with her own feelings, she wished Papa loved Pamela less and her more. Through the years he patiently taught the little girl to accept her mother. Unfortunately, she never understood how to do it.

Katherine watched with new eyes as her mother's lifeless steps brought her to the lounge. *Mother, now I know what hurt you so badly.* She gazed intently at the approaching shadow of a woman. *But…who?* She tried to demand her mother's attention with sheer emotion. *Look up, Mother, look up.* But Pamela did not look up at her daughter standing on the brink of knowledge. She passed her in the doorway—carefully not touching, not acknowledging. It was just another Tuesday.

Katherine suggested a walk on the grounds. Pamela's silence was assent and together they walked to a bench in the sun. It was a pleasant day, temperatures moderate and a nice breeze from the south. The grounds at Spring Haven were dotted with patients and attendants.

"Mother, please look at me." Pamela slowly raised her chin so her eyes accepted the gaze of her daughter. "I have a letter that Papa wrote to you. Do you want to know what he said?"

"That would be nice." She answered in monotone without significance as she reached for the letter which Katherine had withdrawn from her purse.

"I'll read it to you."

Displeasure flooded the older woman's face. She reached again, an unusual insistent action, but Katherine pulled back. This was difficult for Pamela. She did not know how to assert herself but she was sure the letter was hers and should not be in Katherine's hand, much less read by her lips. She began to fidget. Her only solution was to retreat into the building.

Katherine would not allow it—her arm gently crossed Pamela's shoulder, holding her on the bench. "Mother, I'll read the letter so you'll know that I understand what Papa said. This can't be yours alone because we are family. You, Papa and me." She repeated with emphasis. "Family."

Pamela yielded as Katherine unfolded the letter and read aloud.

My dear Pamela,

I love you. I have always loved you. I married you because I love you. I will continue to love you until the day I die. I did not marry you for any other reason. I have told you over and over. Now, I tell you one final time. I love you. That I got Katherine for a daughter was a blessing beyond belief. It's time for you to forgive yourself. What happened so many years ago does not matter. You matter and Katherine matters. Our daughter is an amazing young woman. She can be trusted if you decide to tell her the truth. She knows I am not her biological father but I have kept my promise. She doesn't know who is and never will unless you tell her.

Your loving husband,
James

Katherine offered the letter to her mother and waited until the slow process of accepting was completed. Pamela took the letter in both hands, wrinkling it into a ball. While Katherine watched, she smoothed it out and pressed it to her lap.

"Go ahead, Mother. Read for yourself." She folded over and brought her eyes down to look at the words. Katherine could see a change come over her mother. Her eyes became sharper, her face took on animation, and she unfolded her back and sat up straight with amazing dexterity which Katherine had never seen before.

"You know?'

"Yes, Mother. Papa left me a letter, too."

For an eternity, Katherine waited. Pam read the letter again. "Did he tell you who?"

"No, he kept his promise."

"Do I have to tell you now?"

"You don't have to do anything, now or ever."

"I'm afraid for you."

"Don't do anything out of fear. I'm your daughter. Papa is my father. In that strong love I have nothing to fear and neither do you. Mother, let it go. Please, let it go." Harder than her words was the effort it took to refrain from taking her mother in her arms. "If it will help you to tell me, do—otherwise, don't." Katherine had to risk it—she touched her mother's hand. "I have no *need* to know, believe me. I have had a good life without this piece of information. And I will continue to have a good life. It will not matter to me. My only concern is you."

"Me?" Pamela drew her hand back and began to fade. Her face lost its vibrant appearance; her voice went monotone. "Don't be concerned for me." She began to fidget and repeatedly fold her letter into a small square.

"A pencil?" She asked as she stood to go.

Katherine handed her a pencil and watched as she made a quick mark on the squared paper and folded it to a rectangle and gave it back to Katherine.

"Nurse!" She called to a nearby attendant. "Please, take me inside."

Without a goodbye or look back, Pamela went back into the hospital as Katherine opened the last fold of her mother's letter and read the scribbled notation. *KC Kingsley*

CHAPTER 25

1961

Katherine didn't answer the phone and she ignored a knock on the door. She knew it was Jonas. She couldn't answer either. She needed time to digest it all. Jonas was important but she was not ready to invite him and his wisdom into her feelings.

Learning that Papa was not her biological father was a blow but it really didn't matter. James Ross was her father in every way and her world would not be shaken. However, the small scrap of paper where Pamela wrote *KC* was another matter—that was a horrific blow.

Katherine cancelled her Tuesday night date with Jonas and remained in bed on Wednesday. Lady Fair was delighted to have extra warmth around the curl of her back. Sun streamed in the window and she and Lady Fair took it in to buoy their spirits.

"I'm going to get used to this idea," she said. "Eventually." *Weird,* she admitted. "Always on the verge of telling me something. Always seemed to want to say something and held back. I thought it was my imagination." Lady Fair invited an ear scratch. "Guess it wasn't." She looked into Lady Fair's blue eyes. "KC," she told her cat again. "Get it, wise cat? KC? You're so smart; I'm as dense as a fog. I didn't get it." Vagrant thoughts flooded her brain—thoughts of awkward moments at King's Trace, of KC trying to incorporate her in the family, of her resistance to his power.

Suddenly, she began to sob uncontrollably. "Johnny," she screamed. A piece of the giant puzzle fell into place. "Johnny, you knew…you knew." Katherine fell on her back and gazed at the blank ceiling where everything was coming as clear as print. "Johnny, Johnny, Johnny." Over and over again. "How did you?" Lady Fair felt the atmosphere change and struggled to get away but Katherine held tight. "Oh, Johnny, Johnny. That's what you didn't say that night." With hardly a breath between, she was assailed with wounding revelations. "What about Julianne, Brenda, and Melissa," she drew up the sheet and blanket to cover her face so she could not see the writing on the ceilings and walls. *Oh, Johnny. Johnny! Now I know, too.* "Johnny" *Brother and sister. You tried to tell me.* "Johnny" His name ricocheted in her brain. Katherine could not get his handsome face from her eyes. She could not stop shouting his name. "Johnny, how did you find this terrible secret that will hurt others, maybe more than it hurts me?" She admitted, "Is it hurting you today…*more* than it's hurting me?" Fear gripped her.

Katherine's emotional turmoil became a physical reaction. She threw back the covers. The cat grumbled her displeasure at being disturbed. Lady Fair dashed into her under-bed retreat. Katherine ran for the bathroom and got to the toilet just in time. Her gut reacted to her thoughts. Retching and retching with nothing—because she had not eaten. The tremors came again and again. Bile rose up and burned her throat and mouth. Tears spilled from red eyes as blood vessels exploded. Once again her tongue warned her that this would be easier if she had something to vomit. She thought the pressure would pop her eyes from their sockets. Katherine sat on the cold floor to keep from falling. She grabbed a cloth and reached the tub spigot to wet it and soothe her brow. *Johnny, Johnny.* She saw his face, his pain. The whole strange evening with Johnny marched slowly and deliberately through her brain. His words, his desperation flashed in her mind. *No future. Oh, God. Dear, dear Johnny.*

On the next heave, her mind brought another truth. "The President of the United States fathered me." She spit the words out with a dry heave. "KC!—you." There was no more bile, or body fluid—just pain of betrayal passing from her body into the world that was heaving and retching unmercifully. "This hurts. It hurts so bad." Her arms wrapped around her body as she rocked back and forth. "Oh God, what am I to do? Oh God. Mother! Now I know... I know." She threw herself spread eagle on the floor and cried for Johnny, for her mother, for Julianne, Brenda, Melissa and for herself.

"Call me again, Johnny. Call. Please call. God, please make him call me," she begged and prayed. Prostrate, she took the unyielding knowledge to the extremes of her body and life. Then Katherine drew into the fetal position until she calmed.

Exhaustion stopped the vomiting. Katherine crawled to bed and fell fast asleep—for two hours. Parched mouth, thirst and hunger brought her awake. "It's still daylight, Lady Fair. This day is endless." As she walked to the kitchen, she noticed a note had been slipped under the door.

Kate. I'm outside your door and will stay here until you let me in. I hope it won't be all day and all night, too. J

"Jonas," she called through the door as she unlocked it. "Come in. Don't look at me; I'm a mess. Make coffee. I'll be right back."

Katherine retreated to the bathroom, drank water, brushed her hair and teeth, all the while thanking God for bringing Jonas. She pinched color into her cheeks, donned a pink sweatshirt and hurried to the kitchen.

Jonas hardly had time to turn to her approach when she came into his arms. Her kisses were needy; his were tender. He would not take advantage of her vulnerability. Not this evening, but he put the joy of her greeting away for another time.

"Jonas, take me away," she whispered as she invited his arms to support her.

"If only I had a magic carpet, but I'll take you to the sofa." He tried to lighten the mood. "I'm going to fix you something to eat. I suspect you haven't eaten today. Ahh…" he threw open the refrigerator and noted "…eggs and cheese—two omelets coming up and a cup of hot tea."

"I accept the trip to the sofa and await you and the omelet. I'm famished."

It took over an hour for Katherine to tell her story and face all the dilemmas it presented. Jonas was ruptured by the facts. He hurt—for Katherine, for the pain he heard in her voice, saw in her eyes. Otherwise, he wasn't surprised. It fit too well. It was the kind of thing he, as a lawyer, was trained to see…the reason of it, the sense. Had he suspected before? Perhaps, but he'd refused to think so critically because of Katherine—because of how it would hurt her.

"Truthfully I don't know why, or how this all happened. Only KC knows. I'm not sure I want to know the nitty-gritty, as they say." She took a deep breath. "He *is* the President."

"He's only a man. Let's not forget that."

"The father of Brenda, Johnny and Melissa. Husband of Julianne. The dearest people in the world to me—present company excepted—you're on that list, too."

"I'm glad." He kissed her forehead lightly.

"The terror of today is over Johnny. Not me, not mother, not KC—Johnny. *This* is why he left. Oh Jonas. It's terrible."

He let her vent; he could only listen. There was no point in trying to convince her otherwise. It was the obvious answer to Johnny's disappearance—especially when she recounted his remarks.

When she finally leaned back, worn out by the telling, he held her without saying a word. She appreciated his silence, which told her he knew she would sort things correctly.

"Tell me if I can help you, my love. I'm here for you."

"Have to decide what to do. Has to be what is best for Mother."

"And, what is best for you." Jonas was determined to take care of her. "If your decision-making is helped by bouncing things off me, be my guest. Meanwhile—" He kissed her again as she melted into him. "—if you need me, I'll sleep on the sofa tonight."

"No, Jonas. I'm fine. I really am." She managed a smile for him. "I'm the same person I was two days ago."

"The girl I fell in love with!" His next kiss was full of commitment. Jonas was Katherine's, but he did not get the same assurance from her. He chose to ignore her reluctance to express love. Jonas knew her thoughts were way beyond the sofa and him.

"I know what I have to do."

"Good. What?"

"Have our date on Saturday." She kissed him. "And get myself psyched up to go see KC."

CHAPTER 26

1961

Katherine stood in front of the bathroom mirror preparing for her date with Jonas. She wanted her hair to wave perfectly from her face and so took an extra minute with the brush and her thoughts. *I'm in love. Is that possible?* What had started as a crush had finally become something serious. She enjoyed remembering the realization that feelings were mutual.

"I've wanted him to kiss me for a long time," she admitted to the mirror. Her reflection showed surprise at her words. She finished her hair and went to the front room to wait. Her watch showed she had about eight minutes before he would knock.

"Come Lady Fair." She picked up the reluctant cat. "I have confessions." She nuzzled the cat's head and relaxed her grip. Lady Fair tried to escape back to the window seat and sun. "Not this time, Vixen. I need to tell you something." Lady Fair found a familiar spot in her girl's lap and yielded. "Next to you comes Jonas. I'm falling for him, but I have so many problems." She looked into the blue Siamese eyes. "Mother, oh my. KC? Johnny? Who would want a girl with such huge problems?" Her mood was descending. "Go back to your window. No help!" She pushed Lady Fair from her lap as the sturdy brass knocker sounded on her door.

"Jonas," she whispered. Then she prayed, sighed, and put on a smile as she opened the door.

"Hi, Jonas." Katherine hid her breathless admiration for the man who at this moment could pass for Atticus Finch as portrayed by Gregory Peck. *If he had on his glasses!* She thought. She motioned him in, unable to say anything while her mind was occupied.

"I've looked forward to today." He stumbled for words. "Maybe— we could walk to the Tidal Basin and talk. It's a great day."

"I'll get a jacket and scarf." She smiled brightly at the welcomed suggestion.

"Has it been almost a week since we made this date?"

"A lifetime."

He mustered a professional attitude while following her into the apartment. "I assume you've had time to draw some conclusion...maybe a plan for your mother?" He rambled on to hide his excitement. "I got the written reports from McMaster but am anxious to hear your take on the weekly team meetings. They didn't note any real changes since you took the letter to her."

"No. Mother's handling that in her usual way. She actually seemed angry at me Tuesday. Dr. McMaster thinks any sign of emotion is good but I'd rather have indifference than anger."

"Interesting. How're you doing with all this?"

Katherine led him into the sunroom. "It's been crazy. My classes are requiring a lot. Can't think about Mother all the time. School is a life saver."

"Would be nice if you could just be a student."

"Truly, I can't imagine it. My routine is good and I manage get to the hospital every Tuesday. No small miracle" She put on her jacket and noticed Jonas had neither moved into the sunroom nor taken a seat.

"Let's go. There's a great day waiting for us. I'm ready for it, are you?" His question was full of possibilities and Katherine did not miss the feelings and promise he put in it.

She took his arm and pulled him through the door, tugging and laughing.

It seemed logical for him to take her hand crossing the street. It was pure magic when he did not drop it as they stepped on the other curb. A block later they were still hand in hand and strolling in companionable silence. His grip was not casual; it was strong with purpose. Katherine took heart and held on.

Finally he pulled their hands forward so both could see the fingers intertwined as he looked into her eyes and smiled. She claimed a happiness she thought was only reserved for others. *Me. He wants to be with me!* Her brain screamed as her grip tightened. She wanted to walk hand in hand forever. The sun was strong, the breeze light so the sidewalk around the Jefferson Memorial was full of strollers. They blended in with so many out to enjoy the beauty and the company of someone special. It all seemed so natural—magical.

Jonas led her to a bench with a great view of the water and Thomas Jefferson. "It will soon be time for spring break. I'd like for you to meet my parents. Could you—would you—give me three or four days? It would be good for you to get away." He paused just long enough for her to anticipate his next words. "I want to be with you away from all your responsibilities."

Go away with him? Away from Mother and Spring Haven, can I? Her mind was reeling with those thoughts as her heart was saying, *Yes. Yes.* Holding tight to her emotions, and keeping her breathless feeling from giving her away, she took a light air. "We've had a walk… and on our first real date you want me to go away with you?" He could see the teasing in her eyes. "Where to?" She laughed.

"Okay. Let me back up. Can we go to the movies tomorrow night? Will you have dinner with me Tuesday after the team meeting? And, then I'd like to take you to meet my parents—for three or four days—on the Outer Banks of North Carolina—the most wonderful natural beach in the world. How about it?"

It sounded wonderful. She felt like a schoolgirl, excited and thrilled. Her imagine ran wild. *Me. Jonas. On the beach. Far away from here. Touching...kissing.* Maybe she *could* let go of her responsibilities for some fun time with Jonas. The prospect was exhilarating.

"Tomorrow is good. So is Tuesday. I don't know much about the Outer Banks, but it sounds wonderful." She drew a deep breath as Jonas tightened his hold on her hand.

"You'll love it. Mom will have a room ready for you. I promise it won't take long for the ocean sounds to lull you into total relaxation. It's the best place on earth."

Katherine let her mind wander into anticipation and she realized she had not had the joy of anticipation since her father died. Papa always gave her something to look forward to. Now she knew what was missing, and Jonas Longfellow was sitting here holding her hand and offering to fill her life again with delightful anticipation. She was happy.

CHAPTER 27

1961

Spring came sweetly and quickly to the nation's capital with the Cherry Blossom Festival. Almost as if it could not wait, temperatures soared and children waded in the reflecting pool and park fountains. The warm temperatures were comforting after the bitter winter and cold March. There is no more beautiful place in the USA than the historic center of Washington, DC.

The benefits the first family enjoyed were not difficult to accept. They had always been a privileged family, thanks to the success of William Greeley. But smiles and public images did not accurately portray the first family. KC wondered, as he looked out on the Rose Garden, if Julianne noticed it.

Julianne was busy with her role as first lady and mother. KC and the White House staff quickly learned that she made her own agenda. Melissa would continue to attend Laurel Elementary, so the Secret Service took her to Laurel each day. The black-suited men were in the halls, cafeteria and playgrounds. Two weeks in the President, at the urging of the First Lady, insisted the men wear casual clothes. Melissa was a happy commuter.

Julianne was busy, but not happy. All the luxury and benefits did not soften her stance against KC for his lack of diligence in searching for Johnny. True, he had finally asked the FBI to join the search but instructed them, "Nothing in the media." It was not good enough for Julianne. She wanted KC to go to North Dakota with her to find their little boy. It was unrealistic, but she held to it. After they were settled in and the personal quarters were arranged, she made a trip to North Dakota, praying that God would lead her to Johnny. She visited police departments in twenty-one towns with his picture—to no avail.

"Julianne, I need you. Please come to bed with me," he pleaded one rare evening when they ate alone/together. "We need each other—now more than ever."

"No we don't."

"I need you."

"KC," she spoke with total exasperation. "Will you ever see the true picture?" She put her fork down and looked at him. "KC, this is your world and in it, you don't need anyone. You are a loner; I'm an elbow ornament." She tried to sound gentle but underlying anger brought delivered harsh words that came easily to her. "You're a good President but I only wanted a husband. I don't want to fight or argue—so drop it. I'll help you all I can but, at the end of the day, I don't need a President. And, I can't prostitute myself."

"Really, Julianne?" He was appalled at her language and stance. "I can be a husband and a President."

"You can't. You were not a husband when you were Senator but I was a different woman. I've done it all for you. Even made you a good father in your children's eyes." She yielded her attitude a little. "Not all your fault, mine, too. I'm different. You are the same, I'm not."

"What's our future?"

"That depends. The only family I'm willing to save with you includes our son." His name was not spoken. "Let me know when you are ready to walk out that door and go find him." She closed down, folded her napkin and pushed her chair back. "Excuse me." Julianne left the table. As she walked away she whispered, "Jesus said, leave the ninety-nine and search for one lost sheep.'"

Julianne accepted her responsibilities, and actually enjoyed them when she could put aside her grieving for Johnny for a few hours, never more. It had been many long months since her birthday card arrived, bringing her a burst of faith. Now it was a matter of strength more than faith that got her through the days, weeks, and months since. KC was so busy that during the hours and days that he was absent on official business, she sometimes forgot to be angry with him, but the old loving feelings grew dimmer and dimmer. It was surprisingly easy to live separate lives in this arena. The only thing Julianne had to do was believe what the newspapers said. Lovely, happy First Family.

The day started as usual for the President. He read his morning briefs as he had coffee. Julianne was at King's Trace overnight to attend a concert at Melissa's school. Today at the breakfast table they would not have to eat behind a façade of pleasantness. KC was content with briefs and the ever-present newspapers arranged on the table. He knew what to do with them.

"Mr. President, you have a call from Katherine Ross." Miss Caulkins interrupted his morning routine.

"I'll take it here." The phone was brought as KC took a deep drag of caffeine and even deeper breath.

"Good morning, Kathy. How are you?"

"I'm fine, sir. How are you and the family?"

"We're fine—plugging along. Do you need something?" He hated to rush her but schedules were pressing.

"I'd like an appointment to meet with you, if possible—today. Anytime."

Wow. This was something from her. He was mystified and intrigued that she would call and make a request like this. Katherine was never very far from his mind. His longing to have her close never left him. It was a torment along with his distance from his wife. He would always have time for her.

"Of course, but you won't see Julianne. She is at King's Trace overnight."

"I only want to see you." She wasn't sure how to address him. *KC? Mr. President.*

"Hold the phone a minute while I check with my secretary." It took only a minute. "Kathy, can you come at 10:15? Be at the east gate at 9:55. Someone will take your car and escort you to my office."

"I'll be there."

The morning was ordinary and KC hardly had time to muse over Katherine's surprise request to meet. He was walking to the office at precisely the appointed time. She was seated and waiting for him. The formality of the setting prompted her to rise as he came toward her.

"Good morning, KC—or should I say, Mr. President?"

"KC is fine, of course, unless we are in public. Awkward, eh?"

"Not really. I understand."

"I was surprised to get your call today."

"I know, and I'll get to the point. Your time is precious. By the way, I'm keeping up with news from the White House. Congratulations. You're doing a terrific job."

"Thanks, Kathy. Now about you, are you well? And, I hope you have heard from Johnny. Is that why you are here?"

"Not really, but I do believe he tried to reach me from San Francisco two weeks ago." She took a minute to explain the phone call. It gave her time to settle down and prepare for her real mission.

"KC, I believe I know why Johnny left. I hope your schedule allows us some time. This is vital not only to Johnny but—"

She was interrupted by the sudden entrance of Miss Caulkins, which caused KC to turn abruptly with a stern look for her.

"Mr. President, I must interrupt. You have a call from Paul Forsythe."

"Can it wait?" Aggravation was written on his face and in his voice. She had been told not to interrupt.

"It can't wait, sir. It is urgent." She continued into the room. Ignoring Katherine, she approached the president and whispered in his ear.

"Katherine, please, stay here. I must take this call." Aggravation fell from his face as it turned ashen.

KC rose and quickly exited, giving Miss Caulkins instructions. "Bring Miss Ross something to drink."

Five minutes later, he sent another messenger to Katherine. "You're to come to the private quarters, Miss Ross. Please, follow me."

Katherine was led through the majestic house to the family elevator. The environment gave her awe and she felt the magnitude the place and KC. She embraced a new awareness and felt very small as she walked the grand hallways, passed the reception area and stepped on the elevator to the private quarters. Thoughts flooded her. *I have to tell him. I have to.* Doubts were swamping her brain. *KC needs to know. Needs to know what I know.* The elevator slowed; a small bump as it reached the second floor. Katherine actually began to tremble as the doors opened. *If facing the truth will help Mother…I must.*

Miss Caulkins was waiting and invited her into the room with a gesture before stepping on the elevator and leaving her with the President.

They were alone in a room decorated much like the living room at King's Trace. KC's head was in his hands. When he brought his eyes up to meet hers, his face was distorted and covered with tears. He could hardly speak between sobs. "Johnny's dead." He lamented. "Dead. Oh God… how will I tell Julianne?"

Katherine sat beside him and allowed him to embrace her and put his tears in her hair. Her own crying was soft. For the first time in their lives, father and daughter held each other, sharing mutual feelings and grief. Neither could speak. Independently—each had the same thought—acknowledging the relationship that nature had thrust upon them.

And so they held on to each other, knowing that this moment was lasting too long and knowing that when it is over, awkwardness, beyond belief, would flood the scene.

She didn't move until he pulled back. She drew tissues from her purse, offered him one and dried tears that had flowed unchecked. Then they assumed their usual distant stance.

"Kathy, will you go with me to King's Trace? The whole family needs to be together."

"Of course, I will."

"Let me think. You have your car here. You alright to drive?"

"Yes."

"Go by school and get Melissa? I'll have Miss Caulkins call them and get it set up for you to pick her up. I'll be at home at 11:45. Can you time it to arrive then?"

"Yes, I can do that. KC, please, tell me what happened to Johnny."

His face was again stricken and distorted. Tears flowed freely, this time silently.

"Overdose—drugs." Johnny's father repeated the words John Forsythe had given to him. "My Johnny... overdose...in San Francisco."

CHAPTER 28

1961

Katherine needed to talk to Jonas. She left the White House and made a quick stop at home to use the phone. Going to King's Trace could wait—a short while. It was her intention to take a few minutes, ten at the most, but when the door closed behind her, she stumbled to the sofa and melted down. Salty tears tasted bitter. "How much, how much?" She asked nobody… and, nobody answered her vague question as she rolled over and studied the ceiling until her eyes blurred in the trapped tears.

Katherine saw Johnny. "Oh, Johnny," she cried. He was on the ceiling sadly looking down on her.

"Good bye, Kat." and he was gone.

Startled by the vision, Katherine grabbed the phone and dialed the one person who could save her.

"Jonas."

"Kate." A long pause told him something was wrong.

"Are you alright? Where are you?"

"Johnny's dead. I have to go to King's Trace. Pick up Melissa. I have to go now." Her speech was strange and Jonas was alarmed.

"Where are you?"

"Home."

"I'll be there in ten minutes. Don't leave."

"Okay."

"Promise."

"I promise, if you hurry."

By the time Jonas got there, Katherine had pulled herself together. She had washed her face and restored her appearance. He was relieved to see her grief was within normal bounds as she told of her trip to see KC.

"Oh, no. I'm so sorry." He took her cold, trembling hands "This has been a lot, Kate. You have so much to deal with right now and I want to help. I'm so sorry that Johnny is gone. This new burden is not yours. His death is not on your hands. Can I help you with this?"

"You are, dear Jonas. Just being here…" She pulled his hands around her waist, went into his arms seeking strength.

After a long embrace, he held her back from his chest and looked into her eyes. "I'm here for you. When you accept that Johnny was a victim as clearly as your mother was, you will see that your job—your only job—is to rise above this and bring your mother to love. Love is the only answer. Love for her and hopefully my love for you will see you through this very dark day. I do love you, Kate."

She could not say anything. She could only cling to him. After several minutes of taking in his support, she came back to her place of reason. "I see, and I know you see it, too. Johnny knew. He tried to tell me…he knew." She looked up at Jonas with clear knowledge written on her face.

"Yes," was all he could say as he gently petted her head trying to soothe her frantic brain while they shared a moment of silence.

"I'm to pick up Melissa at school and take her to King's Trace."

"I'll take you." He had a strong need to help her and shelter her, but she resisted with exceptional resolve.

"No, I need my car. I'm fine. I can do this. What I need from you, you have already given me."

"Kate, did you tell KC what you went to the White House to tell him?'

"No. The tragic news from San Francisco interrupted our conversation. I may not have anything to tell him after all."

Jonas walked her to her car and gently brushed her hair from her face. His touch was tender. She took his hand and kissed it. "Call your mother. Our trip to the Outer Banks is cancelled."

"No, just postponed. Call me later."

Somehow Katherine drove to Laurel and got Melissa. The girl's chatter about school was a good distraction. All too soon they were at King's Trace. There was no time for her to plan her entrance or what she would say. Katherine had to go in and let the words come as they may.

"Daddy's here!" Melissa saw the tell-tale black limousines.

Katherine had to prepare Melissa—at least a small preparation, as the little girl bounded out of the car full of exuberance.

"Melissa—" she took her hand. "—let's walk in together." Her firm grip on the small hand calmed the youngster and she fell in step with Katherine. Something in the the way her hand was grasped passed a message. Melissa looked up questioningly at Katherine. Her less than full smile quieted the sweet child. They walked into the imposing foyer, across to the great room where Julianne and KC were waiting. Katherine deposited Melissa on the sofa next to her mother. Then she stepped back to the piano bench and let the grieving family find their way through the first terrible minutes of accepting and believing their loss, just as she had done earlier in her condominium. Katherine's tears flowed with unchecked compassion and fury until the front of her blouse was soaked. The ringing phone told them that Brenda had returned their call.

"Do you want me to tell her.... or do you?" Julianne asked.

KC rose without speaking to go to the phone.

In one of those unexplained urges, Katherine followed KC to the library where he had to tell his daughter about her brother. She stood while KC delivered the facts almost like a state of the union address before he crumbled. Katherine took the phone from the devastated, broken man.

"Brenda, it's Kathy. Are you alright?"

"Oh, Kathy. I can't believe this. No, I'm not alright. I need to be there."

"Yes, you do."

"Dad…Mom…oh, God. Melissa…poor baby… and you." Brenda broke in to sobs.

"Bren, go ahead. I'll wait."

The phone call ended when the two girls settled down to logistics. "The Secret Service will get me there."

Exhaustion took over. Katherine was purged of emotion; she could not think. As she stepped back into the foyer and looked into the great room she saw KC, Julianne and Melissa wrapped in each other's arms. They seemed to be holding the world together. Katherine retreated to the back door and went to the stables to tell Johnny's horse the dreadful news. She hadn't been there long when she heard footsteps and looked up to see KC approaching the stall.

"We had the same thought. There is some comfort being here with his horse, isn't there?"

She didn't answer, she just stepped back so Johnny's father could embrace the animal's warm head. Katherine knew the live, breathing animal was vital in this cold, dead time. She let KC feel it, too. The tears that had been checked, raged again—this time, with sobs that had broken through the barriers of masculine decorum. KC was holding the horse's head so he could stand. Katherine took his arm and led him to the rickety chair in the corner. Without a word she returned to the animal and dried KC's tears from the horse's face before offering him a handful of oats as a reward for what he had done.

Meanwhile, KC rose to find another chair. When Katherine turned around he pointed, inviting her to sit with him. He still could not speak.

"I don't know how…," she tried.

"I've got to go back to Washington. There are press releases and soon reporters will take away our peace. Even Johnny's death is a public event. This is terrible. How can I let our pain be splashed across the papers…but, I can't stop it. I can block them from coming on to King's Trace but they will mob us all when we leave the driveway." He had a faraway look in his eyes. "I want to stay here where I am close to Johnny, but I can't. I'm not going to ask Julianne and the girls to come to the White House. I will return for our mourning and funeral plans. It is the least I can do. Will you stay at King's Trace?"

"No, I won't stay, but I will be here every day. Just make sure the guardians at the gate let me in and out."

KC was quiet.

"I'll leave you and Johnny here." Katherine stood to go.

"Wait, Kathy—" He drew a breath. "I know you are suffering too." He admitted in a few words what he had not allowed his brain to accept—Johnny and Katherine had a special attachment. Death often takes away denial.

"Thank you, KC."

"You said...you came to tell me..." He looked into her eyes, which were so like Johnny's. "You know why Johnny left?"

Now? I have to tell him now? Her brain was reeling. *Is this the time? Oh God, oh God. I know why he left and I know why he did this terrible thing!* Katherine's knees buckled and she reached back for the chair. She had no control. She could not assess. Katherine wanted to run but her legs would not move.

"Kathy, why did Johnny go?"

"KC." She searched for strength and certainty that she was doing right, "Not now. We can talk later." She tried to rise up from the chair. KC took her arm and held tight.

"Within the hour I will be Mr. President again. I know one thing since taking this office, I have to address things immediately or they become lost. I need to know now if you know why he left—," KC pleaded, hoping for understanding, for comfort. He took her hand. "—tell me, Kathy. You came today to tell me." He drew a breath and held his grip. "Tell me." He begged and demanded.

Katherine could not step back from this time and space. Events brought her here and made demands. She looked at the grieving President of the United States and said, "I believe Johnny left because he found out that you are my biological father—that he and I are brother and sister." In a softer voice full of sobs, she told him, "Johnny loved me differently than I loved him." Katherine tried to draw a breath but her lungs were already full of stale air that she had not exhaled. A long sob kept her from fainting.

It was a crushing statement but so full of truth. Neither could deny the depth of Johnny's feelings and thus his tragedy. As she said it, both KC and Katherine accepted the magnitude and grieved in a new and different way.

"Aghhhagh." KC made a sound that was primal and hardly human. He stood and walked out of the stable. Katherine watched him go. Halfway to the house, he turned and looked back at her holding on to the door of the stable. Then he turned back. She did the only thing she could. She sat again in the chair and waited for him. KC sat next to Katherine and did not say a word. She waited.

"Katherine." He invited anything she could or would tell him.

"I came to see you this morning to tell you all that I had discovered about myself…and you. I'm sure, from the things that Johnny told me the last night I saw him, that he discovered the same truths somehow. The terrible turn of events left me bewildered. KC, I did not want to cause any more anguish here today. This could have waited."

"No, it couldn't. I insisted." He turned and looked at her for the first time since returning to the stable. "I had to know." Almost in a whisper, he added, "I suspected."

Katherine rose. She stood tall in front of the man, humbled in the chair. "I am Katherine Ross, always have been. Always will be." She lifted her head. "Is there something you want me to do, now that you know?" Katherine spoke from the place that revealed what kind of person she was. It was a position of strength and confidence in the face of the truth.

"Nothing. I can't think of anything you need to do, Kathy. Just be here for us the

next few days. We all need you as we begin the one thing we have to do now and that is

Johnny's funeral" KC humbly added, "I need to say this. It is true. I am your father."

Katherine stood, inviting him to stand, too. "No, KC. I have one father, James Ross—my only father. In every sense of the word, James Ross is my father, was my father and will always be my father. We may have issues about this biological thing but we won't discuss them now."

There were things KC should have said to Katherine. Concerns he needed to address. But, today the powerful man was a grieving father and a bungling weak man whose past mistakes rendered him impotent. He was nobody's leader; he was nobody's strength. He was nobody's role model; he was nobody's comfort. He could not even lead, strengthen, or comfort himself. KC would have to cross the lawn and return to the house and family circle by himself. Julianne was no doubt waiting for him, but not with open arms and consolation. *Johnny's dead and Julianne hates me.* The President bent over in pain.

It was Katherine's turn to leave the stable. She walked away from KC with her back straight, her head held high and determination in her step. She would go into the house and help Julianne with arrangements for her beloved brother, Johnny.

KC watched Katherine begin her walk from the stable, knowing that they could not walk the path together. "Katherine," he quietly said her name. *What a fool, I am! Thinking I could bring you into our family by calling you Kathy and pretending that made things right.* He left the stable muttering "Julianne." Walking, hardly lifting his feet above the newly mown grass, he hung on to the one thing he knew—he was President of the United States. That arena was where his self-esteem was high and polished. King's Trace was no longer his paradise. It rebuked him. Johnny would never come to the stable again. Julianne had stepped away from their marriage. He only had one choice—be the best President he could.

The knowledge that Katherine had the power to bring his administration down walked around in the dark corner of his mind. *What is she going to do with this?* He had to know—but not today and not tomorrow. Johnny had to be laid to rest first.

CHAPTER 29

1961

It was a long week full of grief and dread as Katherine helped the family prepare for Johnny's funeral. Jonas did all he could, but she only rose above her sadness for short periods. She moved through the whole time as a robot. Julianne, Brenda, and Melissa spent the mourning time at King's Trace. Katherine went there every day, depending on her class schedule. It was good to be with the family and Jonas. It was also good to wander off and think of Johnny and relive their times together. The problem was, each time she started with happy memories, the last night that she saw him blasted through like an off-key trumpet. In the dark, alone in the bed, she recalled the vision she had on the ceiling. She knew it would take a long time to reconcile her feelings with her knowledge that Johnny's love for her led to his death.

The reception following the services was held at King's Trace. Hundreds of people shook her hand and gave condolences without knowing who she was or why she was in the receiving line. They were mostly experienced hand shakers; all looked distinguished. At the first possible moment to slip away, she crossed the lawn to the stables. It took ten minutes to saddle Chessie and gallop away to the wood path that she and Johnny had carved from the virgin forest behind the pond. It felt good. She felt free. Often since Johnny died she would ride this same trail and stop near the river to talk to him. Not today. Katherine was going to let Johnny *go* today. She did not intend to keep him where his torment started. "Go Johnny, go!" she shouted to the breeze rustling the leaves with a sound that could be Johnny running away. "From where you are, we can love each other as we never could before." She went to the bank of the river and urged her horse to go in the water. Standing with the slow current wrapping the horse's hooves, she told Johnny one more thing. "I have always loved you…since the first day of school together." Katherine put her head down in the horse's mane and cried freely. "I have to let you go, Johnny. I've learned from mother what hanging on can do. You aren't holding me any more. I'm not holding you, either." They were her last words to the wind.

Chessie did not move. She put her arms around his neck and with slight pressure from her legs to his side, allowed him to take her to the other side of the river where she dismounted and faced the new feeling coming over her. Deep overwhelming anger filtered through her grief and loss. She, who rarely placed blame, who kept tight control on her feelings, who accepted her mother's plight, who yielded to fate and circumstances, spit out hate along with the name, "KC," Her face distorted and her lips pursed. "You did this!" It was a bitter taste, like bile, that changed her and took her innocence away.

Katherine returned to the house just before dark determined to meet with KC. She wasn't sure what his needs were in this time after the funeral but she was positive what hers were. She needed to say the things that burned in her gut and ask the questions that tumbled endlessly in her mind. *I'll give it two weeks to see if I feel differently.*

Two weeks after Johnny's funeral Katherine called to set another meeting with KC. He was not surprised to get her message.

It lay lifeless and innocuous on his desk among others that were not of an official nature. He rummaged through the pile and took hers in hand.

"Miss Caulkins, did you talk to Katherine Ross?"

"Yes, sir. I asked if she needed to talk to you at the time. She said she would rather you call her back at your convenience."

"Thank you. Please get her on the line." He picked up the phone. "No interruptions until I finish." He waited the long minute or two until they were connected.

"Hello?"

"Kathy, KC."

"I know. The operator told me to hold for the White House." She sounded very matter of fact.

"Do you need something?"

"Yes, sir. I need some time with you. We were interrupted last time if you remember—"

"Remember, Kathy? I'll never forget. I thought we had concluded our talk in the stable that day. I understand all that you said. I know we need to come to an understanding. But, is it vital now? Believe me, I'm not trying to put you off, but I don't have any free time unless you come here."

"Please arrange a time and place." She drew courage with her next breath. "I'd rather not come to the White House."

KC knew he had to see her. He also knew an international incident was about to challenge the country. A quickly planned state visit by the British Prime Minister was on the calendar for tomorrow, the Security Council was meeting at this moment and the Joint Chiefs of Staff were one their way to the White House. Surely nothing else could crowd his schedule—until his biological daughter demanded a meeting.

"Will you be home at the apartment all night?"

"Of course."

"I'll come there but I can't say what time. Most likely very late." He could not spare any time today but would surrender some sleep to see her.

She was very matter-of-fact. "It doesn't matter how late. I'll expect you."

KC put the receiver down and buzzed "Miss Caulkins, get today's duty officer on the line. I need to go see Miss Ross later. Tell the agents."

The President's secretary noted that he seemed more affected by this phone call than the many flying between England and the US all day. She did not realize that he thrived on matters of state. He was a master of diplomacy and unshakeable in his confidence in international circles. It was personal matters that sapped his stamina and strength. He always relied on Julianne for direction and assurance in the family theater. She was no longer at his beck and call. Katherine and Julianne, each in their own way, diluted his power.

<hr />

Katherine waited and napped on the sofa all night. The phone startled her at 6:15 AM. The eastern sky had started to lighten but night held the corners of the room. She shook sleep from her mind and answered.

"Katherine Ross? The White House calling."

"Yes, this is Katherine Ross."

"Miss Ross, this is Amanda Caulkins. He regrets he could not keep his appointment with you. Please understand. He will get back to you as soon as possible."

"Thank you."

"I would suggest that you turn on the news. You will understand why he could not see you. Please write down my personal line. District 9-5555 extension 46. Call me if I can help you before President Kingsley can get back to you."

Katherine heard the urgency in her voice but more than that she heard exhaustion. It came to her that the woman on the other end of the line was worn out.

"Is he alright?" Her anger toward him was dissipating as concern for the head of the only family she had was facing some kind of serious trouble.

"Yes, he's fine. You can offer prayers if you are inclined."

"Are Mrs. Kingsley and Melissa at the White House now?"

"No. They're at King's Trace."

"Please tell the President that I'm going to King's Trace."

The news was terrifying. The whole country was on alert as nuclear war threatened every life, every family, every community, every state and thus—every country. The United States and Russia were head-to-head as the long-festering cold war seemed about to explode into a mighty mushroom cloud of radioactivity. Katherine could not believe her eyes. KC was on the television demanding that the USSR stop shipping building supplies and submarines to Nicaragua. Intelligence reports had confirmed that a submarine base was under construction and Russia was establishing nuclear capability in the Western Hemisphere. His steady, calm gaze into the camera was unyielding. The United States closed the Panama Canal as of midnight last night. Russian ships approaching Central America were surrounded and warned to turn around. Warning shots were fired across the bow of Russian battleships loaded with missiles. The leaders of the two mightiest countries in the world had their fingers on the firing pins of atomic bombs. Tension was extreme.

"Let me be very clear. There will be no proliferation of Russian armaments in this hemisphere. Stop shipping them, Mr. Khrushchev, and begin removing those already assembled in Nicaragua. The deadline is midnight tonight."

Katherine listened to his voice and saw his strength. There was no doubt he was the right man to challenge this Communist threat. KC Kingsley, President of the United States, would lead with strength and conviction. The world was depending on him.

CHAPTER 30

1961

The United States teetered on the brink of war. KC Kingsley was removed from life on the rolling hills of Montgomery County—his focus was global and total.

Katherine turned off the television and lifted Lady Fair from the floor. "I have to go to King's Trace. Lord only knows what I can do to help… but, I'm going." For the first time she admitted to herself that the family on the rolling hills was hers. It was ludicrous to think of a spring break trip—it just wasn't going to happen. She could not ignore the President and scary world and go to the Outer Banks with Jonas now. Life was on hold across the nation and Katherine felt it very strongly.

Classes were over and she did not have to be at Spring Haven until Tuesday. She put a few personal items in the car and yielded to the urgency she felt to be at King's Trace.

The drive was pleasant. There were no signs of the tensions that were pulling the country into puckered seams. Mother Nature had dressed all the trees and forced the grass to green-up no matter what threat was growing in the south Atlantic. Spring was coming to the hills of Maryland in spite of armaments and challenges threatening North and Central America.

The oaks lining the drive to King's Trace were laced with dew that put a sparkle in the canopy as Katherine drove to the portico.

Before going to the door she took a few paces to the left to look down across the lawn. She gave in to the urge to run down the hill to the stables.

The dewy grass dampened her shoes, matching her spirits as she approached the stable. *A little time for me*, she thought as she went for a few minutes of solitude with the horses.

The morning sun was cresting the hills behind the house and although the scene was bright with anticipation, for now, no harsh beams demanded acceptance of a new day. For a few quiet moments Katherine claimed peace, took comfort in the familiar aromas and the early slanted light.

"Steady, boy," she spoke to Chessie as her arms circled the warm brown head. "Miss me?"

"Katherine, I don't want to startle you." Julianne stepped from the shadows. "I came to the stable this morning, probably for the same reason you did—seems the only place that makes any sense."

Julianne advanced to Katherine and offered her embrace, which was immediately accepted.

"I'm so glad you came home."

With that welcome, Katherine broke into tears. She wasn't sure what she wanted to find in the stable but Julianne had it and offered it.

"Don't cry, child. You *are* home."

"I'm crying a lot these days."

"Me, too."

Julianne led her to a pile of warm hay bales that were soaking up the first rays of sun. With a slight tug on her arm she drew Katherine to the amber, aromatic stack. "Sit," she softly invited.

"It's so scary—so scary. What's going to happen? Can KC avoid war?"

"Listen, Katherine. KC can do it if anyone can. Thank God we have him at the helm. There is no doubt in my mind. We are a match for the Russians because of KC. He's an amazing leader."

"You *are* so sure." Katherine was amazed at the sheer strength of the First Lady and her confidence in the President.

"I'm sure. I have this sense that he has been destined to do great things as our President. That belief has made all things possible for us. I mean KC and me. I was destined to be his wife and to see him through to do whatever he has to do—to the point that it doesn't matter what I am or what I think. What matters is that he can do the job that he was destined to do…and that job has just materialized. The only important thing, the only thing that matters, is what he does in the next 24 hours."

"Are you scared?"

"I'm terrified. Here at King's Trace we are scared just as everyone else is."

"Maybe I'm not smart enough to understand what it will take to get out of this situation. Not understanding is another kind of fear. I'm just a college student that just two days ago thought that things in my world were the most important."

"This world crisis sure puts things in perspective."

"Perspective is what I need—I guess."

Julianne straightened her dress and drew a piece of straw to taste the good earth. It gave her time to gather her thoughts for what she had to say.

"Katherine, you have so much on your plate. I'm worried that taking care of your mother and understanding all that goes with that may be too much. I want to help you, if I can."

The moment was emotional. Julianne was so maternal—Katherine so needy. She slouched down into the hay and leaned back to look at the sky through the wide stable door. Julianne took her hand and for the first time, Katherine allowed it because she wanted it. She wanted a *mother's* touch. It was good to relax and let Julianne and the hay straw give comfort. She did not want to talk about problems. She maintained silence so she could be completely in the moment. The lazy joy of the place made her think that nothing mattered—at least for now.

Julianne, with her comforting talk and welcoming embrace, gave Katherine a sense of peace.

The retreat and restful moment was broken by Julianne, who turned her face so their eyes were level. Her gaze was direct; her countenance was gentle but with purpose. She started to speak and hesitated. Katherine could see that she wanted to tell her something. Her gaze softened in response and she felt compelled to accept whatever Julianne had to say. Katherine offered a slight smile.

"I know KC is your biological father."

Katherine sat up with a start and looked straight ahead. *Did I hear right? She knows?* These were the last words she expected and she did not know if she heard correctly or not. Katherine wiped her face for clarity and took a piece of straw from her hair, taking a second to compute the words Julianne had spoken.

"I know KC is your biological father," Julianne repeated—this time as a whisper. "Look at me, Katherine."

Slowly she turned to look at Julianne, who was pale and without emotion on her face. "You are carrying a huge burden and I want to relieve you of…at least this. *It* is not a secret you need to keep."

There were so many questions flying through Katherine's brain that she could not think or utter a single one.

"I hope and pray that if you know I know, you can talk more frankly with me. You, my dear, are the innocent in this. You are not a victim because of your wonderful father, James Ross." She gave Katherine a minute to claim that fact again. "You know you are not a victim, don't you?"

"Yes, I know." Katherine fought back tears. "I understand, even more, how wonderful my father was. I miss him so."

"I know. I know." Julianne offered a tissue as her compassion brought forth Katherine's tears. "If I can do anything to help you, I will. I have held this truth too, too long. It's been heavy on me. Now that you know that KC is your biological father, I cannot sit silently and let the truth be heavy on you." Julianne touched Katherine's back, inviting her to accept or reject all that she offered.

"Julianne, I ju...just learned that my...myself—" She sobbed, stuttered and shuddered. Then she jumped to her feet and began pacing. "When?" A new question became vital. "How did you know...how did you know that I found out?" It was a puzzle. *Did KC confess to her?*

"I want to tell you everything if you are ready." Katherine looked down at Julianne sitting welcomingly on the straw bale and inviting her with a gesture to come back and sit with her.

Here was Julianne, who always treated her as one of her daughters, who always wanted Katherine to at least like her, waiting for Katherine to change her attitude toward the only woman she had observed being a mother in all her life. It was a pivotal moment in their relationship.

She's hurt by this, just as I am, maybe more, Katherine thought, and then another alarming thought crossed her mind, *just as Mother is.*

Before Katherine could return to sit with Julianne she had to recall the years of jealousy she had for Brenda and Melissa. They had the perfect mother. Julianne had always been the glaring example of what she missed.

And now, Julianne opened her arms and asked Katherine to come—physically and emotionally. "Let me try to make things better for you. Let me do something that will help you from this day forward."

While Katherine stood pondering; Julianne waited. *This day had to come. And, here it is. I must be careful. She's fragile. The piper has to be paid.* Even with her brain admonishing, her mother's instinct was strong. Julianne would do all she could to save everyone—especially the children—including Katherine. She was strong and determined because she had already lost Johnny.

"Did KC tell you I found out?"

"KC doesn't know that I know he's your biological father. He told me you called him to meet and then the night after you two met in the stable he said something that told me you knew the secret."

"What did he say?"

"He said simply that he had to make a decision about resigning the Presidency. Walked upstairs and spent the night in the study. We have been married 25 years. A wife knows. I put it together and figured that you told him that you knew he was your father."

"KC is not my father. He may have impregnated Pamela—" Her sobs broke out again—unchecked. "—but he is *not* my father."

Julianne came from her seat to force Katherine to accept the warmth and love she was offering. "Katherine. Katherine. Katherine. Of course, James is your father—a wonderful father. I know." She gently brushed her brow and wiped tears with her bare fingers. Katherine allowed herself this good place and took a seat with Julianne as she continued to embrace her with gentle words. "I love you. Always have. Always will." She squeezed her shoulders and relished the softness returned. "If you'll let me…love has a wonderful quality. It can expand and expand. There is always room to love another person. No need to love anyone else less. Johnny was not the only one at King's Trace that loved you."

Those words went straight to Katherine's heart. She felt love in overwhelming amounts. It was time for Julianne to receive an all-embracing hug—one she had waited for a long time for.

They sat for several minutes thinking while decisions were made. The earthy fragrances and softly approaching daylight magnified every edge, every thought. Finally, Katherine stirred from Julianne's embrace and turned her face toward her, accepting her offer. Without saying a word, she let Julianne know she was ready. Gentleness untied her tense pursed mouth and her eyebrows lifted away the scowl.

"I can answer most of your questions, if you are ready."

"I'm ready. A little nervous."

"I assure you—I love you. All that I say and do comes from my heart. Don't be anxious. Remember you had the good life with James Ross. And *he* made you the woman you are now. Nothing can take that away. You will continue to be the woman you are—in the path you chose for yourself."

Katherine nodded.

"I'll start and you can ask any question at any time."

"As I said before, KC doesn't know that I know. I have known for a long, long time. Pamela told me on her wedding day."

"On her wedding day? You have kept the secret all this time."

"She made me promise. And, I did. We were at the top of those beautiful stairs in your grandfather's house—three stories up. James Ross waited in the grand foyer. Pamela was dressed in a beautiful dress that flowed easily over her swollen abdomen. She and I were both pregnant. I was three months ahead of her—Johnny." She paused so Katherine could put the scene in her brain. "Pamela was shaking and could not go down the stairs where James was waiting. He loved her so much." Julianne paused recalling the scene. "And, Pamela loved him, too. She told me she would not go down and marry him. Couldn't. I have never seen such terror and trembling. I took her in my arms and our wombs were pressed together. Johnny leapt in me at the moment that she felt you move for the first time. It was such a strange and wonderful moment. We were not sure if we felt each other's baby or not." Julianne paused again in revelry. Katherine gently tugged on her hand to go on. "We sat on the top step."

Now Julianne needed time to think. She stood. *Should I tell Katherine everything?* She sat again. With some doubt, she was compelled to pull the truth from the shadows. "Your mother isn't well, although she's very intelligent. Sometimes I think if she were less knowing, life would not have been so hard for her. Anyway, she looked at me and I remember the exact words she said 'It will be your decision, Julianne. You have to decide what I will do. I had meaningless sex one time on my birthday with a man I hate. James knows and now you will know, the father of my baby is KC.' I remember distinctly, Pamela's hand rested on you, Katherine, when she said that." Julianne gently pressed her forefinger into Katherine's abdomen.

Julianne hardly took a breath; she wanted to tell it all now. She needed to release as much as Katherine needed to hear.

"This is your mother's story—not mine, so I won't tell you how I felt about her news. Maybe someday when you carry your own child you will know without me telling you. I thought of Brenda and you and my own unborn child. I was already a mother and I knew Brenda and my baby Johnny would be taken care of—be loved by me and KC. What would happen to you—*Baby you?*" Julianne paused to lift Katherine's chin. "Nothing mattered but two babies bounced together for one unforgettable moment. I would have my Johnny and he would have KC. You needed James Ross. I told Pamela, 'Go to James, Pamela. He will take care of you and your baby.' I never gave her a clue as to how her news tore me apart. I hope I'm not part of the guilt that has ruined her life."

Katherine curled up in the fragrant hay. Julianne stopped talking and rubbed her back.

"I hope I've helped; not hurt."

"You've helped, Julianne. I worried so much about hurting you and the girls."

"They are still a concern."

"I understand. We know what this did to Johnny."

"But, I see that he had to know the truth. Had to." Julianne admitted to Katherine and to herself. "This is KC's burden. Not mine and not yours. I'm trying to make sure that you don't suffer as Johnny did."

Silence settled between them—each lost in thought. It was a comfortable, necessary silence while each thought about the revelations made.

"It is ironic that this has come to a head at this historic time. I have an ironic conclusion, too. KC will handle the world with strength and assurance, but he will be lost with challenges here at King's Trace. And, goodness knows, he will not know how to handle a long denied truth—you." She took a split second to formulate the next thought. "He won't have a clue without me. Not a clue." Julianne felt no softness toward KC—her softness was poured out on Katherine. There was none left for the President of the United States. She could only see Johnny's face, the lost woman in Spring Haven, and the quiet suffering beauty sitting with her on the hay.

"I'm going to be alright but I have to face the truth with KC. Ever since my father died, we have been walking around each other. I didn't know why. Now I do. I'm not sure what it will be in the future, but not the same as the past. Not the same."

"If you want me with you, I will be there."

"No, thank you. I was to see him yesterday and the mess in Nicaragua made it impossible."

The two women stayed quiet for a while, deep in thought. Katherine made a significant decision. "I will go alone and I will face him."

"Good."

"Jonas and I were going to the Outer Banks to meet his parents. It was postponed when Johnny died. I think we can salvage the last couple of days of spring break. Let's go to the house so I can phone him."

"Great idea, Katherine. Go to North Carolina. It'll be good for you."

"I will see KC… just don't know when. I'll pick the right time."

⁓⊙⊙⊙⁓

That night Julianne faced her guilt. *If I hadn't looked the other way, allowing James Ross to save Katherine and KC to sacrifice Pamela, Johnny would not have been a lamb. I did nothing.* "Now, I have to do something!" she proclaimed. Then she went to her knees, confessed the sin of omission and prayed for forgiveness.

CHAPTER 31

1961

At 2:45 in the afternoon—the third Thursday of the month—Julianne, in the back seat of the easily identified black Secret Service sedan, pulled into the back lot of the Prescott Building, Spring Haven Hospital. She gathered her purse and the small bouquet of jonquils and entered the door to the long west corridor.

Barbara Norman was at her post at the nurses' station. "Hi, Julie." She hardly looked up. "You and your ever-present escorts?" she quipped.

"Oh, yes. Coming in right behind me. They're your company for a while."

"She's in her room—waiting. How's the family?"

"Everyone is good. Brenda is coming home for spring break tomorrow."

"How's Handsome doing with the world crisis? It's a bitch, isn't it?"

"Worse than that—scary. You know KC…he's managing."

"Thank God for KC. I have a TV right here, tuned in. I can't get away from it. I have to tell you, I admire that man. What confidence! He makes me feel better, just seeing him."

Julianne waved and went on toward Pamela's room. She did not have time today to chit-chat with her longtime friend—the only person who knew she had been coming to visit Pamela once a month for almost 20 years. The person who made it possible. Julianne did not have to sign a guest register and record her visits, thanks to Barbara.

"Hello, Pam." Julianne advanced to the chair where she always sat in her plain, sad bedroom. Pamela shifted in her chair to acknowledge her guest. She said nothing. She waited.

"You look good." Julianne was aware of the changes the patient exhibited in the year. Her eyes were not glazed and attempts to converse met with greater success. She could hardly wait to see what improvements she would see this month.

"How are you?"

"Today is good."

"That's great. Did you see Katherine on Tuesday?"

"Yes, but she isn't coming next Tuesday. Maybe never again."

"Oh no, you're wrong. She's coming again, just going away this week."

"Away. Yes." Pamela remembered. "She said she was going away, but didn't say where?"

Julianne noted that this was the first question Pamela had asked in her memory. "To North Carolina—spring break. She'll be here Tuesday after next. I know. She deserves a little vacation, doesn't she?"

Pamela nodded.

Julianne went to put the flowers in a drinking glass with water.

"I don't want to play cards today."

"Fine. What do you want to do?"

"Nothing." Pamela turned inward and began to study the flowers printed on her dress. Her fingers traced the design on her lap. Julianne was determined not to let her withdraw.

"Pamela, I want to talk to you. Can I talk? Will you listen?" Many times in past visits Pamela did not allow conversation.

Julianne remembered the raised palm or the hands over her ears. She was relieved that they would not play endless games of gin rummy without talking today. Her silence and statue-stillness was assent and Julianne took heart when Pamela spoke first.

"You have been coming here for a long time." It was almost a question by inflection.

"And I will continue to come."

Relief spread over Pamela as she drew a deep breath. The question she could not ask had been answered. After all these years in a medical fog, she also wanted to know *why* but she could not ask that either.

Julianne was tempted to take Pamela in her arms, but she knew an embrace would terrorize the woman who denied and feared personal contact. And so, she kept her place and waited for the ease that came to their visits after the first volley flew.

Pam straightened her dress as Julianne slipped off her sweater.

"I saw Katherine three days ago. Before she left to meet her boyfriend's parents." Julianne opened the conversation.

"Jonas."

"You know Jonas?"

"Sometimes he comes with Katherine on Tuesdays." Pamela pulled her shoulders in, tightened her knees. Julianne knew the topic was closed.

"Katherine wants me to leave Spring Haven."

"She wants what is best for you."

"I can't." Pamela became agitated "Can't." She got up and began pacing. "I won't." She turned and stepped in front of her visitor. "Tell her. Make her understand. There is *no* place for me." Her face was pained and distorted.

With soft tones she tried to calm Pamela. "It's alright, Pam. She won't insist." Observers were watching through the two-way mirror. If she didn't settle quickly, they would enter.

"She wants you happy."

With that statement, Pamela burst into crazy laughter and the attendant came through the door. Pamela took two steps back from them. "I'm good," she hid her anxiety. "I'm fine," spoken softly without emotion. She quickly took her seat and settled down with a forced smile. No doubt, this incident would be reported in next week's team meeting, noting how well and quickly she settled herself. Julianne was amazed. It was an important event, even to the eye of the nonprofessional.

"My visit isn't over." Pamela announced. The attendant left.

"You are getting better."

"I can't leave Spring Haven."

"You're getting better. That's what matters to Katherine… and if Spring Haven is working for you…well, she'll see it, too. Just as I do."

"Tell her…please."

"I will."

Pamela quieted and her countenance distanced her from her one friend in the world.

"I'm tired."

"Okay, I'll let you rest, now." Julianne picked up her sweater and prepared to leave. She went to the nightstand, pulled out the drawer to place the Hershey bars, which she brought each month. To her surprise, the bars she brought last month were still there. "You don't want the chocolate?"

"No."

"Shall I take the ones here?"

"No, leave them."

This month's visit was over without a fond farewell or loving expression. It was just over.

Julianne spoke to the Secret Service agents waiting in the hallway. "I'm ready."

Barbara looked up.

"Julie, come look." She pointed to the TV. "KC's on. All hell is breaking lose."

She stepped to the desk. KC was on the screen talking. The Secret Service agents came quickly to look too. KC was addressing Americans, Russians, and the world community.

"My fellow citizens, as your Commander in Chief, I am poised to use my constitutional authority to secure the safety and future of the United States of America. I am speaking this afternoon so you will be well-informed of a threat to our peace and security by the Soviet Union's implementation of a nuclear submarine base in Nicaragua. Our surveillance clearly shows the construction of the base, which put nuclear strategic weapons in the Western Hemisphere contrary to Chairman Khrushchev's own words stating that no nuclear missile capability will be established beyond the already established borders. This potential threat is against all the major cities of our Atlantic coast, with extended capabilities depending on the weapons outfitted. The submarine base is a cover for establishing nuclear capabilities from Nicaragua to all points in North, Central and South America. The USSR *cannot* establish offensive military weapons and submarine bases in our hemisphere without consequences. The United States has no choice except to advance against the aggression if the Russian leadership does not abandon this covert plan in Central America. I want you—my family, friends, neighbors, and citizens across this beautiful nation—to know about the Russian actions in Nicaragua. I have sent a message to congress. I have communicated with our neighbors in the Organization of American States as well as our allies around the globe. A shipping blockade has been established; we will inspect all vessels headed to Nicaragua and turn around all that carry equipment meant for this purpose." He paused and looked into another camera for emphasis.

"President Khrushchev, the shipping blockade goes into effect in eight hours. Our nations, the United States and the Soviet Union will have a confrontation unmatched since the end of World War II. Chairman Khrushchev, you can, with a command to your navy or a call on our red phone, end this clear and present danger to the free peoples of the world." He turned back to the other camera, "I will take action with all the power invested in this office and the might of our military forces to end the threat the Soviet Union has created in Nicaragua. It is my duty."

Julianne clutched her chest trying to settle her heart, which was beating fast.

"The USSR holds the fate of the world but…make no mistake, Mr. Khrushchev, our hemisphere will not be intimidated by the presence of your nuclear submarines or your intentions in Nicaragua. We, the countries in the OAS alliance, stand ready to act. I speak for them. We are past semantics about, and denial of, your military development on the coast of our neighbors in Central America. We have the evidence and the pictures." The screen was suddenly full of dated aerial photos. It was obvious that surveillance had been going on for some time.

KC did not blink. He did not miss a beat as he looked directly into the camera and placed his right hand on the red phone strategically placed on his desk. "I await your call, Mr.

Khrushchev, and the world waits for your personal assurances that Russia will maintain the balance established prior to this invasion. We await your assurance that the USSR is abandoning this plan and that dismantling of your submarine base will start immediately."

KC's countenance softened. "I would like to address the citizens of Nicaragua. This military buildup on your coast offers no advantage to you. It puts you in grave danger as the Soviets establish you as a prime target. We are mindful of the danger a strike against this activity would bring to you. Nicaragua is advised to withdraw any alliance with Russia and join us in demanding that the sub base and all the weapons leave your country."

"Lastly, the massive threat of nuclear weapons makes all countries of the Americas one. We are united and strong in our stance against establishing aggressive, offensive weapons that are controlled by a nation outside our hemisphere. It will not be allowed. It will be addressed. Our peaceful nature may be tested, but now as in the past, we have and always will, fight for liberty. Then we can live again in secured peace."

The screen went blank.

"Oh, God. Oh, God." Julianne prayed and tried to gather her thoughts. She knew what she had to do.

"Gentlemen," she addressed her Secret Service detail, "take me to the White House. Please call ahead and have an agent get Melissa from school and bring her to the White House. Barbara, give me a phone. I have to call home."

Suzanna answered with alarm.

"Now, Suzanna. It will be alright. You know KC."

"Yes, ma'am."

"If Brenda or Katherine call, tell them to call me at the White House. Melissa will be there with me. I'll send a car for you. I want you to come to Washington."

"No, Miss Julianne. I'm taking care of King's Trace like I always do. And, I have to feed all those Secret Service men. I'm never alone here anymore and I'll wait here until you all come back home."

"Are you sure?"

"Sure as rain. I'll be here when you all come home. I'll fix a fine meal—everyone's favorites."

It was reassuring just to hear Suzanna's profession of faith. "Don't cook yet. I don't know when..."

"But, you all will come to King's Trace."

Oh, King's Trace, she thought like a prayer. *I'd like to have Brenda and Katherine here—now. Maybe KC can fly Brenda in, but Katherine is on the road somewhere.* Six hours was not enough time for anything. Julianne silently prayed for them and the world as she started for the door that was being held for her. Barbara intercepted her.

"Oh, Julie. I'm petrified." Barbara threw her arms around the First Lady and began to cry. The closest agent stepped forward and warned with gestures that the First Lady could no longer be surprised by an embrace, not even by a longtime friend.

"Barbara," Julianne stepped back, yielding to protocol. "You're a dear. We have to keep the faith. I'd suggest some prayers...and keep calm." She reached out and wiped her friend's tears. "Believe! That's what I'm going to do." She nodded to the men in the dark blue suits. "Gentlemen?" she invited as she went out the door.

The drive to DC was eerie. The roads were empty. At stop lights, no cross traffic waited. The black sedan was waved through the gate unceremoniously. Julianne was back at the White House. "Please tell the President that I'm upstairs." She handed a note to the agent.

CHAPTER 32

1961

She's in the apartment. KC read the note dropped on his desk. "Of course, she came. I knew," he spoke to himself and he slid it into his pocket so he could touch it, whenever. At this time, when nothing was for sure, he knew his wife.

The world was on the edge of disaster. The red phone had not rung in the first hour and battleships advanced against the first Soviet armed vessel. Congress demanded more proof of Soviet intentions. Spain, soft on Russia, was making gestures to undermine the United State's position. *Julianne is upstairs.* It was the President's only comforting thought.

"Mr. President, Prime Minister Diefenbaker is on line one."

KC, with his hand in his pocket, was distracted.

"Mr. President—Canada's Prime Minister—line one." His secretary reminded.

"I'll take that in one minute. Arrange an early dinner in the apartment for me and the First lady. If at all possible, I will spend thirty minutes with my family. Let her know that I will be there at five. Meanwhile, send Joel McGrady to the apartment to brief her on our emergency evacuation procedures." He switched gears. "I'll take that call now."

"Yes, sir," she nodded to his orders before passing the next piece of important information. "The Secret Service will arrive with Melissa in thirty minutes."

For the first time since 2AM yesterday, he thought about his children. "Good." He let a long breath go as he thought of his little girl. "Tell them to set for three. Do you know where Brenda is?"

"She is with the Secret Service at a hotel near Grissom Air Base. She flies in the morning. Arrives 11:45."

"I'll take that call now." He pressed line one and fixed his focus on the Canadian Prime Minister and Nicaragua.

Julianne went straight to the bedroom and plopped across the bed. She gave into crying, not quite sure which of the many concerns she was crying about. The tears left a large spot soiled by her make-up on the coverlet, but she did not care. She was not the organized, poised, controlled First Lady—she was a woman crushed by concern for her brood of children and all the children of the world. A woman, who happened to be in the People's House, upstairs from the most powerful man in the free world and along with everyone on the planet, was marking hours and minutes toward an unknown destiny.

Julianne knew she could not wallow in this pity long, but she did not know how to stop it. The tears continued until her throat hurt. A knock on the door came almost as salvation. She had to do something—answer the knock.

"Just a minute." A washcloth made a minor adjustment to her face. She looked in the mirror. *Terrible, but fitting*, she concluded as she went to the door.

"Mrs. Kingsley, Joel McGrady." He offered his hand. "I'm here to go over emergency evacuation plans."

"Come in; have a seat."

"The President's immediate family will evacuate with him and high government officials. I have a plan outlined here for you." He handed her a laminated diagram. "All you need to know is to come to this point—" He placed his finger on the page, "—as soon as the alarm sounds. An escort will take you from there. I don't have to tell you that you must move quickly. I suggest you place things you want to take beside the door *now*—ready to go. Mrs. Kingsley, in this kind of emergency, there really aren't many *necessary* things. No point. You see?"

"Yes, I see."

"The place of safety will have all your family's toiletries and the personal items that you packed months ago. They're already there. When the alarm sounds there's no time to assemble anything. Understand?"

"I understand."

"You and your family will be taken care of just as the President is. Are you alone here?"

"Yes, now. My youngest daughter will be here any minute."

"Just need to inform you. If any personal friends or staff comes here, they will not go with the President as you and your children will. You are instructed not to invite anyone here for that purpose. If you have guests, they will be secured with White House personnel—not with you and the President. It is all outlined on the back. Please read all the instructions before you need to. Consider this briefing as insurance against ever needing it." He smiled, trying to lighten the message.

"Thank you, Mr. McGrady. I will."

"Now that you understand all that, I have to tell you one more thing. There'll be a drill later tonight. The alarm will sound but the light—" He pointed to the blinking lights over the door. "—will remain green." His demeanor changed for emphasis. "If in fact, it is a drill. Gather your things and go to the assigned place at the head of the stairs. If that light is red—it is not a drill. The danger is real." He started for the door and turned. "I'm assigned as your escort for tonight's drill. It is a pleasure serving you, Mrs. Kingsley." Joel McGrady made his exit.

She had hardly taken a seat to read the emergency plan when another knock on the door brought Melissa, who did not wait to be invited in.

"Mommy! What's happening? They wouldn't let me see Daddy. Made me come straight here when I knew I was passing his office."

Julianne embraced her and led her to the sofa. "I'll explain." She hadn't noticed Miss Caulkins standing in the door. "Oh, Miss Caulkins, come in. I was excited to see Melissa."

"That's fine, Mrs. Kingsley. Nice to see a warm family greeting on a day like today. Dinner is going to be served in the family dining room at five. The President is trying to clear things so he can eat with you. I hope he does. Frankly, he needs that. Does that meet with your approval?"

"That's fine."

Julianne turned to Melissa. "See, Daddy'll be here for dinner. He has a lot of work to do today. We'll be lucky to have him at dinner."

Brenda's call came next. "Mom, I'm frantic. The White House or the Secret Service or somebody decided not to fly me home tonight. I'm upset I can't get there today—it will be tomorrow. How's Dad?"

"I haven't seen him yet. Won't until dinner. If you can't get to the White House, you are probably better off out there. The Secret Service will bring you here. You're coming home. Remember, Sweetie, you are the daughter of the President. Things are not done our way. What time will you be at Andrews?"

"11:25—in the morning. I hope those crazy Russians don't do something foolish. I'm scared for Dad, you, and Melissa. Not sure Washington is the place to be."

"Don't worry about us. They won't let anything happen to him and we are going to be right beside him. There are families all over the eastern seaboard scrambling. I think we are more fortunate than most. I'll talk to your father about whether or not coming tomorrow is a good idea. Stay close to that phone."

"Where's Katherine?"

"She left for the Outer Banks of North Carolina about noon. I can't call her while she is on the road. Katherine's a smart girl, she'll figure out what is best. I do wish she were here, though. I'll tell the switchboard that calls from you and Katherine are to come right through—no matter the time. Don't hesitate. I want to keep you assured. The television can scare the bejeebers out of you."

"Okay, Mom. It's terrible, isn't it?

"Keep praying, darling. And, I love you very much."

"I love you, too. I know I can't call Dad. I talked to him for about a minute on the Secret Service phone. He's too busy to call me again. Make sure he knows I love him, too… and he's the man who can save us. I know." Mother and child were fighting tears. "Can I speak to Missy?"

While the girls talked, Julianne re-read the emergency plan and put family pictures by the door.

Another tense hour passed. Fervent activity filled the war room where the Joint Chiefs, the Security Council, and Secretary of State circled the table. TV on every wall updated every Soviet position on land and sea as well as the United States Navy's. KC was tied to the phone where he spoke to almost every leader of the free world. He was an amazing bundle of positive energy and only paused momentarily to touch the folded note in his pocket and write a quick note to Julianne.

I'm glad you and Missy are here—makes it possible to do what I have to do. See you at 5:00. Keep the prayers coming.

Love, KC.

PS I talked to Brenda .She'll be alright.

Upstairs, Julianne went through the difficult task of explaining the tension and danger to a ten-year-old. It was impossible to use the television as diversion as her father or military experts were on every channel discussing the situation and showing Soviet ships approaching the United States Navy blockade.

Downstairs the third hour was flying by. KC glanced at the clock and the ominously quiet red phone. KC laid his hand on it. "Son-of-a-bitch. What are those crazy Russians thinking? No way to figure them."

"Mr. President, we have a new intelligence report. Take a look at this. They are talking to Spain. Here's the decoded transcript. Can you believe they think we are bluffing?"

"Bluff nuclear war? We have two hundred years of history—we always mean what we say. God, how could I be more convincing?"

"They are waiting for a showdown, sir. The Joint Chiefs are always ready to act on your command. Invasion plans for Nicaragua are prepared."

KC had to stay alert to their agenda. He paced as intelligence reports were handed to him minute by minute. The ever-changing reconnaissance pictures flashed on the screen. The Russian ship looked like a magnet drawing three US Navy ships closer and closer. "Admiral Busby, are we ready to intercept?

"Yes, sir. Ready to board or blow them out of the water."

"I've given them an ultimatum. Now I've got to give them a way out. I don't believe they think we are bluffing. That is just an intelligence smokescreen. They know we are getting their communications with Spain. Makes me wonder how we deciphered this so easily? Give me some time to think, gentlemen."

"Four hours and eighteen minutes, sir," he was reminded.

KC left the war room and went to the unusual quiet of the Oval Office. The ultimate decision was his—he needed at least fifteen minutes to think. He took his seat at the desk and read the clock. "4:45." Julianne, Brenda, Johnny, and Melissa smiled back at him from pictures taken at King's Trace. He touched each face and traced the line of their chins. His moment was broken by Miss Caulkins.

"Sir, Katherine Ross is at the gate, asking to come in."

"By all means bring her in and escort her to the apartment. Get Mrs. Kingsley on the phone."

The first words the President said to Julianne during this crisis were, "Julianne, I just let Katherine in."

CHAPTER 33

1961

KC had pitted hope against hope. Prayed and prayed. By five o'clock when he went to dine with his family, hope and prayers had not affected the crisis. The Soviet ships were still moving toward Nicaragua and the deadly line the US had drawn through the waters. There had been no dialogue on the Red Phone. Alas, he had to leave the war room without the news he wanted to carry up to the apartment where Julianne, Melissa and Katherine waited. *Three more hours. If only Brenda were here. That damned Khrushchev.* His mind bounced between never-ending concerns.

KC was tense but looking forward to the small escape this half-hour would bring. He deposited his constant companions, holding the ever-necessary brown briefcase outside the apartment door. "Gentlemen, I'll leave the door open." He went in pretending he entered with privacy.

"I hope we don't have to interrupt," the agent remarked as he pulled a chair over to the door and sat.

'Don't we all," was the President's terse reply.

"Julianne," he whispered as his hand grasped the doorknob. He knew when he saw her, the first time in a week, he would see Johnny's face. Would feel the wash of feelings that caused this riff in their relationship. That's how its been for the last five months.

He drew in a breath and opened the door feeling less like the President.

Katherine was at the table. *Oh, God, Katherine.* He realized he had not even thought of his other daughter until her arrival was announced. He took a sense of relief seeing the three women at the table and smiled for the first time in days. *If only Brenda...*

KC had taken two steps into the room when the alarm sounded and he went into action—looking first at the blinking light. "Green!" he announced.

"Julianne! Girls! Move!" He reached out for Melissa's hand and pulled her from her chair. Julianne took Katherine's as napkins scattered. They had hardly gotten into the hallway when Joel McGrady arrived, out of breath.

"This way, Mr. President. Stairs, no elevators." He looked at the stream of women following the President and led them down the stairs to the point where the war room personnel were rushing toward them. The Secretary of State, Generals, and Admirals, and several Congressional committee chairmen watched as KC, Julianne, Melissa, and Katherine approached. At this somber moment there was no talking except muttered relief that the blinking light was not red.

Joel McGrady took a quick look at his charges, noting the unknown girl with Julianne. "Is this your daughter?" he asked Julianne.

"No, this is Katherine Ross,"

"Only your children." He replied before addressing the problem. "Sorry, Miss Ross. You must wait here for staff evacuations. Please step over—" He pointed to the far wall. "—and wait for further instructions—only the Kingsley daughters can go. Let's move!"

In a pause that was only a second or two, but seemed an eternity to Julianne, her heart screamed, her brain demanded—*honesty, KC…courage*. Julianne stepped across the corridor with Katherine.

"Katherine Ross is *my* daughter. We are with you, McGrady. Move." The Commander in Chief barked with authority.

The drill went smoothly down the corridor to the back of the White House and through the sub-basement. McGrady moved everyone quickly to a door marked *No Admittance*. He stopped and checked his watch.

"Two minutes, forty-nine seconds. Good…for a drill, but we can do better, if we have to."

"Sir," he addressed the President, "we will not go into the underground now. On the other side of this door my counterpart is completing the move to the remote White House. The drill report will be on your desk in twenty minutes." Catching his breath, he advised. "I'd like everyone one of you to challenge yourselves to move out quicker. We did well but we can do better, I'm sure."

"Thank you." KC acknowledged McGrady, and turned to his staff, excusing them with a nod. "Julianne—", he took her hand, "—girls, we can have our dinner now." They began to retrace their steps without talking. "We'll use the elevator." Katherine and Melissa fell in behind them, still silenced by the seriousness of the last few minutes.

The dining room was in order—napkins replaced, chairs arranged. Dinner was brought again to the table, warm and fresh as if it had not been interrupted. KC, Julianne and Katherine sat looking at their plates, stunned by all that had just happened

"Daddy, will we have to do that again? Fire drills at school make us go outside. Was that a fire drill?" Melissa took a big bite of chicken and looked up to her father. "Why did we stop at that big door?"

"Missy, that was not a fire drill. It was a drill to protect the President of the United States if ever someone tries to hurt him. Since I'm the President we have to practice going to a safe place. The safe place is beyond the big door. If it is a real emergency, we'll go through. It's important to move quickly if there is another drill or real danger." He smiled but she saw through it.

"Who would try to hurt you, Daddy?" She was frightened.

"No one is trying to hurt me, but they may want to hurt the President. I just happen to be President. Don't worry, dear. I'll be taken care of by our powerful and wonderful country. You, Mommy, and Katherine, too. So we practice for safety's sake, just like your school fire drills."

"Tell you what, Dad. If that alarm sounds again, I'll save time by going right to the door." You won't have to come take my hand."

"Good girl." He smiled the smile that won hearts and votes.

Julianne noted his handsome smiling face with a pang in her chest. She took the first few minutes at the dining table to sort her feelings. She watched KC and Melissa talking and wished she were back at King's Trace eons ago—when her family was intact. *Strange how what seemed so perfect, never was.*

Miss Caulkins appeared at the door and without a word summoned KC from dinner to the war room. His fork was dropped, his dinner uneaten. He left without looking back.

Katherine waited until she was settled in Brenda's room to review the evening events. Downstairs in that tension-soaked corridor her world was challenged, not by nuclear war but by KC's pronouncement. She recalled the words—*Katherine Ross is my daughter*. They had an immediate impact when KC spoke to the security officer, to all the powerful assembled, to Julianne, to Melissa and Katherine, too. Each of them would recall and evaluate his words when the present crisis was over. Katherine had to think about it as soon as she was alone. But first, she needed to talk to Jonas.

"Oh, Kate. I've been waiting for your call. Thank God you are at the White House. When you turned around and headed north, I feared you would change your mind and go to your place."

"No, they're my only family. Just as you needed to be with your family, I needed to be with mine. It is just so hard to be so far from you—especially during all this."

"They will take good care of you there."

"How are things on the Banks?"

"Beautiful, but would be better if you were with me. Looking out on the ocean, it's hard to believe this is real—all this peace is threatened."

"It's real. We just had an evacuation drill. Very real. I can't describe the tension here. Unbelievable" She paused to regroup. "Strangely, you and everyone else in the world know what's happening better than we do. The television is turned off to protect Melissa. And, KC doesn't have time or even want to tell us. We're right above the war room but know nothing."

"I never thought of that. God, the TV's scary. I don't recall ever seeing anything like this flashing on the screen. I see the Russians and our ships, wakes splashing. The showdown time is approaching and so are those warships. It's all on the TV screen." He changed pace. "We have to believe the Russians will turn back. We have to."

"You and I deserve more time—in a world that isn't devastated. I feel like I just found you. Oh, Jonas, I wish I were with you, right now. I didn't expect this desperate, separated feeling."

"Me, either, Kate. But I knew they wouldn't let me in the White House and I was afraid you would stay with me instead of being safely there. I was sure if Julianne or KC knew you were at the gate—."

"Not a problem but, more than that, in order for me to participate in the drill, or the real thing, if it happens, KC had to tell them I'm his daughter. We were at the evacuation door when I was told to step aside. Only the president's wife and children can go with him. I thought I would have to stay with the staff but he spoke up for me."

"Really! What did he say?

"'Katherine Ross is my daughter.'… to security and all the bigwigs. To Julianne. To Melissa. Of course, Melissa didn't give it a second thought—she has looked on me as a sister. Julianne showed no emotion."

"Oh, my dear. How did that feel?" The phone went quiet. "Kate?"

"It shocked me, mostly. I'm still mulling it over. Affected me like Papa's letter and you remember our conversation about that. I'm not letting anything change who I am."

"I can't imagine in that setting with the President speaking. It must have been overwhelming and powerful. Wow!"

"Julianne keeps it real for me. She's a rock. Comforting Melissa, embracing me, and without saying anything, forcing KC to do what is right. Without a word, she expected, even demanded, that I be counted and be allowed to escape any possible danger. I can't imagine what she would have done if KC had left me against the wall in that corridor. Most likely, she would have refused to go without me. I need a role model and she has been in front of me for years. I had to grow up to see it and finally, I have."

"This has been quite a day for you, hasn't it?"

"Yes, but it isn't significant that KC claimed me as his daughter. I don't care about that. Meaningless. My eyes opened to Julianne. I definitely got something important today and it wasn't another father."

"The line is beeping. What does that mean?"

"We have to hang up."

"Call me when you can. I love you." The line went dead before Katherine could tell Jonas how she felt. She turned over in bed and missed her pet. *I could tell Lady Fair—I love Jonas very much.* The tender thoughts in the highly charged atmosphere brought the first tears of the day; she wiped them away with determination.

"I'm not going to cry, because everything will be alright. KC will bring us out of this terror. Jonas will come and get me. Julianne will save us all." She said it out loud because she needed to hear it. "Save us all," she repeated.

Julianne talked to Brenda for the third time that evening. "I can't wait to see you tomorrow." They said in unison and laughed. "Let's talk again after the Soviet ships turn around…and they will. Brenda, never forget we love you, Daddy, Melissa, Katherine, and me." She replaced the receiver slowly not wanting to jar the last words she said.

She glanced at the clock. 6:55. "One hour and five minutes." *I hate electric clocks*, she thought. *We need tick-tocks.* She smiled at her own foolish thoughts that had nothing to do with the crisis at hand. Then she realized she was longing for one of her favorite sounds in the great room at King's Trace. Her head went back on the sofa. Katherine's approach awakened her.

"Hi, Sweetie,"

"I just checked on Melissa. She's asleep."

"Sit, let's talk. How are you doing with all this?" She fluffed a pillow and invited Katherine to sit.

"Most of all, I miss Jonas. Do you think Mother is upset?"

"No, I don't think Pamela cares about the world situation. I'd like to think she is concerned for you."

"I'd like to think that, too." Katherine leaned back and allowed a quiet minute to bond with Julianne. "I was surprised by KC."

"I was pleased. So it took a world crisis for him to do the right thing for you. About time."

"I really don't care except it feels good to have the truth out. I don't need him. He doesn't need me. There is only one thing that matters—he gave his daughter away—," she drew her hands to her chest. "—to the best father in the world. Maybe he had selfish reasons but it turned into a good thing. Oversimplified? Maybe. But, that's *it*—as far as I'm concerned."

Julianne slipped her arm around Katherine, each admiring the strength in the other. And without saying a word, she let Katherine know she agreed with her.

"Less than an hour." Julianne checked her watch. I'm going in to watch Melissa sleep."

Julianne sat in the darkened bedroom and allowed thoughts that had hammered her brain all day. In this quiet place, with only the sweeping sweet puffs of a child's innocent breaths interrupting, she started the evaluation she needed to do. The first thought was the way KC left the dining room without looking back.

That's who he is, she thought. *He has never looked back to see how or who or why about us. I've been in this marriage alone.* She reached over and pulled a lock of hair from Melissa's mouth. She tucked the quilt in tightly and her heartstrings tugged, overwhelmed with love. A sudden epiphany came. *KC never felt his heartstrings tug over me or the children. His heart is in this house.* "Pure and simple." She whispered as she kissed her sleeping baby girl. "Pure and simple." This time, thinking of the child.

Julianne stood up and straightened her back for what she knew she had to do. "KC is who he is and right now he is the President of the United States, trying to save us all. That is a kind of pure love, too. And, it is the *only* thing he *can* do." She talked to herself as she left Melissa's bedside.

The bedroom reverie was interrupted by Katherine. "Miss Caulkins is on the phone." Julianne planted one more kiss on Melissa and rushed to the phone.

"Yes."

"The President wanted you to know that the Soviet ships have altered their course from Nicaragua. He'll be speaking to the American people at 9:00. And, he would like you to come to the oval office when he speaks."

"Please tell him I'm on my way."

She spoke to no one, only the tense air. "I stand corrected. He looked back at me, just now."

"Mrs. Kingsley, you have twenty minutes. Please be in the oval office ready to appear on camera." She was used to such demands, even from a generic Secret Service agent. Her navy blue basic dress with a red scarf would do. No doubt the president would have on a red and blue tie. She recovered her ignored hairdo with amazing products she kept on hand for just such an emergency. It was easy to go into gear with such good news. Her relieved heart renewed her energy.

"Katherine," she gently called to the dozing girl. "The crisis is averted. The Russians turned back, praise God. We can breathe easier." She rushed in to give and get a warm hug. "I have to go down to appear with KC on TV."

"Oh, that's the greatest news. I got you covered with Melissa. I'll be watching."

Julianne took just a minute to kiss her sleeping baby's forehead before joining the agent waiting in the hallway.

"Good, Mrs. Kingsley. You're ready with time to spare." He led the way to the elevator.

"Let's go." The change in atmosphere was permeating the residence. Relief was on every face as she approached the Oval Office.

The door was opened for her and she went into the epicenter of KC's world. Lights, camera, newspeople, cables, microphones and producers all focused on the presidential desk. Julianne expected to see KC seated there, but it was empty.

"The President will be arriving in a moment, Mrs. Kingsley. Your seat is right here." She was guided to a chair behind and to the right of the desk. She nodded to the cabinet members and military men in full regalia seated to the left of the desk.

New excitement permeated the office when KC entered as applause and directions exploded. He took it in stride and came in with sure steps and complete confidence, accepting and rejecting directions— it was obvious— he was in charge even in this media frenzy. Julianne smiled to herself just as he noticed her. He pushed a make-up artist aside so he could come to where she was sitting.

"Julianne," he greeted her. "Julianne," he repeated. "I wanted to bring you the news myself." He stepped close so he could speak privately. With a quick motion he signaled to his assigned agents to make room for him to talk to Julianne. Three agents moved all the television crew back three steps as he took the chair next to her.

"Give me a few minutes," It was a demand, not a question.

"KC— a great day. Congratulations."

"Thank God. I've never been so scared in all my life. Are you alright? Melissa? Katherine?"

"Fine. I'll call Brenda as soon as this is over."

"Thanks for being here." He smiled his winning smile and she responded with a look of joy as they embraced. A camera flashed. This image of the President and First Lady at this historic moment was published all over the world.

KC went to his desk to tell the world that disaster was averted. The United States and Russian had moved back from the brink of nuclear war.

"My fellow Americans, I bring you good news tonight...."

It seemed like a terrible nightmare, a horrible dream. Relief spread across the nation as it moved through the beautiful halls and rooms of the White House like a light. Truly everything looked brighter. It was hope, and until it was restored, no one had noticed how dim the world had seemed.

President Kenneth C. Kingsley took a place in history— likened to Lincoln and FDR. These events did not build his ego, they justified him. Today put his life in perspective.

Julianne took his hand as he offered it and they walked together out of the Oval Office.

CHAPTER 34

1961

Julianne and KC walked out of the Oval Office together. "You're going to call Brenda?"

"I'll call her now. She must have seen us on TV." KC took her arm gently.

"Have the operator transfer the call to me, too. I want to at least say hi." They
walked in silence until they reached the elevator. "I'm tied up for a while. Will you come
back down later? I'll send a message when all this," he waved his arm at the television
crews wrapping things up, "is gone."

"Certainly. Official?"

"No, casual—you and me. It might be late—not sure if I have another agenda
back in the war room but there are things on this desk."

"Not a problem."

It was late when the message came. Julianne had dressed down and dozed in a chair in the new quiet that seemed to blanket the White House. As she looked in the mirror, she remarked, "Amazing how tensions and relief spread though this house, in and out of offices, up the stairs, too. Tonight *feels* so different." She ran her fingers through her hair. "I'm different." She drew her fingers across the deeper lines around her eyes. "Changed."

The First Lady went to meet the President in the Oval Office again. He was waiting at the door and without a word took her elbow to guide her to the patio. The temps were moderate and the croaking of spring frogs filled the air.

"I had jackets brought for us," he said as he slipped into his and wrapped her shoulders.

"Thank you." Julianne pulled the jacket close. "Lovely evening. Surprisingly warm." She relaxed a bit, glad to be beyond the powerful white walls of the House—albeit barely. She took a deep breath of fresh spring air and gathered her strength, which always seemed to be diluted when inside. Things were not right between them, but years of marriage removed static and she relaxed in that comfort. *He cares, as much as he can*, she thought.

"We can talk freely here. You know I want to take you in my arms, don't you?"

"KC—," she admonished. His arms fell after placing her jacket.

"I know." He backed away, paced a circle and stopped to face her across the patio and went to the reason he *had* to talk to her tonight. "Katherine *is* my daughter, Julianne." He started with the words—the reason—the explanation. "The emergency drill was not my choice of time to tell you." He walked toward her believing that he had to explain his admission and expecting her recriminations.

In the soft light, he saw her unchanged countenance. "I already knew that, but in that moment, I didn't know what you would do. You needed to speak up."

He drew her to a chair. "You already knew? Katherine told you?"

"No, Katherine didn't. Pamela told me on the day she married James."

KC went to his chair and sat down heavily. "You knew. You've known all along?" His head went down on the table. "All this time?" He wrapped his arms around his head. His psyche was having trouble shifting from his exalted position of hours ago to this defeated place. "All this time," he repeated as a dark cloud of ugly truth engulfed the gentle spring evening. Julianne waited for KC to say something, but the man who could explain nuclear crisis to millions could not find words to explain anything to the woman he loved.

Classic, she thought. *Hopeless*, she knew.

"Katherine is remarkable—smart—level-headed and beautiful. And James was a wonderful father for her. Your loss." His first reaction was to nod agreement and let his posture relax. She was not going to lash out at him. He wanted her words, which would tell him how to think and how to feel. When he tried to speak, Julianne put up her palm; she was not finished with her thoughts. "I see no way for you to get back what you have given away—your daughter." She let her words soak in. Silence filled the suddenly intimate patio. "Fortunately KC, Katherine does not need you."

"I wanted to tell you. And when fate brought her to live with us, I wanted to tell the world." He spoke slowly and deliberately

"But, you didn't." Her words cut him like a knife. "See what happened because you didn't?" It was rhetorical; she did not expect an answer. "You could have given your responsibility a shadow of validity but, you didn't."

"Julianne, the lie had its own life—the beautiful girl... I... James..." He stammered. His sentence did not make sense, his logic was confused.

"Beautiful, yes."

"I came to love her while she lived with us."

"Unfortunately, so did Johnny." She let her words hang in the night air. They did not evaporate or fade. They echoed with life, born from truth and swaddled with utter despair.

If Julianne had looked at KC she would have seen tears that ran unchecked from his eyes. She might have seen the shudder that went down his spine, and the ugly look on his face. But she kept her eyes down to keep her pain in check. "Katherine will be fine. I'm going to make sure of that."

Anger flared. She had one question that had to be thrown. "You knew Pamela's condition. How could you touch her?" The anguish was deep. Julianne stated the one thing she could not rationalize. For two decades she suppressed this thought and with a voice two octaves lower, she repeated. "How could you touch that poor girl?"

No answer passed across the patio. KC wished he knew the answer. Julianne was sure she knew it. She drew a breath and went on.

"Pamela is the crime." She spoke with a catch in her voice, hardly above a whisper. "And, I share your guilt."

"Guilt? You have no guilt, Julianne." For the first time he spoke with authority. "God, if I could go back…change things. No guilt, Julianne. Not you."

She rose to stand before him and give a testimony that she had rehearsed for years.

"I'm guilty, too. I knew and I let the lie, that you decided to live by, stand." She spoke slowly as though she were on camera and the world had to understand. "I let Pamela suffer. I stood by and let you give your daughter to James. I watched Pamela go out of her mind. I did it to save my family. Little Brenda, unborn Johnny, you and me. I'm as guilty as you, for different reasons. I saw the happy child with a wonderful father and, like you, I thought that justified the means. I lived with the lie and so did Pamela." Julianne turned to face the anonymous city and spoke into the universal darkness. "Compliancy, weakness, expediency are no less a sin than seduction." She gently let her fist hit the table with a dull thud that echoed through the night. "I am guilty, too."

"Oh, God. Oh, God." KC was sobbing. "I never wanted to hurt you and—," he could hardly say it. "—and, Johnny."

"No, you didn't and neither did I... but, we did. You decided to live a lie and I decided to live the same lie. Katherine is a blessing in all this, but Pamela and Johnny paid the price." She whispered, "KC, there is always a price." He did not say a word; he knew she was not finished. "Sometimes the cost is never paid and can be owed a lifetime. I cannot forgive you for not going to look for Johnny. You," she pointed, and although he was more than an arm's length from him, her finger burned his chest, "did not go."

The man who only hours ago saved the world from nuclear disaster sat broken on the patio of the Rose Garden, the White House, Washington, DC, shaking his head from side to side. He needed Julianne so much and she was lost to him. All he could do was wait. He was a failure in this arena, but just inside the tall French doors, within his house, KC was strong, powerful and most importantly—loved. He wanted to run inside but he waited for Julianne and words he knew were coming.

"I'm going to support Katherine as she works through this. Her future will not be tainted by the past, if I have anything to say about it. Not sure what I can do for Pamela."

"Brenda and Melissa?" He asked.

"They are all that is left of our family. I don't have to tell you their priority. It's my question, KC. What about Brenda and Melissa? You still have time to be a father to them. Let them in…do for them all that is too late for you to do for Katherine and Johnny."

"I love them. You know that." His words were soft.

"Yes, I do and I promise you I will not do anything to diminish their love and respect for you. It isn't easy to be the daughters of the President, but they are good, strong young women. I want them to grow and learn about their father and his years at the helm…here." She pointed into the White House. "If you want me on my terms, I will fill my official capacity here. Melissa and Brenda will be here, too. If you want me as First Lady, I will be—for the last two years of this term. I'm sure you will have a second term and Brenda would make a perfect hostess. You can explain me into a minor role. No one beyond this patio needs to know the changes in our personal lives. I challenge you to get to know your girls. You'll be surprised. We must do all we can to keep them nurtured in spite of our—," she paused, "—situation."

"I love you, Julianne."

She turned away and faced the worst part of this juncture in her life. If she was determined to go forward she had to deny what was left of her feelings for him.

"I can't love you anymore, KC." In her simple words she told him the finality of her feelings without denying the past.

"Divorce?" He paused.

"No. Let's postpone that discussion. This has been a remarkable day for you and our country. You've just done a great job and I will not take any of that away from you. Go, KC, do what you were born to do. I've never made your road more difficult and won't now. Somehow we will find a way to live in the public eye and we will not be the first couple in the White House who have provided a false picture of ideal. Won't be the last, I'm sure."

"No chance? No chance we can... get back to our life at King's Trace... no," defeated he admitted, "none."

"You're right. I don't see any possibility that we can go back to what we were at King's Trace. It's up to you, tell me what we can do...say, starting tomorrow."

It was too much, coming too fast. He needed clarification. "You'll live at the White House and be First Lady?"

"Yes. I'll stay in the apartment in separate bedrooms," she pointed to the upstairs window, "when necessary because of official duties. But, my home will be King's Trace. That will be my private place, if you will agree."

She was asking him to give up King's Trace. It was a terrible blow. *No King's Trace? I'm exiled.* He paced back and forth. He started to speak twice—first to fight; then to yield. Julianne was the epitome of patience. She knew what she was asking and she knew he would give it to her. She only had to wait until he realized it was the only way he could have what he wanted.

"I agree, and I'll get a townhouse in the city. The media will get tired of trying to second-guess where you are between the three places." He spoke as a politician, already managing implications.

"I'll be at King's Trace." She reiterated.

"Understood...but a townhouse here may give you even more privacy at King's Trace. Thank you for continuing here." Gratitude oozed in his voice. "I'll always try to make it easy for you...and I'll always want you back."

Julianne did not respond; she would not even look at him. She used the black night to shield herself against his handsome, winning ways and soft smile.

"Brenda graduates next May." Julianne changed the subject. "You need to ask her to be your official hostess the last year of this term, surely for your next term."

"I'd love to have her here, perhaps as your secretary. You are my First Lady." He began to apply diplomacy, hoping for a better outcome. "She can step in at times as hostess and you can give your special philanthropic interest your attention. Best for both of you."

She tried to keep her tone soft but she began to feel his power. "No. No more than this term. "I can't," she touched his hand. "I've already left this life. It's your life; not mine. A curtain has pulled back and I see exactly who you are and how perfect you are in your world, but more importantly, I see who I am and I cannot act as if it were otherwise. Can't you see? I've struggled to support you, knowing what I have known, while holding on to what is important to me. It's time, KC, for me to have a voice. Here, under your—" again she searched for the word, "—your influence, your power, our marriage becomes less and less as you belong more and more to the world. Here I have to be someone I don't want to be. And, you must be all that you can be. I must go and do the things I must do. Please don't work to keep me here any longer than I have to stay."

KC's shoulders bent down and inward. "Julianne, I can't do this without you."

"Oh, Ken. You just did." She softened her tone and seduced him to yield to her thinking. "You don't need me to sit for the cameras for ten seconds. I will admit that if I still loved you, I would bask in the light with you. But, we have moved in different directions. I'm seeing clearly for the first time in years. And, I believe you'll come to see things as I see them. I don't love you. You don't really love me either; you just haven't admitted it to yourself.

"That's not true. Just not true." He could not give up.

"You love your work. It's your life. I gave you a background and at times the background you assigned to me was ugly, very ugly. I've got to do something about that."

"You're being unfair. I don't understand. Ugly background?"

"Ugly, yes. The truth about Pamela."

"Please, Julianne, let's keep this to us and what is important."

I was! Her brain screamed. He still did not get it.

"Sure, Ken. I'll just say this." She spoke in sympathetic tones because she knew, in all honesty, that he never could understand the very reason she had to leave him. "I cannot mourn our son without doing all in my power to correct what was done to Katherine and Pamela."

KC rose suddenly to his feet. He could not stay in this conversation any longer. He was finished. Like a political caucus or a government meeting—enough was enough. He knew that he could not answer her points and he would never see why Julianne was concerned about Katherine, who was obviously doing well, and Pamela, who would never do well, no matter what anyone did. He closed down.

The patio and warm spring night became stifling. Julianne was finished with the night and KC. She could tell he had given all he could. She crossed the patio without emotion. If she had learned one thing in their marriage, it was the limited attention span KC could give to family matters and he had exceeded that tonight.

They went through the tall French doors different people than an hour ago. The President escorted the First Lady to the staircase.

"Good night."

"It will be fine, KC. You'll see." Julianne, always the comforter, gave him all she could.

He turned without another word to go his way. After two steps he felt her hand on his arm so he paused to listen without turning toward her.

"Katherine's upstairs. She needs to see you tomorrow before she leaves."

"I'll see to it."

"I hope you'll think about what you need to say to her."

"I will do all I can," he turned to face her, "to protect her from the press by admitting my parentage or hiding it…whatever is necessary. That's what *you* want. Right?"

"I have no say in this but I want her protected and I think she wants that too."

"Last night everyone in the hallway believed I said what I said, to keep her with you in the emergency. I doubt they took my pronouncement literally. This is not fantasy land. No magic will give everyone what they want but rest assured, Julianne, I'll do all I can for Katherine. I know that is what you want…and I want it, too."

"When she comes to see you, ask her what she wants."

"I'll do whatever she asks." It was a generous offer but Julianne doubted he could.

"Good. KC, if there was ever a time for you to think beyond yourself, it is now… with her. Be nothing but a father. It is your *first* and last chance."

He could only nod agreement.

"Sometimes we can show our children love by giving…other times by taking away."

KC was not sure what she meant, yet hoped when he was with Katherine, he would.

CHAPTER 35

1961

Katherine was on the phone with Jonas when Julianne walked sleepily from her room the next morning. The sun was pouring in the wide window lighting a new day for the nation, for the President, for the President's family, and especially for the First Lady. She felt good—satisfied that today her life was *right*.

"I'm driving to the Outer Banks this afternoon. Jonas is meeting me at Manteo. He said it will take about six hours. I'm sure I can do it…and I want to go" She said with unusual drama and emotion. "What do you think, Julianne?"

"I'm sure you can do it. Please leave early enough so you meet him before dark."

"Yes, that's what he said, too. I'm all packed. If I leave before noon…"

"Good." She walked over and gave the sweet girl a kiss on the forehead. Katherine surprised her with a hug around her waist.

"Katherine," she whispered lovingly as she returned the hug. "If you want to talk to KC, he's expecting you."

⁂

"So, you are going to North Carolina? To be with Jonas' family?" KC greeted Katherine warmly. "Come, let's walk on the grounds. The early flowers are in bloom." He still had jackets from last evening. With a nod he dismissed Miss Caulkins and opened the door. "I know we need to talk. I'll talk about anything, everything, whatever you want. The White House is daunting—" he pointed at the ever-present Secret Service agents who joined their walk several yards behind, "—and doesn't invite relaxing, but we will do our best. Okay?" He took Katherine's elbow and guided her to the path. "Nice, isn't it?"

"Yes, beautiful." She was anxious to start and moved quickly to the path. "My thoughts are very simple, KC. James Ross is my father."

"Of course he is. An excellent one."

"You—" She started to speak, he interrupted.

"Kathy, I—"

"Katherine," she corrected.

"Katherine, it is," he smiled to put humor in her correction. "Ever since you were a tiny little girl, I have thought of you as James' child. His love for you left no doubt in anyone's mind as to who your father was. If it seemed that I abandoned you or forsook you or did not care for you—I understand and admit that shame. For many years it seemed important that the biological secret be kept. And—" He paused before saying the difficult words. "—I was selfish."

"I don't care about you or this biological thing or even your motivation. I know who I am."

"Of course you do. I'll do whatever you want. Tell the world or not."

"I don't want to tell the world anything. I'm not the daughter of the President and don't want to be. I don't want to be on tabloids." She was finally lashing out in anger. "I *am not* a lie." Her eyes flashed with unusual ardor. "My life *is not* a lie."

He wanted to put his arms around her, pat her back and say it will be alright but KC knew his sperm planted long ago did not give him that right. He took an unusual stance for a politician; he let his adversary speak without interruption.

"I'm Katherine Ross. Not Kathy, that's for sure. I appreciate all you and Julianne did for me when Papa died." Her heart felt an old pang at the mention of his death; then she took a breath and continued. "If I owe you anything, anything..." It was hard beyond belief.

KC interrupted. "Nothing! You owe us nothing."

"I want to clear the air and look you in the eye." She stopped and faced him. "I am not a lie," she reiterated in a soft whisper.

For the first time since the rainy night that James Ross died, KC looked Katherine in the eye. Each saw the swelling of tears in the other. He did not look away.

"Katherine," he spoke softly. "You are not a lie because of James. I'm in awe of him and you, too.
And, I hope that because of James, you will not hate me. Because of James my mistakes have not kept you from being the lovely person you are." He had said the right thing with absolutely no political benefit. *Validation, she wants validation.* It was hard to keep his mind focused in such an emotion-charged time. *Not what I want, not what had to be admitted to the world, not what had to be a secret— but validation.* The daughter he had given away wanted to be validated and KC Kingsley was the only one who could do it.

He reached and took her arm with a firm grip. With a slight tug she pulled and then let him have it.

"You are Katherine Ross. Daughter of James and Pamela Ross. Strong, capable and definitely not needing anything from me. The future is yours and, Katherine, your past is yours also. It is pure, right, and true because you have had a father, a good father, to guide you. I will thank God every day for James. I want you to know one thing." He demanded her gaze with his own. "If there is anything I can do for you, it is done."

"Someday I may want to know all about my grandfather and the business arrangements but now I have no interest. None. I will say without knowing the circumstances—I'm grateful for Papa and prefer to think that God made sure I got the *right* father."

She made a strong, cutting point and then eased in her passion as the conversation continued. They sat and talked, even smiled a bit as they recalled efforts to make her into Kathy Kingsley. Miss Caulkins came twice to interrupt and he sent her away. This time had come and both he and Katherine knew it would not come again.

"Mother hates you."

"I'm sorry about that. Very sorry. I kept up with her treatment and she never seemed to improve." She went quiet with the mention of her mother. "All I can do is offer any help you think would improve her situation. Should I go to Spring Haven and tell her I'm sorry?"

"No, KC. Absolutely not."

"I'll do whatever you want me to do."

Katherine could only nod. Neither intended to talk about Pamela. He took a deep breath of relief. "Katherine, you can bring my administration down with this, you know that. I will not stop you or deny the truth. This lie has been way too costly. You are here in the White House. If you want a press conference to reveal the truth, I will arrange it. I ask you not to do it. I have no right but I ask it."

"Here are the only things I want from you. Maybe I have no right to ask, but I will."

"As I said, anything."

"I need a family—Julianne, Brenda and Melissa." There was a small sob in her voice but sheer determination held it back. "I need King's Trace, the place where Johnny's memory lives. I need to finish school and make a life but still have a place to come home to."

KC was well aware that she did not need him—that her recitation, which seemed hard for her, did not include wanting anything from him. He swallowed hard. "It's yours, Katherine, without asking. Those are things you don't have to ask for."

"I don't want to tell the press anything. Keep me out of your life here." She looked at the White House sparkling in the spring sunshine like a flower.

"Of course, you are the daughter of my deceased business partner." He paused for emphasis. "No more; no less." It hurt for him to say it but it was the only way he could hope to have even a small part of her. And he knew, with the parting of ways with Julianne, he would not be at King's Trace when this daughter was there. He would not even have a minute part of the daughter he gave away.

Katherine was ready to leave. She stopped walking and turned to KC. The sun lit the back of her head and gave a glow that burned into his memory bank. He was overwhelmed with her beauty, her sharp focus and her *transparency*. With a slight smile below her serious eyes she gently touched his arm.

"I will not come to the White House again."

They parted without saying good-bye. KC and Katherine simply walked into the White House and separated. He could not help himself. He turned and watched her until the elevator door closed.

Like a starburst everyone scattered from the White House. Only KC was left in the center. He got the call from the Secret Service that Katherine had departed and he knew she was going to Jonas on the Outer Banks. Then Brenda stopped in the office before going shopping with friends and then to King's Trace for the last days of her spring break. Julianne's secretary called to say Melissa was coming down to say good-bye before she and her mother drove to King's Trace.

In the fading light of the starburst, KC sat in a dark mood—for a short time. In truth he was pleased and contented with Katherine's position. She was not going to be political. Brenda and Melissa were lights in all of this darkness. And, he believed someday he would get Julianne back, almost like a running for office. He always won.

Then he looked around his arena. The Oval Office, the mighty seal, the power fired his spirit and he thought of his family with a sigh and a short comment, "I'll be the best damned President." Then he slammed his fist to the desk.

CHAPTER 36

1961

Jonas wanted to walk on the beach as soon as possible after Katherine arrived. She met his parents and had barely opened her suitcase when he tapped on the door with an invitation. "The beach is calling."

It was a typical spring day on the Outer Banks. The breeze was warm and the sun strong. Soon the strollers had their sweatshirts tied around their waists.

"It's so warm. I didn't expect it."

"Time to soak in the sun, Kate. We are close to the Gulf Stream here. Nice," he agreed. A large piece of driftwood offered a seat. Gulls circled in and landed, hoping for a picnic. The panoramic view of the Atlantic and the beach that was stretching miles and miles to the north and south left her breathless. The roaring surf sang to her sagging spirit as the vast ocean embraced her. Her mother, the White House, and school seemed far, far away. Suddenly she ran to the water's edge to splash and giggle as the water soaked her rolled-up jeans. Her feelings magnified and her kicking became less fun and more intense—almost symbolic. *Spring Haven,* she kicked. *KC* she kicked. *KC!* She kicked again. When she turned from the ocean to look back at Jonas, she stopped splashing, stood spent at the edge of the surf and yielded to the love she had for him at this time, in this place.

Jonas had no idea what was going through Katherine's mind. He watched her with delight. *I love you…and today you are free on this beach.* He watched her embrace, relish, and claim it. He saw her accept the true gift—one of release and definition with the universe. And he loved her more at this moment than he thought possible.

Jonas ran to the surf and Katherine as if ten seconds was an eternity. Finally, she was *here*. He slipped his arms under hers and lifted her from the foam. Katherine arched her back and pointed her legs behind her and spread her arms—she flew like a gull as he lifted her high and went round and round. In mid-laugh, he kissed her open mouth. His lips were gentle, searching. She came back to earth and waited for the next kiss. "Jonas" she whispered. "Jonas" she repeated. They were the only words he allowed when she drew a breath between his kisses. In a lover's dance, they swirled together over the warm sand and fell together at the base of the dune. And for the first time in her young life, Katherine felt the full body embrace from a man. Kisses were sweet, hinting passion. Katherine was generous. Jonas was cautious.

Two strollers smiled at the young lovers claiming a place by the dunes. Katherine was embarrassed and sat up.

"You've seen people kissing on the beach before. So now it's us. Get used to it, we have three more days!" He kissed her one more time, this with a message of future passion and necessary parting. He pulled away gently. "I'm sure dinner's ready. Let's go." He drew her to her feet and happily helped her brush off the sand clinging to her wet legs. He slipped his hand around her waist and invited her to match his stride back toward the house. "I thought you would never get here. Some things are worth waiting for."

"Jonas, can we stay forever?" It was a lover's question.

"Of course, forever." It was a lover's answer. "As long as you follow two rules," he added, "up for every sunrise and no shoes."

Early the next morning Jonas was waiting on the top porch step for her. She came from the house at the exact appointed minute. "Look," he pointed to the waning moon that was lighting the western sky and without a word kissed her lightly and offered his hand. The barefooted pair went down to the beach.

The beauty of the sunrise on the Outer Banks was pivotal. Neither Jonas nor Katherine would ever separate this setting from their feelings—from this day forward. The clouds high on the horizon began grabbing the peach, yellow, and pink colors, creating a picture any artist would envy. The colors spread to the high sky and around to the west demanding that human spirits climb. Jonas and Katherine were both elated by the view. Soft rays pushed up from a spot on the edge of the world. The grey ocean turned multi-hued, first rosy, then cotton candy pink with blue. The first blast of brightness marked the sunrise and a silver pathway to the eternal orb.

Katherine sat on the sand mesmerized. Her happiness was defined by the coming sun. She was rising like the glowing orb and felt as promising as the new day. Just as the sun needed to rise in this place in the universe, she needed to rise into her place.

"Jonas..."

"Yes, my darling."

"I want it all—just like the sun wants the day." She pointed at the bright ball for the last time before it became too bright to look at. "The sun is nothing without the day and the day is nothing without the sun."

"I want to give it all to you. I want to be your sun and your day."

"I want to be your sun and your day, too." She took a deep breath. "I'm in love. I love *you*."

"I love—," She covered his mouth with a sandy hand.

"Wait, Jonas. I need to tell you some things."

"Okay," he replied ,spitting sand and laughing.

"I don't know much about love…as I'm feeling for you. I love my family and I loved Johnny but that was all different. I needed something from them. It was a grateful love. This is a sharing-giving love. Am I making sense?"

"Yes." He tried to take her hand, but she pulled back for concentration.

"I feel different about you."

"That's good."

'I want to be with you. Never want to be apart. I want to explore life with you and I feel very… I don't know how to say it. When we are close I want more and more. Oh dear." She was suddenly embarrassed.

He reached for her and she did not pull back. His kisses found her mouth and her neck. She followed his lead and returned his passion in the dawning light. Her hand went into his hair as she buried her face in his neck.

"We'll go slowly, Kate, but we both know where we want to go with our love. I love you very much—have for a long time. This is a passionate love that's meant for a lifetime. I want you for a lifetime."

Katherine looked up wide-eyed. A sudden tear ran unbidden down her cheek.

"I'm talking forever. I love you and when you're ready I'll propose marriage."

"I—." This time his finger crossed her lips and stopped her words.

"I'll know when. I want you to know that I *will* propose because you are my life, my future." He took both of her hands and drew them to his chest. "You're sorting out some very troubling things in your life. I understand…and I believe…" He searched for the right words as he squeezed her hands. "I believe you're close to realizing that things in the past, and care of your mother, can't keep you from the wonderful life you deserve. You are on the brink of a lot of good things and I'm the lucky man holding your hand, your body and your love. I'm going to take good care of it all." He opened her arms and pulled them around his body. Her breast pressed his chest and she gave into him with a sigh. "When you want me and can't live without me, I *will* make you my wife. I love you with all my heart, Katherine Ross." He kissed her and proclaimed, "You will let me know when you love me with all your heart." And kissed her again.

Katherine was silent, but except for that one tear, did not cry. Her body was quivering with passion and desire that she knew she had to contain. In the moment, while her body ached with a desire, her life flashed before her—her responsibility—her parentage—and knowledge that her mother had, somehow, gotten pregnant before marriage. Katherine moved back from Jonas frightened and inhibited. *Can I be this happy? Can I love Jonas this much?*

"I hardly know how to be so…happy."

He held her trembling body hoping that somehow through his embrace her doubts would melt away.

Katherine was beaming; her eyes reflected the fire of the sunrise. She felt his hands across her back and felt a comfort she had never felt before. A broad smile gave her face new beauty. Her hair was flying in the breeze that comes with the rising sun—freely underlining her new emotions.

"You are so beautiful," he whispered.

"Not now, I'm not." She said as she tried to straighten her windblown hair. "I'm content. There is no place I would rather be than here, with you. Jonas, you have become my world. How'd you do that?"

"I'm not sure," he quipped. "Just glad to know I did." He gently pulled her hand from her blowing hair so it could fly free.

Her smile suddenly left her face and her mood changed. A blank look crossed her face and she was gone. Jonas knew it immediately.

"Kate, what is it? Don't shut down. Talk to me."

She resisted all urges to run from this new happiness. And although she did not move from his arms, she stiffened and deep furors etched her brow. "Talk to me. Don't turn away." Jonas tried to look in her eyes but she turned away.

"Why, when I'm happy, does thinking of Mother take it away?" She moved six inches from his embrace and looked at him with sad eyes. "I'm my mother's daughter. Suppose I have her sickness. Suppose I can't have a relationship. Mama loved Papa but couldn't….and, she gave me away." Katherine's emotion was strong; her words emphatic as she voiced the fear that stayed just below the surface ever since she was old enough to mourn her mother's life. Now, with Jonas' profession of love and her own desire, fear welled up and spilled over, taking away the beauty of the sunrise and the joy of moments ago.

"I don't want to hurt you as my mother hurt Papa. And if we have children—"

"Stop, Kate! Stop right there," he interrupted knowing she was voicing demons that had plagued her for a long time. "I have read the team reports on your mother. You—" he cupped her chin and brought her around to face him. "You—are your mother's daughter, but you are not her. Nothing in your makeup or your past would take you to the place that Pamela is. Nothing! No warped childhood. No domineering parent! No unwanted sexual encounters! No leftover, unfinished, undefined psychological trauma!" He lowered his voice for emphasis. "From all I've learned and all I've seen for myself, your mother's illness is not in her genes but rather, in her unfortunate life. You *are* your father's daughter, too and he gave you a fortunate life, my darling. Come here." He took her to his breast again.

She calmed and moved into him, allowing his embrace fully. "Oh, Jonas," was all she could say as the sun poured its first warmth on them and the breeze came to move the sea oats on the dunes. He rocked her gently.

"When you get back home, go see Julianne. She was there. She's known your mother since she was a young girl. Have you ever sat down with her and asked about your mother?"

"No. Never thought about it."

"Does that seem like a good idea?"

Katherine was quiet and pensive for a while. "I think that's a very good idea." She turned the thought over and over in her mind. "Yes, Julianne."

CHAPTER 37

1961

Sweet anticipation swept over Julianne when Katherine called wanting to meet. *She reached out. Katherine called me!* The call was an answer to one of Julianne's constant prayers. *Please, God. Bring Katherine to me.* Even before tragedy brought her into the Kingsley family, Julianne had wanted to mother the motherless child. She could not force the issue—Katherine had to come to her. *Was this the happy day?*

"Of course, I can meet you. I'd love to. I want to hear about your trip to North Carolina and I'll bring Melissa's school picture. Got one for you."

Julianne cleared her desk and let the Secret Service know she was going to the Woodward and Lothrop's Restaurant on K Street at eleven o'clock.

The day was warm and the late spring flowers bobbed in the soft wind. Julianne was happy—meeting with Katherine felt good. The two women greeted each other warmly. Julianne held her hug an extra second or two.

"Katherine, you are glowing! I hope that means you are happy. I see a bit of a tan."

"I'm happy. Jonas and I had a wonderful time on the Outer Banks. I fell in love with that place and his family is great. I learned a few things about myself."

"Tell me." This was turning into a rare time with Katherine. Julianne took an instant to put the young girl's radiance, beauty, and animation into her memory.

"I left all my concerns, even school, behind. It was easier than I thought. That beach is beautiful. And the house! —a perfect beach house that sits right behind the dune—up high. My room faced the ocean and I could hear it all night. The ocean and roaring surf soon washed my cares away." She was rambling on with happy recollections. "And there was Jonas…" Her voice trailed off for a moment of reverie. "We had a marvelous time."

The conversation settled down over steaming cups of coffee and a shared giant banana nut muffin. After describing the beauty of the Banks, Katherine went to the purpose for their meeting.

"Jonas and I are serious. He's wonderful." She let Julianne fill in the blanks as she gazed wide-eyed and repeated. "Wonderful." A shiver of delight passed over her. "I've never been so happy."

"Plans?" She asked, needing to know and not wanting to push too much.

"Yes, for the future. Not right now. I have to finish college first." Katherine took a long draft of her sweet coffee and drew strength. "I love Jonas." It was not easy to say to anyone except Jonas. "I'm in love." Even as she said it she knew it was time to tell the world and she wanted to. "Me and Jonas."

Julianne sensed the milestone Katherine was reaching and took her hand. Her slight pressure gave assurance that being in love with Jonas was good. "That's wonderful. He's a fine man."

"Julianne, I can't think about getting married…or think about having a family without understanding my mother." Her face reflected a change in mood. "Suppose I become ill like her. What if I can't raise my own child?" She paused to weep. This was bringing forward old fears and voicing them was admission that they were real. Katherine had to dig deep to ask the disturbing questions. "I'll never understand how she could give me away, even to Papa. But, she did. I wonder if I would ever do that. Would I give a child to be raised by someone else...or reject Jonas—a man who loves me and that I love?" Her lovely face distorted with pain. "God!" she exclaimed. "That's really *sick*. Sick! Sick! Now I'm in love and I'm confused and mystified."

Julianne passed her a tissue and said, "Dry your tears, Katherine. We're going to walk in the park. Some good Spring air is needed for our talk. It will refresh your thinking because I'm going to fill your mind with things that'll make your life easier—even new. You need the truth." She smiled broadly and took Katherine's hand. "Come."

Julianne held tight and Katherine took courage at her words and her strong grip. They walked toward Lafayette Park without talking, each deep in her own thoughts. When they reached a bench she pulled Katherine to sit. It was a good place with dogwood and tulips providing a soothing, pastel background.

"Look. The flowers have the colors of an Outer Banks sunrise—pink, orange, yellow. Beautiful. Jonas and I shared every sunrise. It was so special. I know he loves me, and I him, so very much, but..." Again, she trailed off without words.

"Take your time. Don't be afraid."

"I'm scared." She took her words to a whisper. "I'm afraid of becoming my mother. How can I be sure I won't lose it all in childbirth...like she did?" Her back straightened. "I've been afraid to discover Mother's story. Now, I love Jonas enough to ask for help, for answers. I need to know things that aren't in the hospital's clinical reports. I almost have to travel back in time."

"Dear Child, I see where you are going with this. Of course, I'll help you. I'll tell you all that I know and answer any questions you have. Anything to put your heart at ease and to help you know that your mother's illness is not, never will be, part of you."

"You're so sure?"

"I *am* sure—positive. I have known your mother since she was 16—the age you came to King's Trace." Julianne began the story, holding nothing back. She did not hesitate to paint a clear picture of Katherine's grandfather, William Greeley. The distasteful man came to life on the bench in Lafayette Park. "He twisted Pamela at a very young age." Her story continued and included her grandmother, Genevieve, and all the problems that boiled over on their young daughter. "Pamela was mentally abused and sick when James Ross came into the picture." She told the unusual circumstance that brought James and KC into the Greeley business. "As amazing as it seems, your grandfather picked and hired James to marry Pamela and they fell in love. He loved her and, for a while, seemed to bring some sanity to her life. But, I believe if you could ask your father, he would say that even his love could not correct the mental conditions set in Pamela. Add to all this, unsought attention from KC and a pregnancy." She took a breath. This part of the story hurt. "It's only right that I comment on that. Omission would be unfair. I'm not going to make an excuse for him. KC was an animal. I don't know how it happened—never asked, never will." She paused a moment to gather strength and waited for Katherine to ask questions about this part of the story but she only said, "Go on."

"He obviously had opportunity and no man will stop to assess the mental condition of a lovely available woman." Julianne gave this part of the story as little emphasis as she could.

Katherine sat mesmerized and saddened. "Are you saying Mother was mentally ill as a girl? Before my father? Even before I was conceived? Before I was born?" A heavy burden lifted from her shoulders. Even she was surprised at the weight she had taken on herself. For the first time she admitted to that she had taken responsibility for her mother's illness. *I didn't put her in Spring Haven? I didn't push her over the edge?* She looked up at Julianne. "I'm not the reason Mother is sick?"

"No. No way." Julianne cupped her chin and clasped her wide-eyed gaze with her own eyes. "If she hadn't already been sick, James and you, sweet baby, could have saved her."

"Already sick when I was born?" It was such a revelation that she had to repeat it.

"Yes, my dear. Before you were even conceived, Pamela was…self-destructive, eating disorders, paranoid. I saw it all and the reasons for it. Your grandmother wanted to get her help, but she was weak against your grandfather."

"It didn't start when I was born?" Katherine had to ask again.

"No. Absolutely not."

The time had come for conversation to stop. Julianne waited for the truth to settle into Katherine's life. Not only for truth to be believed, but also time for false ideas to be replaced—a more complicated adjustment.

"I'm so afraid of rejecting my children."

"Do not torture yourself fearing that you will reject your child, because Pamela never meant to reject you."

"She did!" Katherine stood, challenging Julianne's words.

"Sit Katherine. Sit, and listen." She opened her palms, inviting her to rejoin the conversation and accept the truth. "You felt rejection. I understand…and your father did all he could to keep you from feeling that. You longed for your mother and were rejected…how could you feel otherwise? But, Pamela believed with all her heart and soul that she did what was best for *you*. She didn't reject you; she gave you to be loved totally by James. She sacrificed herself for you."

"I never saw it."

"Of course not. You hurt too much. Your mother believed the only way she could make sure you had a whole life was to stay out of it." Julianne's eyes became sad. "She said those words to me hundreds and hundreds of times. And, hundreds of times I tried to tell her she was wrong. I could have saved my breath." She brightened her countenance, not wanting to bring Katherine down. "Pamela Greeley Ross is an intelligent woman. She's mentally ill, but it is an unusual brain that is so distorted and can still assess surprisingly. I have been visiting her for almost twenty years at Spring Haven and she never ceases to amaze me. If there is anything I want you to take away today it is this: Your mother's illness did not come with childbirth. I've told you most of the things that took her mental health away." She paused for emphasis. "She did not reject you. You were given away because she wanted you to have a good life."

"I wanted her."

"Yes, I know…but she could not know that longing. Nor could she assess her warped thinking. Actually she denied herself the right to love you and that exacerbated her mental illness. A mother who loves and wants her baby cannot deny herself that natural love and remain sane…or become well, if already ill."

"Most of us live our lives trying to do good in the world and we have many opportunities. Pamela believed with all her heart, soul, and intelligence that there was only one good thing she could do in her life. It was to give you to James. She would not let doctors, or anyone else change that." Julianne drew Katherine to her chest, put her hand in her hair and drew her head close to whisper in her ear. "And so she denied her love and you were given."

Katherine cried with abandonment. Her tears flowed and her sobs racked her body. Julianne held her tight until the emotions ebbed.

"Think it over but believe me, I have given you the truth as I saw it. I love you, Katherine, and want to help you all I can, at no expense of my feelings or KC's responsibility."

"Oh, I believe you, Julianne." Katherine put her arms around her and held long enough for each to feel the importance of the other. She composed herself and let her first thought come into the lovely May day. "Actually, KC has nothing to do with this."

Julianne quietly rejoiced in those words—Katherine *was* going to be alright.

"Thank you, Julianne."

"Please let me, Brenda and Melissa be your family. Come and be with us when you can—at King's Trace. It is no longer KC's home, even after he leaves the White House."

"Are you saying—?"

"—I'm saying the family at King's Trace is me, Brenda, Melissa, and you… and, Johnny's memory. And Jonas, if you are the smart girl I think you are." She added with a twinkle and wink.

"Oh, Julianne, how can I thank you enough?"

"Come to King's Trace. Never forget the family you have there."

"I will…and Jonas will be with me."

CHAPTER 38

1961

The sun felt especially good this morning. Katherine took her coffee to the window and folded into her favorite overstuffed chair, and picked up the phone receiver. Lady Fair followed uninvited. Slightly perturbed, the cat settled on the back of the chair and waited. She was not her girl's confidant any more—not like she used to be. Lady Fair came to hate the sound of a phone dial. She hopped down.

"Good morning, Jonas."

"Good morning, Sweetheart. Nice to hear from you so early."

"Couldn't wait until our date tonight. Wanted to talk now."

"That's always good. I'm yours and…I'm in my office alone. Lucky for me."

"My mind is going back to my conversation with Julianne today. Really can't stop."

"Tell me."

"I can't wait to tell you some things that are important to you and me. Things that Julianne wanted to tell me. Come over early, right after work. I'm studying for finals all day. I'll be finished by five and I'll fix our dinner."

"I'll be there a little after five."

She felt so warm toward him that she hesitated to say goodbye. "Jonas, I love you more than ever."

"Maybe by five, you'll love me even more."

"No doubt."

When Jonas arrived, she had put her books away and had a big chef's salad ready. A bowl of ice floated bottles of Coca Cola and a large bag of chips filled a bowl. Katherine was waiting. She threw the door open and jumped into his arms. Her excitement was contagious and Jonas wondered what it was all about.

"Kate, what is it?"

"I have such good news to celebrate. Julianne gave me a gift today."

"A gift?"

"A gift of knowledge, a gift of relief, a gift of the future. I can't wait to tell you about it. Come, let's eat and talk." She stopped on the way to the dining room to kiss him once more. "I do love you more than this morning. Just like I thought I would."

He responded with kisses that weakened her knees and caused her to laugh and slip away from him. "We'd better eat."

"Okay, maybe you will love me even more after dinner."

She looked across the table at him with puppy eyes and he had to laugh gazing back at her. "I'm not sure what is going on but, Darling, I think we can be happy like this forever."

'Yes, we can. More salad?"

She gave him her mother's story as Julianne had told it. Jonas was enthralled and attentive. Her narrative told him things he needed to know about Pamela Ross, but also things he had to understand about his beloved Kate.

"Kate, I had no idea you had these concerns." He went to sit beside her. "You never told me."

"I know and I'm sorry. It wasn't until *you*…that I had to know. Thanks for suggesting I go to Julianne. She was the only one who was there and knew Mother through it all." She went around the table and climbed into his lap. "I'm so relieved."

"We have nothing to worry about. You and I will marry after you finish school, we will have children. You will love your children and we will care for them together. You will love me forever and I will love you. We're a team." He recited as he wrapped his long, strong arms around her.

Katherine took a deep breath and drew his strength into her lungs to circulate through her body like oxygen.

"I'm thankful Julianne was so helpful. She's a wonderful person—honest and strong—and trusted. The next time I see her, I'll give her a big hug, too." He squeezed Katherine to demonstrate. They laughed the healing, bonding glee that would earmark their lives for generations.

"Kate, we can live out near Spring Haven if that would make you happy."

"Thanks for that…but, no need to think about that now. I love the city and so do you."

"We will do what is best for everyone."

"I love you more every moment." She tossed a chip to his mouth and he caught it. Their joy was complete.

After eating and cleaning up, Katherine and Jonas moved to the sofa. The mood remained light and wonderful. They opted to put music on the turntable instead of television. She went into the spot right under his shoulder; he put his chin in her hair.

"One more thing. KC and Julianne are not living together. She said when he leaves the White House he's not coming back to King's Trace. I'm invited there to be a part of the family that doesn't include him."

"The President and First Lady are separated? Really!"

"She's fulfilling her position as First Lady, but...I don't know how that works but really don't care."

Jonas reached down and took her shoulders, turning her to face him. "Kate, is there anything else to be settled between you and him? Any buried agendas like the ones you straightened out with Julianne? I think it's important to get everything right for you. We have a great future ahead. I want to know everything that makes you tick, even thoughts about KC."

"Tick-tock, darling." She laughed and kissed him with that special kiss that included a smile.

"KC. Hmmm, KC." She gave his question deep thought. Her answer was not going to come quickly or off-handed. The time was right for her to voice how she felt, not only for Jonas, but for herself.

Jonas allowed her plenty of time. He did nothing to distract her, instead paid close attention to the music from *Carousel* pouring from the turntable. Finally, Katherine sat up straight and demanded his attention with her posture.

"Okay, here's how it is with me. I've observed him, even studied him and all the different times when he left me puzzled. Now that I know why things were...let me say...awkward. Lady Fair and I tried to figure it out."

"You and Lady Fair?'

"Yes, we often talked it over. She was a big help before you came along. Now that I know the whole story, I've reached some important conclusions."

"Tell me."

"He delivered the sperm that gave me life and that is a bigger problem for him than it is for me. KC worried all his political life that his image would be ruined if the secret got out. I didn't have any concerns. Mother was mentally ill and he had to worry about that, too. Then he had to worry about questions when I went to King's Trace to live. Poor man had so much to worry about. Meanwhile, life with Papa prepared me for the future...for you, my love." Jonas leaned in as more thoughts poured from her.

"KC is a good President. Actually I'm very proud of him. Good for him. Morally? I've decided not to pass judgment. What he is—is not my problem. But I know, he has always been, a poor husband and father. I'm not sure he can make it without Julianne but that is not my concern, either. When I'm with him, I'm tempted to say 'forget it'. It's very simple." She stopped to think one more moment. "Maybe I *should* say to him: 'forget it.'"

"Good for you, my love. You're wonderful as well as wise." He kissed her with so much passion she had to pull back which she did gently, letting him know it wasn't easy.

"Popcorn?"

"Sure. We'll eat to keep passion in check." He was half-serious. "By the time you graduate, we will both be blubber balls."

Katherine went to the kitchen as the phone rang and Jonas heard one side of the conversation. "Yes...Yes, sir. I'm sure I did well. No, Jonas is here. Of course...I will...that works for me, KC." The phone went back on the cradle. Then Jonas heard the sounds of popcorn popping. He was alert to catch the look on Katherine's face when she returned to the sofa. Her demeanor was unchanged—it was confident, bright and happy.

"Popcorn's ready." She handed him the bowl. "That was KC. I never ceased to be surprised when the operator says, 'White House calling.'"

"And?" Jonas tried to keep the same bright happy attitude.

"He asked about my exams and he wanted to be sure I would go to King's Trace to be with Julianne and the girls—an invitation of sorts. Then he asked for something."

"Are you going to tell me or tease?" He tickled her, causing a handful of popcorn to scatter over the rug.

"KC asked me to forget." Katherine got serious. "KC asked me to forget his part in my life—the very thing I would ask him." She looked Jonas square in the eye, clear and honest. "I didn't tell him but… I already have."

"Tonight is a special night. We have it all."

"I'm contented. KC gave me three gifts besides life. He gave me to Papa. He gave me his family, and he gave me King's Trace. That's what I'm going to remember."

Katherine settled down into the sofa next to Jonas. He reached up and turned off the lamp so they could give promises without words.

CHAPTER 39

1961

Pamela sat looking out at the budding summer across the lawn. She was waiting. It was Tuesday—the only day of the week that mattered. Lunch was over. There was nothing to do but wait.

Katherine arrived on time and they left the lounge for a bench on the lawn. "It's lovely. Let's go outside." She was happy that she could take her mother outside the hospital walls today.

They crossed the wide lawn on a well-worn path. "Sit or walk?" Pamela pointed to a bench and opted to sit. She pulled her plain dress tight around her knees and sat ram-rod straight looking ahead.

Katherine smiled to herself, knowing that it could take minutes before her mother acknowledged her with a gaze. *Mama.* She begged in her mind. *Me!*

She noted how her mother's hair was streaked with shiny strands of silver. It was hard resisting the urge to touch her head and hair. Instead, she ran her fingers though her own.

"I brought you something. Look." A large tote bag was placed at her knees. "I found this packed away with Papa's office. It must belong to you." Katherine reached in and brought out an unfinished afghan, large balls of yarn with knitting needles stabbing through. "Do you knit, Mother? I never knew."

"Used to." With a gentle kick she pushed the bag back toward her daughter. "No more." With tight shoulders she dismissed the yarn, needles and suggestion. "They have knitting here—if I wanted to."

It was hard to start another conversation after such rejection, but Katherine was determined. She sat quietly and waited. Through the months, she learned that her mother wanted to talk, but had to find the subject and words herself. The last thing Katherine could do was start the conversation herself. Knitting was not going to do it today.

The time did not hang heavy—mother and daughter seemed comfortable waiting for conversation. Katherine did not know if her mother wanted to touch her as she longed for it. She could not guess what was in her mind. But, she came to wait, and wait she did. *My normal*, she thought as she wondered what mothers and grown daughters did when they had an afternoon together.

"Julianne visits me."

"I know. She told me. I'm happy to know it."

"Sometimes, we don't talk." It was an explanation—and excuse for not finding words today. Pamela could not get beyond seeing the knitting bag. Just like everything from her past, the yarn, needles, and unfinished work left Pamela lost.

Katherine understood. She would have to do all the talking today. "Julianne and the whole family have gone to Brenda's graduation. They invited me to go, but I have final exams this week. Can't go. Jonas and I are going to his parents' for a few days as soon as my exams are over." She went on talking about things, watching carefully for a nod or indication that something sparked interest. "Mother, you do understand that Jonas is very important to me, don't you?"

"Of course, I do." Her head rose slightly...and dropped again.

Katherine did not know what else to say about Jonas "This summer I'm taking more classes." She allowed some silence, which seemed to please her mother.

The visit was over for today except for her weekly parting words. "You'll come next Tuesday?"

"Yes, Mother. I'll be here." Katherine walked her in and handed the tote bag to the attendant, who nodded her understanding.

Earlier that day the team meeting introduced a new idea to Katherine. The social worker addressed an item on the agenda. "We have reviewed and decided that Pamela Ross is not a candidate for the new half-way house program."

All agreed around the table.

"Why?" Katherine blurted her question.

Dr. McMaster pulled a report from his file and handed it to Katherine. "Your mother has been here almost twenty years. This program is designed to reintroduce the world to patients who have not been isolated so long."

"Not because she is too ill?"

"We would not have evaluated the half-way house program if we thought Mrs. Ross was too ill. She's approved for home visits, but you remember how upset she got when you suggested leaving Spring Haven?"

"I remember."

"Have you brought the idea to her again?"

"No, sir, not since then."

"Read this over, Katherine. You will see that acclimation is the issue. Your mother has made some good progress, but the consensus is that she has been removed too long from society to expect her to progress with a group in a half-way environment." He paused to give her an assuring look. "Come see me. We'll talk about this. I'll be in my office all afternoon."

※

Katherine walked slowly to Dr. McMaster's office after leaving her mother with the attendant. The idea that her mother could leave Spring Haven churned inside her.

"Is he available?" she asked his secretary.

McMaster heard her voice and called from the adjoining office. "Come in, Katherine."

He pushed back from his desk and invited her to sit. "Good visit today?"

"Fair. I didn't ask her if she wanted to come home for a day as you suggested. The visit wasn't that good."

"I see."

"I don't want to lose ground with her like I did when I suggested leaving Spring Haven. She is so entrenched here."

"It's all she knows—her comfort zone. Your mother's sick but, just like many ill patients, does not need to be hospitalized twenty-four/seven. However, she is terrified of the world and would not be able to function in a half way house. Nor could you take her to your apartment to live. She just cannot do it. I'm sorry, Katherine, but that is the opinion of the whole team."

Katherine wanted to cry. "This is as good as it will ever be for her? Living, until she is an old woman…in a hospital?" The doctor could hear her pain.

"A half-way house is a group home. It will not work for your mother. This has been her life, her environment, her home for too long. Patients like your mother cannot function outside and that is the purpose of the half-way house program."

"I can't expect to see her anyplace but the patient lounge or lawn bench—for all her life? I don't want her to live here forever. I don't want to visit her week after week *here*." She paused to assess what emotion she was trying to voice. "Is this all I will ever have with my mother?"

Dr. McMaster knew she was questioning more than location. His patient's daughter wanted more. She always had, but he could not give her even this hope.

Truth was settling in, but acceptance was not easy. She faced her future and her mother's. The vision was overwhelming. "Doctor, I know she will never be my mother in the traditional role. I'm grown up now and my expectations are grounded. What has to be; has to be. But it is hard to accept that I'll never share our time in a softer place. Never sit at breakfast in my home. Never have her in my life."

"I'm going to be blunt with you, my dear. Patient care has improved much and we are so pleased with where Pamela *is* compared to where she *was*, but—"

"But." Katherine cried. "But. There is always *but*." She was surprised with herself. She had not planned to have such a showdown with her feelings and expectations today. Dr. McMaster saw desperation on her face.

"Easy, child. We are facing some difficult truths here. I knew the time would come when you would ask these questions. Do you want the answers?" He walked from behind his desk to sit next to Katherine.

Katherine regained her composure. "I want to know. Today is as good a day as any. Tell me Doctor, will I spend the rest of my mother's life visiting her here at Spring Haven?"

"She could have day visits with you, if she would go. Pamela cannot be left alone. She panics and her attacks are violent and severe. You can't be with her all day. You cannot attend her all night."

"Money is no object. I can buy the best home care."

"A busy city apartment is not the answer. She needs calm hours and a place that makes no demands. She could go to a home environment where twenty-four hour companionship is available as long as she is seen regularly by her doctors. Perfect for her but impossible for you. My dear, you need to finish college, marry, and raise a family. Don't blame yourself for what must be. Your father understood this and he understood your mother. If he could have brought her home, he would have." He stopped so she could think about his words. "And we cannot ignore how she feels about it." He took her hand in a fatherly way. "You have a life to live and your mother is savvy enough to refuse to burden you or interrupt your life. If she sees you abandon your life for her, she will go over the fragile edge she has scaled." He patted her hand for emphasis. "She has some choices too, you know."

It was a long drive home and the only bright spot Katherine could find was her Tuesday night date with Jonas. She chewed and digested facts the doctor gave her today. Maybe she had to shout out about the reality, but she also had to admit to herself he was right. *Mother can't come home. If she could, Papa would have brought her. Oh, Papa you are still helping me today.* She picked up his picture and kissed it. "You know that Jonas is very important to me, don't you? Of course you do." The picture went back on her nightstand.

"I'm not going to spoil our date," she told Lady Fair. "This will not be one of those Tuesdays when Mother comes with me on our date." She brushed her hair to a shine and waited anxiously for his arrival. She carried Lady Fair to her bed, looking into her blue eyes, "I'll tell him what the doctor said. He will figure for himself how I feel about it. That's the wonder of Jonas. He'll know without me telling him. He'll understand."

CHAPTER 40

1962

It had been weeks since Katherine had been to King's Trace. Final exams and the chance to run-away to North Carolina were immediate demands on her time. Julianne's invitations had to be put off twice. She called again. "I'd love for you to come to King's Trace. In fact, I was hoping today or tomorrow." She would not let Katherine slip away into a busy life. Julianne was determined to keep her—and bring Jonas—into her family circle. "Jonas, too. I'd love to see him."

"We got back from North Carolina today. Tomorrow is good for me, but Jonas can't. He's tied up with depositions and leaving in the morning to go to New Orleans. I don't go to Spring Haven until the day after. Perfect." Katherine was happy to fill her days while Jonas was gone—especially in this way. The summer heat and humidity was unbearable. It would be great to get out of the city. King's Trace would be refreshing. *Ahhh. A breeze across that broad lawn.* Just thinking about the breeze and a visit with Julianne and the girls at King's Trace made Katherine happy. "I hope Brenda and Melissa are home."

"Melissa is at camp and Brenda is at the White House doing duties for me. Come for lunch. Stay overnight if you like."

"Great. I can leave from there to see Mother Tuesday."

After a quick call to Jonas, Katherine packed up, anticipating a wonderful summer day and evening in the country. As she drove she recalled how much she loved King's Trace—the place where she'd found a family. "It will be nice to be in my room and look out at the hills again," she told Lady Fair sleeping in her carrier. Katherine thought about the stable and Johnny, and discovered that she could recall those happy days without tears. *Time does heal*, she thought. Katherine even allowed that going to King's Trace and to Julianne was almost a homecoming now. Her mind and heart were aligned. She had figured things out. She knew who she was, where she was going, and more importantly, who she was going with. Her mind settled happily on Jonas while driving the last few miles through the Maryland countryside.

Suzanna met Katherine at the door. "Hello, Miss Katherine. Miss Julianne's tied up right now. She said to make yourself comfortable. Lunch'll be at one. Can I take Lady Fair and your things up?"

"Thank you, Suzanna. I'm going to the stable. Chessie is probably wondering what happened to me."

"Quiet at the stable. Not here." Suzanna complained as she pointed to the Secret Service command center set up in the library. "Nice young men…and I'm getting used to them being here. They call us the *Country White House*. True enough, the house is white." She talked as they walked down the kitchen corridor toward the back door. "Tried to send a cook but I told Miss Julianne, 'it's like cookin' when all you kids was home. I don't need no help.' Now, I enjoys them."

Katherine smiled at Suzanna's rambling. "Tell Julianne I'm here. One o'clock lunch. I'll be back."

"So good to see you, Miss Katherine—so good."

Katherine could hardly wait to tread the familiar path to the stable. She started out leisurely but her pace picked up as she got closer. She felt happy, contented, and finally at home.

Johnny. She knew he was not here but she was sure that from some distant plane, he knew *she was.* And so, she smiled for him as she entered and spoke aloud, "Johnny." It was not a question. She was not calling him. It wasn't seeking. It was just a statement, a pronouncement, an acceptance, a fact. "I'd live in this stable with your memory if I could, but I'm not a girl any longer and you are not here. Please love my life. Johnny— if you can." She walked on in.

The stalls were empty. The smells included earth, manure, horse, and wood. Katherine breathed in deeply, loving every aroma as she ran her hand across the saddles and tack. A waxed cloth hung loosely on a nail, so she dusted Johnny's saddle and continued her conversation with him. "Always be here, Johnny. I'll come to the stable whenever I can. Isn't it funny? I tried not to let King's Trace be my home and now…Oh, Johnny—" Gentle tears came. "—You loved this place and now, so do I." She wiped them with the waxy, leather-smelling cloth. "I miss you."

"I miss you, too. Kat." His voice whipped in the wide door on a breeze, swirled around Katherine and drifted to the loft.

She whirled to see him, but wisdom, deep within, made her keep her eyes closed. She heard his voice and saw him in her mind. And, she was content. Her arms dropped to her side in submission to claim their love and acknowledge their innocence. Katherine went to the hard earth ground and suddenly she knew. "I understand, now. Clearer than I ever did. We would have suffered greatly, my dear, dear brother. Love isn't meant to hurt so much." The breeze came again and moved her hair.

"We're free."

Did I say that? She wasn't sure.

"Johnny, if you are listening, hear me now. I love you—always will. We're both free to love." She twirled around with arms extended and her hair blowing free. "Always."

Katherine felt suddenly exhausted from emotions that had purged her. She came back to the girl who had crossed the lawn minutes ago. It was time to find Chessie.

Across the pasture, the horse was grazing like an ornament in the lovely landscape. When he turned to her whistle she laughed out loud. Chessie looked comical with green blades pointing from his mouth. "Hey, Chessie." She whistled again, this time shaking an oat bucket. It was irresistible to the horse. "Yeah, not me, the oats, I know." She reached around his broad warm neck. "Nothing stays the same, Chessie—except maybe you." The horse was unwilling to let her and the oats go, and followed her back to the stable door.

Just for the fun of it, she donned boots from the corner and began mucking Chessie's stall. The work was rewarding and grounding. "I'm not doing this for you, Chessie. I'm doing it for me," she called to the horse. She dug and swung the pitchfork in an old remembered rhythm. With each toss of muck and straw, Katherine grew stronger. Her mind joined her heaving muscles as she symbolically made room in the stall and in her life for the forces that would drive her. "I love Jonas." She pulled and tossed. "I love Mother." Another swing and pitch. "I love Julianne, Brenda, and Melissa." Katherine lifted and threw. She pushed the fork lightly into the old wood floor and leaned against the handle. "I love Johnny and this place." She walked to the door and looked out at Chessie again. "I love you, too, Ol' Friend." Her heart was full of realization.

Stepping out of the boots, she ran her hand across the saddle again. *I'd rather be riding*, she admitted to herself, knowing she did not have time before lunch. Katherine checked her watch. *Someday soon…*

Her steps as she crossed the lawn again were light, almost a dance. Suddenly she noticed the waxy, leather-smelling cloth tucked into her pant pocket. Katherine did not remember putting it there but it was a happy discovery and became an instant treasure. "You will always remind me of the girl I was," she said as she tucked it back into her pocket and resumed her dance away from the stable.

Again, Suzanna met her at the door. Suzanna, I'm showering. I'll be quick."

"Miss Julianne's in the morning room when you finish. She 'bout running the White House from King's Trace these days."

Katherine thought about her morning at King's Trace as she showered. The warm water refreshed her body and cleared her mind. *Home. I'll never live here again, but I hope there is always a place for me.*

Julianne was waiting with hugs and smiles. "Sorry for the late greeting. I knew you'd go to the stable. That smelly ol' place was welcoming enough for you."

"I have to admit, you are right. But I've missed you. I think with all my new plans with Jonas, I tend to reminisce about the past. So much has happened since that rainy night when destiny brought me to live at King's Trace. Have I ever told you how grateful I am for all that you did for me?" She turned from Julianne and made a 360-degree turn in the room to take it all in. "I am—more than you'll ever know—so thankful. I realize how lost I would have been without you and my new family. I love you all and I love King's Trace, too."

"That's thanks enough, Katherine."

"Julianne, can I talk to you about Johnny?"

"Of course." She kept her smile strong for Katherine.

"This is where Johnny is. He came to me in the stable—his voice—as clear as it could be. I believe he is happy that I come to King's Trace."

Julianne could only take her in her arms and hold her. There were no words to express the feelings that they shared. Then Julianne stepped back; they had to go forward.

"Suzanna has prepared a nice lunch. We're taking it upstairs. I've moved some rooms around." She pointed to the stairs. "Let's go."

They climbed together. Julianne took Katherine's hand as she reached for the latch to a room beyond her original master suite. She paused a moment and turned to Katherine. "Sweetheart, I have a surprise for you."

She opened the door to a large brightly lit room. Sunlight poured in from four south-facing windows, curtained with white gauze. Everything was new and fresh—carefully prepared. The walls were a faint gold straw color. A light blue carpet was circled with beautiful overstuffed chintz sofa and chairs. A breakfast table sat in one corner, set for three with an arrangement of fresh flowers. In another corner, a twin bed was neatly made up with a light blue coverlet. A nightstand featured a framed picture of James Ross—the same one that sat on Katherine's nightstand in her apartment. On the walls were pictures of Katherine taken at different ages. All framed in white and arranged chronologically.

In a rocker at the far end, in the bright light from the windows, Pamela Ross looked up from knitting and smiled at her daughter. Katherine could not believe her eyes as she cautiously approached the sunny part of the room. "Mother." She looked at her mother in this beautiful setting and crossed to sit on the floor at her feet. To be with her mother away from the hospital was her eighteen-year-old-dream and it took her breath away. "Mother," she whispered as she drew oxygen to calm her trembling.

Pamela hesitantly reached out her hand and then drew back.

"It's okay, Mother. It really is."

Pamela touched Katherine's face for the first time in her memory, and, said the most wonderful thing.

"Katherine Marie."

The End

EPILOGUE

Julianne's plan to bring Pamela to King's Trace for home visits had not been easy. She was determined to make it work. There were so many unknowns, not the least of these Pamela, herself. But Julianne was a strong woman with a mission.

Spring Haven and Dr. McMaster spent weeks preparing their patient for time away from the hospital. It was an unusual halfway house arrangement for a very unusual patient. Her team agreed that this experiment not be presented to Katherine until they knew Pamela could function outside the hospital. It was also recommended that they try a one-night visit and work toward three-day visits—maybe twice a month.

The success of the venture really was credited to Julianne and her single-mindedness. She took a positive attitude. And Pamela Ross, who was not always malleable, was led by the one person she had come to trust.

"I don't want to see KC."

"Of course. I know."

"I'll go with you, Julianne. One time." She did as she was told and did not fight against the only friend she had in the world.

"One time, that is all I ask now. Come to King's Trace. I will bring you back to Spring Haven tomorrow."

"I'm frightened."

"It will be fine and tomorrow you will be back here."

Julianne enjoyed getting the rooms arranged for her intended regular visitor. Three rooms were set aside and redecorated.

A bedroom for Pamela, a bedroom for her private nurse/attendant, and a bathroom.

They traveled the road to King's Trace without conversation until they entered the long drive. Pamela kept her head down and had some nausea. "I feel sick."

"I'm sure this is a lot of motion for you. Relax and eat this cracker. Look, we are turning into the drive."

Pamela followed instructions—ate the cracker and looked at the big house that she knew so well. "Take me back." She began to fidget.

"Pamela, you promised. Come in and eat lunch. I'll take you back in two hours if you insist."

"Just you and me?"

"Just you and me…and Suzanna."

"Not KC?"

"Not KC. I told you, he will never be at King's Trace when you come. I promise."

They went into the beautiful suite prepared in Pamela's favorite colors. She seemed to relax as they waited for Suzanna to bring lunch. Julianne did not push for conversation. She had learned over the years to let Pamela lead, if she wanted to.

"Is my daughter here?"

"No. Not today."

"Pam, I have only one request." Pamela dropped her eyes. "Look at me. This is important." She looked at Julianne. "I hope you will want to come here again and again. It is up to you. But, when you do…when you are here…when you see her… please, say her name."

Pamela tried to look away but Julianne's gaze seemed to hold her eyes with a loving look that touched the fragile woman.

Julianne said, without words, *love is good and I have it here—for you.* Her eyes spoke eloquently of love. "Please, Pamela, say her name."

The first visit happened. Two weeks later, she more willingly traveled with Julianne in the shiny black car with Secret Service escort. And Thursday she returned the same way. By the time Julianne urged Katherine to come to King's Trace, Pamela was staying for three days at a time.

As time went by, Pamela began to look forward to her time away from Spring Haven but was always ready to return and go into her comfort zone. Her one constant question at each visit, as Julianne turned the car into King's Trace was: Is Katherine here?

Sometimes, as frequently as Katherine could manage, it was *yes.* Katherine came to see her mother at King's Trace and gradually stopped attending Tuesday team meetings unless Dr. McMaster called her with important news. The hospital was pleased with the home visits and the improvement in their patient. It was life-changing for Katherine to visit her mother in the home setting that Julianne provided. Katherine and Pamela began to relax. Julianne and either Brenda or Melissa joined in the visit. Pamela had progressed far, but still could not maintain a one-on-one conversation with her daughter. The added person made it easier.

Time passed quickly in Pamela's new routine. For eighteen months, Julianne kept the schedule unless family or White House demands interrupted. During these months, Katherine went to Spring Haven if Julianne could not bring Pamela to King's Trace.

One Monday a call came from Dr. McMaster. "Katherine, I need to see you before the team meets tomorrow. Would that be possible?"

The next day, Katherine walked into Spring Haven and hurried to Dr. McMaster's office.

"Doctor?" The old apprehensive feelings came along with this summons.

"Yes, yes, Katherine. Come in. Relax." He saw her concern. "All is well with your mother." He pointed to a chair. "Please, sit." He rounded his desk and took a chair beside her. "The team wants to recommend Pamela's release."

This was more disconcerting for Katherine than the doctor could imagine. "Release?"

He took her hand. "We have a special responsibility toward Pamela Ross. I remember clearly our agreement when Dr. Sherman died. I have not forgotten our promise to you and to her. She will never *have* to leave here. There is no doubt in my mind, especially as we have seen her function with home visits, that she would have progressed out of the hospital years ago if she had received good treatment at the onset of our care. It is unprecedented that decisions on her residency will not be decided by me and the team. It is yours, and Pamela's decision. Solely."

Katherine and Dr. McMaster reviewed the patient history and progress. Nothing new was introduced. Katherine had all the information that could and would be used for the important decision. She left the doctor's office unsure of what the answer would be. Lost in thought, she turned down the corridor that led to her mother's room and surprised herself when she looked up and saw 'Pamela Ross' on the door. She tapped lightly and opened the door.

"It's not Tuesday." Pamela said with a look, slightly animated, not quite surprise.

"No, Mother. I need to talk to you."

☙❦❧

Pamela Ross stayed at Spring Haven. She could not—would not—-leave. Everyone was good with that—Dr. McMaster, Katherine, and Julianne. It was a workable solution for everyone, mostly for the patient, who was touched by happiness and joy in small increments and yet could not move further. She learned to take small amounts of love as it was offered, yet never learned to give.

Pamela Ross did not attend Katherine's graduation. The crowds and situation would have been too much. She waited at King's Trace for the family to return from the event and for Katherine to come to her room.

"I should have a gift for you," she said as Katherine entered, carrying her mortar board and tassel.

"Thanks for coming to King's Trace today. That is gift enough, Mother."

⁂

Jonas and Katherine were married on the south lawn of King's Trace that fall. They planned very carefully to have the bridal arch in clear view of Pamela's window. At the moment when Jonas took Katherine's hand, she looked up and smiled at her mother. She did not know if the smile was returned but she was content. Julianne gave Katherine away and her attendants were her sisters, Brenda and Melissa. Katherine was sure her father was watching over her. In fact, just before she started her vows, she spoke to him. "Papa, look at Mother's lovely face in the window." Her wedding was perfect.

⁂

The following year Katherine and Jonas climbed the stairs at King's Trace. She had not seen her mother for four weeks and was most anxious for this visit. Pamela was in her usual rocker, knitting in the sunshine. Katherine walked to her without a word. Tears streamed down her face past the broad smile as she placed her baby girl in Pamela's open, waiting arms.

"Mother, look. Our baby girl."

Pamela finger caressed the tiny cheek, outlined the perfect chin.....

Discussion Questions for Book Clubs

1. What role did forgiveness play in this story? Who forgave? Who could not?

2. What led to Pamela's admission to Spring Haven and what affect did it have on James, Katherine, KC and Julianne?

3. What feelings does William Greeley generate with his life, his success, his legacy?

4. What is the group dynamic between William Greeley, James Ross and KC Kingsley that made it possible for them to set up a business together?

5. What impact did Katherine's abrupt arrival at King's Trace have on the Kingsley family?

6. What created awkwardness between KC and Katherine when she came to live at King's Trace? Explore his feelings and her reaction to him.

7. What were the stumbling blocks that prevented Julianne from having a stronger relationship with Katherine? What finally made their close relationship possible?

8. KC's run for president affected Julianne, Katherine and Johnny differently. Discuss how each felt about it and how they dealt with it.

9. Would you describe Pamela as weak or strong? Why? Pamela was an isolated, hidden, quiet force. In what ways did she 'speak' volumes throughout the book?

10. How did Katherine begin showing her strength through James, KC, Julianne, Jonas, and Johnny?

11. Johnny made a difficult decision. What options were available to him?

12. Katherine and KC met in the stable after Johnny died. Their walk back to the house was significantly and symbolically different for each. How? Why?

13. Katherine easily handled learning that James Ross was not her biological father. Why? She had more trouble after learning who her biological father was. Why?

14. How did moving to the White House change Julianne? Contrast her before and after.

15. Describe Julianne's guilt for allowing the lie about Pamela and Katherine to stand for twenty years. How did KC react to her profession of guilt?

16. In what way was Katherine affected by being in the White House during the international incident? Attitude change? If she had confronted KC before the crisis, what do you think she would have done it differently?

17. How did your feeling for KC change as you read the book? Sympathetic? Why?

18. Historically, how was KC different from—or like—other presidents?

19. Who was the heroine of the book?

20. What were your thoughts on the ending? Evaluate the importance of the epilogue?

21. What was the main theme of the book? What were the sub themes?

22. How does Pamela's treatment differ from how people are treated today?

Faye Green will join your book club discussion by pre-arranged speaker conference call or in person, if possible. Contact her by e mail. greenvine@verizon.net